THEY HAD THE COURAGE TO ANSWER THE CALL OF THE WILD FRONTIER...

NORA CRANDALL—She was stunned by what the remote Alaskan wilderness required of her, but nothing would make her leave the land she had learned to love.

SAM BENNETT—A rough, hard-hewn engineer, he fought to tame the wild land. Some said he was a man to trust, but Nora had yet to discover how far.

ANTHONY LOWERY—A gifted young painter, he had no talent for hardship. He found solace at the gambling tables and gaming houses, aching to flee the harsh frontier.

MAURY HILL—She knew what kind of love could hold a man in the lonely wilderness and keep him happy through the long, dark winter nights.

THEY FOLLOWED THEIR DREAMS TO...

A DISTANT EDEN

A DISTANT EDEN

Donna Grundman

A DELL BOOK

Published by
Dell Publishing Co., Inc.
1 Dag Hammarskjold Plaza
New York, New York 10017

ISBN: 0-440-12136-1

Printed in the United States of America
First printing—February 1982

Dedicated to my loved ones,
who understood when
I took time out
to go and pick some daisies

A DISTANT EDEN

CHAPTER ONE

I sat in my bedroom absently watching the early-evening shadows begin to play across the soft-blue flowers on the walls. The sun was just setting, and only a low flame was needed on the gas hearth to chase away the chill of dampness. It was near the end of February in the year 1905, and here in San Francisco the days were already becoming noticeably longer and a little warmer. Patches of grass were just starting to turn green, and only this morning I had found a haze of spring buds sprinkled over the dead-looking twigs on the hedge around my father's gardens.

I should have been restless, pacing the room with worried nerves keyed tight. Instead I forced myself to sit quietly—though it was not my nature to do so. But the half-completed needlework still lay neglected in my lap. I was waiting, as I had been told to do. Waiting for and yet dreading to hear the outcome of the family discussion going on in the library one floor below, where they were planning my future for me.

I could picture the scene all too clearly in my mind. My father would be sitting in his great chair, the black leather pulled stiff across the puffs of mohair. He would be frowning, I knew, because he was angry with me, and he resented the domestic family problems that took his attention away from his import business. My father—handsome, graying at the temples, always so serious and dignified—spent most of his waking hours engrossed in the intricate problems of making money since Mama died nearly fourteen years ago. Since Mama died . . . How easy it was to use that phrase, because it was what I had believed for so long. And now . . . I didn't know. I was no longer sure what to believe. I loved my father and I used to spend hours, when I was younger, devising ways to draw his attention to me. I was sure he must have been very fond of me too, in his own way, but he hadn't looked at me closely enough in the last years to be aware that I had grown tall and slender. I wore my hair up now, and I had a blossoming figure that suited the latest fashions even if it did cause a great deal of distress to my aunt.

Perhaps that is one of the reasons my father was so upset over this whole affair. He had not been aware just how much I had grown up until he was confronted with this problem I had caused.

My aunt would be there, sitting in her straight-back rocker, her back stiff, her chin high. Outwardly trying to appear calm, she would keep her hands folded neatly in her lap. But I knew better! I knew that inside she would be in an emotional turmoil, once again at a loss as to how to cope with the problems of trying to rear her brother's children. Poor Aunt! She did try so hard, but most of the time we were just too much for her.

My brothers would be collected there also. Paul, my eldest brother, would be leaning against the hearth, a cigarette burning heedlessly in his hand. Paul was ten years older than I, and he had entered the import business with my father as a junior partner. He was a good businessman—shrewd, calculating, dedicated—and I knew my father depended on him a great deal.

Thomas, my other brother, my dear Tom, would be standing at the window looking out at the evening. He would not be listening carefully to the angry discussion behind him. Instead he would be thinking of me, trying to understand what drove me to cause this new family crisis. Of all the family, Tom knew me best. He was only two years older than I, and he too was a rebel, sharing my restlessness now as he had shared so many of my games and adventures of childhood. Yes, of all of them, I felt I could count on Tom to understand.

As I sat waiting, I thought back over the whole string of events that led up to my present situation. It really all began soon after I met Anthony Lowery at a tea given to feature a new artist. It was becoming quite fashionable here in San Francisco for a family of wealth to sponsor young and struggling artists. Self-acclaimed art critics were popular, and fortunes were being invested in oil paintings, with much speculation as to their future value. I went to the tea that afternoon because all of my friends would be there. I had not understood Anthony Lowery's paintings, nor was I particularly attracted to them, but the artist himself intrigued me. I flirted discreetly and I encouraged his attentions. He was quite different from anyone I had ever met before, and I found him exciting and just a little daring. His dark-brown, laughing eyes, his carelessly handsome features and bohemian ways drew my attention again and again, and I sought invitations to gatherings where I knew he would be.

When Tony began appearing at our door to escort me to a party or invite me for an afternoon drive in the park, my friends turned green-eyed with envy. My family, on the other hand, frowned openly. Tony was everything my father disapproved of in an escort for me. He had no family background, no obvious income, and no plans for the future beyond his painting. But to me Tony provided the laughter I missed in my formal, dignified homelife. He gave me the open affection I needed, was someone who noticed me, someone who made me feel like a woman. I was drawn to him like a moth to a flame, knowing the dangers yet unable to resist.

When Tony's courtship became serious, I hinted to my father that I might marry this artist and asked if he would give his permission. Father was furious, and the conversation ended with him forbidding our friendship to continue. There was an ultimatum: We were not to see each other again.

Never so easily discouraged from something I am intent on doing, I continued to see Tony. I would slip out under the pretense of shopping or visiting friends, and we would meet secretly, holding hands in small, out-of-the-way cafés and walking in the park, stealing kisses by the fountain where it was sheltered from view by the flowering shrubs. I found it all quite romantic and daring. We talked often, and I told Tony about my mother dying when I was five, and how much

I missed her and felt I needed her as I grew older. I confided how lonely I was, raised in a household with a bereaved father who lost himself in his work, one brother much too old to notice me and another nearer my age whom I had been very close to but who now was leading the life of a young bachelor about town and had little time for me.

Tony never spoke of any family. His world was his art, and he talked to me of his dreams of being a famous artist, someday very wealthy, with his paintings sought after by collectors. They would sell for exorbitant prices, and when they did, we planned how we would marry. We would spend our time traveling to faraway places and we would have all the luxuries I had always taken for granted. He spun his dreams and I clung to them as though they were promises.

But I am an impatient person, and there were times when I was not content just to dream, times when I despaired at the waiting. I was not content with talk of a sometime future, but wanted to marry immediately, even if it were without my father's approval.

Tony wouldn't listen to me, insisting that it was important for us not to turn my family against us. He was most popular in all of the fashionable circles and was sought after as a guest in the wealthiest homes because of his handsome good looks, his excellent manners, his charm. Yet despite all of this his paintings were not selling, and thus he could not support a wife. If we were to marry, he explained, we needed the approval and the financial support of my family until his paintings brought in an income.

It was not until I had finally almost become resigned to waiting that I made an astounding discovery, and as a result a plan began to form in my mind.

I knew my father's desk in the library was forbidden to me. From the days of my childhood I had never been allowed to touch a thing that lay on it, because that is where he kept all of the important papers he was working on while at home. But that day I had lost my pen and I needed to write a note. I searched everywhere, finally thinking I could go to the library and borrow one from his desk, returning it before I was discovered.

While there was no pen, there were several papers laying open, as though he had been reading and for some reason had left hastily, not taking the time to fold and put them away. I started to leave when the name "Amelia Crandall" caught my eye and curiosity made me turn back. My mother. Why would her name be on papers Father was working on? She had been gone from us for so long.

The letterhead was from an attorney in Alaska, a town called Valdez. The lawyer's name was Garth Williams. He was writing about my uncle, James Crandall, and my mother. How could he possibly have known her? And in Alaska? My mother was dead. I had always been told that she died soon after the last time my uncle visited our home. One of my last memories of her was the way she laughed as she watched my uncle playing a silly game with me. I skimmed over the papers, not taking time to read the text, seeing only the familiar names that caught my attention. Then I picked up the papers to start reading from the top.

"What are you doing?" My father's voice thundered across the room at me.

Guiltily, I dropped the papers back in place. "I was only going to borrow a pen. I lost mine somehow. . . ."

My voice trailed off. I had almost forgotten the real reason that I was there.

"Then why are you standing there snooping among my papers?"

"I'm not snooping, Father. I had no intention of reading anything on your desk." I watched him walk over to me and pick up the papers, open the top drawer, and put them inside angrily. "Why was a lawyer writing to you from Alaska and talking about my mother?" I asked.

His face was flushed with anger. "It is just settling some old estate problems. It is of no concern to you." His voice was sharp; clearly he wanted to put an end to the conversation.

"But I don't understand," I persisted. "Why should he link Mother's name with Uncle Jim? She has been gone such a long time. How could he possibly know about her? Father, I don't understand." My eyes searched his face, pleading for an answer. "I'm sorry. I don't mean to upset you. I know that you never like to talk about her. It is painful for you, I suppose, because you must have loved her as much as I. But don't you see? I have missed her so, and to see her name on those papers . . . Won't you tell me what it is all about?"

"Really, Nora," he answered, "you are allowing yourself to become upset about nothing. It is just some paperwork that I must take care of. I don't want to talk about it any further."

"I know. That is what you always say. There are times when I would like so much to just be able to talk about her to someone—someone who knew her and could tell me what she was like. You have refused to mention her name, and Paul never has time for me at all. Tom doesn't remember any better than I do, and besides he never wants to talk about her either. There are times when I need her and there is no one else to turn to."

"Rubbish!" he snapped. "You have your Aunt Margaret. It is quite a chore to take on three children when they are someone else's. She has done an excellent job of managing the household."

"Handling the servants, yes. But how can she help me with my problems in facing life—understanding love—when she has never lived or loved herself?"

"Enough!" he roared. "I won't have you talking this way. It is that no-good artist who has caused the change in you—disrespectful of the way you were brought up. I even suspect you have been seeing him, though you were forbidden to meet him again. Love, you say? You don't need to know about that until after you are married—and there is plenty of time for that yet."

"Oh, Father, you are so gruff!" I hoped to coax him out of his mood. "Didn't you love Mother before you married her?" My eyes went to the small framed picture of her that sat on his desk. It was the only picture we had of her. "She was so beautiful, how could you help but love her?"

He raised his chin defiantly, his mouth a firm, hard line. "Our marriage was arranged by our families, who had the sound judgment to go with the responsibility of making a match involving a great deal of money and the lives of two people from very important families."

My mind raced to the small portions of words I had been able to read, and slowly I began to understand why the two names were linked together. "She married you, and loved your younger brother," I breathed softly into the room, stunned by what I had said. "That is what is the matter, isn't it? Why you will never talk to me about her."

I feared for my father's well-being; he became so angry. He picked up the lovely framed picture and smashed it against the stone of the fireplace, seeming unaware of the shattering glass. "You are just like her!" He turned accusing eyes on me, making me shrink back. "You are foolish! You show no judgment, no taste! You would rather spend your hours laughing and dancing than think about your future!" He took a step toward me, and I retreated a step toward the door. "Love!" he exclaimed. "You want to know about love! It is nothing but the caterwauling of the immature, crying out to satisfy the sexual feelings they are too young to understand. Your mother is dead! Do you hear me? *Dead!*"

"That is why you are so angry, isn't it?" I asked, my voice calm now, watching him closely for the answers I no longer believed. "Tell me, Father, am I not right? My mother didn't die, did she? She ran away. She left you and ran away with your brother."

He turned back, his anger gone now, and for a moment he looked very tired, very old. I caught my breath, wanting to take back the words, wanting to reach out and comfort him. He leaned heavily on the back of a chair, looking deep into the flames of the fire. When he spoke, I had a feeling he had forgotten that I was still standing there, waiting intently for his answer. He spoke to the years that had gone by, leaving him a lonely man. "Yes. You are right. I loved her. But she is gone. She is finally really dead."

I turned quietly and left the room, closing the door softly behind me, leaving him to his grief. I had no wish to hurt him further. My mind was in a turmoil, numbed by what I had learned. I went to my room where the note I had started to write still lay on my table, but I was not able to concentrate. My mind raced back and forth like a ball striking the walls of an empty room, not getting anywhere, not finding any answers. I had to know what was in the papers on the desk! Somehow I had to know if my mother was alive and living in Alaska. I had to know why she left me behind, letting me think she was dead. Father had said, "She is finally really dead." What did he mean? Could I ever believe him again? All of those years without a mother. Had she failed me or was her reason for going so overpowering that she had no choice? I *had* to know.

Suddenly the confines of my room were stifling. I had to get out of doors and walk briskly in the cool, sharp air. I had to somehow slow my racing thoughts and be able to think clearly again.

I picked up my hat and my gloves, the unfinished note to my school friend forgotten and no longer important.

I stopped outside the closed library door, hoping my father would have left and I could perhaps steal inside and finish reading the papers. Voices came to me through the heavy wood, and by listening carefully I could make out the muffled words of my aunt.

"I always knew something like this would happen," she was saying. "Sooner or later . . ." I was listening intently now. "He always showed an unnatural favoritism for the child, singling her out in his affections. Have you noticed? She does tend to favor him in her actions. For instance, this infatuation she insists on pursuing for that—that painter! She certainly has been brought up to be much more selective. Goodness knows, Martin, I have tried! I have done the best I could to make her realize what it means to be a Crandall—even if her mother didn't."

"What are you trying to say, Margaret?" Father's voice had a harshness, a challenge.

Margaret sounded a bit hesitant. I could almost feel her embarrassment through the heavy door. "Considering what happened—well, really, Martin, stop and think. How long had she been carrying on with James before she came to you and admitted her guilt? Perhaps she had been indiscreet earlier." She took a deep breath and finished with a note of defiance. "Perhaps James is the child's natural father!"

I heard Father's fist hit the desktop and I knew my flighty little aunt must be shrinking back, intimidated.

"I'll not have that said ever again in this household! *Ever!* Do you hear me? Amelia died the day she walked out of this house and left my daughter—do you hear me? *My* daughter!—and my two sons behind for me to raise. For me she died, but I will not have her memory sullied."

I turned and ran blindly out of the house and down the walkway, into the bright sunlight. I must have walked for miles, forgetting where I had been, not seeking any special direction, just wanting to be away by myself for a little while. I looked up and saw the building where Tony had his studio room, and I knew that unconsciously I had found my way to him, wanting him to hold me while I told him what I had learned.

* * *

His back was turned toward me as he bent slightly toward the easel, impatient to catch what light he could from the February sky. He ignored me completely as I stood watching him work. I allowed my eyes to trace the lithe lines of his shoulders, smiled over the way his white shirt was tucked so carelessly into his tight black trousers, aware of the easy grace of his slim, lean body. Slowly, absently, I removed my gloves and reached up to untie the ribbons on my large straw hat.

"Tony, I need to talk to you." I know my voice must have sounded slightly critical because I resented him not turning, not coming over to me, showing his surprise at seeing me there in his rooms. After all, it had been quite daring of me to go there, alone, to see him. If he loved me, he should be able to tell that I was distraught.

It was a long moment before he acted as though he heard me, and then with a sigh he laid the brushes aside, wiped his hands on a paint-soiled towel, and turned to let his eyes play over me, affection showing in his smile. He reached out for my hands with both of his and drew me to him.

"All right, my darling. What is it that is so important I must stop my work to listen to you? You know that even though it's late February, there still isn't enough daylight for me to work for very long each day, and I hate it when I'm disturbed."

"Surely you must know that it is important for me to come here like this—" I began. "I had to talk to you." I moved closer into the circle of his arm. "Hold me for just a moment, Tony."

He looked down at me in sudden concern. "Why,

Nora, you're trembling. My poor darling, what is it? What has happened?"

"I found a letter—some papers—from a lawyer in Valdez, Alaska." I turned in his arms, feeling the softness of his shirt against my cheek. "Tony, I think my mother is alive."

Gently he led me to the sofa and sat down beside me. "What are you talking about? You said your mother died when you were small. What do you mean?"

In half sentences, my words tumbling together from my disorganized thoughts, I told him of the papers I had found and of the terrible conversation I had had with my father. He listened carefully to every word I said. I went on to tell him about listening at the door of the library and hearing the cutting accusations of my aunt, wondering what truth, if any, was in her words.

"Oh, my poor Nora," he crooned, and I was touched by his sympathy. "How awful this must have been for you."

"I think she is alive, Tony. All of those years when I missed my mother so—when I needed her—they let me think she had died." My voice was bitter but touched with sadness as I tried to picture what must have happened. I gave a sigh. "How terrible it must have been for her to have to make a decision like that! To have to choose between her husband and her children or her lover! Oh, Tony, she must have loved him so desperately to have this happen."

Tony gently dried the tears that had formed in the corners of my eyes. I felt better now that I had someone to talk to, someone to hold me and listen to what

I said. Someone who cared about my feelings. "Their marriage was arranged, you know," I murmured. "I'm sure that Father was terribly fond of her. I'm convinced of that. He has never paid any attention to another woman since she . . . left. His business has been his whole life."

"Do you think she is really still alive?" he asked.

"I don't know. I don't know what to believe. I asked him. He was so angry—he said 'she is finally really dead.' I don't know what it means. I don't know if I can ever believe him anymore." I was silent for a moment. "He was quite a bit older than she, and always so dignified and proper. She loved to dance— and she would sing for us—she laughed so easily. She was very pretty, Tony."

"You remember her then?"

"Yes. There is a small portrait of her in the library, but I remember her even without it. I was five when she left. Father told me she took ill and went away for a rest. Later I was told that she had died. I believed them. That was when Aunt Margaret, Father's sister, came to stay."

"Well, Nora," he said thoughtfully, "you certainly have stirred up something now, haven't you. What's going to happen next?"

I sat up, pulling away from him. "I don't know." I stood up and walked away, going over to where I could study his canvas, looking at it without really seeing it. I stood there, lost in my thoughts for a few moments. Then I turned and looked at him across the room, suddenly knowing what I wanted to do. "I think I will go to Alaska. I want to see her again. Yes, that is what I have to do!"

"But what if she isn't alive? What if he is telling the truth?"

"I want to go anyway. I want to see where she lived. To learn what her life was like. I want to know more about her. I want to see Uncle Jim again. That is all I have left of her, Tony. I have to go."

"Alaska is a big country—so little known about it. How will you find her?" he asked.

"Through the lawyer in Valdez. He seems to know them both—he is the one handling those papers Father was working on. I remember his name."

Tony took both of my hands in his. "You're sure that this is what you want to do?"

"Yes," I answered with conviction. "Yes, I am going up there to see if I can find her."

"Then, my love, we shall go together," he answered.

I raised my eyes in surprise, unable to believe what he had said. "What do you mean?"

Tony laughed at me, enjoying my bewilderment. "Is it so hard to imagine that if you were going away, I would want to go with you? I love you, Nora. I couldn't let you go up there alone. We've talked of marrying for a long time, but there was no money and we didn't have your father's approval. Now we shall marry without either of them. Do you think that between the two of us we can scrape together the price of steamer tickets?"

I stared at him in disbelief. Today had been a series of shocks for me, and now I was receiving a marriage proposal from my dearest Tony, who held my love so easily.

"I—I have my savings," I said haltingly. "It is a sizable amount. Father has always been very generous with my allowance and I have managed to save the greater portion of it. It should be enough, if we are careful."

"Then what are we waiting for?" he cried, swinging me around in a circle in his arms. "We're practically on our way!"

"But Tony . . . can you leave, just like that?"

"And why not? I'm tired of this city anyway." With that he bent and kissed me soundly, doing away with my reason for the moment.

After spending the afternoon making plans with Tony, I went to my father with my chin just as firm as his, my mind just as determined. I told him that I had grown up without knowing my mother and that now I was leaving, going up to Alaska to find her. I stood up to my father, with fire in my eyes and stubborn determination in my voice. I admitted then that I had still been seeing Tony and that now I intended to marry him, with or without his approval. Tony and I were going to travel north, to find my mother.

"But she is dead!" he shouted back at me. "*Both* of them are dead. In an accident. I tried to tell you."

"You shouldn't have lied to me for so many years, Father." My voice was low, tightly controlled. "Now I don't know whether to believe you or not. I am going to find out for myself. But I won't be alone. I will be going as Tony's wife."

It was a terrible session—a true nightmare as our two strong personalities clashed. Wringing my lace handkerchief until it tore into shreds, I refused to back down. And he, his face a fiery red as he paced back and forth, roared out his anger continuously at me.

"And what does this Anthony Lowery say to all of

these plans you have talked him into?" he sneered.
"He has nothing to gain by marrying you now. Does
he know there will be no money from me? How does
he plan to support you? And let me tell you, girl,
those velvet jackets and lace-trimmed shirts he wears
when he bows and scrapes in front of the ladies will
do him little good when he has to break a trail through
the snow to bring in wood to try to keep warm!" He
threw out his arms in a gesture of disgust. "Who will
take care of you then, Nora? You have been spoiled,
never wanting for a thing all of your life. Do you have
any idea at all of what you are doing? You aren't an
adult—you're still acting like a headstrong child, having a tantrum, not using good judgment. What will
you do when the money runs out? I won't be there."

I glared back at him angrily, refusing to listen to
his arguments.

"It doesn't matter what you say, Father. I won't
listen. I won't let you stop us. Tony is just as excited
about the trip as I am. I didn't talk him into it. I
wish you could understand—would give your approval—
but even without it, I am going away with him."

I heard him shout "We'll see about that!" as I
turned on my heel and fled to the shelter of my room.

So it was that the next evening I sat quietly in my
room waiting, as the shadows grew longer on the walls
and darkness crept into the corners of the room. Finally, with an abrupt impatience, I stood up and let my
needlework fall to the floor unnoticed. I moved to the
window to stare unseeing out at the green-tinted lawns
below, fighting within myself until I made a decision.
Then, with determination I turned and stole silently
from my room. I slipped cautiously down the flight of

stairs, remembering in time the loose tread that squeaked, to stand at last in the dark hallway below, my ear pressed to the keyhole of the library door, where the family members were gathered to discuss the situation, thinking they were deciding my future for me.

They underestimated my willfulness.

They still didn't realize that no matter what the outcome of this family conference, I was going to go to Alaska, and I was going with Tony, with or without their blessings. Several hours ago I had hastily packed my trunk, and it had been secreted away from the house. I knew that Tony was packing too, and he was waiting for a message from me.

The only real decision to be made was whether I was to have a lovely wedding as befitted our position in society and leave on a ship with a stateroom filled with flowers and baskets of fruit or whether Tony and I were to slip away secretly on a steamer leaving at dawn tomorrow, to be married later, on board, by the ship's captain.

Because I knew my family so well, we had taken the precaution to reserve passage on the steamer leaving at dawn, and my trunk was already waiting at the dock.

CHAPTER TWO

I drew my heavy cape closer about my shoulders against the penetrating chill of the drifting fog and the clinging sea mists. We had boarded the steamer while night still lay heavy across the city, but now the sky behind the mountains to the east was becoming tinted with color and the murky waters below us were reflecting the lights, turning them into pools of deep scarlets and dark blues.

I stood beside Tony at the rail, looking down, watching the scene below us, my every nerve tingling with excitement as I tried to gather all of the strange sounds and sights to me so as not to miss a single thing. The seagulls were making their noisy swoops among the pilings in search of scraps, paying little attention to the stevedores loading the last-minute cargo or the people hurrying aboard. From every side of us were the unfamiliar sounds of men shouting back and forth to each other as they worked, hidden engines throbbing in the din of creaking cables and pulleys, crates bump-

ing together, frightened horses being led aboard unwillingly, dogs protesting from cages, their sharp barking cutting into the air, and everywhere there were
laughing, shouting, pushing, milling people. Mixed
with the noises were the odors of the sea lying heavy
on the air—the seaweed, the fish, the tangy smell of salt.

Despite the early hour, small groups of people collected on the docks to watch and wave tearful good-
byes. I felt the ship shudder beneath my feet, and
finally we began to move slowly, carefully, away from
the berth, away from the lights of the awakening city
that had always been my home. We were finally on our
way! In my excitement I reached out for Tony's hand,
and he put his arm around my shoulders, drawing me
close. I looked up at his dark eyes smiling down at me,
his unruly black hair ruffled carelessly across his forehead by the light breeze, and I sensed that now he was
as impatient as I was for the journey to start.

I knew that my father and brothers would still be
sleeping and my empty room would not yet be discovered. We would be leaving the shelter of San Francisco Bay and entering the Pacific Ocean about the time
the sun could be seen balancing above the horizon and
my family would be waking up.

The family meeting behind the closed doors of the
library last night had been disagreeable and lengthy. I
had listened at the keyhole long enough to realize that
there was little hope of their deciding in my favor or
even trying to understand my feelings. My father stood
firm in his belief that I should be sent East to visit rela-
tives until I forgot my infatuation with Tony and my
foolish plans to travel north in search of my mother.
He had carelessly brushed aside Tom's offer to go to
Valdez and meet with the lawyer, saying he felt it not

only unnecessary but foolhardy for any of the family
to travel up there. It would be much better to have his
attorneys handle the entire affair. Tom gave in easily
without much protest. I was hurt at Tom's lack of
support or understanding. I had counted so heavily on
him. After all, she was his mother too. Did he still
resent her because she had left us? Didn't he ever wonder what had taken her away from us? Had my father's
bitterness so influenced him that he had no compassion
for a woman so torn by love that she left her home,
her children? Why couldn't he understand that I was a
woman now too, loving Tony, needing his love in
return?

I knew then that somehow, in growing up, we had
also begun to grow apart, and I hated the thought of it.

Paul and I had never been close; there were too many
years between us. When I was a child, bubbling with
the discovery of the world around me, he was already a
serious scholar, patterning his life in our father's foot-
steps. I hadn't expected him to understand me now.
And in my aunt there was no hope at all. Life beyond
the secure boundaries of our household left her confused and bewildered.

Again I wondered what had been in the papers I had
caught such a brief glimpse of, and what matters needed
to be settled by the attorney in charge. Could an accident really have taken the lives of both my mother and
my uncle? Even if both were dead, I still had to continue my journey. With all my heart I wished for my
mother to be alive, wanting to see me, making me welcome. But if it were not so, I must go there anyway. I
had to learn more about her, something to fill in all of
the years that I had missed.

Though I felt a sorrow for the pain I had caused my

father by deciding to go, for me there was no turning back.

We stood at the rail for a long time, each of us lost in private thoughts as we watched the skyline slip farther and farther away and the sun appear bright above the eastern mountains, turning the morning into brilliant shades of blues and greens and yellows. The light wind touched my hair and the crisp air made my face tingle. I shivered from the delicious excitement racing within me, but Tony thought I was shivering from the cold, so he drew me closer into his embrace, giving me a tight but tender kiss as he suggested that it was time we went below and inspected the cabin he had booked for us.

Neither of us had traveled by ocean before. I don't know what I had expected, but it certainly was not the tiny, cramped quarters I saw through the doorway. I looked up sharply at Tony as I stepped inside. Two narrow, uncomfortable-looking bunks occupied one whole wall. On them were lumpy mattresses and lightweight quilts of uncertain origins. Against the back was a porthole, letting in only a glimmer of light through a dirty glass. A small stand held a water basin and an empty pitcher. In the center of the room, almost filling the walking space, sat the trunk I had packed with such haste and secrecy, looking out of place in this poor cabin. A smaller trunk that I knew must be Tony's was beside it, along with several canvases, an easel, and his case of paints. I turned to ask him why they were together like this, but he was studying something beyond the porthole and I felt that he was avoiding my eyes.

"Hasn't someone made a mistake, Tony?" I asked.

"They have brought all of our luggage to one cabin. Is yours close by?"

"Now look, honey, we are traveling together, aren't we?" he answered casually. "I registered us as Mr. and Mrs. Lowery. I don't think you realize how everyone is fighting to be able to get passage north right now. It's difficult to get a cabin, at any price. We were lucky to get this, small as it is. A lot of men are bunking three and four into spaces this size, and a few are even sleeping in bedrolls out on the deck. How would you like to have to travel like that? Besides, I didn't have much choice—especially since I didn't have much money to bargain with."

I frowned slightly as I thought of the small pouch of coins I had taken from my savings and given to Tony the day before to pay for our fares. When I had counted out the money, I felt that it would be more than enough to see us north if we used care. We would have other expenses along the way, and I had been careful to set aside what I thought it would cost for us to cover these before giving the rest of the money to Tony. I had really counted on him buying our passage and having money left over to use for any other incidentals that might come up. Evidently I was misjudging the cost of things already, and we weren't even away from the city yet.

Tony saw my frown of concern and he reached out, drawing me into his arms. "Don't look so worried," he cajoled, a little mockingly. "What has happened to your sense of adventure? You must learn to take things as they come, to relax a little. You know, Nora, you're going to have to expect things to be a little bit rougher than what you are used to. We're headed into a frontier country, to a land where nature plays no favorites. The few inconveniences here on the ship are the least that we will have to learn to cope with. Don't let me down, now, before we've even started." He tipped my face up with his fingertips and gave me a lingering kiss. "What does it matter about the trunks, Nora? We're going to be married as soon as I can talk to the captain, and then we would have to move our things around anyway."

"Do you think he will be able to marry us today?" I asked. "I thought that it might take several days. I don't know, I didn't know just what to expect."

"Honey, you worry too much. You should have thought of these things before you decided that you wanted to run away. Now, smile for me. Everything is going to be all right."

I'm being foolish, I thought, remembering the hasty way we left, without time for planning or packing properly, and I slipped my arms up around his neck, relaxing against him, wanting to be kissed. "You are going to see the captain as soon as possible, aren't you?" I murmured as he held me close. "We will be married today, won't we, Tony? I have waited so long to be your wife!"

Though he held me tenderly, I sensed the hesitation in his voice as he answered. "Of course I will. As soon as the captain is free, I'll talk to him. Right now I imagine he is very busy getting his ship out of the harbor and onto the high seas. I really don't think he has the time or the patience to be interested in our problems, no matter how important they may be to us. But soon, my dear, soon."

The events of the past two days had been a very heady experience for me, and I felt a little faint from it all. And now, the thought of finally being Mrs. Anthony Lowery, Tony's wife, after so much plotting and waiting, seemed almost too tantalizing to be true. I pushed away from him, suddenly a little frightened by the smoldering emotions that were coming to life within me, making me tremble.

"Please, Tony. Let me go," I whispered. "It won't be long now."

I turned and looked about the cabin. "I've got to get us settled and the trunks opened." This tiny, unpleasant cabin, confining and depressing as it might be, was to be our home for a while. I set out to unpack the few things that I thought we would need, hanging our heavier cloaks on the pegs provided and putting out odds and ends of our toiletry items to brighten the square, plain washstand. I felt a certain thrill in handling Tony's clothing in such a housewifely fashion, but my domestic chores did nothing to hold his interest. He left me to take a turn on the deck to talk to the other passengers and, I hoped, to see if the captain was available to talk to him.

He returned soon after I finished with the unpacking. He seemed to have caught the contagious fever of the prospectors headed toward the Klondike or the interior of Alaska, and his eyes flashed as he recounted the tales he had heard on deck and described the men he had talked to. I listened, trying to seem interested, but it was not what I was waiting to hear.

"The captain, Tony?" I coaxed. "Did you talk to him? What did he say?"

I saw his handsome features turn dark and a scowl tug at his forehead. I knew he resented my bringing up the subject again, and I began to feel that something was wrong.

"The captain suspects that we're eloping, Nora," he explained as he dropped down to sit on the bunk. "He is reluctant—no, that isn't quite right—he refused to perform the marriage ceremony for us."

"But why?" I cried. "I don't understand. Certainly if he suspects that we are eloping, he must realize that since we share the same cabin, it would be much better that he marry us!" I shook my head. "I just don't understand."

"It isn't the captain's fault, Nora. Your father is a very important man in the import business and in shipping. He pulls a lot of strings, has a lot of influence. The captain is only looking out for his own best interests. You can't blame him for that. If he looks the other way, he isn't involved. If he marries us, he becomes a part of the plot." He took my hand and pulled me down to sit on the edge of the bunk beside him. "Don't look so worried, my dearest," he consoled. "It really isn't that big of a problem, you know. We will be in Seattle before too long, and then we can go ashore and be married there. I understand that the steamer will stay there overnight, to transfer cargo and pick up more freight."

I pulled my hand away from his and moved away from the bunk toward the center of the room. Unhappily I glanced around. The bunk seemed to grow and take up the greater portion of the cramped quarters.

Guessing my thoughts, Tony seemed amused. "Stop worrying about so many small, unimportant things," he chided. "You are the one who is the great adventurer! At first you even thought of traveling up to Alaska alone, remember? Well, my little mouse, if you are going to travel up into the gold fields you had better understand that the rules of San Francisco society hardly apply to us now, out here," he said. "If you were going to be such a prude, you should have stayed home—safe in the watchful care of your family."

"I'm not a prude!" I flared. "It's just that . . ."

"I know." Unexpectedly he smiled reassuringly at me, his eyes holding a gentleness. "I was only teasing you. Don't be upset. It will be all right. I'll take the top bunk, and we'll tack a blanket around the lower one to make plenty of privacy for my timid little virgin."

It was then that the full impact of what we were doing finally caught up with me. Until now things had moved along so fast, I had been completely caught up in the intrigue of running away with a very handsome and fascinating man to a faraway place, headed to an unknown future of challenge and adventure. But now my courage faltered slightly as I confronted the reality of the unplanned details that were a part of our elopement. My strict upbringing rose to the surface to challenge and confuse my feelings of adventure and freedom. I was irritated by Tony's amusement at my discomfort, but I shrugged my shoulders and struggled to toss a smile of casual indifference toward him. "You are right," I said. "It is only temporary, anyway. We can manage."

Our route carried us up along the high, rocky cliffs of northern California, past the heavily wooded shoreline of Oregon, and into the bustling port of Seattle. The weather held, with only a few clouds in the afternoon and the customary early morning fog. I was beginning to feel very worldly, congratulating myself on being an excellent sailor. I delighted in standing on the deck, letting the wind toss my hair and tug at my clothing as I watched the rolling seas. I was fascinated every

moment, wanting the trip to stretch on and on. My
only regret was the captain's refusal to perform the
marriage ceremony for us, and it embarrassed me a
little when I saw him on the deck so I avoided him
whenever possible.

Though Tony honored the boundaries of the
blanket-curtained lower bunk, I still felt uncomfortable
closeted in the cabin with him. I found excuses to stay
as long as possible in the dining room, visiting with the
other passengers, coaxing Tony away from the confines
of the cabin on one pretense or another. I dreaded
night to fall, alarmed at Tony's increasing ardor as
soon as the door closed behind us.

"No, Tony!" I pleaded, pushing him away. "Not
until we are married! You promised!" I turned my
head away so I couldn't see the anger in his smoldering
eyes, and I wondered if it was his passion that frightened me or rather the unfamiliar turmoil of emotions
burning within me that I feared I couldn't control.

Only a few more days, I kept telling myself. Just a
few more days until we are safely out of Seattle and
then everything will be all right. I will be Tony's
wife, and we will be on our way to find my mother.
My dreams, my plans, would all be coming true—unless
my father found a way to send someone overland in
time to meet the steamer at the docks in Seattle. . . .

Early in the morning on a day when the sun was
shining clear and the sea was calm, we first sighted the
deep emerald-green shoreline and steamed our way into
the noisy, bustling port. It was filled with all sorts of
seagoing vessels, from small fishing boats to the large
lumber carriers. I had heard my father and brothers
talk so often about this fast-growing shipping center

that I looked forward to being there and seeing it for myself.

How I would have loved to explore the streets of this city with Tony. We could take an overnight lodging in a nice hotel where we could have a lovely meal served in the dining room and I could spend my first night in Tony's arms on a large soft bed that didn't pitch and roll with the waves. . . . But I knew we didn't dare spend all that money if it wasn't necessary. As far as I knew, the only money we had brought with us was what I had drawn from my savings, and after the money I had given to Tony to purchase the steamer tickets there was not a large sum left. I had never really concerned myself with budgeting or the problems of money before. I always had whatever I needed at my disposal and never gave too much thought to where it came from or what would happen when it stopped coming in. Not until now.

Tony and I stood side by side at the rail, watching the beehive of activity going on below us on the docks as the steamer was guided into place and secured. The crisp air ruffled Tony's hair and his handsome face was alive with the excitement around us as we stood there watching, his arm protectively around my waist. The air was filled with the smells of fresh-cut lumber, exhaust from noisy gasoline engines, fish, and seaweed, and the sounds of men shouting back and forth, dogs barking, the creaking of lines pulled taut as cargo was swung from the dock to the decks of waiting ships.

Tony loved the people, the large crowds, the noise, the laughter, and the artist in him responded to the new and strange sights all around us. We both felt the exhilaration of two children on an unexpected holiday

as we ran down the gangplank and stood unsteadily on
the wharf after so many days on the ocean. We looked
about for the walkway that would take us to the streets
toward the shops. I felt so confident with Tony at my
side, his easygoing smile there to reassure me if I hesitated, his hand holding mine, but I couldn't resist
quickly scanning the crowds along the wharf, looking
for a familiar face. There was still this last chance that
my father had found a way to have us stopped before
we continued on our route to the north.

Once away from the confusion of the wharfs, we
found a number of shops all within walking distance. I
saw so many things displayed in the windows that I
wished I could fill out the hastily packed wardrobe. For
the trip ahead of us we would both need warmer clothing than what we had always worn in San Francisco.
Tony saw me looking wistfully in the shop windows
and suggested that I go through the stores to find some
heavy outdoor clothing while he went in search of a
minister and made the arrangements for us to be
married.

We stepped off the boardwalk into a sheltered doorway, and I opened the money pouch that I had hidden
away in the folds of my clothing. I kept out a portion
to cover my shopping and handed the rest of it over to
Tony. He pulled me close, kissing me, ignoring the
stares of passersby.

"In only a few more hours, Nora," he whispered. His
sensuous smile and the promise in his eyes left me weak,
and I clung to him for a moment, not wanting him to
release me. And then I reluctantly pushed against his
chest and stepped back.

*   *   *

I spent the next few hours going from shop to shop, selecting items for each of us, a heavier cloak for me, a sturdy coat for Tony, woolen stockings for us both. I moved from one store to another, happily engrossed in my shopping, my mind on the evening ahead of us. As I stood looking at a display of new hats in a window, the sun reflected the crowd behind me off the glass. Suddenly I thought I saw a familiar face. I turned quickly, my eyes searching the strangers about me, but I found only people going on their private ways and paying me no mind. Still I felt a chill and my interest in shopping waned. Tired of being alone, I turned back toward the restaurant where I was to meet Tony.

He was already there, sitting toward the back of the room where he could watch the door, frowning over a steaming cup of coffee. As I hurried toward him, his dark expression increased my feeling of foreboding. I waited until I was seated across from him and the waitress had placed a hot cup of coffee in front of me before I asked what was wrong. I sensed that something had happened once again to upset our plans, and I feared the answer.

"Tony, you didn't find a minister, did you." It was a statement, not a question, but my eyes pleaded with him to tell me differently.

He reached out and covered my hand with his. "We will have to eat our dinner quickly and return to the ship. The sooner we do, the better it will be."

"But what is it, Tony?" I was becoming a little frightened.

He glanced toward the door before answering. "Paul is here—in Seattle. I saw him get out of a carriage and walk toward the wharf."

"Oh, no!" I whispered. "That is what I was afraid of. What are we going to do, Tony?" I wailed. "He'll find some way to make me go back, I just know!" The last of the lighthearted feeling I had earlier melted away into a dark cloud of despair.

"No, he won't." Tony's face was grim in spite of his efforts to reassure me. "He doesn't know for sure that we left on that ship, and he won't be able to find us here if we watch our step. We'll go back and stay close to our cabin, out of sight until we sail."

"But what good will that do?" I asked, wondering at his plan. "He must have reason to suspect we are on this ship or he wouldn't be here. All he has to do is check the passenger list and talk to the captain. He will have no trouble finding us at all." I felt the warm tears threatening in my eyes as I thought of meeting with Paul, of seeing him wear the same dark look my father wore when he was forced to deal with my misadventures.

Tony leaned back and gave me a confident, conspiring look. "More trouble than you think, Nora. You underestimate me. There is no way he can trace us. Our names aren't on the passenger list."

"I don't understand." I looked at him in bewilderment. Tony had secured our tickets, we had a cabin, we certainly weren't stowaways. "How could we possibly not be on the passenger list?"

Tony answered me a little defiantly. "Quite simple. I didn't book our passage under our right names. The cabin is assigned to a Mr. and Mrs. Lowden. Wayne Lowden."

I stared at him, understanding slowly coming to me. "Then when the captain spoke to you on board, he really did call you 'Mr. Lowden,' didn't he? I thought at the time that I just misunderstood. He really believes that we are Mr. and Mrs. Lowden!" Then I had another thought. "Oh, no, Tony! If he believes that, then he thinks that we are already married. You never did ask him to marry us, did you?" I whispered in horror. "I don't understand. Why did you lie to me?"

Tony was becoming distant now, playing absently with the silver on the table, not meeting my eyes. "I thought we would have less trouble this way, and I didn't see how there could be problems getting married in Seattle."

"Why didn't you at least tell me?" I asked. "Why did you lie to me? I don't understand why you did it this way. We are only eloping, not criminals escaping from the law! If you had only told me, I would have understood."

I could sense that he was losing his patience at my lack of trust, and his irritation lay heavy in his answer. "I did it to protect us—in case such a thing might happen as is happening right now. That was my reason. In case we were followed. In case someone tried to find us and stop us." He leaned across the table toward me, catching both of my hands in his, softly pleading now as he looked into my stormy face. "Ah, Nora, I was only trying to protect you. To take care of you. Please, just have a little patience. Trust me. We will be married as soon as we reach Valdez. I promise. Then we will go together to see this lawyer you talked about, and we will find your mother—*if* she is living up there. Think, Nora! Isn't this what you have wanted? And I will be painting. The gold fields are in everyone's minds right now. I will paint things that I see, and they will sell! We'll have all the money we need. I'll be able to take care of you, Nora." His voice was low. "Just try to believe in me."

He smiled that endearing, boyish smile that had always worked before, and his eyes were softly pleading, but this time I had my very first doubts as I studied his face intently. "You had other reasons for booking us under a false name, didn't you? Why, Tony? Who else, besides my father, were you trying to keep from finding us?" The thought had never before occurred to me that Tony might have reasons of his own for wanting to leave San Francisco when he did, not wanting to be traced. What were they? Debtors he wished to leave behind?

The soft smile faded and he closed his fingers about my wrist angrily. "You have hardly touched your dinner. You are going to be hungry before we have a chance to have a hot meal again. And we still have to get back on deck and into our cabin without being seen."

"Please, you are hurting me. Let go, Tony." My voice was soft, my eyes accusing. I pushed back the plate the waitress had set on the table while we were talking. I didn't feel as though I could swallow a bite, even though the food was attractively served and smelled enticing. For the first time since we had started out on this escapade my enthusiasm wavered. Remembering the angry scene with my father, I wondered now if he was right after all. Was I acting like the mature adult I thought I was, or was I in truth just a headstrong child without good judgment, as he had accused me of being? Had I been spoiled by too much wealth and an overly indulgent family? Was this just another game I was playing that had gotten out of hand, or would I have the stamina to face what lay ahead of me? And what about Tony? Had I been like my mother and chosen to love a man because he could make me laugh and feel wanted, finding a love strong enough to endure any barriers? Or was my father right again, and it was only a sexual thing, a web of passions that I wasn't mature enough to understand?

My hands trembled as I took Tony's arm and we made our way out of the restaurant, heading back to the safety of the ship. Carefully we checked the faces of the people along the walkway, ready to dodge into a hidden doorway if necessary. We didn't laugh together and hold hands as we did on the trip into town. I walked quietly beside him, my mind a whirlwind of confusion and doubt. It would be so easy for me at this point to just admit that it was a foolhardy adventure and to refuse to go back on board with him. I must confess I considered the possibility—I could turn back and let my brother Paul find me, give in to his anger, and let him take me home. I knew if I did, there would be the expected storm to go through, but it would pass in time and once again I would be the sheltered daughter content with her needlework, having my life carefully planned out for me.

But I was my father's daughter, full of stubborn pride! I knew that there was no way I could turn back now, giving up the search for my mother and losing Tony's love in the process.

I sighed heavily and followed Tony aboard. We reached our cabin without meeting anyone, and we slipped inside, shutting the door quickly behind us. I drew off my gloves, tossed my cape carelessly across the top of the trunk, and went to sit on the lower bunk. My mind was busy, worrying away at our new situation as I tried to sort out my feelings.

Nothing had really changed. We were still headed north to Valdez to find my mother, or to find where she had lived, to learn something about her—and I didn't want to turn back now. Though my moments of distrust had caused us to quarrel, I still loved Tony and I wanted to be with him, to know that he loved me in return. I looked across at Tony's dark face and I knew I wouldn't bring up the subject of marriage again until we reached the shores of Alaska. His distant coolness left me hurt and unhappy, and though I was angry at the way things had turned out, upset with him for lying to me, I was lonely too.

After a long and restless night, I didn't wake until eleven o'clock. By peering out of the porthole and listening to the noises from the outside, I could tell that the crates from San Francisco had been unloaded and the cargo to be carried from Seattle to Alaska was being stowed away. I slipped from my bed, anxious to complete my toilette and be dressed before Tony woke up. When he did, we were very quiet, speaking to each other in polite short sentences and then only when necessary. Neither of us could leave the cabin yet and the air lay heavy with the tension between us. I picked up a book and tried to read. Tony paced back and forth and often went to look out of the porthole. Finally he threw himself across his bunk and pretended sleep as I read, and reread, the same page in my book. It was nearly four o'clock before the tides were right and we felt a shudder run through the boat. Finally we were in motion, moving out away from the docks and

murmuring endearments as he led me into a world that
I had not known existed—a world of hot, driving, all-
consuming fire and passion begging to be fulfilled. I
clung to him instinctively, following where he led, my
body responding to him with a knowledge of its own
until I felt an explosion race through my veins so vio-
lent that for a moment I thought I would perish right
there in his arms. Together we fell back against the
damp pillows, panting, exhausted, entwined in each
other's arms. We lay quietly now, sleepily content in
the wonder of this new love we had found together.

I heard Tony breathing softly at my side. I knew that
he was sleeping. I lay quietly looking up into the shadows of the darkened cabin, relaxed and happy, drowsily
trying to sort out and understand these new emotions
of love and fulfillment as a woman. I was sure now,
without any doubt, that I was really in love with Tony
and held his love in return. I wanted to be with him
like this forever. He stirred in his sleep, murmuring my
name. I turned slightly, adjusting my body to his, and
sighed happily as I drifted off to sleep too.

Our ship moved slowly but steadily northward, and
the air became sharp with the bite of cold. Even
though it was almost spring back in San Francisco, here
the days were still short and carried the feel of winter.
Tony hated the fog and dampness that hung about us
most of the time. He sat in the dining room playing
cards with the other men hour after hour, seeking the
companionship of their rowdy conversations. I would
slip out onto the deck and watch the sea until the rain
and sharp wind would drive me back inside. I missed
the books that I used to read on rainy days back home,
and I was restless and impatient with the slow progress

that we were making. The days seemed endless to me.
I looked forward to our nights, because then Tony
would draw me close to him, wrapping me in warmth,
as we lay together in the narrow lower bunk and he
would teach me the mysteries of a man and woman in
love. He was again the carefree, handsome man I had
known in San Francisco and I was happy in my confidence of his love.

Each night I thought less and less of home and
looked more and more to the days, and the nights, that
lay ahead of us. I refused to allow the doubts I had in
Seattle to bother me.

We were about four days out of Valdez when I discovered I was not the ocean traveler I had thought I
was. It was about noon, and Tony had come out to
stand on the deck beside me, watching the black clouds
roll in closer and heavier overhead. The wind came up
sharp and cold, and I felt raindrops hit my face. The
sky grew darker and the wind stronger, until I huddled
against Tony for protection. It wasn't long until we
were forced to seek the shelter of our cabin, not only
from the cold and the rain, but for protection from the
pitching of the ship. It was almost impossible to maintain a footing as the high seas tossed and rolled us
about. Water slashed against the porthole and the ship
creaked and snapped in agony, as though it were being
torn apart. For the first time in my life I knew real
terror. We sat clinging together on the bunk, clutching
at the sides to keep from being tossed across the cabin.
I stared in horrified fascination at our cloaks swaying
back and forth on their pegs and watched the basin on
the washstand as it clattered to the floor. Each time the
ship rolled up to the top of a wave, then dropped
with a bruising crash, my stomach rolled too, and I

retched until there was nothing left but an aching hollow. I tried to cling to Tony for reassurance but I think he was as scared as I, and just as sick.

We gave up trying to keep our balance on the edge of the bunk and lay back against the pillow, cold and frightened. Finally I was able to stop retching and I held Tony in my arms as a mother holds her frightened child, murmuring to him each time he bent toward the slop jar. He was so desperately ill my heart ached for him, but I could do nothing. With each crash of the ship we tensed, sure that this time it would not be able to withstand the punishment it was receiving and would break in two. Sometime late in the evening, numbed by our terror, we fell into a restless sleep.

When morning came, I slipped carefully from the bunk, holding on to the sides for support until I could wrap my shawl around me, trying not to wake Tony. I worked my way across to the doorway. As I opened it, a wave of water hit me full in the face, leaving me drenched. One of the ship's crew was there, just outside, and he caught my arm and steadied me.

"Are you all right, ma'am?" he shouted to me above the roar of the wind. "You shouldn't be out here. The seas are high and will wash a mite like you overboard!" He was wearing a rain slicker and boots as protection against the storm, and the water ran in rivulets from the brim of his hat. "Is there anything I can do to help you?" he asked.

I clung to his arm for support as I shouted to make myself heard above the storm. "Would it be possible to get some fresh drinking water? We can't eat a thing, but my . . . husband is very ill. A taste of cold water would help, I think."

He nodded. "Go back inside. I'll bring some." He

pushed me back inside the shelter of the cabin and disappeared into the mist. Before long he was back with a jug of water and a small tin of clear broth. I must have looked nearly as bad as I felt because he patted my arm and tried to smile reassuringly at me. "Just stay inside and try to keep warm and dry, ma'am. If you can drink this cup of broth, it will do you good. You mustn't worry. This old ship has ridden many a storm a lot worse than this one and she is still afloat."

I tried to smile back but the effort was too much. I thanked him and pushed the door shut, leaning against it, with water dripping down from my clothing. So she's been through worse storms than this, has she? I thought. Well, not for me! I would be only too glad to see land again—if we were to be lucky enough to reach it, that is.

The ship gave another great heave into the air, and as it dropped with a crash I was thrown across the cabin, spilling the hot broth. I managed to set the water pitcher down on the floor and block it with our shoes to hold it in place. The next roll of the ship set me to retching again, and afterward I curled up weakly on the bunk beside Tony and closed my eyes.

It was the quiet that first woke me. I opened my eyes and slowly looked around the small cabin. The coats were hanging from the hooks on the wall, without swaying. The water jug was on the floor where I had left it, still with some water inside. Sparks of sunshine were filtering through the porthole and dancing on the wall. I lay listening to the silence. We were moving, but with the gentle, rolling motion I had felt in the waters off the shores of Oregon and northern California.

Tony lay beside me, and from his easy breathing I

could tell that he was sleeping restfully. I threw back the blanket and crawled on my hands and knees to the foot of the bunk so I could see out of the porthole. The ominous black was gone from the water and the sky. Patches of fog drifted about and through its haze, the sun was brilliant, striking the water in ribbons of yellow.

I washed myself hurriedly and changed into clean clothes, then I attempted to straighten up and air out the cabin before Tony began to stir.

With the good weather, my high spirits returned. "Tony! Wake up!" I coaxed. "The storm is over! Come on, please wake up." He stirred and stretched slowly, unwillingly. "Wake up. Let's go find breakfast. I'm so hungry!" Tony groaned at the mention of food and pulled the covers over his face, but I was ravenous!

In spite of my enthusiasm, it took a great deal of encouragement to get him out of the bed and on his feet. Dark circles smudged his soft brown eyes and his hair lay limp across his forehead. My poor dear Tony. But I coaxed and pleaded until I got him up and washed and into a clean shirt so could leave our cabin and go in search of hot coffee and food. I felt as though I hadn't eaten in days, and even the poor ship rations tasted like a banquet. Not many other people were in the dining room with us, only the hardiest of passengers—and all showed the stress of the storm, no matter how sturdy they were.

I could not face going back to the confines of the cabin so we went to stand at the rail of the deck, looking out over the beguiling, calm seas, rolling lazily in the sun. The cool air smelled so fresh and clean to me. Bits of sunlight, burning through the fog, fell warm on our shoulders and danced on the water. Even Tony began to respond. He put his arm about my waist, drawing me close to him, and smiled down at me as he reached to brush my hair back from where the wind had blown it across my face. I rested my head against his shoulder, and we stood breathing in the crisp, clear air following the terrible storm.

Gradually I could see high, sharp cliffs forming on the horizon. Here and there jagged rocks protruded from the sea, forming islands, and as we drew closer I could see something moving about on them. Black-and-white birds, foreign to me, nested in large numbers in the crevices, and there were seals basking in the sun. Off to the right was a huge mountain entirely of ice— ice different from that which I had ever seen before. It held a rainbow of colors in its depths, with large patches of brilliant blues and turquoise. Never had I seen anything to quite match the splendor of this.

"I see you've spotted the glacier." I turned to see the same crew member who had brought the jug of water to me the day before standing nearby, his eyes crinkled in a friendly smile.

"I've heard of glaciers before, but this is the first I have ever seen." I stared in wonder. "It's beautiful!"

"That ice floe has been there for thousands and thousands of years, they say," he answered. "She has the colors of the sky and the sun frozen right into her. Aye, she is beautiful, but she can be deadly too."

As I watched a large chunk of the glacier ice broke loose and fell into the water, sending a spray of water high into the air. My eyes fell to the other large chunks floating in the water. Icebergs!

"Is there danger here?" I asked.

"Aye," he nodded. "She's calving now. She spawns those chunks of ice big as buildings, and they can be treacherous. But you're not to worry none, ma'am. Our captain knows these waters well. We're in the sound now, and in a couple of hours we'll be anchored in Valdez and you will be walking on solid ground. Your trip on the water will soon be over."

He tipped his hat and left us then because the activity of the crew had increased and every man was needed.

Tony and I stood together and watched the land move closer. High mountains covered in snow, their tops disappearing into curtains of mist, completely circled the sound except for where the sea made its entrance. The air carried a cold dampness that penetrated through our clothing. Seagulls swooped and cried. Small islands of ice floated by us in the water. Rock crags protruded from the waves, daring us to come too close. I saw one or two small fishing boats venturing out from shore. An occasional log could be seen riding on the crest of the tide. The rocks had large groups of seals, sleeping or lifting their heads to bark a warning at us for intruding into their territory. Other seals were in the water, and I watched them as they dived and rolled near the ship, as curious of us as we were of them.

Every nerve in my body tingled in excitement as I stood there watching, my face into the wind, feeling so . . . alive!

CHAPTER THREE

The little town of Valdez lay huddled in mist at the back of a finger of the sound. On the day we arrived very little sun was able to reach up into this fjord. The whole area was damp, surrounded by dreary shadows of a heavy green undergrowth. Beneath the twisted evergreens the tundra grew knee deep in a spongy marsh.

The town itself was bustling; it looked as though it was springing up too quickly for any organized planning to take place, pushing against the mountains for a place to set its feet. Close to the water's edge were fishing and cannery buildings. Behind lay homes and businesses, built along the few streets that were roughly graded and ended abruptly at the foot of the ring of tall mountains. Snow was still heavy on the surrounding peaks but down every gully and crevass tumbled waterfalls from melting snow and ice, capturing the bits of sunlight that escaped the clouds, turning them into dancing rainbows.

Evidence of new building was everywhere. I heard the sounds of saws and gas engines from the sawmill, shouting and confusion from the streets, and everywhere, dampness and mist. Most of the town must have been there to meet our ship, turning our arrival into a sort of holiday. Merchants, anxious over delayed supplies, were eager to see the crates unloaded. Men were sorting out their equipment, eager to get their gear in order and begin their trek up into the gold fields. There were a few women here and there in the crowd, and young boys offering to help carry luggage, curious about everything that was going on.

Tony and I walked the several blocks from the dock to a hotel. The walk was not too difficult because there were walkways made of boards laid across log planking, raised several inches above the mud of the streets. However, we had to cross two sidestreets. I raised my skirts as high as I could and still maintain my dignity, but my boots sank into the ankle-deep clay-like mud, and I had to cling to Tony's arm to keep from slipping.

The hotel was on a corner, a wooden structure with heavy board siding, painted white. It looked totally respectable. A clerk wearing wire-rimmed glasses and a black suit studied the big ledger open in front of him on the counter and assigned us a room on the second floor in the front of the building, with a window looking down on the street.

The room was quite comfortable and modern, with a thick down comforter on the bed, a welcoming wooden rocker, a bureau for our clothing, and a kerosene lamp with roses painted on the shade sitting on the small table.

I crossed to the window, and by leaning against the

glass I could see several stores. Directly across the way were large log pilings sunk into the ground with the beginnings of a flooring attached about three feet above the dirt, evidence of another new building going up. To the left, back up the street we had walked, I could see a general store, a bank, and at least t̄ ̄ ̄ ̄ taverns.

I sat on the edge of the bed, testing its softness, and stretched wearily, only too content to stay here, with firm floors beneath my feet, and let Tony return to the docks to collect our luggage.

I must have fallen asleep because a late-afternoon sun was pouring in through the white lace curtains on the window when I heard Tony drop my heavy trunk on the floor near the bed. I was awake and on my feet by the time he came back up the stairs with the other trunk and his canvases.

The hotel clerk sent a husky young lad up to our room with a steaming bucket of water, and while I attempted a basin bath, Tony left to seek a barber for a hot bath and a shave. How I longed right then for the big white enamel tub in my father's home, and a long, soothing soak in hot water deep enough to cover me and smelling of sweet, fragrant oils!

The evening sun was just resting on the rim of the mountains when we set forth to look for a restaurant. My handsome Tony was smiling confidently, and I felt clean, rested, and lighthearted as I walked at his side. The mud in the streets didn't seem so discouraging now, and at least we didn't pitch and roll with the seas. The ground stayed solid to the step. I was so glad the ocean trip was over.

At dinner we recaptured some of the warm and wonderful feelings we had shared back in San Francisco when Tony was courting me. We held hands and Tony's eyes caressed me tenderly across the table, in the candlelight.

We laughed together over the menu that contained such foreign-sounding dishes as caribou steak, moose roast, and wild berry pie plus the more familiar macaroni and cheese. Evidently up here in this country they ate sturdy and starchy meals. Fresh green vegetables obviously were not available at this time of year. I wondered if they had gardens up here in the spring, and what sort of things would grow in the spongy gray earth.

Tony ordered a bottle of white wine to add to our celebration, surprised to see that it was available. Solemnly we toasted our future together here on this frontier, and I had not felt so warm, so happy, so loved, in many days.

There were perhaps a dozen other people sharing the dining room with us, and at least four of them were women. At one table was a couple with two small boys. Knowing that people were moving into this distant land and families were being raised comforted me. All was not wild and rough and unfamiliar. As forward and headstrong as I might seem, I was still a little frightened inside at the venture we had undertaken. To have Tony smiling at me and holding my hand was reassuring. I felt the warmth of the wine in my veins and I relaxed, feeling as if all the pieces of my little world were falling into place at last.

After dinner we strolled the boardwalks, looking in store windows. My fingers rested on Tony's arm and we exchanged light banter about the buildings, the streets, and the people we saw. The townsfolk looked as though they were clinging determinedly to the dress of the outside cities, while other men wore the grime of the mines or looked like trappers. I saw ladies heavily made up and smiling a little too freely, and there was a scattering of military uniforms.

My eyes went often to the high wall of mountains that rose so close to the edge of town, with their snowy peaks turned pink in the sunset, and to the many waterfalls. It was a sight and feeling that drew me, held me, and I knew I would never tire of it.

Back in our room, I dropped my cape onto a chair and ran to Tony's arms. "Oh, Tony, I am so glad we came up here," I cried. "Everything is going to turn out all right! I am so sure of it!"

Tony held me close and returned my kisses tenderly, but then he pushed me away gently. Teasing me a little over my forwardness, he suggested that I unpack our clothes and get us settled for our stay while he would look about the town. He wanted to talk to the other men, ask some questions. He kissed me on the forehead and laughed at my frown of displeasure, reassuring me that he would be back before I had finished. If I managed to keep my eyes open that long, he added with a teasing laugh. "You look like a sleepy kitten," he said as he left.

The bed was soft and inviting, with a thick down comforter. The pillows were large and fluffy. Quickly I unpacked our nightclothes, laying Tony's out across the foot of the bed. I put on my favorite soft-blue gown with the sprigs of embroidery and touches of lace. I brushed my hair until it shone in the lamplight and added a tiny touch of my favorite perfume.

Tony still had not returned so I unpacked the heavier garments, shook them out, and hung them on the pegs. The sun had completely disappeared and outside it was very dark. Evening came much quicker in this northern land than it did at home this time of year.

I had finished what unpacking was necessary and I searched for something else to do to occupy my time. I took out my notepaper, because a twinge of conscience demanded that I write my family to assure them of my well-being and to ask forgiveness for the hurt I knew I had caused. Though the dispatch would not reach them for weeks, I would feel better knowing it had been sent.

I would ask my father and Paul to try to understand why I had left as I did, why it was so important to me to come up here where my mother had made her home, why I had to find some part of her life to replace the years I had missed. I needed them to accept my becoming Tony's wife because I loved them and their acceptance was important to me.

To my aunt the words were difficult to find. Her need for a well-planned household, strict schedules, her set rules of social behavior, and her limited knowledge of the outside world and its ways made anything I could put on paper about my trip so far totally beyond her understanding.

To my brother Thomas, my beloved Tom, who had shared such a large part of my life until now, the words came easily. My problem was not what to say but how to limit myself to the boundaries of the pages in my letter. He would have stood on the banks of Valdez with me and marveled at the glaciers, the high, forbidding barrier of mountains, the multitude of waterfalls that tumbled from their ridges. Even the clouds that covered the tops most of the time and hid the sun would have held their own attraction for him.

Tom would have felt the same excitement inside that I did, and I tried to share this with him on paper.

By the time my letters were finished Tony still had not returned.

I pulled a chair close to the window where I could sit and look down on the street. With my shawl drawn closely over the thinness of my gown, my forehead resting on the windowpane, I sat and watched Valdez at night. Across the way and to the right I could see a tavern. There were bright lights inside, and through the stillness of the night I could hear a piano and loud laughter. Up the street in the other direction the other taverns were throwing their bright lights out onto the walkways, and I could hear music and voices. Beyond that row of buildings was a log cabin. At first glance it appeared to be a house, with a full front porch. Each window was brightly lit, and I could hear women's laughter, loud and coarse. As I watched, a number of men came and went through the single front door. This was Valdez at night, and I wondered where out there my Tony was.

I must have drifted off to sleep, sitting there with my head resting on the windowpane, because I woke with a start as someone fumbled with the latch on the door and Tony stumbled in. He was having difficulty in walking and fell heavily against the side table. At first I thought that he had been hurt, but when I rushed to his side to help him, I caught the strong smell of whisky.

I had never seen a man inebriated before, at least not so close at hand, but I knew instinctively what was wrong. My Tony, whom I had only seen sipping at wines in the drawing rooms of my friends in San Francisco, never drinking enough to have his tongue stumble on his words, was totally drunk and he smelled bad.

I helped him with his coat and, propping him up on the side of the bed, I removed his shoes and stockings. Somehow I managed to get his shirt off, but it wasn't an easy task because he kept tipping over and grabbing for me, trying to pull me down on the bed beside him. I kept shushing him, afraid his singing and talking would arouse our neighbors in the adjoining rooms. At last I was able to get him to lie down, and I covered him with a quilt as his voice faded away into a mumble jumble of words about cards and people he had met. Then finally he quieted completely as he fell into a sound sleep.

I crawled to the side of the bed away from him and curled beneath the remaining covers. Then I closed my eyes, tears slipping silently onto my pillow.

This was my first night in Valdez.

The next morning soft fingers trailing little patterns across my face and down the line of my throat awakened me. I didn't open my eyes but lay there pretending to sleep. I was still angry with him for the way he had gone out to explore the town the night before, leaving me alone.

Though my eyes were still closed, I sensed that he was resting on his elbow looking down at me as he made small tingling sensations on my flesh with the tips of his fingers. I wanted to lie quietly, pretending that I was not aroused by his touch, but when he bent his head to send light, flickering butterfly kisses across my breast, the quickening of my breath gave me away.

"Go ahead, pretend you are not awake," he teased. "See how long you can ignore me." His hands continued in their searching, moving in slow, lazy circles around my breasts, downward across my stomach, following the curve of my hips until he was gently stroking my inner thighs.

"Oh, Tony!" I scolded, moving closer to him under the covers, unable to keep up the pretense any longer. "How can you treat me like this? Last night I wanted you. I needed you and you left me alone while you went out and sought entertainment in the town. Now you expect me to fall into your arms at your first kiss."

"I'm sorry about last night, Nora," he murmured into my hair as he continued to caress me. "I didn't mean to stay away so long. It's a new town and I wanted to talk to some of the men. I wanted to find out about the conditions of the trail we will be taking to find your mother. I couldn't take you with me. The rowdy saloons in a frontier town are no place for a woman." His lips sought mine hungrily but I turned my head, still not quite ready to forgive.

"You didn't need to stay half the night, did you? You didn't need to drink so much. Tony, you were an awful sight when you came back." Despite myself I had to giggle at the memory. "I thought you were going to wake everyone up in the rooms nearby with your singing. I had a terrible time trying to get you to be quiet."

He had me in his arms now, cradling me against the warmth of his body. "The whisky they drink up here is strong stuff!" He chuckled. "I have to admit I'm not used to liquor with so much backlash. You ought to see how those tough old miners line up at the bar and drink it straight, just the way it comes out of the bottle without any water to put out the fire." His kisses were more demanding now, making it impossible for me not to respond. "Forgive me, Nora," he whispered between kisses, as his lips nuzzled the hollow of my throat. "I intended to come back sooner. The men were talking about the trapping up north of here, about finding gold nuggets as big as eggs. They kept setting up drinks— timbering the house, they called it—and I was fascinated by their stories. I didn't realize how fast the time was going or how much I had drunk."

He held me with one arm while the other hand was continuing its explorations as he talked, gently bringing my passions alive, making me forget my anger. I felt the pressure of his knee against my legs, the weight of his body as his mouth came down hard against mine, demanding now, bruising my lips. My arms crept up around his body, my fingers digging into the flesh of his shoulders as I cried out for him to love me.

In each other's arms, we found a joyous fulfillment that blotted out the rest of the world, leaving only the two of us, with nothing else mattering except the love we shared.

It was later, as I stood brushing my hair in front of the mirror tacked to the wall over the dresser, that Tony told me of the plans he had made the evening before. He sat back and watched my delighted face as he told me about our eleven o'clock appointment with the justice of the peace.

"You see, Nora, I told you if you would just have trust in me, and have patience, everything would eventually work out as we wanted it to," he said. "I want to give you so many things. And someday I will. But it isn't going to all come at once, and it won't be easy."

"I know," I answered, laying down the brush and going over to sit on the bed beside him. "I just need to know that you love me, Tony. If you love me, then nothing else matters. I don't need all of those other things."

He reached for me, pulling me down to lie beside him. "Love you? More than you realize," he answered. "There are going to be times when you will find that hard to believe, I suppose. I'm too used to living an easygoing, carefree life, and you are too serious, your background so different from mine. But I love you, Nora. You can believe that."

We were married in the small office of the justice of the peace shortly before noon. His housekeeper and a man from the store next door were the witnesses. I wore a dress of soft pale-green lawn with tiny pink flowers embroidered around the collar. It was a dress that I had brought from San Francisco with me and had been a favorite. Tony gave me a ring—a small, delicately carved bit of gold, set with two tiny rubies. It had been his mother's wedding ring.

It was a far cry from a young girl's dream of the romantic wedding she would have someday, but I was happy. I was in Alaska, I was so close to finding my mother, and I was Tony's wife.

That afternoon we sought the offices of my uncle's lawyer, the man whose name I saw on the letterhead on my father's desk. The man who could tell me about my mother.

His offices were in a single-story log building with a shingle roof, only a short walk from our hotel. A hand-carved sign over the doorway announced GARTH WILLIAMS   ATTORNEY AT LAW. Smoke curled lazily up from the stovepipe chimney and I could smell food cooking as we opened the door, so I took for granted that his living quarters were in the rear of the building.

As we entered, Tony closed the door a little louder than necessary. At the sound, a tall, slender man of middle age came in from the doorway to the back of the room. His smile was friendly and I was instantly at my ease, feeling comfortable and welcome.

"We are looking for Garth Williams, the attorney," Tony explained.

"I am Williams." His voice matched his smile.

I was startled by his answer. He wore a rough plaid wool shirt and dark trousers. On his feet were comfortable-looking leather moccasins. Obviously he had been cooking his noon meal when we had interrupted. I thought of the lawyers who came to my father's home from time to time to discuss business. They wore dark suits, white shirts, stiff collars, and ties, their hands were soft and well manicured. I smiled to myself as Tony and I accepted the steaming mugs of coffee he offered and settled down in comfortable chairs facing his desk.

"I am Nora Crandall—" I began, and then my face flushed slightly in embarrassment as I realized my error. "Nora Lowery. I've recently married and I'm not yet used to my new name," I added softly.

Tony interrupted. "My wife is the niece of James Crandall. The daughter of Martin and Amelia Crandall. I believe you are the attorney handling their business affairs."

Williams looked at Tony with curiosity. "Yes. I was Jim Crandall's attorney. We were also good friends. I have been corresponding with Martin Crandall about the distribution of the estate."

"The estate?" I asked. "Then . . ." Somehow I couldn't put the question into words.

He turned to me, a slight frown tugging at his brow. "Yes. Didn't you know? They were killed in an unfortunate accident over two months ago. I sent a letter with the details and copies of the will to Martin Crandall—to your father. I took for granted that he had told you. I'm sorry you had to hear it this way."

I felt the color drain from my face. Up until this time I had held out hope that Mother might still be living. "Both of them . . . then it's true that my mother was alive all of these years—and living up here, wasn't she?" My voice was low and full of pain. "Did you know her very well?"

"Yes. I knew them both probably as well as anyone did. Jim and Amelia came up here ten, maybe twelve years ago. Jim did some prospecting around the country. He had two claims. One didn't amount to much. The other gave him the stake he needed to build Ravenwood."

"Ravenwood?" I asked. "What is Ravenwood?"

He smiled warmly and I began to relax again. "Ravenwood is a lodge that he built about a hundred miles or so north of here, right in the heart of the Copper River mining country. He and Amelia loved it there. They had a lot of plans—plans they never lived long enough to finish."

"Did they ever have any children?" The thought had just occurred to me.

"No." He shook his head. "And it was a shame. She was a very warm, loving woman; they would have been good parents. She had so much to give. But Amelia and Jim were very much in love and they found happiness together. The only thing that gave her sadness was knowing she had been forced to leave her children, especially you, behind. It was probably the most difficult thing she had ever been forced to do."

"Then you know about—" I didn't know how to word what I wanted to ask.

"I think I know the whole story." He nodded. "They seldom talked about it—but as I told you, we were close friends. Amelia told me how her first marriage had been arranged by her parents. She had not resisted and at the time there had been no one else. She respected and trusted Martin. He was older than she, and I think she was a little bit in awe of him. It was not too much before you were born that Jim came home from the East where he had been living. It was against everything she believed in for a married woman to be attracted to another man, particularly her own husband's brother, but she could not help herself. They fell in love. For a while they did what they could to keep from acknowledging it. Jim even went away—this time up to the Klondike. He was unhappy and drawn back to the city where she lived. The next time he left, she went with him. I know Amelia loved you and your brothers, but she was also desperately in love with Jim Crandall. It was a terrible time for the both of them; making the decision nearly tore her apart. The only way your father would release her was for her to agree to leave you children behind, for him to raise. It hurt her to leave the boys behind, but she knew that at their age they would soon be entering school and be gone from her anyway. At least with Martin there would always be the home, more than enough money to see to their education, and a business waiting for them when they were adults. But to leave you, her small daughter, behind was a torture that she never was able to get over. She lived with the hope that when you were old enough, you would understand and forgive her, and that she and Jim could bring you up here to their beloved Ravenwood. Jim loved you as though you were his own daughter too. I can see why now. You look so much like her."

"As though I were his daughter?" I asked. "But he was my uncle."

Williams nodded. "Rumors can be vicious. I know what you are thinking. Somewhere you have overheard some of the guesses that were made. Jim returned to visit his married brother and found a young, beautiful desirable woman struggling to survive an arranged marriage that gave her security and respect but not love. Not the kind of love that she and Jim found. It was a difficult time for them, and it was a long time before she gave in to her feelings and left with Jim when he came up here. She knew that if he went back to Alaska he wouldn't return, and she would never see him again. It was more than she could bear, and she had to make a choice. She kept hoping Martin would relent and let her bring you up here with them. She never stopped hoping until she discovered that you thought she was dead. She knew then that Martin would never allow it to happen. Not until you came of age, at least, and were able to know the true story."

I sat quietly, lost in thought. No one spoke, letting me try to absorb all that he had told me. I felt a terrible sadness, as if I had lost my mother a second time, if that was possible. It is hard to grieve for one you had already thought dead for so long—the sorrow is there, but not the shock.

Garth Williams's voice was gentle. "That is why I was corresponding with your father. If anything happened to them, Jim and Amelia wanted Ravenwood to be yours. Martin thought that it was the best idea to sell the property and put the funds into a trust. I think he was wise. You will want to go up there and see it, I would imagine. After coming this far to see your mother, you would like to see where she lived, the place she loved so well and where she found her happiness. Then I can go ahead and work with your father's attorneys to take care of the arrangements for you."

"No." My voice was sharp, and both men looked at me, a little startled. "No. I won't sell it. I'm going up there, and Tony and I will live at the lodge, just as they did." I turned to Tony, wanting him to understand. "I think that is what they would have wanted."

Williams had been leaning back in his chair, watching us as he talked. Now he chuckled softly. "Mrs. Lowery, have you ever been to Alaska before? Do you know anything at all about the territory, the climate, the way of life?"

I felt my face turn pink but I met his eyes defiantly. I was conscious of the thin, delicate dress I still wore and of Tony's jacket and vest, so out of place in this setting. "We arrived yesterday. On the *Dauntless*, from San Francisco. What does that have to do with anything?"

"Nothing. And everything. I was just wondering. Tell me, how much do you know about running a lodge? Better yet, how much do you know about running a lodge in the Alaskan bush? About living away from city conveniences? About survival in the bush? This is not going to compare with anything you have ever seen in San Francisco."

I felt that he saw through my bluster and suspected I had been genteelly raised, a product of the pampered upper-class society. I didn't feel it was the time either to acknowledge Tony as an artist. "Tell me, Mr. Williams, just what sort of a lodge is it—this Ravenwood?"

He folded his hands thoughtfully, looking past me, out the window toward the street. "Well," he began slowly, "to begin with, it is a large, well-built structure of logs, set among the trees not too far off the Valdez Trail, near a small village that is just starting to grow. There is a dining room—no, that's the wrong word—a kitchen that serves hot-cooked meals for the folks traveling through, and for the lodgers. There is a large barroom—people eat in there too. It gets a little loud sometimes, but there's not too much rough stuff—Jim always kept them in line pretty well." His eyes drifted to Tony, taking measure of his well-fitting jacket, his satin vest, his polished boots, the soft white hands. "Jim and Amelia had their living quarters behind the barroom—sort of a combination living room and office—and there's a bedroom attached." He paused. "Upstairs there are six or eight rooms for lodgers."

Listening to him talk, I caught myself relaxing, imagining what my mother's life must have been like there in the bush.

"This lodge is north of here," he continued. "Up in the copper mining fields. You will be isolated from any sort of a city life. It is a rough country, my dear, and the people are rough. They have to be to survive. There aren't many women up here yet to keep us mindful of our manners. The summers are beautiful—nothing anywhere to compare to it—but the winters are long and hard, and I'm wondering how you can handle having it stay dark most of the time. There will be days on end when you won't be able to get in or out because the roads and trails will be blocked with snow. The dark will close in on you, wearing on your nerves. It does to the best of them. There are none of the conveniences that you have been so used to. It will be a hard life—no place for a *chee-chako*, an untried greenhorn. You and your husband seem so young—" He gave a heavy sigh and shook his head. "I just don't know."

"You are quite right," Tony interrupted harshly. "You *don't* know."

I frowned at him, shocked at his rudeness, but he continued. "I am quite capable of taking care of my wife *and* her affairs. Your responsibility ends with seeing that the property and whatever funds might be involved are transferred to her."

"Tony, please—" I implored. I liked this kindly man, and I was embarrassed by Tony's sharpness.

"Not quite there." The attorney's voice became businesslike and formal, his eyes lost their friendly twinkle, as he answered. "I'm afraid that the money remains in trust until Nora is twenty-five—whether she is married or not. It is one of the provisions of the will. She can have whatever she wants, as long as I approve of the bank withdrawal."

He turned to me now, giving me his full attention. "There is five thousand dollars in the bank here in Valdez. Jim earned that money the hard way. It was his and Amelia's fondest dream that when you were old enough to be on your own that you would choose to come up here and stay with them. They always intended that someday it would all belong to you, but of course they had no idea it would be so soon." His voice softened as he talked. "They were both very fond of you, Nora. It's too bad things turned out as they did."

I nodded. "It's been so long. I had no idea she was alive until I saw her name on some papers left out by accident on my father's desk." I folded and refolded my gloves in my lap and my mind was busy planning ahead. "I want to leave for Ravenwood as soon as possible. I want to go there—to see where they found their happiness. I want to live there. I think they would have wanted this, even though they aren't there any longer. It's the only thing I have left of my mother. It is where I will find something to replace all of the lost years when I didn't have her. And where I can try to understand her reasons for leaving me." I looked up at Garth Williams and smiled. "Will you tell me more about them, please? What was their life together like? Was my mother really happy? They must have been so much in love to have sacrificed so much. They must have loved Ravenwood."

"They did. It was a hard life, and a demanding one, but they were happy together there," he answered.

"I want to know more about my uncle. I remember so little about him. Just hazy memories of a man who laughed so easily and played games with me. It isn't much to go on, is it? There had to be so much more."

"Later, Nora, later." Tony was impatient. "Let's get the business end of this settled first. We'll want to leave for the lodge as soon as possible, and there are so many things to be taken care of first. There will be plenty of time to visit later."

We spent the next half hour or so on paperwork. Tony was restless, only half listening, walking to the window to stare unseeingly out up toward the mountains. When the conversation turned to our trip north to Ravenwood, he again joined the conversation. He listened carefully as Garth Williams began to list the things we should purchase here to take with us.

"These things that you are talking about—telling Nora we will need—this is all going to cost a great deal of money, if I am guessing anywhere near right. Where is it going to come from?"

Garth Williams looked at me questioningly. "I have some—" I faltered, my thoughts going to the money pouch I had given to Tony in Seattle. I looked toward him, but his face was expressionless. "Yes, we will need money," I answered with a sigh. "Is it available for me to draw on?"

The attorney hesitated a moment, then went on to repeat that the money was in the bank in Valdez, held in trust for me. He mentioned again the terms of my uncle's will with the clause that any withdrawal must be made with his approval until I was twenty-five years of age.

"I will make arrangements with the bank so that you can draw out five hundred dollars," he agreed. "This will more than cover your expenses here in town, and leave extra to take with you."

I listened eagerly as Garth Williams described the lodge and the people who worked there. A couple had worked for my uncle and now were keeping the lodge open and running until other arrangements could be made. Maury Hill was doing the cooking and taking care of the rooms. Her husband, Abe, was tending the bar and doing the other necessary chores.

Williams suggested that we contact Logan Aldridge and make arrangements to travel with him on his freight wagon. He would be leaving tomorrow on a regular haul, taking mail and freight on up as far as Chitina and McCarthy. He often carried a passenger or two, if he had the room.

He went on to explain that the village near where we were going was built on mining property. Jim Crandall had first built the lodge on that site because the fishing

and hunting was so good, and it was near where he had
several gold claims. He eventually let the gold claims
go but kept the lodge. The village, which is within
walking distance of the lodge, was flourishing in a remote wilderness in the mountains, quite a distance
north of Valdez, not too far from where the Chitina
and Copper rivers met. Some large veins of copper had
been discovered in that area. A copper mining company
had been organized and was now operating. The Copper River and Northwestern Railroad was being built
to carry the copper to Cordova for export. When this
railroad was completed, the town would boom and
stood a chance of becoming one of the larger ones in
south-central Alaska.

Enthusiasm glowed in his eyes as he talked, and I
knew that he too believed in this land and its future.
It showed in every word he spoke, as well as in the
things he left unsaid.

We left Garth Williams's office with my excitement
running high. In just a short time our travels would be
over. We would be at Ravenwood and settled into our
new way of life. And perhaps I would come to know
more of my mother. I walked along at Tony's side with
a light step, chattering to him about our future plans.
He, however, seemed unusually quiet. If I had bothered
to turn and look back, I probably would have seen
Garth Williams standing in the doorway watching us
walk away, a worried frown shadowing his face, and no
wonder. A young man who showed by his dress and
manner that he was more suited for the life in a large
city and a young girl so obviously raised in a sheltered
home protected from the realities of the outside world
—two young people eagerly looking forward to living
in the bush, where only the sturdy survived.

CHAPTER FOUR

The next day found us on a horse-drawn freight wagon
driven by Logan Aldridge, headed out on the Valdez
Trail toward Ravenwood.

The wagon was loaded with odd-shaped forms of
freight, covered with canvas and secured in place with
ropes. Tony sat up forward on the seat beside the
driver. He was wearing the new fur hat I had bought
in Valdez and the heavy coat I had found in Seattle.
Even with the woolen scarf pulled high around his face
and the rough, heavy clothing, Tony managed to look
dashing and handsome. Wrapped in warm fur robes,
I was wedged in behind them, tucked in among the
crates like another piece of freight.

The horses leaned heavy into their harness, making
slow progress in the spring "breakup" mud. There was
not enough snow left to use the sled, and yet the spongy
mud made it hard for the horses to pull the wagon.
The wind scuffled and whined down off the mountains,
stinging the men's faces with the particles of snow it

carried with it, but I was snug and warm in my burrow of fur robes, mittened and scarfed almost to the tip of my nose.

The two men talked together as we rode along, but I was too far back to hear what they were saying or to enter into their conversations. I let my thoughts ramble around lazily, in rhythm with the rolling, jolting wagon. Mrs. Anthony Lowery, I thought, smiling to myself. I touched my lips to my mitten where it hid the ring Tony had given to me and I daydreamed about our future.

We left the buildings of Valdez behind us, moving steadily toward the Valdez glacier. The sky was overcast but even so the colors were there, the blues, the greens, wearing the mask of serenity while it hid the secrets of the ages.

We had traveled for quite a while—perhaps ten or twelve miles, maybe a little farther—when Logan pulled the team off the trail into the yard of Fort Comfort. "Got to rest the team here," he announced. "We'll be getting into Keystone Canyon pretty soon and I want them to be ready for it."

Fort Comfort was a way station—a place to stop and rest, eat a warm meal, look at the glacier up close, and spend the night if it was getting too close to evening to go any farther. There were two other wagons in the yard when we pulled in—wagons loaded heavy with supplies, driven by men in army uniforms. When he saw me watching them curiously, Logan explained that we might see quite a few of these army wagons. This trail was used as a route for carrying supplies from Valdez to Fort Egbert, in Eagle, up north in the interior.

We went inside and had hot coffee and sandwiches.

Afterward I walked around outside, wanting to stretch my legs a bit before returning to the confining wagon. I stood looking up at the glacier, awed by the cold, distant beauty of it, when I heard Logan walk up behind me.

"You may think this a pretty uncomfortable trip before I get you to where you are going, ma'am, but just think about the men that took that route in 1898, up across that glacier, and on foot they were too, trying to get to the gold fields." Tony joined us then, and together we stood and listened to Logan as he pointed out the route the prospectors had taken. He told us stories of men who went to the gold fields, of the hardships they endured, of a winter so fierce that it drove them back toward Valdez, many of them freezing to death in the wake of its fury. He told of the fighting over claims, of stakes being moved and shootings in the night—and of the few who had really struck it rich and went back outside with a treasure of gold. And, in looking for the gold, an even greater wealth in copper was discovered. He told of "big money" groups moving in, gouging open the primitive land to take the precious ores, and how right now they were fighting the U.S. Government and the elements, trying to build a railroad up to their mines.

He told us how Major Richardson and Captain Abercrombie had been instrumental, each in his own way, in the surveying and opening of the Valdez Trail we were traveling on. We wouldn't have to cross the glacier to get inland.

Even so, the trip was not all that easy. We loaded up again, and Logan checked the ropes holding the freight, walking around the wagon, giving it a last inspection before we started out toward Keystone Canyon.

We followed the road, which was in fact little more than a wide, muddy trail, climbing slowly, twisting, turning, winding along beside a noisy stream that raced past, down toward the sea. On each side of us the sheer rock walls of the canyon rose high into the air, as straight as the walls of a giant corridor, boxing us in, shutting out all daylight except what was directly over-head. There were waterfalls along these rock walls, caused by the spring thawing of glaciers lying hidden at their snowy tops. Each falls seemed more beautiful than the one before—except for one that surpassed all of the others. I tipped my head back in breathless won-der, trying to see up to where it tumbled from, over six hundred feet up, at least, enveloping us in a mist of wet spray as we passed.

Though we were leaving the dark canyon, we were continually climbing higher and higher. The air be-came colder and the wind stronger. After what seemed like an eternity of bumping along in the wagon, we broke out onto a high plateau-like area and Logan pulled the team over onto a turnout.

"Sorry, ma'am," he apologized. "I'd like to take time to build a little fire and boil some coffee—imagine you could really enjoy some—but we're running late. That mud really slowed us down. We got to get to the next way station before it gets dark." He reached up toward me. "Here, I'll give you a hand down and you can walk around a little and stretch your legs while I tend to the horses."

I accepted his offer gratefully because I was begin-ning to feel so cramped that when he helped me down from my nest in the blankets I wondered if my legs would hold me well enough to stand alone.

It had taken us most of the day, but we were on the

top of the summit, headed for the nearest roadhouse where we would spend the night. I had thought that when Logan said we would spend the night in a roadhouse, it meant a warm meal, a soft bed. I'm not sure how I thought a hotel like the one we stayed at in Valdez was going to find its way out here into the bush! I was not prepared for the rough, tentlike structure, crowded with prospectors, trappers, several men in uniform, and a couple of Indians. The hot meal I looked forward to was a large, cast-iron kettle filled with a stew of some sort, dished out into tin plates. There was only one other woman in the group—the Indian woman who was cooking.

The sleeping arrangements were a bit casual, to say the least. Bunks were built along the wall—nothing more than frames filled with tree boughs with a blanket thrown over the top. I watched skeptically. It seemed whoever went to bed first got the choice of what was available. And I saw one man take boughs from another bunk, filling his own up more. I stayed as close to Tony as possible, wondering what was going to happen to us when it came time to try to get some sleep.

Logan winked and motioned for me to follow him. I was hesitant at first, glancing at Tony, but he gave me a nod and a brief kiss and I picked my way across the room. Logan led me through a side door into a lean-to.

"You'll rest better in here." He grinned. "This belongs to the woman you saw out there who does the cooking. She says you can sleep in here—they got two beds. Her old man will sleep out in the main room tonight." Relief must have shown plain in my face because he patted my shoulder. "Don't get that many women up here. I put the fur robes off the wagon over there on that bunk for you. See you in the morning."

I sat down on the edge of the bed, testing it carefully. I felt rope, tied back and forth across the frame, instead of tree limbs as I had seen earlier. I didn't undress at all, except to pull off my shoes, and curled up inside the warm robes. Uncomfortable as it was, I was almost asleep when I heard the woman come in and settle herself on the other bunk.

We were on the trail early the next morning, trying to make as much time as possible in the daylight. Logan stopped at all of the way stations and roadhouses, bringing in their freight and mail. Our wagon was watched for and eagerly met by these people anxious for their supplies, thirsty for word from the outside.

We stopped at places like Wortman's, Ptarmigan Drop, Beaver Dam, gratefully accepting the hot, strong coffee and lunch that they offered, each time my aching muscles a little stiffer than the time before. We reached Tonsina just before dark, for our second night's stopover.

That day we had forded places where the water ran axle deep across the roadway, the wagon tipping first one way and then the other. We had clung onto sides of banks, the horses lunging into their harness, doing their best to keep us rolling, while Logan shouted encouragement to them. We had passed a wagon or two headed south and moved as far as possible to one side, trying to make room for two where there had barely been room for one. It seemed to me that the trip was taking forever, that we were not making any headway at all along the trail, but Logan assured me with a confident smile that we were running right on schedule. He was allowed seventy-two hours for a mail run from

Valdez to Copper Center, or what amounted to three full days, and if nothing happened tomorrow along the route, he would have left us off and be in Copper Center by evening.

In spite of the enthusiasm I had felt when we left Valdez, by this time I began to grow bone weary of the hard and uncomfortable wagon. I stretched and twisted as much as possible, trying to ease my aching muscles. Now, instead of fantasies of homemaking, I dreamed longingly of a hot tub of soapy water and a soft, clean bed. I wasn't sorry when toward late afternoon of the third day Logan pulled the wagon to a halt and announced our arrival at the lodge.

Excitedly I pushed aside the robes for my first look at Ravenwood, where I would make my home from now on. I saw a large, sprawling building, two stories high, set in a clearing of spruce filtered through with birch. It was built entirely of logs, with a large rock chimney on each side. Eagerly I reached for the men's helping hands, clamoring to be let down from my perch among the crates.

The Hills came out onto the porch to greet the freight wagon, smiles of welcome on their faces. Logan introduced us, and we turned over a letter from Garth Williams. In no time at all we were inside, warming our hands in front of the largest rock fireplace I had ever seen.

Abe Hill was in his late forties, with his dark hair just beginning to show a trace of gray. He was a quiet man, not given to wasting words, but his friendly eyes told us we were welcome. Maury, who talked enough for the both of them, took over immediately, bustling about to get us settled in. Once Logan was assured that all was in order, he left to carry his load of freight and mail down the road into the village, promising to stop in tomorrow on his return trip.

Abe helped Tony carry the trunks into what was now to be our living quarters. It was a comfortable apartment and surprisingly well furnished. In the sitting room, a lovely tapestry sofa sat against one wall. Two leather chairs were pulled up invitingly by a large stove with isinglass windows in its door. There was a heavy oak desk near the window, with a lamp on it, ready for someone to sit and work.

There were several paintings of Alaskan landscapes on the walls, and soft velvet drapes hung at the window. The whole room spoke of warmth and comfort. I walked about, trailing my fingers across the spines of the books in the bookcase, and stopped to inspect a small picture of me, as a child, sitting on a reading table. It gave me an odd feeling, seeing the forgotten picture, and I felt as though I had been expected. I knew I would love the hours that I would spend in this room.

The bedroom opened off the sitting room, through a doorway behind the desk. It was very small, quite plain but comfortable, intended only for sleeping. A double-size brass bed with a handmade patchwork quilt took up most of the room. A plain chest of drawers of undistinguished background, a straight-back chair, and a small bedside table were the only other furnishings.

Abe brought in a basin of hot water, and after we had time to freshen up and inspect our quarters, we went back to the main room of the lodge. Maury was waiting with a delicious meal for us, spread on a table near the fireplace. She set out large plates of hot, bubbling caribou stew, with light, flaky biscuits, wild currant jelly, and to top off the dinner she brought out a blueberry pie fresh from the oven. Tony and I ate with such gusto that Maury beamed at us.

At last, warmed through, filled with food, and relaxed, I could feel my eyelids grow heavy. It was with real effort that we roused ourselves to leave the fire and bid the Hills a good night. Together we walked sleepily back into the quarters that were to be our first real home. The bed was soft and clean, smelling of dried rose petals. I slipped between the covers to curl drowsily in Tony's arms, needing only his love to complete my happiness.

I woke up the next morning with the first signs of daylight, eager to explore, slipping quietly out of the bed so as not to wake Tony. Maury heard me moving about the sitting room and tapped at the door. She will never know how grateful I was to see her standing there with a large copper bathtub. Together we brought it in and placed it in front of the fire. Abe followed her in, carrying two buckets of hot water. After several trips the tub was filled, and I spent the next hour in the most luxurious treat I had experienced since leaving San Francisco.

After a brief discussion the Hills agreed to stay on, helping us as they did my uncle. For that I shall be forever grateful, for as I began to know Maury, a deep friendship developed. She had come from a good family, of that I was sure, though she never spoke of it. She was such an odd mixture of prudishness, flavored with a touch of vulgarity, showing itself in her outspoken manner and a quick, contagious laugh that was just a bit too loud. Maury had no children of her own, and to fill that need, she domineered her husband to a certain extent and bossed, mothered, and loved all of us. She certainly did more than her share of the work, laughing and talking all the while. What she lacked in the social graces, as I had known them, she made up for in warm humor and a real down-to-earth outlook on life. Everyone liked Maury.

Abe was a very quiet, reserved man, and though I liked him, he was not as easy to know as Maury, who was so open with her affections. The two of them lived comfortably in a small cabin built to the back of the lodge, easy to get to in the winter snows but giving them a privacy of their own.

Tony found the lodge constricting, and with his quick smile and easy ways he soon became acquainted with the settlement down the road. It was much easier for Tony to meet new people than it was for me, and he sought the company of the men collected there.

We had four lodgers living in the rooms upstairs, men who worked in the copper mines. In the evening after one of Maury's filling dinners and a few relaxing drinks at our bar, they would often drift on down the road toward a place called "Beth's" to play poker, they said. Beth, with the help of several girls, ran a roadhouse here in copper country.

It wasn't long before Tony started joining them on an occasional evening. He would come home early before the others and laughingly tell me of how serious the men took the games and how high the stakes ran. The bets were backed not only by their wages from the copper mines, but by little pouches of gold dust, nuggets, and even fur pelts. It was all quite new to Tony, and he found it tremendously interesting and amusing.

One evening I saw Maury watching him leave. She had such an unreadable expression in her eyes it aroused my curiosity. When I asked her about Beth's place, she turned away and pretended not to hear. I did begin to notice that Abe never joined the men, although he was frequently invited, and I began to wonder.

I loved Ravenwood and for me the days passed quickly, each one filled with new things to learn. Maury handled all of the work easily. I was her assistant and student. Every part of it was foreign to me, from the huge, wood-burning cookstove and its temperamental oven to the kerosene lanterns we used for light. The preparation of food was not as simple as I had imagined in my fantasies of taking over the cooking. No neat packages of meats from the butcher shop here. Abe shot most of the fresh meat that we used, and I watched in revulsion as the carcasses were dressed and brought to the kitchen table to be cut up, before storing them in the meat cache. Even the meat cache, built to look like a miniature log cabin sitting high on poles out of the reach of marauding bears, was new to me.

We picked currants that grew lush and red in the nearby woods and made jelly for the winter. I learned to recognize blueberries and where to find patches of low-bush cranberries. I soon knew which leaves left you scratching and burning if you touched them. I found hidden vines of wild strawberries and felt my heart beat faster as Maury pointed out fresh bear droppings to me.

My fingernails broke and my hands were rough and scratched. My face took on a light tan that my aunt never would have permitted, but I loved every moment of it.

Maury taught me to make pie crusts filled with the wild berries we had picked. I worked very hard to imitate Maury's quick, deft handling of the rolling pin and the confident way she worked the flour with the lard. Maury's pie crusts would melt in your mouth. Mine were leathery and pale, or burned around the rim, but I kept trying.

Abe would come into the kitchen and sit at the table with a mug of coffee, watching us working over the stove. He sampled all of my cooking with a serious look on his face while I would wait anxiously, holding my breath, until he either frowned his distaste or beamed his approval.

Maury laughed at my disasters in the kitchen, and there were many. She gave me soothing creams for my hands chapped by the laundry and the scrubbing, and she sympathized with my sore and aching muscles.

The cleaning was not fun. I had never had to clean my own room at home or to make my own bed. I had never cleaned or pressed my own clothing. But here, fun or not, it was necessary, and I tackled it with the same vigor I did the rest of the chores. As we worked, Maury talked. She loved to talk, and I was a good listener. There were so many things I wanted to know.

She told stories of my mother, a lovely woman, warm and loving, liked by everyone who knew her. She talked about Uncle Jim, describing him as he had been in the last few years when I didn't know him. She told me how much they loved each other—and the only sadness in my mother's life was when she spoke of me, wishing there was some way she could see me again. When I became angry, telling Maury that it was all so foolish—that I would have come up here sooner if only I had known—Maury just shook her head. "You are only thinking of yourself when you say that," she told me. "There are times when things happen in our lives and someone has to be hurt. Your father loved you too, whether you believe it or not. Your mother knew that. Some folks just love more openly than others. Some are afraid of showing their feelings. When your father refused to let her take her children, giving her the freedom she wanted but insisting the children stay behind, each was doing what they felt they had to do. She left to follow a very special love. He kept the children because he could not bear to lose both his wife and his sons—and a little girl who looked so much like her mother. Think about it, Nora, and don't judge too harshly."

She told how she and Abe came here three years ago and stayed to help with the work at the lodge. "And now, just like when they were still here, we will stay and work with you. They would both be happy if they knew that you were here and fit in so well."

She told how Uncle Jim had first selected this site for the lodge because of the excellent hunting and fishing, and then when the big copper mines started up, bringing so many men to work in them, how they had started taking lodgers until the next thing they knew they were so busy they couldn't handle it all by themselves.

At first they had lived almost isolated from the outside world. Other than the Copper River Indians who roamed the area, there were few settlers. The entire area had been very remote, hard to reach. Then copper had been discovered and people began moving in. The cabin or two down the road grew to a small settlement. The railroad from Cordova and Valdez to Chitina and McCarthy was being built, and if ever they were able to finish it, this whole area would expand and grow. Uncle Jim had such high hopes, so many dreams. It was too bad that his life was cut short before he was able to see them come into reality.

I listened carefully to everything Maury told me, thirsty for anything that would explain what could have caused my mother to leave me or for her to allow my father to let me believe she had died. "Will you tell me where her grave is? Where my mother and my uncle are buried?" I asked. "I would like to go there, to see for myself."

"It isn't far from here," she answered. "There is a small wooden church with a cemetery in the back of it, at the edge of the village. They are there, side by side, as they would have wanted to be. If you'll wait until morning, I'll go with you and show you where it is."

"No. Please. I don't mean to be rude, but I would rather go alone. It's rather a private thing."

Maury nodded. "I understand. You won't have no trouble finding it. The church is right alongside the road and the cemetery is small. They are toward the back, in a quiet corner near a clump of wild currants."

That afternoon I slipped away, walking alone along the road toward the village. As Maury had said, the church was not hard to find. It was a small, one-room building of rough-hewn lumber with a window on each side. I looked about but there was no one in sight, so I walked around to the back. There were several scattered rows of wooden markers, hand carved with names and dates.

I wandered about, reading the markers, wondering what strange, unknown chain of events had brought these people up here to this unsettled land, having their lives end before they found what they were seeking. A small child's grave; a prospector, shot down in an altercation over ownership of a claim; a trapper caught in an unexpected blizzard. There was a woman who had died in childbirth and a young man known only as Klondike Kelsey.

I found where my mother rested side by side with my uncle. I sank down onto the grass near the foot of her grave, wondering if somehow she might know that I was there at last. I felt no sudden grief, no deep sorrow. The years had mellowed those emotions. What I sought now was an answer to why it had been this way at all. I remembered Garth Williams's words as we sat in his office in Valdez a short time ago. "Amelia and Jim were deeply in love. . . . Their only sorrow was in knowing that your father would only give her the freedom she sought if she would leave you behind." The sun was hidden from time to time by the drifting clouds and a light breeze caught at the branches of the shrubs nearby, but I scarcely noticed, I was so deep in my own thoughts.

Maury tried to explain to me in her own down-to-earth way that Mother honored and respected my father, even though she loved another man. Both my parents loved me very deeply. My mother was leaving to travel to an unsettled country where there would be hardships and perils too severe for a small child. Logan Aldridge had pointed out the route to me that they would have taken, traveling on foot up across the glacier, because the Valdez Trail had not been completed at that time. My father's home offered comfort and security, an education and a future.

Gradually I began to feel at peace with the past, to understand the reasons she had left me behind, entrusted into my father's care. With a feeling of serenity

I stood up and brushed the grass from my skirt, ready to return to the lodge—to Ravenwood, my home.

As time went on, Tony began to spend less and less time helping Abe at the bar in the evenings. He was gambling more. When he won he was exuberant; when he lost he was sullen. His only consistency was that on the evenings he spent at home, he was restless. Thus I was delighted when he finally unpacked his paints and canvases and began to work out of doors in the strong summer sunlight.

The first painting that he completed was a lovely view of the valley, showing the first signs of autumn. The birch trees were resplendent in touches of brilliant reds and yellows. High granite cliffs formed the background, with a distant view of the peak of White Mountain, wreathed in a light fog. I thought it was beautiful —the finest yet of any of his paintings.

Tony did several other landscapes after that, each one taking a little longer to complete than the one before. Finally the last painting stood half finished against the bedroom wall, forgotten, along with the uncleaned brushes standing on end in a jar.

The days were rapidly becoming shorter now, and I blamed the poor light for his losing interest in his work. When late fall and early winter come to this North Country, they move in quickly, as though suddenly nature is caught in a frenzied rush to close the distance between the long hours of sunlight in the summer and the few twilight hours of a winter daytime. We were lighting the lamps by midafternoon now, and letting them burn until long after the breakfast hour. Overhead we heard the call of the geese, and when I raised my eyes to search the sky, I saw their determined "V," headed for warmer climates. The wild animals we saw in the wood were growing heavy coats for the protection against the cold.

Abe shot a moose and brought it in piece by piece, as it was too heavy for him to carry all at once, even with Tony's help. We took salmon, pink and sparkling, from the cold waters of the river, and cut them into strips, to smoke to a shiny glazed finish for a winter delicacy.

I watched each night stretch out longer and longer, until I wondered if by the time December got here we would have any daylight left at all. I wondered too if I was going to be able to meet this new challenge— the dark—with the same bravado I had faced the others.

The summer had flown by so quickly, with so many new things to learn—the cooking, the canning, the preparing for winter—that I had sadly neglected to keep up the paperwork the way I should have. Each day when we closed for the evening, the day's receipts had been put into the same tin box that my uncle had used, with hasty notes written on slips of paper for future reference, but I had not taken the time to sit down and enter them in my uncle's big ledger and total up the columns.

Now, with time finally on my hands, I sat and studied his neat columns of figures and tried to copy his system of bookkeeping. No matter how I added or subtracted, I couldn't get the totals to balance. I went back over the rows of figures, trying to find my errors. I had kept receipts each time I had taken money from the tin box to pay bills and freight. But when either Tony or I had wanted pocket money, for spending money for him or for my shopping at the general store and hardware in the village, we had been careless about marking it down. This would make some difference in the totals, but I didn't see how they could be this far off. At first confused, and then uneasy, I began again, going back to the day we arrived, taking the daily receipts and the paid-out bills and putting them in neat stacks, checking each day carefully. The difference between the money we took in less the money we had paid out should have shown the amount of cash in the tin box. The figures in the book showed a tidy sum, and yet there were only a few stacks of coins left in the tin box, and the difference between the two left me stunned.

I went back, trying to remember how often I had gone to the little store down the road and how much I had spent each time. We bought most of our supplies wholesale and had them shipped in, buying only small items we ran out of in the village, like a can of cinnamon or perhaps some thread, or once in a while some nails for repairs. I stared into the fire, remembering how many times Tony had taken his coat off the hook on the wall and followed the men down the hill to Beth's. I tried to remember how many times he returned laughing and joking, how many times sullen and restless. How much had been taken from the tin box to cover the gambling debts without my being aware of what was happening? How much did he still owe? How blind had I become to what Tony was doing to fill his hours while I was so engrossed with the lodge and its care? I thought of how many empty hours he must have had while the rest of us were so busy. Tony hated to hunt. He was a sensitive man, and the sight of a bloody carcass needing to be dressed left him pale and nauseous. And, of course, I didn't expect him to help with the berry picking or the canning and cleaning. As I sat staring into the flames, I realized just how frequently he was away lately and how seldom I waited up for him.

Tony had started drinking heavily too. Not the wines that we both were accustomed to, but the strong, biting whisky common up here, and if I was not asleep when he stumbled in, I pretended to be. But tonight, with the figures and the small stack of coins in the money box playing on my mind, I stayed awake, waiting for him to come home. The longer I waited, the more I thought, and the angrier I grew. Carefully I rehearsed over and over what I would say. I had my whole lecture, word for word, all planned out.

When Tony came in, well after midnight, he was surprised to see me still up, sitting in a chair by the fire trying to read.

"Well, well, awake and waiting for me, like a dutiful, loving wife," he slurred.

"Tony, we need to talk—" I began.

"Talk? At this time of night?" I saw the challenge in his eyes and sensed he was on the defensive.

"We haven't done much of it lately. Maybe we've waited too long." I took a deep breath and started again. "I have been working on the books tonight, and we are in trouble, Tony. The money is gone—"

He took off his tie and tossed it carelessly across a chair. He began to loosen his vest. "The money is gone," he mimicked. "What money, Nora? The petty cash you keep for expenses in that tin box? How far did you expect those coins to go?"

I stood up then, my feet planted firmly on the floor, my hands on my hips. My chin jutted out and I knew my eyes flashed with fire. "Far enough to pay the expenses for the lodge, that's how far! There is no reason why we shouldn't be able to pay our freight bills and the Hills' salaries out of the money we take in, and have enough left over to cover our own living expenses."

Stray strands of my hair had slipped loose from their neat roll in back and my shirtwaist pulled tightly across my breasts as I stood straight and angry. I realized I was shouting, but I really didn't care. It felt good to finally release all of the pent-up resentments that had been building inside, and once started, I couldn't stop. I railed at him for the hours he could have been helping at the bar, leaving Abe free to lay in our supply of meat and do the repairs before the cold weather came. I accused him of not carrying his own weight, leaving the work to the rest of us, while he spent the money we earned at the card tables. Bitter, angry words I threw at him, emphasizing my anger with phrases learned from Maury.

Tony sprawled on the sofa watching me, not saying anything, letting me shout my accusations without interrupting. Finally I stopped, partly to catch my breath and partly because it is very hard to have a good, air-clearing, noisy argument all by yourself.

Tony was amused. "Have you looked in a mirror lately, Nora? What has happened to you?"

I stared at him. It was not the answer I had expected, and he caught me off guard.

He went on. "What would your aunt think of the new words you have learned up here?" He clicked his tongue and shook his head. "And do you realize that you were shouting? My God, you look and sound like a cheap, unkempt . . ." His voice drifted away.

I couldn't believe what I was hearing. My hand

moved unconsciously to my hair. "If you stayed here, helped more—" I faltered. Then, regaining my composure, I went on. "Where has the money gone, Tony? I have just spent the whole evening working on the books. I should have done it before—not let it get ahead of me the way I did. It just seems that no matter how much comes in, there never is any left over. I went over the figures. The money came in, but the tin box is almost empty. I have freight coming tomorrow and I have to have the money here to pay for it, but there just isn't any. And Tony, what about the Hills' salary? They are going to expect to be paid too, you know. What do you think I am supposed to tell them? Sorry, I can't pay you this time? My husband lost it all at the poker tables? Is that what I'm supposed to tell them?"

"Now we're getting to the real reason for your anger, aren't we?" He straightened up and leaned forward. "This is why you were waiting up for me to come in tonight. It isn't how many evenings I've been gone, or who I might be spending them with, is it? I'm surprised that you even noticed that I wasn't here, you're so wrapped up with this lodge of yours—and asleep when I come in—not caring enough to stay awake. All you care about is the money, isn't it? It's *your* lodge, *your* money, *your* bank account in Valdez. Never once have you made any attempt to make it *ours*. That's not the way you sounded in San Francisco, when you wanted to get married so badly, is it? All you could think of then was how to get a ring on your finger."

"Now wait a minute, Tony!" Angered by his insolence, my eyes were flashing fire. "When I learned that my mother might still be alive, I could think only of

coming up here, to try to find her. You were the one
who offered to come with me. And, now that I think
about it, I'm beginning to wonder if you didn't have
reasons of your own for wanting to leave San Francisco
in such a hurry. You wanted to leave without anyone
being able to follow you, and I provided the means.
And all the time I thought you loved me."

He was becoming sulky again. "Think back, why
don't you. Who was it that said we should wait—not
turn your family against us? You forget so easily. You
couldn't wait to come up here to Alaska. But after I
brought you up here, things have really changed,
haven't they? You resent every single penny I spend.
The money is all tied up in your name, needing
Williams's approval to draw it out. *I* am your husband.
I should be handling your affairs, not him."

"No, that's not true. You're wrong, and you know
it, Tony. I haven't refused you any of the money. I
know it costs a great deal for supplies—for food, clothing—and you have to have spending money too. I
know that. I want so much to have Ravenwood survive.
My mother lived here; she found happiness and love
here. My uncle Jim loved me and wanted me to have
this place after they were gone. It meant so much to
them. I can't betray the trust and let anything happen
to it. And, Tony, Ravenwood is doing well. We should
be able to live on its profits without touching the
money in the bank. I'm trying as hard as I can. I want
to make my home here, as they intended. I want
Ravenwood to be the place they intended it to be. I
want it to be my home, my security, where I will find
the love and the happiness that they knew here. I
know that I don't know how to manage money—I don't
know so many things. But I am trying to learn. I've

worked so hard. I need your help, Tony. The money is coming in, and yet each time I go to the tin box to pay the bills, the money isn't there. Where is it all going?"

"You worry too much," he answered with a shrug. "The money in the tin box isn't enough to become upset about. But if money is so important to you, we should make different arrangements about the money you are hiding away so carefully in Valdez, with Williams as the keeper. You can pay all of the bills, and control how it is spent, if this is the way it is to be. But Nora, if I don't have the right to take out the money, I will just have to present you with my bills." He stood up and walked over to me, the sulkiness gone from his face. "Alaska is a very expensive place to live. Everything costs twice as much as it did back in San Francisco. But if this is where you are determined to live, then we will just have to make do, won't we? I've had some debts too, you know, that I have had to pay. I can't just sit here all day and watch you making jam and pies and being a little homebody. I need people. I need to hear someone laugh once in a while."

"Oh, yes, I know. How well I know." I was getting angry again and, keeping my voice low and controlled, I fought not to lose my temper. "You are not a hunter or an outdoor person, are you? It would be too much to ask if you were to help Abe with the meat supply we're going to need for this winter. Or to cut wood. It is hard work, and you aren't used to it. The evenings here are boring for you—the rest of us are tired, after working all day, and we just want to relax, read some, maybe, or visit quietly. You find me dull, don't you, so you must go out in the evening, where there are people who will laugh with you and keep you entertained. And it takes money. There are the card games at Beth's. Are you really losing that much? Drinking that much? Tell me, Tony. How much are your gambling debts?"

He got up and walked over to the fire, near where I stood. "Do you want the answer, Nora? Let's talk about all of this money of yours. When Aldridge comes in with the freight tomorrow, I want you to go back with him to Valdez and see Williams."

"Why?" I asked. "Why should I go see Williams?"

"Because you are going to draw some money from the account he is holding for you."

"Am I, Tony? Is that what you think? Am I going to Garth Williams and tell him I can't manage on what we earn here? And just how much do you think I am going to tell him I need?"

"One thousand dollars."

I spun around, staring in disbelief. I drew in a sharp breath. "One thousand dollars! You're mad! No, I won't do it. I refuse!"

He took me by the shoulders, his fingers biting into my flesh. "Let's don't fight, not anymore, Nora. In my own way I love you, although you may not believe that. I want to take good care of you—I really do. We had a lot of happy dreams when we came up here, both of us." He kissed me on the forehead. "Remember the jewels I was going to give to you, the rings for your soft hands? The traveling we were going to do? France? Italy?" He drew me closer. "Other than the two paintings I sold to the bank and the mining office, there is very little call for an artist up here. We both know that. I'm not a very successful gambler either, am I?" He chuckled ruefully, as he nuzzled my cheek softly. "Lord knows, I've tried. I want to be

successful here. You have got to have more patience
with me." He lifted my chin, so I had to look at him.
"I want you to go to Valdez on the freight wagon. I
want you to stay over for a few days. I want you to do
some shopping for yourself. You've earned a vacation.
You have been working hard and you are tense and
sharp tempered because you need a little rest, away
from here, that's all."

I stood stiff, my hands clenched until the nails bit
into the flesh as he trailed kisses down to the hollow
of my throat. "Go see Williams." His fingers undid
the buttons on my blouse and I felt his warm breath
on my breast. "Because if you don't, Nora, you will
probably be a widow. They play rough games up here.
They will collect, one way or the other," he murmured.
And I knew that this time, at least, he was probably
telling me the truth.

I left the next morning, perched high on the wooden
seat of the wagon beside Logan, trying to lift my chin
in the holiday spirit.

Winter was close at hand now, and the horses and
freight wagon would not be making many more trips
before the snow stopped them. We carried plenty of fur
robes, extra food, and I felt safe and secure, traveling
with a seasoned freighter like Logan.

I checked into the hotel where Tony and I had
stayed on our arrival in Alaska. I was no longer timid
about traveling alone, but I would have preferred having company. I delayed my visit to Garth Williams as
long as possible, touring the shops, selecting fabrics to
take back for dresses, setting aside warm winter clothing, a few gifts, to be picked up and paid for later.
The shopping trip was a chore to be done, rather than

a treat, because my mission to see Garth lay heavy on my mind.

I ate a quiet supper alone and returned to my room to read. Finally I fell asleep listening to the noises drifting up from the street.

When I appeared unannounced the next morning, Garth Williams greeted me warmly, anxious to hear my version of our settling in at Ravenwood. I didn't know how, but I felt as we talked that he was already informed of the affairs at the lodge. He seemed interested in everything I said, laughing heartily when I recounted some of my disasters in learning and beamed his approval at my accomplishments.

"I have it from a very good source," he told me, "that you now turn out a real tasty berry pie."

"Oh, really?" I answered. "It must have been Logan that you were talking to. He's becoming my number-one taster when he is up there. But if he told you that, I wonder if he told you that my first few pie crusts would have made excellent shoe leather!"

We laughed together, and I found myself relaxing and completely enjoying my visit, until Garth turned serious.

"I've got to be frank with you, Nora," he said. "When I saw you come into town yesterday I was hoping it was to tell me that you had given it a try, had your adventure in the bush, and were now ready to return to San Francisco."

I bristled defensively. "Never!"

"You have no idea how rough the winter is going to be."

"I am prepared," I said, my chin high. "We've

worked hard for weeks now, and we are ready for the winter."

"You really do like it there, don't you?" Garth said, studying me closely.

"Yes." My answer was solemn as an oath. "I've grown to love Ravenwood as much as my mother did. It meant a great deal to them, and I am going to stay there—to take care of it—just as they would have done if they were still living."

He shook his head. "I worried so about you, that day you left here to go up there." He paused, his voice thoughtful. "You looked so young—so inexperienced. And Tony—well, Tony belonged in the city, not on the frontier. I didn't have much hope of the two of you making it. My biggest worry was having you run into trouble and lose the lodge. It would have been so much better for you to go up and see it, maybe stay a few weeks to see what it was like, and then let me sell it for you while I could. Running it takes a lot of hard work and guts, and a careful handling of money. I didn't feel that you had a great deal of experience in any of those things."

"I'm growing older every day, Garth. I won't be a green *cheechako* forever. I'm learning all of the time."

He nodded. "Some of the lessons are pretty hard to take, aren't they?"

I knew then, from his tone, that he had heard of Tony's gambling and his drinking. I squared my chin defensively.

"Forget it, Garth! I'm not going back to San Francisco." I looked down at my rough hands, with the broken nails, folded in my lap, and gave a sigh. "Besides, I doubt that I would feel comfortable in my father's drawing room any longer." Then I laughed goodnaturedly and held my hands out for him to see. "Just look! Lately my days have not exactly been spent serving tea in thin china cups and dreaming over fashion magazines. But I'm not really as ashamed of them as I probably should be. I'm a little proud of those scars, if the truth be known. They represent some very hard work."

"I can't argue that with you, Nora. And it must be agreeing with you. You seem much prettier now than when you sat in this office the last time."

"Such flattery!" I laughed. "So, it's prettier I am, is it, with my face tanned from the sun and my hands scratched and dry?"

"Yes. Then you were just a headstrong, willful child, playing the game of being a grown-up lady. Now you are a woman—a very warm, attractive woman."

I blushed, but my thirsty ego soaked up the compliments. Sobering, I remembered the real reason for coming to Valdez. "I need to talk to you seriously now, Garth. I need some money—" I faltered a little. "As you said, I wasn't too good at managing at first." He was watching me closely. Lord, it was hard to lie to this man. "I overspent. I was not used to budgeting."

"How much do you need?"

My voice cracked. "One thousand dollars."

Garth answered, his voice harsh, cold. "It's to cover Tony's gambling debts that are piling up, isn't it?"

"How did you know about them?" I whispered.

"There's an old expression in Alaska—sneeze in Fairbanks in the evening, they will know it in Nome in the morning. It applies to this part of the country also. Don't do it, Nora. As your lawyer, I am advising you. As your friend, I am telling you. *Don't do it.* He'll cause you to lose Ravenwood. It would be so much better to sell out—now—while you still have something left clear of debt to sell."

I stood up and walked to the window. "I've got to. I am his wife." I turned. "You can't stop me from using the money, you know. Not really." I grew defiant. "But I will promise you one thing. I won't lose Raven-wood! I love it too much not to fight for it. I'll fight, as hard as I am able!"

"Will that be hard enough?"

"I told you—I am learning, every day. I won't be a *cheechako* forever."

The worst was over. I sighed tiredly. The part I had dreaded so was over and done. I had made my demands and weathered his disapproval. I moved across the room to stand beside him.

"Garth, I have a very good idea. I saw the loveliest hat in a shop window. I really wanted that hat, but I had no use for it. If I were to go back and buy it, would you consider taking me to dinner tonight?" A little startled at my own forwardness, I added hastily, "That is, if you had no other plans already made?"

He put his hands on my shoulders, and for just an instant I thought I saw veiled desire as he smiled at me. "When the prettiest girl in Alaska has just asked me for a date, how could I possibly have anything more important to do?" He walked with me to the door. "Go and buy that hat! A new gown too, if you see one that suits you. Take extra care with your hair and put on your nicest perfume. I will call for you at six."

As I started out of the door, he added, "I'll bring the money that you want with me."

* * *

I stood in front of the mirror for a long time, studying the image, taking close assessment of what I saw.
Yes, I had changed. I had a small frame, I was slender
but not thin. I had a small waist, but my breasts rose
round and firm. I had tanned, yes, but not too much,
I didn't think, and my skin glowed from being out of
doors. My eyes were a soft gray, not the bright blue
I would have wished for, but my lashes were thick and
dark. My hair grew in a thick heavy mass, the color
of highly polished walnut. Beautiful? No, I would
never be beautiful. But attractive? Desirable? I hoped
so because inside I felt that I was, right now. I tied
on the new bonnet and went downstairs to meet Garth
Williams.

We had a lovely, carefree evening. He didn't mention
again selling Ravenwood or my returning to San Francisco. Other than handing the envelope to me, which
I tucked into my purse, money wasn't mentioned
either.

Garth may have been comfortable in wool shirts
and moccasins, but he also knew how to dress with a
quiet, elegant style. No backwoods bumpkin lawyer,
this one! He escorted me to a restaurant that by these
frontier standards was very plush indeed. Even in San
Francisco it would have been worthy of attention. Soft
lamps put a warm glow on the richly brocaded wall-
paper. Velvety, wine-colored drapes hung at the windows. Oil paintings graced the walls and graceful green
ferns filled the corners. A fire burned on the hearth.

A number of people were dining there, but the
tables were placed at discreet distances so we could
converse easily. Garth ordered wine, and we toasted
Ravenwood and its future. With a twinkle in his eye,

Garth proposed a toast to the disappearance of a *cheechako*, replaced by a sourdough.

"Not yet." I laughed. "But soon, Garth. I still have a winter to go through, remember?"

The dinner was all that I could have hoped for, but I discovered I had also developed an appetite not altogether acceptable for young ladies of society. It just wasn't proper to enjoy food this way!

I longed to ask if he had heard any word from my father, but the conversation was kept light and impersonal, away from painful subjects, and I didn't want to change it. Garth told me of news from the outside—we talked of current plays and concerts, of fashions, of scandal, of books we had read.

We walked for a bit after dinner, along the board sidewalks of the town, and then Garth escorted me to my hotel.

When we parted, Garth took my hand. "I just want to tell you one thing, Nora. If you run into trouble, need help up there and can't reach me—I want you to promise to look up a man by the name of Sam Bennett. He is a close friend of mine. He is an engineer for the copper mines and has his quarters up there in the village. Remember that name. Just tell him I sent you, and he will give you any help that you need."

I stretched to my tiptoes and kissed him lightly on the cheek. "Stop worrying about me, Garth," I whispered. "I'll do fine, really I will. And thank you for the lovely evening. You have no idea how much I enjoyed it—and your compliments. My ego was a little wounded, I'm afraid, before this evening." Then I turned and ran lightly up the stairs to my room.

* * *

Logan stopped the wagon at the path leading up
to Ravenwood, helped me down from the seat, and
stood watching until I reached the door. We had met
with a heavy snowfall at the top of the pass, and it
had slowed us down so much that Logan was anxious
to be on his way. I couldn't talk him into coming in
for a cup of hot coffee. He knew the fire would be out
and Maury already gone to her cabin. I came in the
front door, into the darkened barroom. Maury and
Abe would have retired for the night because both of
them had been working since early morning, leaving
Tony to finish up in the barroom for the evening. The
fireplace, banked for the night, still threw enough
flickering flames for me to see the tables with the
scattered dirty glasses. The air was heavy with stale
beer and tobacco odors. Chairs were at odd angles,
left as they were when their last occupant departed.
Tony's hat and coat were gone from their hook in the
corner. It filled me with anger, but it didn't surprise
me. I knew where he was. As we had come over the
top of the hill toward the town I saw the lights at
Beth's and heard the music from that broken-down,
out-of-tune piano she prized. Tony couldn't even take
time to clean up here when he closed in his haste to
get down to the noise, the drinking, the poker games!

Bitterly I thought of how he had not touched his
paints in weeks. Here, where there was so much beauty
just waiting to be put on canvas, Tony had completely
lost interest in art.

Ahead of me the door to our living quarters was
standing ajar, and I could see the lamp had been left
on low, throwing a warm welcome out to me. How
considerate of him! I took off my boots at the door and

moved tiredly across the barroom to our apartment. I kicked the door open the rest of the way, taking some pleasure in hearing it slam against the wall. Directly ahead of me was the desk where I sat to do my paperwork. In the lamplight I saw the tin box sitting on top of it, the lid open.

"Damn!" I muttered out loud. "Why not spend it! There's a refill on the way!" I picked up the box and hurled it across the room. "Spend it all, Tony! There's always more, isn't there, in the bank in Valdez!" I drew off my gloves and dropped them, with my coat, across the back of the chair. I reached for the hairbrush and, removing my hairpins, I began to brush furiously. My hair had grown longer since I had been up here, and released from its pins, it fell into a heavy mass about my shoulders.

The dry, cold air caused static electricity and as I worked off my frustration by brushing so hard, my hair soon tangled. I worked the brush loose from the snarls and threw it as hard as I could across the room, where it clattered to the floor, taking a small glass vase with it. I sank into the chair and dropped my head to the desk, beating its top with my fist. I was too hurt and too angry to cry.

A match flared in the shadows and I smelled the aroma of a cigarette being lit. I realized I was not alone. I raised my head sharply and looked into smiling hazel eyes, mocking me from across the room. Flustered, I lowered my eyes to see a strong, firm jaw, long, angular figure, a woolen shirt pulled taut across hard muscles, heavy whipcord pants tucked into leather boots, all draped quite relaxed and comfortable on my sofa.

"Are you quite in the habit of entering without being announced? Making yourself at home in other people's houses?" I snapped.

His eyes lingered on my face like a caress, then traveled slowly down to the front of my blouse where I had torn loose a button in my tantrum. When he spoke, his voice was low and vibrant.

"I came to see Tony Lowery. Since I seem to have a great deal of trouble finding him at home lately, I decided to come in and wait for him. The door was open—I didn't break in," he added softly.

"Then why didn't you speak up when I came in?" I flared.

Those mocking eyes again. "I was going to. But I didn't quite know how to do it without interrupting. You seemed a bit preoccupied."

My God, the nerve of this man! I wanted to be cold, hard, my voice precise and calculating. Instead I felt my pulse beating hard in my throat and I was breathless, as though I had been running.

"I am Tony's wife. What is it you are waiting to talk to him about?"

"I don't think it's anything for you to be troubled with." He got up and walked with an easy stride across to where I had thrown the tin cash box. He picked it up and returned it to the desk in front of me. "My problems with Tony are money matters, just between the two of us. But it seems as though I am too late. Again. I've been wasting my time sitting here waiting for him. Obviously he has found another use for his money today."

I stood up and went around the desk. "Money?" My hands were trembling but I hid them in the folds of my skirt. "What do you mean? Does Tony owe money to you?" He stood quite close to me now and I could smell shaving soap and leather. Every nerve of my body tingled with an awareness of him.

"Yes. Quite a bit, in fact. Your husband has a bad habit of joining in poker games with other men, over-bidding his hand, and leaving markers instead of cash on the table." His eyes played across my hair and fool-ishly I wondered if it shone in the lamplight. Em-barrassed by my thoughts, I stiffened defensively.

"Who are you? I don't think I've seen you around here before. I don't recall Tony ever mentioning a large debt to you either, for that matter."

"No, I doubt that he would have told you," he answered with a shrug. "A man doesn't usually talk about his gambling losses if they are high—especially to his wife."

I wished he would turn away. He was standing much too close now and I couldn't understand the feelings racing through my body, my response to a total stranger. My breathing was constricted and yet I couldn't look away from his eyes that held me, leaving me weak. I wanted to turn and run while there was still time—to tell him to get out, to come back during the day when Tony was at home. I saw him hesitate for a moment and then reach out toward me, and still I didn't turn away. I felt the strength of his lean muscles as his arms slowly, gently, tightened around me, drawing me close until I felt the scratchiness of his wool shirt against my cheek. He touched my chin with his fingers, tipping my face up, and I saw the warmth and desire in his eyes as his lips sought mine in a hungry kiss. I felt my arms slip up and circle his neck. We seemed drawn to each other by some un-explainable magnetism, and we had no control over

our desires or our responses. I only knew that I didn't
have the will or the strength to pull away. I felt his
hand moving to the torn button on my blouse, and
my breath caught in my throat but I only moved
deeper into his embrace.

Quite suddenly he pushed me away roughly and his
eyes turned cold, sending a chill through me. "My
God—what are we doing?" His voice was husky with
emotion. He stood looking down at me for a long moment and then turned and walked briskly to the door.
There he paused only long enough to pick up his hat
before he disappeared into the night.

Shaken by what had happened, I clung weakly to
the desk for support. "Wait!" I cried out. My breath
was ragged as I spoke to the empty room. "You didn't
even tell me your name."

CHAPTER FIVE

In the days following my return from Valdez, Tony was more at ease, more willing to spend his time at the lodge doing repairs that were long overdue, helping Abe at the bar, taking over completely at times, giving Abe a chance to do some ice fishing.

Maury and I went over the dress materials I had brought back with me, trying to decide which fabrics to use first and in what styles. I had brought woolens for shirts for the men and ginghams for aprons and new curtains. My aunt had taught me to sew, and I was very good at it. Maury had never learned to cut and fashion a dress so for once I was the teacher and she the student. We enjoyed our sessions together at the cutting board, and the winter hours flew by.

There was an awkward tension between Tony and me, but we didn't talk about it. We were each doing our best to keep the rift from growing deeper. Having Maury, with her easygoing nature, and quiet Abe with us made it easier to pretend nothing was wrong. When

the conversation dwindled, Maury took it up. When
time lagged, Abe decided I should learn to play cribbage.

If not warm, we were at least amiable, and somehow
the days passed without our quarreling again.

It was a quiet evening in the middle of the week.
There hadn't been too many people in during the day
and our work had been light. I left Maury in the
kitchen to finish up the end-of-the-day cleaning and
went in to work at my desk. I had vowed never to let
the paperwork get ahead of me again, and I diligently
spent several hours each evening keeping all the
rows of figures current. Chewing on the end of the
pencil thoughtfully, I spent hours going over and over
my uncle's ledgers, studying them, learning from them.
I enjoyed the time I spent there, with the fire crackling
cheerfully and the lamp casting warm, friendly shadows
about the room.

But tonight I was finding it hard to concentrate.
My thoughts kept drifting back and forth, going across
the room to the sofa, and I remembered hazel eyes
mocking me in the soft light. Then into my mind
would come a tall, lean figure; I'd recall strong arms,
the way they held me, and I would hastily pull my
mind back to the books in front of me.

It was a little frightening the way my body had
responded to his touch, the way my lips burned from
his kiss, the way I had wanted him. . . .

I had said nothing to anyone about this stranger,
this intruder in the lodge, but I couldn't forget his
eyes and the way they looked at me with desire.

I could hear the murmur of voices sifting through
the wall, and once in a while I heard Maury's laughter
above the others. The sounds were warm and friendly,

and I felt left out . . . lonely. So tonight I closed the
ledger early, pushed back the chair, and went out to
join the others in the barroom.

I paused in the doorway, looking about. The fireplace was popping from a fresh piece of frozen wood
someone must have just placed on it. Maury sat on a
stool at the end of the bar, and she and Abe were
listening intently to a fellow spinning a yarn, accented
with gestures of his hands. Two men sat at a table near
the fire, playing cribbage. There were only a few
others at scattered tables, laughing, talking, arguing.

I spotted Tony at a corner table, in deep conversation with another man. I stood watching them for a
moment, wondering who the stranger was. His back
was turned toward me, and I didn't recognize him. He
was tall and sandy-haired, and wore a long rawhide
jacket that fit smoothly across broad shoulders. I
moved across the room to join them.

Both men stood when I approached.

"My wife, Nora," Tony said, holding a chair for me.

I looked up, squarely into hazel eyes that were
smiling in recognition.

I flushed in confusion and turned away to catch
Abe's eye, to cover my embarrassment. Abe brought
over a mug of hot coffee, laced with my favorite
brandy, and set it on the table in front of me.

"I believe we have met before," the stranger was
saying. "But not formally. I'm Sam Bennett."

I caught my breath sharply. Sam Bennett was the
name Garth Williams had mentioned to me when we
parted in Valdez. Sam Bennett, the man I was to turn
to if I needed help. I watched him as they talked. He
was a soft-spoken man, a few years—probably six or
seven—older than Tony. He sat completely at ease,

confident, and I felt he was a little amused at my discomfort. My eyes fell to his hands resting on the table —strong hands.

"I'm sorry. I didn't mean to interrupt," I apologized. "If you were talking . . ."

"It's all right, Nora," Tony answered. "We were just discussing the copper mines. Sam, here, is an engineer."

"Really? How interesting! The mines are doing so much for the growth of the village. There are new people coming in every week!" I said. My God, I thought. Couldn't I say something more intelligent than that? No wonder Tony was frowning at me.

"The village is built on mining property," Sam explained. "With the exception of Ravenwood, the mining companies own most of the land around here."

Tony interrupted, turning to me. "The railroad is finally moving ahead faster. If the winter isn't too bad and doesn't cause them a lot of trouble, it should be completed before too much longer. When they get it up as far as the mines so that the ore can be hauled out by rail, watch the boom that will happen!"

I looked at Tony's face, alive with interest. I wondered what they had been discussing before I joined them. What was this all leading up to?

But the talk turned to the killing of a large brown bear behind the assay office in town. From there the talk drifted to the number of gold claims filed during the summer, and onto predictions of what kind of a winter was ahead. Sam asked if we were prepared for it, and Tony told him of all of the work we had put in, to get ready.

Finally Sam stretched his long legs and stood, pushing back his chair. He reached over to shake Tony's hand.

"It's a deal, then, is it?" he asked. "If you still think this is what you want to do—if you want to give it a try, I'll see you in the morning."

"I'll be there," Tony answered.

Sam nodded to me and left.

"What was that all about?" I asked.

"It should make you happy, Nora. I'm going to work up at the copper mines." He leaned back in the chair, looking smug. "For a good salary too, I might add."

"To work? At the copper mines? What kind of work? Why?"

"And why not?" he snapped. "Things are going to be slow here at the lodge, now that winter has closed in. Money has become so important to you . . . not only won't I be spending any of your precious money, I will be adding to it."

"Have you known Sam long?" I asked. Throughout the conversation my mind kept going back to that other evening and Sam saying his business with Tony was "of a financial matter."

"A month or so."

"I haven't seen him around here before."

"No. He plays poker sometimes down at Beth's. That's where I met him."

"Does he win often?" I whispered.

"Quit picking, Nora. What do you want me to say? Do I lose? Do I owe him money? My debts are all squared away now, so quit worrying." He was angry with me. "Come on, let's go up and sit with Abe and Maury."

Maury was in the middle of repeating a funny story, and everyone was listening intently and laughing at her when we joined the group. God, how I envied her. Was there ever a time when Maury wasn't able to look around and find something to laugh about?

Tony was up early the next morning, full of enthusiasm for his new job at the mines. I sat up in bed, watching him dressing, and listened to him talk of his plans. The salary was high, and Tony told me of the things we were going to be able to do around the lodge. First of all, he was going to send out for some glass and enclose the rest of the front porch, to keep out the cold in the winter and the mosquitoes in the summer. After a few months of working, he was going to put away the bigger part of his salary. By next summer we would be able to take a trip back to San Francisco! His eyes glowed at the mention of it, and I think I realized then, for the first time, how much Tony missed the big city. As I listened to him talk my mind wandered to another conversation. I wondered how much Garth had to do with this job being offered to Tony. . . .

The first week went by quickly and smoothly. Each morning Tony was awake before I was, looking forward to his day ahead of him. He returned in the evening, eagerly relating what had happened during the day. He told how the mines were stockpiling ores, waiting for the completion of the railroad, and he became frustrated with their slow progress. He was enthusiastic as he talked of the future of the mines and the town nearby. "The mines need the people in order to operate—and the people need the mine to

survive! We should take steps to organize a city coun-
cil. We ought to elect a mayor!" He turned to me.
"Do you have any idea at all how big that village could
grow, when the railroad gets here? It could be a city!"

Abe shook his head and frowned.

"What's the matter, Abe?" I asked.

"Too many people already," he grumbled.

"Why, Abe." I laughed. "I thought you liked people!"

"There's too many of them around here already,
without the railroad. Too many drifters, rainbow
chasers, wanting to get rich quick. And I'll bet you
can count at least eight women, not including you and
Maury."

"That's called progress, Abe," Tony said. "That's
what builds a country. If you think this is getting too
crowded, wait until that last leg of the railroad is
done and they start hauling that ore out of here by
rail! It's not going to be much longer either."

"It will be kind of nice to have more women
around," Maury mused. "We need some reinforce-
ments. You men are too darned independent."

"Didn't intend to live in a city when we moved
here," Abe said. "Don't intend to now. Keeps on
growing, we may just have to pull up stakes and move
on somewhere else—where there's more breathing
space."

"Fat chance of that, Abe." Maury laughed. "I was
here when it all started, and I want to stick around
to see it grow." She reached over and pinched his arm
playfully. "And you ain't going nowhere without me,
honey. I've got you too spoiled with my cooking and
my lovin'."

"Yeah, Maury—guess you got a point there," he said dryly. "Got to admit, you are getting to be kind of a comfortable habit." She flushed and we all laughed.

I was content, because once again Tony showed an active interest in something. He stayed home in the evening, sometimes helping Abe at the bar, joining in the good-natured ribbing and storytelling that went on among the men there.

Once more I began to look forward to our nights. Tony was a skillful lover, and I responded to his touch with a warmth I thought I wasn't capable of feeling any longer. Later we would lie together in the big brass bed, my head resting on his shoulder, and he would drowsily talk of our making a trip to San Francisco next summer. He talked of the opera, the theater, going to parties, carriage rides in the park. I listened and felt guilty because I couldn't share his yearning to return to the things I was only now realizing how much he missed.

We saw more of Sam. He began to stop in at the lodge for his supper, sometimes staying for a drink or two at the bar. Other times Tony would join him at his table, and they would linger over dinner, Tony's face animated as they talked.

After that first night when he had kissed away my reason, I never saw Sam alone. The lodgers were there every evening for their meals, and other men strayed in, stomping the snow off their boots, beating their hands against the cold, going to stand in front of the fireplace while they waited to be served their supper. Once in a while a trapper stopped in wanting nothing more than to share our fire and to feel for a little while the companionship of others. And there were prospectors, driven in from their claims by the blizzards, already restless and quarrelsome with the winter not yet half gone.

There would be noise, talking, glasses clinking, dishes rattling—I would be hurting with tiredness—and then the noise would fade into a low hum and I wouldn't feel my weariness, for Sam would be standing in the doorway. His eyes would find mine across the room and I would feel the warmth of their caress. Then the moment would pass.

"Even', Nora." He would nod casually and walk over to the table Maury had waiting for him. I would move instinctively to Tony's side, as though seeking protection from my traitorous emotions.

Sam praised Maury's cooking and she beamed with pleasure. I noticed how often we had Sam's favorite desserts now, and I smiled to myself at how open Maury was with her friendships.

On the surface things were going well as we all waited out the winter. Tony would be completing two weeks today at the mine office. He had spent every evening at the lodge, seeming content with our quiet evenings and our casual conversations. I felt cautious, wanting so much to have our lives have a meaning again and yet afraid to take anything for granted. Each day I must try a little harder. I must somehow find a way to believe in Tony again.

Despite all our troubles, Tony was still able to fan the fires of our passions into life at night. He was a gentle, thoughtful, persuasive lover, and my young, healthy body responded to his touch. And yet I was becoming more and more aware of something missing in our relationship. Something much deeper than just being sexually compatible, a closeness that faded with the first early-morning rays of sunlight. When I first met Tony I was completely captivated by his handsome looks, his charming manner, the bohemian difference in his background. Gradually I began to sense how different we really were. Tony missed the people, the excitement, the parties, the San Francisco life style, and tried to find some substitute for it in the gambling and the drinking at the roadhouse, while I sought a different dream. I wanted the love my mother had known in the arms of Jim Crandall. A love so lasting that it could still be felt here in the rooms of Ravenwood long after they had gone. I remembered the heady thrill of a first romance, dancing with a young and handsome suitor, feeling the envious glances of my friends, the stolen kisses. . . . Without realizing it, was I trying to change Tony into the image I had of James Crandall and finding him lacking? Or had he been wrong for me right from the very start, and had I been too young and inexperienced to realize it? Somehow I had to find a way to bridge the gulf that was growing between us, even though my pride was refusing to acknowledge that it existed.

On Fridays we usually had some sort of fish for supper and I was just lifting a large baked salmon from the oven when I started in surprise at the sound of Tony's voice.

"You're home early," I called. "Everything all right?"

He shrugged in return, taking off his heavy coat and going over to the bar. I stood watching him for a moment, thinking that he looked as if he had lost some weight from his already thin frame, and his face looked drawn and tired.

I filled two plates and carried them out to the table near the fire where we could have a quiet supper by

ourselves. Maury and I usually took turns eating in
the evening, and she liked to wait until later when
Abe could join her.

We ate quietly, not talking. Tony was moody and
his thoughts were somewhere else.

I caught myself watching the door each time it
opened. I glanced over at the clock on the mantel.
"Sam hasn't come in for his supper yet tonight. I
wonder where he is?"

"Who cares!" Tony snapped at me. "Time he found
someplace else to eat. Being with him all day and then
having him hang around here in the evening too was
getting too damn much."

I raised an eyebrow in surprise, but I didn't answer.

Maury came over and sat down with us, bringing a
cup of coffee and a piece of pie with her from the
kitchen. She began telling Tony of things that had happened around the lodge during the day, laughing as
she talked, finding humor in little things so easily, but
he only half listened, boredom showing plainly in his
eyes.

He pushed back his chair and stood up. "I'm restless
tonight," he said, trying to sound casual. "Been cooped
up too much lately. Think I'll just walk on down the
hill and watch the game for a while." He dropped a
kiss carelessly on my cheek. "Stop frowning. I'm not
going to play—just watch. I'll be home early; tomorrow's a work day."

I watched him go over, take his coat off the hook,
and wrap the scarf up tight as he went out into the
swirling snow and darkness.

Maury picked up the dirty dishes, and as she headed
toward the kitchen I heard her mutter, "Wondered
what would happen on pay day at the mines."

I curled up in a chair and read until late that night before giving up and finally going to sleep. I didn't hear him come home.

The next day I was tired, my nerves on edge. The walls of the lodge were confining; they closed in on me. Often I went to the window and stood looking out at the deep snow that shut us off from the outside world. When Maury complained that she was running low on cinnamon for her pies, I eagerly took it as an excuse for me to walk to the village. The air was cold and crisp, burning my nose as I breathed. The trail was well packed, and I felt my spirits rising as I walked briskly along to keep warm. I slowed down on the walkway in front of the row of shops that had sprung up in the last few months, looking in the windows. The low winter sun played on the rough board siding, softening their crudeness, and the white snow made everything look fresh and clean. I glanced up and saw two drifters watching my progress from where they stood in a darkened doorway. I didn't remember seeing either one of them around town before. They wore dark clothing, a little the worse for wear, and muddy boots. One pushed his hat back on his head as I passed, and I felt his sharp, cold eyes as they brazenly roved over the entire length of my figure. I had seen that look in the eyes of men before but never directed so openly at me, and I shuddered in distaste as though he had touched me. The other man was built heavier, with a thatch of unruly dark hair and a prickly beard. Neither spoke to me, but I frowned as I saw that look of raw animal hunger twist their mouths into lewd grins as I passed. I shivered as I hurried to walk a bit faster.

The bells tied to the door rattled a greeting as I entered Walker's General Store and Hardware. The odors

that assailed me were strong of dampness, leather, tobacco, and foodstuffs. Mrs. Walker had her back to me,
folding a bolt of cloth. Her husband was bent down,
busily sorting out his new stocks, ready to set on the
shelves. Both turned to greet me warmly. They asked
about Maury, about Ravenwood, and then the talk
turned automatically to the latest word on the progress
of the railroad. A large blue granite coffeepot steamed
on the heavy, pot-belly stove in the center of the room,
and I accepted a cup gratefully as I warmed my hands
at the fire. I took my time to look around leisurely and
select a few items. Besides being a convenient place to
purchase things the lodge had run out of, the store
also housed the local post office, built into a corner
against the wall, and it was a source for all the town's
gossip.

Mrs. Walker pointed out a new supply of handicrafts
the Indians had brought in for sale, and I chose a
lovely pair of beaded moccasins. They would make an
elegant pair of house slippers for my brother Tom. I
would pack them into the Christmas package I had
almost ready to ship to my family. They still had not
answered my letters, but I couldn't let my first Christmas away from them go by without sending some token
of my affection. I found a small, delicately carved piece
of ivory shaped into a ring for my aunt. I really wasn't
sure she would like it, or ever wear it, but maybe she
would treasure it as a keepsake and know that I was
thinking of her.

The shadows were growing long now and the sun
would disappear soon, so I had to hurry. I walked
quickly past the bakery and the assay office and started
up the path toward the lodge.

I looked about but the two men I had seen earlier

were gone. Yet I had an uneasy feeling of being watched. I quickened my step, suddenly eager to be home. As I followed a turn in the path, the two drifters stepped out, blocking my way. Every instinct warned me of danger. I glanced quickly over my shoulder, but there was no one to hear me if I were to cry out. I knew it was useless to try to run.

The one with the cold eyes reached out and grabbed my arm.

"Well, if it isn't the pretty lady from the lodge!"

The other tipped his hat and bowed low. "May I carry your packages for you, ma'am?"

I was surprised at my calmness and the hardness in my voice. "Let go of my arm. You are in my way."

"Now, easy, gal. We ain't aiming to scare you none, just want to brighten your day a little. Come on, don't you want to be even a little bit friendly?"

The other moved in closer, taking my other arm. "Sure now, ma'am, we can make you real happy, my buddy and me. We ain't seen too many women for a long time now, and we got a lot of loving stored up inside." I caught the smell of whisky strong on his breath.

"Sure, li'l gal. That husband of yours leaves you alone too often. If a pretty li'l thing like you belonged to me, I wouldn't be spending my evenings down at that roadhouse, playing cards and feeling up the girls. No siree, not me!"

His fingers dug into my wrist and I cried out in pain, kicking at him with all of my strength. My kick was well directed and I managed to throw him off balance, but the other man grabbed both of my arms from behind. My package fell to the snow-covered ground. The first man was angry now, and he slapped me hard across the face, jarring the pins from my hair. I was pulled to the side of the path, and though I fought as hard as I was able, kicking, biting, scratching, I was tumbled to the ground, hurting my arm as I fell. Pure, raw panic seized me now, and I screamed and screamed.

"Stupid bitch!" the first man snarled. "You shouldn't have done that, now!" And he clapped his rough dirty hand across my mouth. I still struggled, but I was no match for the two of them.

"A real wildcat we've caught ourselves here, buddy."

"Just makes the game more fun. Don't be so slow, Davy." He was breathing heavily, his eyes glazed in anticipation.

One now had a firm hold on my shoulders and I felt the other solidly pinning my legs, pushing at my heavy clothing. "No, no, please! No," I moaned, terror taking hold on me.

Suddenly I heard the loud thud of splintering bone. The one trying to push my legs apart yelled a curse of agony and fell sideways to the ground. The other released my arms, rose, and started to run, but strong arms caught him. I sat up in time to see a heavy fist catch him full in the mouth. Blood flew. I crawled a few feet away. Clinging to a young tree, I pulled myself to my feet. My head was reeling dizzily and bright spots of light spun in front of my eyes. I felt sick inside, afraid I was going to faint.

Everything was out of focus—just a mass of swinging arms, grunts, and heavy oaths, whirling in front of me.

It all ended as suddenly as it started. The two strangers were on the ground. One appeared to be out cold. The other was conscious but showed no signs of wanting to get up. He held his hand to his bloody mouth and his eyes were bright with fear.

Sam nudged him with his foot. "You aren't hurt that bad. Get your friend there and get the hell out of here."

He turned to me then, and I felt the strength of his arms holding me, making the world stop spinning. I stared up at him, wanting to speak, feeling a chill seize my body. I saw his strong face look down at me with such compassion that I wanted to lean against him, stay within the protection of his arms.

"It's all right now, Nora. It's all right. It's over," he soothed. "It's over—you have had a bad shock, but it's over now."

I looked up and for a moment our eyes held, saying things, admitting things our lips dared not speak. I looked away first. I was disturbed by him, and I didn't understand why. Or wouldn't admit why.

"I'm all right." My voice was shaky as I moved out of the circle of his arm. I bent to pick up the torn package. "Guess I was lucky that you happened along. . . ."

"I was on my way to see Abe."

"Sam, don't tell Tony. Please. He would—"

"He would what?"

"Just don't tell him, that's all. No harm done. I'm not hurt. I'd rather just not speak of it again." I didn't know what Tony's reaction would be. Relief that I was all right? Anger at a raw, unsettled country where this could happen? Resentment that it was Sam, not he, who was there when I needed help? Or would he somehow twist it around to find a reason to place the blame on me? It was better just to say nothing at all.

"If that's what you want." Sam grinned at me. "You better smooth your clothing and repin your hair, though, if that's what we're going to do. Otherwise Tony might suspect me . . ."

I handed him my package while I tucked my hair

back awkwardly. Then, standing in front of him, once again composed, I asked, "There, do I pass inspection?"

His warm hazel eyes appraised me critically. "I think I would have enjoyed it more if you had thrown yourself into my arms, crying in fright, so I could feel the hero. But, yes, you'll do. You'll do very well, Nora."

He took my arm and we walked on, in silence, to the lodge.

Maury saw us come in and her sharp eyes raked over me. "My God! What happened to you!"

"Nothing. I wasn't watching and I slipped and took a nasty tumble on the ice. Luckily Sam came along, and he was good enough to pick me up and escort me home. Really, I'm fine. Just collected a few bruises, I think, nothing to mention. Sam was coming this way anyway to see Abe."

As I went through into my sitting room, I heard Abe ask Sam, "And what happened to your eye? Fall on the same patch of ice?"

I stayed close to the lodge for the next few days and tried to forget those two drifters. I sewed diligently by day, in between busy spells in the kitchen. Maury and I each had a new dress now, and I was working on a second. Maury had cut out a shirt for Abe, and I was showing her how to put it together. Evenings I spent with Tony, trying to encourage his interest in the lodge and listening to him talk about his work at the mines. I was attempting to understand what he was doing there and why he liked it.

He surprised me by suddenly saying, "I don't want you to be so friendly with Sam Bennett anymore."

I looked up quickly. "For heaven's sake, why?"

"No real reason." He shrugged carelessly. "It's just

that I see so much of him during the day. He's watching me all the time—expecting me to make mistakes. It's beginning to get on my nerves. He thinks he's always right. Thinks no one else can do the work like he can."

"Come on, Tony," I cajoled. "You're just tired tonight. I thought you liked your job. You seemed so interested. . . ."

"I like the work all right. Or at least I did. I'm just tired of Sam playing the boss—giving me all of the dull, routine chores that any errand boy could handle, while he does the interesting, challenging jobs. The big chief! It makes him look good that way. He's got a pretty good 'in' with the company up there, you know. I think he must be a stockholder too. That guy has really got it made!" Tony gave a sulky frown. "I have to put up with it during the day. I'd rather not see so much of him in the evenings."

"This is a pretty small settlement, Tony. There aren't too many places for a man to go in the evening to visit."

"Then let him stay home," he said grouchily.

"Oh, come on, Tony," I said. "You're just tired tonight, and you're being crabby. Sam, along with a lot of other people up here, has been a good friend to us, and you know it. Besides, I can't be rude for no reason at all. He's a very good friend of Garth Williams." I have no idea why I had to add that. As soon as I had, I knew it was the wrong thing to say. But it was too late.

Tony's head came up sharply. "How do you know that?"

"Well, I—I don't really," I stammered. "It's just when I was in Valdez last, when I was talking with

Garth, he told me that if I—if we—ever were in trouble and couldn't reach him—to look up a friend of his here at the mines. He said to look up Sam Bennett."

"Oh, great!" Tony exploded angrily. "That's just great! Why didn't you tell me before this?"

"It just didn't seem important. I had forgotten."

"I suppose Sam knows I sent you to Valdez for the money I needed."

"Not unless you told him. I certainly didn't."

Tony leaned back in his chair, his mouth grim. "I think I see it all now. Protect poor Nora. Give her worthless husband a job. Williams must have arranged it with Sam to offer me that job." Then Tony's eyes narrowed. "Or was it Williams after all? Maybe it was you, Nora. Did you ask Sam?"

I pushed back my chair and stood, fire sparking in my eyes. "Sometimes, Tony, you can be extremely exasperating!" With that I flounced off to the kitchen to help Maury finish the cleaning up.

Two days later Tony quit his job at the mines.

After Tony left the mining office, Sam still dropped in at suppertime for Maury's cooking, but not as often. He and Tony often spoke, just a casual greeting, or nodded across the room. But Sam never attempted to draw Tony into a solitary conversation, and Tony, though not avoiding him, did not make any effort to be more than impersonal. Sometimes Sam stayed, sitting at the far end of the bar, playing a quiet game of cribbage with Abe and enjoying a pipe as they talked, but most of the time he left early.

I received a letter from Garth Williams. He had a buyer for the lodge. The offering price was more than fair, and once again Garth urged that I consider it. The winter was going to be rough, and he felt that I would be much better off back in a city outside. I read it thoughtfully, then slowly tore it in pieces and dropped them into the fireplace. Tony must have seen the envelope because he asked, "That from Williams? What does he want now?"

"Nothing much." I shrugged. "Just a note asking how we are doing, wondering if we were ready for the winter." Then I turned away before he could see the lie on my face.

Saturday was an unusually bright, clear day. Tony was helping Abe take advantage of the weather by cutting and stacking more wood in the shed off the kitchen. There were no lodgers around, so neither man was needed inside. I stayed in the barroom so I would hear if anyone came in. Sitting at the table nearest the window, I was taking advantage of the full sunlight to read a novel I had found in my uncle's bookcase. The book was interesting, but I didn't realize how deeply I was lost in it until I heard someone talking to me.

"Must be very good. I said hello twice but you didn't seem to hear."

I laid the book aside reluctantly and tried to make up for it by smiling warmly. "Hello, Sam." I stretched and yawned, realizing I must have sat there in one position longer than I thought. "Sit down, won't you? Yes, it is a good book. I was lost in it. . . . Gosh, didn't it turn out to be a nice day? The sun coming in through the window is so warm that it feels good on my back. I just want to sit here and soak up every bit of it that

I can. I guess I'm just not adjusted to the short days yet."

Sam pulled up a chair, bringing with him a mug of coffee that Maury must have given him in the kitchen.

"You looked so relaxed and content, curled up there like a kitten in a spot of sunlight." He smiled. "I hesitated to disturb you."

"I *was* content. We have the work caught up, and I had time on my hands for a change. I love to read, and this book is well written. It's a romance that takes place in the Regency period in England. I was surprised to find it among my uncle's books."

"And you were escaping in its pages."

I made a face at him. "Escaping? Well, yes, maybe you are right. Maybe I was, for a little while."

He was watching me thoughtfully. "Ever think of going back, Nora?"

"Oh, no! Not you too!" I cried.

"What do you mean, me too?"

"You and Garth Williams." I frowned. "Or is this a joint plot between the two of you, to get me to sell the lodge and return to San Francisco?"

"No. I just wondered. No plot. Be honest, though. Aren't there times, once in a while, when you think it might be the best thing to do?"

"Absolutely not." I looked him squarely in the eye. "Is that what you want me to do, Sam? Is that what you would like to see me do? Just call it quits and leave?"

He returned my look, answering evenly. "You know better. No. I would hate to see you leave. A part of me would leave too." He shrugged. "I was just thinking of you—what would be best for you, you and Tony."

"Don't, Sam. I know what you are thinking. Don't interfere."

"Are you happy here, Nora?"

"I love Ravenwood. It's my home. I have no intention of leaving."

"What about Tony?"

"What *about* Tony?" I flared. "Sam, don't take this role of 'big brother' too seriously. I'm quite sure Garth asked you to look out for us, check on us once in a while, but we don't need it—or want it, either," I added.

"Okay, okay." He held up his hands, laughing. "You can spit like a kitten too. I wasn't looking for an argument."

"Then don't meddle, Sam." I was firm. "You are so very sure of yourself, aren't you? So much a part of this country up here. You don't bend very easily. Tony is trying very hard, you know. He isn't strong like you are—but he is trying." I felt like a traitor, talking about Tony this way. "Sam, you have got to understand. He resents you! Don't you see? He looks upon your advice as interfering in our lives, as though you doubt he is capable of caring for me and the lodge—as though you are expecting him to fail and are waiting to catch me when I fall. I would like very much for us to be friends, Sam, but we can't if you keep this up."

He reached out to me. His large hand covered mine, his tiny golden hairs glistening in the sunlight, his fingers firm and strong. My nerves tingled and my pulse raced in response. Oh, dear God, what was I going to do? I had no right to feel like this!

I jerked my hand away. Color flooded my face and my breath caught in my throat. "Don't!" I turned

away. "Don't, Sam. I am Tony's wife. Don't ever forget it, because I won't."

Sam pushed back his chair and stood. "If ever the
time comes—"

"It won't," I snapped.

"Don't be too sure," he said as he turned away. He
waved to Maury as he went out of the door, letting it
slam behind him.

I glanced up toward the kitchen and saw Maury
watching me thoughtfully.

CHAPTER SIX

Christmas was just two weeks away. The nights were long now, very long, and I felt closed in, smothered in darkness. The weather had been bitter cold the last week and the snow was deep, with drifts reaching to the eaves of the Hills' small cabin. It was a continuous task for the men, working with snow shovels, to keep the entrance to the lodge open, with a wide path out to the road. Once in a while we would have a clear day, and then the sun would rise to just above the horizon and balance there on the treetops for a few short hours before dropping out of sight again. It was a depressing, confining time for me and the others. Any sort of diversion was welcomed, and the coming of the holidays was eagerly anticipated, more out of an excuse to get together than out of sentiment. I threw myself into a flurry of planning. That year I made most of my Christmas gifts. For the women on my list I dried and crushed wild rose petals, herbs, and spices and sewed them into satin sachets, trimmed with bits of ribbon.

For Abe and Sam I made hats from pieces of fur, as I had seen the Indian women do in the village. Somehow I found the time to knit a long, heavy scarf for Logan and a pair of stockings for Garth.

I had a gift hidden in a closet for Tony, ordered weeks ago from Seattle. I had sent for two brightly colored silk vests, with two black silk ties, like the men wore in San Francisco. There was a jacket too, well cut and smoothly fitting, along with several white shirts. He loved to dress, and I finally realized how much he missed the elaborate affairs he attended in San Francisco. The few parties we had here were a poor substitute.

But the special gift that I had for him could not be wrapped in a package and tied with a bright ribbon. I knew now, without a doubt, that I was carrying Tony's baby. I didn't want to tell him yet. I wanted to keep the secret to myself, holding it close, treasuring it, for just a little while longer. I would tell him on Christmas Eve, and it would make our holiday complete. I was sure that he would be as happy as I. A child would draw us closer together, would help to weave a bridge across the gulf of indifference that was pulling us apart.

I spent those two weeks before the holiday in a whirlwind of activity. Like an avalanche, what started as a small idea rolled downhill picking up momentum and other ideas until what started out as a small party for our close friends turned into a potlatch, with an open invitation to all our friends and neighbors along the Valdez Trail. Logan promised that he would be here, and everyone else answered with the same enthusiasm. Maury and I baked cookies and cakes and made candies. We planned on cooking the two large geese Abe brought back from one of his hunting forages, gar-

nished with the low-bush cranberries we had picked
last summer, along with all of the other trimmings. I
insisted that we put up a Christmas tree. The evergreens here struggle too hard through the long and
cold winters and grow too fast in the full hours of summer sunlight to match the thick green of the trees back
home. However, I found a passable tree and wove in
extra branches to achieve the fullness I wanted. Abe
and Tony grumbled a lot as they followed me around,
floundering in the snow, while I chose the tree and we
hauled it indoors. But they worked with me, making a
stand for it, hanging evergreens around the room under
my direction, and bringing in the ladder to tack up
decorations I made of bright red berries and pine
cones, bits of pretty ribbons and colored paper. Tony
got caught up in the mood and spent hours on repairs
that were needed and helping at the bar. We relaxed
into easy, happy ways, and the hours flew by for all of
us. Others in the village seemed to catch the festive
air, and the bar was crowded most of the time in the
early evening, as though everyone felt the need to get
together, to visit, to laugh, to join forces to push away
the darkness.

I hugged my inner secret to me, and though Tony
commented that the starchy diets we had here were
making me put on weight, he gave no other indication
that he had guessed.

On the morning of Christmas Eve, the temperatures
warmed up above zero and it began to snow lightly.
The sun came out briefly about noon and then it
snowed the rest of the day. Our guests began arriving
in the late afternoon, depositing armloads of packages
under the tree, hanging steaming, snowy coats on the

hooks, and filling the room with loud voices and laughter. They came in horse-drawn sleighs, with dog-sled teams, or on foot. The horses were unhitched and put in the small storage barn behind the lodge. The dogs were unharnessed and staked out in the shelter of the trees, with a safe distance kept between each team.

When Logan Aldridge came in, stomping the snow off his boots, I was delighted to see Garth Williams with him. I ran across the room to him and was folded into a big bear hug. He looked about the large barroom and his face broke into a wide smile.

"It's looking good, Nora," he said. "I can see for myself now that you are happy here. You and the lodge seem to suit each other."

"Thank you, Garth. That is one of the nicest things you could say," I answered. "Let me help with your coat. Have you ever seen so many people? I think you probably know most of them. . . ."

Dinner was a tremendous success. I had insisted on preparing the geese myself under Maury's worried eye, and the tables were heaped with things the two of us had been cooking for the past several days. Many of our friends brought special dishes they had prepared to add to the feast. Tony stayed behind the bar at first, until everyone got their coats off and started relaxing. Then they all served themselves, both at the tables and at the bar.

I had slipped away into our sitting room, to freshen up and change my dress after the meal was prepared, when Tony joined me. He watched me struggling with the buttons at the waist of my skirt and looked at me thoughtfully. "Nora, you really should watch it closer," he said. "Your clothes are becoming too tight."

I laughed merrily and ran to put my arms around him. "Yes, aren't they! But Tony, I'm not going to be able to do much about losing weight until about the middle of next June. Isn't it wonderful? Tell me you are happy too—please, Tony."

I watched the puzzled look on his face, then slowly understanding came into his eyes.

"I was so afraid you would guess ahead of time," I whispered. "I wanted to tell you tonight—as a Christmas present. Merry Christmas, darling!"

Tony gathered me into his arms. "I had wondered several times," he said. "But I thought if it were true, you would have said something. I didn't know you could keep a secret like that."

"Aren't you happy about it, Tony?" I asked softly.

He kissed me tenderly, with emotion. "Of course I am. If you are happy, then I am too. It's just that it was a surprise. I need some time to get used to the idea. Me—a father."

He spun me around and smacked me on the backside. "Hurry up, we need to get back to our guests. They are going to miss us."

Later Maury drew me to one side. "You finally told Tony about the little one, didn't you?"

I raised my eyebrows in surprise. "How did you know?"

"Of course I knew. What do you take me for, not to have guessed?"

"Yes, I told him. It was his Christmas present from me."

She put her arm around me and gave me a warm hug. "Nora, don't be disappointed if Tony isn't as enthused as you think he should be. Men are like that. But once it gets here, he will be as proud as you are. I'm sure of it!"

For a moment a shadow crossed her face, and I knew she was thinking of the two she had conceived and lost, without a chance to hold them in her arms. Then a big smile broke out and she squeezed my arm.

"I'm so happy for you, Nora. You will do all right too. You're healthy, and you have me here, right beside you, to help you all of the way. We are going to have the most beautiful and healthy baby ever to be born in this godforsaken wilderness."

The evening seemed to go too fast. I wanted to slow it down, catch it in my hands, hold it, to make it last.

We exchanged gifts. Tony gave me a dainty locket, fashioned of small gold nuggets, with a jade inset. Inside was a small lock of his hair. When I opened Sam's gift, I found a lovely antique music box, engraved in delicate filigree. As I lifted the lid, the soft, tinkling notes of the "Blue Danube" drifted out. I looked up and caught his eyes watching me across the room. My cheeks flushed and I looked away quickly.

There were several novels and a book of poetry from Garth. There was a lovely hand-painted china teapot from Logan, and as I held the fragile piece of china in my hands a tear came into my eyes at his thoughtfulness. What dear friends we had, here in the bush!

There was laughing and boisterous singing. Tables were pushed back, and people danced to an accordion played by one of the men. I spotted two different games of cribbage going.

Tony had changed into one of the new vests and

jacket. He looked so handsome, lounging against the bar.

I looked about the room at this odd collection of people, all enjoying each other's company. There was a store merchant and his wife, a trapper and his Indian squaw, an executive from the copper mines, and a madam from a roadhouse. Yes, Beth was here too. When I had realized she might come, I hadn't known what to expect. I had never met a madam before that I knew of. I imagined someone gaudily dressed and overpainted, I suppose. But Beth was beautiful—pale white skin against raven hair, unfathomable dark-green eyes, a tiny thing, quiet, carrying her chin high with a delicate poise.

The men who roomed upstairs were all here, and there were others from the town as well as the Indian village nearby. I even saw several that I didn't recognize, drawn in by the laughter and the music and drinking and joining the fun.

I had never seen a group of people enjoying themselves so thoroughly in such a relaxed manner. I thought of Christmases at my father's home in San Francisco. They were stuffy, black-tie affairs, with outrageous presents picked to impress. I couldn't help but wonder what my aunt would think if she were to suddenly appear right now, right here in the midst of this gala Christmas party in our barroom. The very thought of the shock she would receive made me laugh out loud.

I danced with several of the men—a wild sort of cross between a war dance and stomping on bugs—and then, breathless, I sought shelter behind the tables.

"Are you hiding, or can I have the next dance?"

I turned and saw Sam standing there, waiting for

me to answer. I hesitated for a moment and then held out my hand to him. "All right. But only because they are playing a slower number now." I laughed. "I really don't think I could last through one more like the last one."

He danced so well—a gliding waltz that left me feeling as though we were floating around the room on the air. It was ridiculous for me to stumble slightly as he placed his hand at my waist. I kept my eyes lowered, refusing to look up even when he spoke to me, because I didn't want him to see the emotions that might be showing on my face, but I felt his eyes watching me. The other times I had danced this evening, I thought the music would never end, but this one ended almost before I realized it had started.

I stepped back only to find Tony waiting for me. "We really should have a dance, don't you think?" He smiled at me. "You are the belle of the ball tonight. I've had a hard time catching you free."

I turned and placed my hand on his arm. We danced as we had danced so many times before, and yet it was not the same. Somehow the enchantment that held me wasn't there any longer. I looked up and studied his face. My eyes told me he was the same man who had led me out onto the ballroom floor to the envy of all my girl friends. I remembered how my heart had fluttered when he had smiled that easygoing, charming smile. He had captivated me so easily with his winning ways. I knew now in my heart that it would never be the same. And yet I knew also as I looked up at him that he was the same. He had not changed. It was I who had changed. . . .

The last of the guests finally left in the wee hours of the morning, some going out into the dark night to their homes close by, others upstairs, the men bunking three and four to a room. The barroom was a shambles of empty glasses, displaced furniture, discarded pieces of bright paper and ribbon, and two sleeping trappers on a pile of coats. I was tired to the point of complete exhaustion but I hated to see the party end. For the last few weeks my world had been as I wanted, with no arguments, no crises. And Tony was always near, content to be at the lodge, taking part in the work with the rest of us. Though it lacked the passion we had once known, our lovemaking was satisfying and Tony seemed content for once. Like a child, I wanted to be able to wake up the next morning and discover it was Christmas all over again.

The following days were dull by comparison, and I turned my thoughts to preparations for the birth of the child I carried. Maury showed her happiness openly, taking over with her usual zest. She watched over me constantly, becoming an overnight authority on diet, exercise, and the amount of rest I must have. She bossed and fussed and worried over me, as was her way, but she didn't pamper me. She knew that to remain healthy and strong, with an easy delivery, I must also be active.

Tony accepted this child as he accepted all new things—with a burst of enthusiasm, daydreams, and a great many big plans. He decided the child could spend his early years under my tutelage, but then he must go to Seattle for his first schooling. After that, boarding school in San Francisco, and finally, college in the East.

"But Tony"—I laughed—"what if it is a girl?"

He looked at me blankly, as though the possibility had never occurred to him.

It was quiet, unsentimental Abe who surprised me. To listen to him, a person would think this was the only baby ever to be born in this northern land. He admonished Maury not to allow me to help with the laundry. He glowered at me if I didn't eat all the food he thought I should. He appeared at my elbow out of nowhere, taking baskets and trays from me, insisting I shouldn't be lifting.

And thus we four waited the arrival of this babe, with Abe and Maury acting as much the expectant parents as Tony and I.

Though the winter still held me prisoner inside the lodge, I spent many happy hours making a layette, each tiny stitch sewn with love. It was bitter cold outside, with the temperature often dropping twenty or thirty degrees below zero. The snow fell and drifted, covering the paths the men had shoveled. Though the equinox had passed and the days were becoming longer, it was not fast enough to suit me. There were still too many hours of darkness and so little daylight. I grew restless and irritable. It made me angrier still when the others overlooked my bad temper because of my condition. Abe put on snowshoes and did some hunting. Tony made several trips into town for supplies, coming home late, and I suspected he stopped at Beth's. I envied them their freedom.

Not as many people came to the lodge now, and only two rooms upstairs were filled. The bad weather was causing severe setbacks in the railroad's progress and slowed the work at the mines. Sam's visits were infrequent, and when we saw him, his face looked tired and drawn, etched with little lines of worry.

Now the freight and mail came on a long sled pulled by a team of dogs. We watched for it eagerly because it was our main contact with the outside world. Maury and I waited for the magazines from Seattle and San Francisco, but Tony and Abe scanned the newspapers from Cordova and Valdez with worried frowns. Our future, the future of our Copper River country, depended on the building of the railroad, but it seemed as though the men were working against almost impossible odds. The weather this year was unpredictable. We had heavy snows, followed by warm, melting chinook winds, then unseasonable rain and breakup muds that were followed by more blizzards, snow, and below-zero temperatures. When nature changes her natural order of things, it causes havoc with the land. The papers that Logan brought to us carried stories of a huge lake imprisoned within the Miles glacier breaking loose during a thaw and completely devastating a valley. When it broke loose from its barriers, it took several miles of newly laid track with it and stranded some of the workers.

I listened to the men talking about it at the bar. One had just come up from that area and he described vividly the destruction. Though the railroad workers were discouraged, still they kept working, forced on by Congressional time limits allowed to complete the line. They had to work in temperatures of forty to sixty below zero, and with the strong winds that blew in that area, who knew what the chill factor was. It was too cold for me to even imagine. I shivered, though our room was warm, as I thought of what it must be like for those men, trying to push their way in to where the others were stranded and to continue the fight to extend the railroad despite the weather.

To me the whole thing sounded hopeless, yet the

men continued their battle, building, rebuilding, inching their way forward. We waited, we watched, and we listened to the stories, trying to sift out the facts from the rumors.

One day we all collected around a table as Abe spread out a newspaper. It was late March, and Logan had brought the latest edition of the *Cordova Alaskan* to us with our freight. The headlines carried the message: "COPPER RIVER CONQUERED!" The track had finally been laid across its treacherous waters and a train had crossed the lake at Childs glacier. For that many miles, at least, the road was open to traffic! I heard it estimated that the train could carry more freight up to Abercrombie Canyon in one afternoon than could be taken over the Valdez Trail in six months. The railroad teams were working long hours now, moving ahead fast, pushing the line toward the mines. Our Copper River country was changing!

From the window I could see the black-and-white magpies coming into the yard to collect the bread crumbs we threw out to them. The huge black ravens, looking ominous, perched in the tops of the leafless birch trees, swooping down from time to time to steal the bread. I hated their sharp, raucous cry as it split the air, sounding like a child crying. We would see tracks in the snow in the mornings where nocturnal moose had been in the yard and often would catch sight of caribou. Other than that, the rest of the world seemed to be just burrowed away, waiting out the winter.

The first weeks of queasiness had passed now, and I blossomed as my figure thickened. Gradually the nights became shorter, and the sun came out, bright against the white snow, noticeably longer each day. I saw the first pussy willows on tall sticks protruding from the snow, and I knew now for sure that spring was somewhere ahead of us. I watched them from the window and, sighing, wished for a bouquet. I heard Abe grumbling under his breath as he took his coat off the hook and went outside. Then he came back in carrying a dozen long, furry-coated willow switches. Delighted, I put them in a blue crockery pot on the table, but when I tried to thank him he only shrugged and turned away.

One blessed day when the mail pouch was opened, a letter tumbled out addressed to me in a handwriting I knew so well. I had written home several times now, and I sent a package to all of them at Christmas, but this was the first answer I had received. I snatched up the envelope and slid it into my pocket, not wanting to read it until I was alone.

I kept patting my pocket for reassurance that it was really there, and it seemed forever until I was able to slip away unnoticed. Finally I curled up in the deep chair by the stove in our sitting room and drew out the precious letter.

It was from Tom, and it had been written only three weeks before. I scanned the pages hurriedly, then went back and began to read slowly, savoring every word.

Tom began his letter by apologizing for letting me down when I needed his support. He said he still did not understand my romance with Tony, and he hadn't believed that I would really leave. But since I had done it, he sincerely hoped that I had found happiness.

He wrote that my father was a proud man and still had not forgiven me for marrying Tony and running away as I had, but the news of his expected grandchild had noticeably affected him and he worried about my well-being. Have understanding, Tom begged me, and patience. Father's pride would not allow him to answer my letters, but my brother felt the arrival of the baby would mend the rift and he would weaken.

Tom said my aunt was in her usual flighty turmoil, not able to understand at all how I could possibly survive having a child up in that unknown land, living among a bunch of savages. Would there be any chance at all of my coming home to have the baby?

Paul had married, the letter said. His bride was an attractive young socialite from a very wealthy family. Father was quite pleased with the match. There had been an enormous, well-attended church wedding, which he described in detail to me. They were living in the old Parks mansion. Tom wondered if I remembered it.

Tom ended his letter by telling me he felt guilty for not answering sooner and begging me to keep them informed on my health and the arrival of the baby.

I read and read the letter over again, searching between the lines for the words I wanted to hear. I had tears in my eyes, and one dropped down and blurred the ink. There was not all that I had hoped to find in that letter, but at least it was a starting place. Maybe later, maybe after the baby was born. . . .

As though to make up for the disastrous winter, spring came earlier that year, and was milder than usual. The snow was going fast, and I heard the words "breakup" in every conversation. "Breakup" time was more dreaded than winter, I learned. During breakup time the warm chinook winds blew and the snows melted quickly, turning the hard-packed frozen ground into a wet, clinging mass of claylike mud. It didn't matter how many hours we spent cleaning, the mud was always there. It stuck to your boots, tracked across the floors, and clung to your clothing. But worst was trying to travel anywhere. In summer the ground was hard and dry, making it easy for the horses to pull buggies and wagons. In winter the dogs pulled the sleds on runners that glided across the snow and ice. But during breakup time nothing could move. It was my first breakup and I too learned to dread it, to despise the constant cleaning that never kept ahead of the new mud brought in on the men's boots and their clothing.

I was growing heavy now, and awkward, moving slower and stopping oftener to rest. Other than the tiredness I felt most of the time, I was in good health, I thought. Just impatient. Impatient with the way time moved so slowly. Impatient with wanting to be out of doors in the fresh air, wanting to take a long walk. I felt as though I could not stand the confines of the lodge any longer, and I was determined to escape. Abe had his trips out on snowshoes, when he went hunting or ice fishing. Tony spent his evenings down the road at Beth's, mingling with other people, laughing and drinking, playing poker, not tied down by his share of the role of becoming a parent. Even Maury got outdoors, going with Abe to the village several times, leaving me behind because the drifts might prove too much for me to navigate. I had to get out of doors! Only a thin blanket of snow was left on the ground now and the temperature had climbed to fifteen above. I drew on my heavy wraps, determined to go into the village. At first I met a heavy opposition from both Abe and Maury, but finally they relented, realizing it would probably do me a great deal more good than harm to get out into the fresh air, if I walked carefully and if Maury went with me for company.

The road was deep in mud and slippery in places from ice where the sun didn't reach, but I picked my way carefully, breathing in the cold, clean air that carried the heavy hint of spring. I reveled at being outside, finally released to walk along the trail and feel the sun touching me, to listen to the quiet of the country. It was what I needed to still the sulky, rebellious impatience that had plagued me lately.

We knew several people who were in the Walkers' store that day. Obviously I was not the only one feeling the crush of winter, eagerly anticipating the coming of the summer months. Soon we were all engaged in a lively exchange of gossip, and I felt my tangled nerves stretching and relaxing.

As we came up the path to the general store I had noticed several shops that had recently opened, and I wanted time to explore them. Maury was deeply involved in a conversation with Mrs. Walker, so I slipped out to go next door. The window was filled with a display of mouth-watering delicacies: a birthday cake, with pink rosebuds and dark-green leaves; cookies in neat stacks; fresh loaves of bread. I pushed the door open and went inside, feeling like a child pressing its nose to the candy counter, I breathed deeply of the tantalizing aromas. Against one wall was a small table, with four chairs. A coffeepot was nearby.

I looked about for the clerk, but the room was empty. Evidently no one heard the door's bell when I entered. There was a door leading to the back, to what I assumed were the living quarters of whoever owned the shop. I walked back toward it. The low sound of voices blended into a murmur could be heard from the other side of the door. I had raised my hand to knock when I realized that I knew one of the voices drifting out to me.

With my hand suspended in midair, I listened to Tony's rich, warm voice with a terrible sort of fascination as realization of what I was hearing flooded over me. I wanted to put my hands over my ears to shut out the words, to turn and run away—back to the shelter of the lodge—to erase the sounds, deny I had listened. I wanted to scream out in my anger and my hurt, but I couldn't move. I stood frozen to the spot, staring at the door, feeling as though I were having a terrible nightmare and was not able to wake up.

I could imagine the two of them, unaware that I was standing on the other side of the door. In my mind's eye she was but a blur, a shadow without features, dressed in gingham, leaning close, face tipped up, listening and believing. His dark, crisp curls would be untamed, as usual, his smile teasing, his voice coaxing for understanding as he told his lies. He was lying—everything he said about me, about us, about our relationship together—was all a slanted fabrication to evoke her sympathy. I heard the murmur of her reply, her words too low to distinguish. Were her arms moving up, to caress, to comfort, to hold him close? I clenched my hands until the nails cut into the flesh, and it was that pain, rather than the searing ache in my heart, that finally stirred me into motion.

I turned and stumbled blindly toward the door, suddenly needing to be in the cold, clean air. I couldn't think. My mind was a whirl of confusing faces, words, feelings, that I had to try to sort out. I had to get away!

Maury was on the walkway, coming to look for me.

She saw my white, stricken face and reached out a hand toward me. "Nora, what is it?" Her eyes traveled back, to the shop door behind me. "Oh, my God!" she swore softly, and I wondered how much she already knew and how much she was guessing at.

"Let's go home, Maury," I said, my voice dead, my body moving like a machine.

Maury fell into step beside me and we walked along in silence for a while, she not knowing what to say, I not knowing how to say it.

I was the one to speak first. "Who is she, Maury?" I asked.

"Says she is a widow. Her husband was killed in a mining accident. She started up the bakery instead of going back outside to her family."

"He was in there, Maury. In the back room. They didn't hear the bell on the door when I came in."

Maury nodded. "I figured something like that must have happened. It's been pretty plain to folks around here that she don't intend to stay a widow for very long. She ain't too fussy."

"But surely she must know that Tony is married," I cried. "If it is a husband she is after, why?"

"Sometimes that doesn't matter much, to some women, if they are lonely. They believe what they want to hear. And sometimes what they hear is mighty convincing."

"But doesn't she have any pride?" I raged. "Doesn't she care if the man already has a wife?" Anger was surfacing and I was searching for someone to blame. "In a village this small, she must know that people see what is going on. Must know how they gossip. Doesn't she care what people say?"

"Maybe not," she replied. "But don't turn blind to

things you don't want to see, Nora. It doesn't make them go away. No matter how you cut it, it still takes two—"

Knowing she was right but refusing to admit it, I called the conversation to a close by hurrying along a little faster on the trail, my lips closed in a grim line, my eyes hard, to hide the hurt that lay behind them.

I was not as careful as I should have been. My thoughts blurred my vision and I didn't see the icy spot caused by a small trickle of water draining across the path. It all happened so quickly I hardly knew what happened. My feet went scooting out from under me, my parcel went flying into the air, and I fell, hard, landing on my side at the very edge of the path, my shoulder striking a rock. Maury made a desperate grab for me, but my coat slipped through her fingers and I started to slide—over the side of the bank, off the trail, rolling over and over until I came to a stop in a pile of feathery soft snow below the pathway. I lay quiet a moment as brilliant circles of light flashed in front of my eyes, and my breath came in ragged gulps. Then, slowly, awkwardly, I got to my feet.

"I'm all right, Maury, really I am." I tried to reassure her when she reached my side. "I have so many clothes on to bundle against the cold that it didn't really hurt me at all. I'm just a little shaky." I attempted to laugh as I stood, stretching cautiously to check my arm and shoulder.

Together we crawled back onto the path, grasping the willow shoots for support. Maury was half laughing, half crying, as she tried to help me brush the mud and snow from my clothing. I was shaking, chilled.

We heard a shout and looked up to see Sam running toward us. It was then that everything became a hazy fog and I felt myself falling again, this time slower, slower, and before I reached the ground I was wrapped in a dark, enveloping, smothering blanket of black, and I remembered no more.

An awareness of sounds reached through my numbness, drawing me back to reality. I knew somehow that I was back at Ravenwood. I sensed that I was in my own bed. Through a blanket of bitter pain, as I drifted in and out of consciousness, I was aware of Maury beside me. There were other voices, talking softly, but I was too tired to listen. I thought I saw the doctor from the mines bending over me, and I struggled to speak to him but the effort was too great. I could not form the words I needed to say.

In the distance I heard a woman screaming and wondered who she was—then I realized that it was me. Great waves of searing, tearing pain pulled me and I stopped fighting, giving in to it, drifting away into a long, black tunnel of echoing sounds and lights and faces.

I was so warm—burning. I fought to throw away the covers but someone kept pulling them back. Then I lay chilled, shivering. Someone had left a window open somewhere and the snow was coming in, cold—so cold! Please, close the window! Please, someone!

I was so tired. So deadly tired. I just wanted to be left alone. Why wouldn't they let me sleep? Father, I am so sorry I hurt you as I did. Are you ever going to forgive me? Tom? Tom, where are you? Why aren't you here? I was drifting on soft clouds of down—white billowy clouds. There were faces all around me but I couldn't make them hear. The pain—it hurts—Tony, dear Tony, what have I done to you? You really didn't want to come up here, did you? It is my fault. I'm sorry, Tony. It's so warm. I am so tired. If only you all would stop—let me sleep—sleep. Sam! I screamed. Sam, help me! Sam! Then, finally, blessed blackness and I slept.

I woke slowly, feeling cool and without pain, but very tired. Lifting my eyelids was an effort. Slowly I turned my head on the pillow and looked about the room. I saw Maury sitting in a chair nearby, her eyes rimmed in red, lines of weariness written on her face.

"Maury, what happened?" I said softly.

At the sound of my voice, she came quickly to my side. "You've been a very sick little girl." Fresh tears flowed openly down her face. "Thank God! You are awake and your fever is gone."

I reached out and took her hand. "Don't cry, Maury. Please don't cry. It's all right. Everything is all right. I am fine now," I soothed her.

"Yes, thank the good Lord. I think your fever has finally gone down. Your forehead is cool. I'll get you some broth."

"No. Wait. You look so tired. How long have I been here?" I asked.

"For nearly a week. We've all been so worried."

"Tell me, Maury, was it a boy or a girl?" I whispered.

"A boy. . . ." Hurt lay open in her eyes.

"Is he . . . ?" I couldn't go on.

Maury didn't answer, just shook her head as new tears filled her eyes.

I reached out and patted her hand, trying to comfort her somehow. "It's all right, Maury. Please don't cry—it's all right." I turned my face to the wall and closed my eyes.

Later I slept, a long, healing sleep.

The others came in, one at a time, with pain and sympathy in their eyes, but none of it touched me. My feelings—no, my very soul—had swirled and shrunk to a small hard knot buried deep within me to where it couldn't be touched by anything or anyone. Since I couldn't be touched, I couldn't be hurt anymore. I couldn't feel anymore. I was aloof—distant from the others' pain, as though nothing would touch me deeply or hurt me, ever again. The thoughts of my father and my brothers sank into the farthest depths of my consciousness and became unimportant. Thoughts of love or passion were buried and lost. The dreams of the child I would never hold became swathed in a thick, protective fog, with only the self-protective need for survival merging as an armor against the world and its demands.

My recuperation was gradual. At first I was up for a few hours, sitting in a chair in my room, reading or just staring into the fire. But I was young, and I began to feel the twinges of restlessness. I stayed up longer each time, walking out into the barroom, on into the kitchen, helping with the lighter chores. As my strength returned, I took on more and more, until finally our days were falling into a routine. But my temper was short. Maury's fussing over me only annoyed me. I snapped at her, and the hurt looks I received only annoyed me more. Quiet Abe tried to draw me into conversation. I knew they meant well and were fond of me, and I was ashamed. I tried to reassure them that I was fine. Not only had I regained my health, I had completed my growing up. I no longer was the green, wide-eyed *cheechako* who came North with dreams in her eyes, but I didn't know how to tell them.

I would catch Maury watching me thoughtfully, and I would turn away. Abe would challenge me to a game of cribbage when I knew he had other things to do, but I was too restless to sit still.

When my strength had returned completely I threw myself into a frenzy of cleaning. I polished the walls until the paneling shone. I scrubbed floors and cleaned cupboards. I worked until my arms ached and my legs trembled with tiredness and yet I could not sleep at night. When I turned out the light and shut my eyes, thoughts and sounds of the past closed in on me, and I would turn the light back on and reach for a book I kept on the bedside table. Tony would turn toward the wall, pulling the covers up to shut out the light, but he never objected. I longed for summer, and warmth, and the long periods of sunlight that would chase away all of the night.

Tony and I saw little of each other alone, without the protective company of Abe and Maury. It was not that we were avoiding each other. It was just that we didn't seem to have anything to say to each other anymore.

Only once had he said something that made me wonder if Maury had told him I was in the bakery the afternoon of my accident.

"I wish you could understand . . ." he began one night after he had settled into bed.

I looked toward him, turning my attention from my book. "Understand what, Tony?"

"I'm not like you—I'm not a loner. You are able to open a book and spend hours by yourself, content to be alone. I need to be around people. I need to have friends—a lot of them. I need to laugh once in a while, Nora! I need fun and noise—"

"And cards. And whisky. And other women," I added.

He knew then that I knew. He turned away and pulled the covers up, wanting to go to sleep.

Something—the distant howl of a wolf from up on the ridge, maybe, or the wind brushing a tree limb against the edge of the roof—penetrated into the shallow places of my sleep and I turned my head on the pillow, opening my eyes to the darkness of the room. I could hear the loud ticking of the clock on the nightstand, but there wasn't enough light to see the time. I had no idea how long it would be until morning, when I could get up, wash, dress, and begin another day of pretending.

Carefully, so as not to wake up Tony, I stretched my legs out straight, feeling the ache of muscles held tense, not able to relax even in sleep. I was fully awake now, not able to return to that warm, sheltering escape of sleep where thoughts and worries did not penetrate.

I lay quietly, looking back into the shadows of my memories, my mind refusing to rest. When we ran away from my family in San Francisco, when we eloped, to travel to the mystery and adventure of the northland, I had known it would not be an easy life I was going to. In fact, the challenge of wondering if I would be able to cope with the hardships was one of the things that had drawn me on. And, because of it, I had Ravenwood. My wonderful Ravenwood. How much I loved my home in the Alaskan bush! I had been so captivated with my romantic dreams that I didn't once think of the possibility of Tony's not being as deeply in favor of this venture as I. When did things begin to go wrong? When did I stop pretending not to notice the bitter twist to Tony's mouth when he was crossed? The way his face darkened, his eyes turned away, shutting me away from him, when money was tight and I let him know I resented his gambling and drinking?

Things would be better now. I was learning not to show my hurt so plainly when he preferred the poker games with the other men to spending the evening with me, just as I was learning not to lash out in anger when I went to the tin cash box and found it empty.

Tony was sensitive and artistic, not a bush country homesteader, and dressing him in rough woolens would not turn him into one. Was losing my illusions too high a price to pay for Ravenwood? How long could I go on, building my house of cards, pretending from day to day that everything was all right? That nothing mattered?

The railroad was pushing hard now, making a full-scale effort to regain the miles lost at Miles glacier. Every conversation hummed with news and rumors of its progress and its problems. Armchair engineers pointed out the errors being made, telling how it would be done if they were calling the shots. Forecasters of gloom still predicted that it would not reach the mines, let alone push on to Fairbanks as the long-range plans called for.

Sam stopped in for his supper two or three times a week now. The good weather was a boon to the mines as well as the railroad, and he didn't have to work such long hours. His eyes would find mine across the room, and for a moment we would allow ourselves to pass unspoken thoughts. Then I would turn away and he would begin a conversation with someone near. His face was drawn, and I saw hard lines around his eyes that I did not remember being there before. I wondered if it was only the mines that were putting them there.

Once again money, or the lack of it, became the cause of an open rift between Tony and me. I knew he was gambling and drinking heavily, and when I commented on it, he blamed my irritable disposition for making him want to stay away. We argued bitterly. The tin box was emptied often these evenings, and I knew he was losing heavily.

I firmly refused to appeal again to Garth Williams for help. Though I couldn't keep money in the tin box, I refused to draw more from the dwindling account in the bank in Valdez. We were going to live on the earnings of the lodge, one way or the other. If it was not enough, then Tony was going to have to learn to survive.

In defiance, Tony took a job with the railroad. I was startled at his announcement because Tony had never done a day of physical work in his life, but I was too stubborn to try to talk him out of it, as he expected me to do. Rather than resent the days and the nights the job kept him away from home, I welcomed the hours alone. . . .

We had a surprise late-spring blizzard. The temperature fell, the winds blew, and the snow came down thick and heavy, lasting several days. When the sun finally came out again, the ground and the trees carried a blanket of white, making everything look clean and new. This snow wasn't depressing because we knew it was just an afterthought. Summer wasn't far away.

Abe tried to teach me how to use snowshoes. He spent several afternoons making a pair especially for me. He cut the straps to fit my boots and showed me how to fasten them securely to my feet. My first lesson was in the side yard, with Maury watching from the window. Abe moved from the doorway to the meat cache and back again with an ease that made it all look so simple. My first efforts to copy him were stumbling and awkward, bringing merry laughter from Maury and chuckles from Abe. At last, catching on to the long sliding steps, I was anxious to prove my agility and took off at a faster speed to catch Abe. I looked a little like a disjointed puppet as I flopped the long snowshoes down and waved my arms for balance, more intent on speed than caution. I wasn't doing too badly until the tip of the one snowshoe caught on something and sank below the crusty surface of the snow, bringing me to a rather sudden, unexpected halt. I tumbled, somersaulting into a drift.

"Come on, get up," Abe encouraged. "You can't just lie there!"

"I can't!" I wailed. Each time I tried to regain my footing, I tumbled again before I could stand upright.

Tired of trying, I tossed my arms out, deliberately letting myself fall backward full length into the soft, cushiony snow. I was laughing by now, laughter that brought tears to my eyes and left me too weak to try to regain my footing and walk.

"Abe—please! Rescue me!" I pleaded.

He was laughing too, as he came over and put a hand under each elbow, lifting me to my feet, holding me until I got my balance.

"Blasted things," I sputtered. "Who invented these miserable things anyway?"

"Okay, okay. If you can make it back to the door under your own power, the lesson will be over for the day," he promised. "But you should learn to walk on them, Nora. Who knows? It might be necessary for you to use them someday."

Several mornings later Abe was waiting for me in the kitchen. "Ready for another lesson, Nora?"

"Goodness," I protested, "what did I do wrong to deserve this? I still have bruises from the last time." I tried to frown.

"Today I've decided it is time you learned to shoot a gun," he announced.

"Shoot a gun!" I exclaimed in surprise. "For heaven's sake, why!"

"You want to be a helpless *cheechako* for the rest of your life?" He scowled. "You think I'm going to be around to take care of you forever?"

Maury was setting a steaming-hot bowl of oatmeal on the table in front of me. "Eat!" she commanded. "It takes a good hot breakfast to give you the courage to stand up to Abe."

I ate, without argument.

Less than an hour later, with my snowshoes on and bundled in my fur parka, I stumbled along behind Abe through the timber. He carried a heavy rifle over his shoulder. I caught him looking back over his shoulder once in a while, but other than that I received no special attention. Remembering the bear stories I overheard recounted at the lodge, I had no desire to fall behind or become separated from him, so I struggled along, putting one awkward foot ahead of the other as fast as I could.

When I felt that I could not possibly pick my feet up for one more step, I saw that Abe had stopped beside a large fallen tree. Silently he motioned for me to move up beside him and keep quiet. I crept up and tried to see what he was watching. Off to the left, some fifty yards or so ahead of us, were two moose. One was huge, the biggest I had seen, with powerful muscles that rippled when she moved. The other was younger and smaller, but almost full grown. Eating the willow twigs with a loud crunching sound, they moved about as though they were completely unaware of us watching.

Carefully Abe leveled the rifle across the log, motioning me to move closer. In quiet whispers he showed me how to sight along the barrel and where to aim. I nodded to let him know I understood.

"Then, shoot," he said.

I drew back in horror, shaking my head no.

"Hold the gun firm against your shoulder, Nora. Pull the trigger slowly." His voice was low, patiently encouraging.

I did as he said. A terrible explosion roared through my head. I fell backward into the snow and would have dropped the gun if Abe hadn't caught it. Bark flew from a tree at least ten feet from the nearest moose. They raised their heads in alarm, listening. Then, as though deciding they were in no real danger, they ambled away in that curious, awkward gait of theirs. We sat watching them for a few minutes.

"Always give a moose a lot of room when you meet

one out in the woods," Abe said. "It is one of the most dangerous animals you are apt to meet."

I looked at him in surprise. "They don't look mean. Kind of like an oversized, lumpy horse."

"They got to be the dumbest animal there is," Abe explained. "Bears will usually go the other way. They don't like people and don't want to meet them any more than you want to run into them. Bears are smart. A moose is so dumb it doesn't know what it likes or doesn't like. One time an old cow will be content to go on eating and not even look up at you. The next time she'll whirl around and lower her head and charge! Mean critters. Especially around this time of year when the food supply is running short."

I sat quietly, thinking over what he had said.

Abe made no further remarks but stood up, held out a hand to help me back onto my feet, put the gun over his shoulder, and motioned for me to follow him.

I could tell we were moving in a circle, working our way back to the lodge. My legs ached from the unaccustomed exercise and, to my embarrassment, my stomach was making rumbling sounds.

After a bit Abe slowed and found a large rock to sit on. "Must be a little out of practice," he said. "Think I'll rest a bit." Gratefully, I sank down at his side, on the rock.

"You all right, Nora?"

"Sure. I'm fine," I lied.

Abe laid the rifle across his knees. As I rested, I watched, and he explained again how to sight, to aim, and to fire. He got up and moved across to a log.

"Here, Nora. Stand here beside me. Take the gun in your hands and rest it on the log until you feel comfortable. Then practice aiming."

I tried to do as he said and slowly moved the front sight in an arc, taking aim at leaves, twigs, rocks. Unexpectedly a wild rabbit appeared directly in line, and without thinking I squeezed the trigger. To my astonishment, the rabbit flew into the air, shuddered, and dropped in a heap.

"What did I do?" I cried. "Abe, I didn't mean to hit it!" In dismay, I looked at the small white ball of fur lying in red trickles of blood on the snow.

"Looks like you got yourself a rabbit, li'l lady. Let's go see how much of it you blew away." Abe chuckled.

Apparently I had just barely nicked it with the powerful rifle, because the head was almost gone but the body was intact. I looked at it in revulsion as Abe held his hand out to me.

"You shot it, you carry it," he told me. Then, seeing me shudder, he grinned. "Take it home to Maury, honey. She'll show you how to fix a real tasty dinner with it."

Maury had been watching out of the window, and when she saw us coming down the trail, she met us at the door. Hesitantly I held out my dubious prize for her to see. She started to laugh, but catching Abe's eye, she took the ragged carcass from me and began to talk of the good supper we were going to have, with fried rabbit and hot berry pie.

As we were cutting it up and getting it ready for the kettle, I confided to Maury, "Golly, am I ever glad I didn't hit that moose we saw! Abe told me that what you shoot, you carry, and if I had shot that moose I would be out there still, wondering what I was going to do!" We both chuckled. It was a heady feeling to be so relaxed and laughing with Maury again.

I realized what Abe and Maury were doing—quietly

seeing that I worked hard throughout the day, inventing ways to get me out of doors to exercise, breathing the clean fresh air, keeping me too busy to brood. They were showing their love and worry for me in this silent way, and I was so very grateful to both of them.

That evening, after a long soak in the old copper tub to take away the stiffness from the day's hiking, I tumbled into bed. My shoulder was bruised and my legs ached. I had a blister on one heel. But that night I fell asleep almost instantly and slept a long and dreamless sleep—for the first time in weeks.

The days were long now, with sun still streaming in the window at the supper hour or later. I could read in the evening without turning on a lamp. The last of the snow had melted, except way up on the mountaintops. The mud dried, leaving clouds of dust in its wake, and almost overnight the whole outdoors turned green, from the light lemon green of the birch to the deep blackish green of the hemlock and the spruce. The woods hid tiny, fragile lady's-slippers and bold trilliums. I saw small squirrels in the trees and heard the insistent tapping of the woodpecker. Birds were busy selecting a place to build a nest, calling back and forth to each other as they worked. The very air was alive with the sounds of spring, and all of nature was in a burst of frantic reproduction before the season slipped away as quickly as it came.

A new restlessness caught me now—the fever of summer and the urge to be out of doors, to dig in the dirt, to plant something, to watch something grow. I needed to feel the warm soil of the garden in my hands and to dream of the bright flowers I would grow in my garden. I wanted to live.

CHAPTER SEVEN

I dug up a small patch of ground in the side yard where it would get the most sun. Abe helped with the first breaking of the hard ground, and then I pulled weeds and roots, picked out rocks, and worked the soil until it was soft.

Logan had brought several packets of seeds as a gift on his last freight run, and I planted them. I had little hope that my garden would grow well because the soil was poor and the season too short, but working in it proved to be a very soothing occupation for me. It kept my hands much busier than it did my mind, and I would daydream as I dropped the tiny seeds into the soil and gently covered them with my fingers, sifting the dirt across where they lay. The sun was warm on my arms, and I found an old straw hat among my uncle's things that I wore on my head. The hours spent in my garden were peaceful.

One day a shadow fell across where I was working. I heard someone walk up behind me and sit down on the log bench at the side of the building. I knew, somehow, without turning my head, that it was Sam.

"Time for an old friend to visit?" he asked casually, scuffing the toe of his boot in the loose dirt.

"I suppose so," I answered without looking up. "Just don't start an argument, please. I'm enjoying myself too much out here in the sun to allow you to ruin it for me."

"I promise to keep it light," he said. "I'm very good at small talk, you know, when I make the effort."

"I am too," I answered. "At least in that I've had a lot of training."

Relaxed in the warm sunlight, he watched me for a few moments in silence, his long legs stretched out carelessly, his hat pulled down to shade his eyes.

"What are you planting?" he asked.

"Some carrots and lettuce for fresh salads. I have a few cabbage and tomato plants in the kitchen window that I'll bring out and plant pretty soon. They are about ready, I think." I leaned back and surveyed my work. "I think a border of petunias, about here, around the edge, would be pretty, don't you?" I picked up another handful of rocks, which constantly seemed to work to the surface. "I don't know if they will grow, but I'm going to try."

"You like flowers, don't you? Have you had gardens before, back in San Francisco?"

"Yes. We always had large flower gardens. Father had a gardener, so I never did the planting myself, but I used to love to watch him, and I always picked bouquets for the house. The rhododendrons were so beautiful! And this time of year we always had tulips and daffodils. I think I missed the daffodils this spring as much as anything." For a moment I let my mind linger on those delightful patches of color that grew so easily in my father's well-tended gardens. I was almost able to smell their heady fragrance.

"You look very desirable, you know, there in the sunlight, with a smudge of dirt on your nose—"

I stiffened. "You're breaking the rules already, Sam, talking like that." I frowned at him, but I turned my head and tried to brush the dirt from my face, wondering how much was there and how bad it looked.

"Sorry." He didn't sound sorry. I felt the warmth of his hazel eyes as they seemed to caress me there in the sunlight. "Give me a second chance before you send me away. Books. That's it. A very good subject. Always good for lots of small talk. Have you read any good books lately, Nora?" His voice held traces of hidden laughter.

"As a matter of fact I have, whether you are serious about the subject or not." I turned around and sat down on the ground, wiping my hands on my apron. "I mentioned one day to Logan that one of the things I missed most during the winter was my collection of books. I always enjoyed reading in the evenings. When he came up here this last time, he brought these packets of seeds and some books, as a gift."

Sam chuckled. "You know, I think that hard-hearted grizzly old muleskinner has got a bad crush on you!"

I laughed merrily at the compliment. "It isn't me he has the crush on. It's the hot blueberry pie I always manage to have ready on freight day and the jars of wild currant jellies he carries away with him in his pack. But, nevertheless, I'm fond of Logan, and I think it was dear of him to bring the books to me. And the seeds."

"I order books from Seattle every few months. The

shipment is late this time. Right now I've read every-thing—the magazines twice or more."

"Then come inside," I invited. "I need to get washed up, and I'm ready for a hot cup of coffee. I imagine Maury has the pot on. And since you have done such a good job of staying with the small talk, I shall reward you by sharing my loot! You can borrow one of my new books. Uncle Jim kept quite a library too. Maybe one of his books would appeal to you more."

I picked up my garden tools and placed them in the corner as we went inside. Sam stopped in the doorway leading into our sitting room. "Tony's not here?" he asked.

"No." I didn't want to talk about it. "Come on in. You can be picking out some books while I go and wash up."

"I heard he came back in from where the railroad crews are working."

"Yes." I intended to let it drop there, but added, "He went to Fairbanks with Benson."

Sam didn't answer, so to fill the silence I said, "There was some work up there. He wanted to check on it." I walked across to the bookshelves and Sam followed me.

"Not prospecting this time? Thought he might try that next," Sam answered. "The job in the office for the mines didn't work out—and apparently neither did the railroad."

"The mine job was too confining," I defended quickly. "Tony is an artist. He isn't used to being shut in an office all day. He is a gentle, artistic person—not hard and rough."

"And he didn't like having me for his boss, did he?"

Sam answered sharply. "And the railroad didn't suit him either, did it? He had to work—to get his hands dirty. Apparently he has quit that too. What is he after this time, Nora? Do you know?"

I turned away, feeling the anger building inside. I reached for the books I had promised. Sam had no right to put me on the defensive like this!

"Do you know why he went to Fairbanks, Nora?"

"I *told* you. To see about some work he had heard about." My voice crackled with annoyance.

"Is that what he told you?" He reached out to cover my hand with his but I drew back. "Nora, Nora, how long are you going to keep this up?"

"As long as I am able," I answered with a sigh, feeling the weight of his remark.

"And how long will that be?" he demanded.

"We'll manage, Sam." I was suddenly tired. The warm happiness of my afternoon in the garden was fading. "Mind your own business. We don't need you telling us what to do."

"And I suppose one of these days Tony will grow up, will take over his share of the responsibilities around here and run this place as it should have been run—as Jim intended. He will take care of you as you deserve. You'll have some new appliances to make your work easier—some new clothing—maybe a trip outside."

"I don't need or want luxuries!" I didn't like being on the defensive like this. Why did he always do this to me? Why couldn't we just talk without striking sparks?

"They aren't luxuries, Nora. They are things you work for and deserve. But you are going to go on, taking the money from that tin box of yours to cover Tony's ventures until one day when you reach in for more, it won't be there. What then, Nora? Even Garth Williams won't be able to help you then. What will you do?"

My hands were clenched at my side, and I wanted to lash out, to hurt back. "Stop interfering, Sam! You and Garth never believed that we could make it up here, did you? But I'll show you! The both of you! I am Tony's wife because I wanted to be. We'll make it just fine, the two of us, without anybody's help!"

"You speak with a lot of anger but not a lot of conviction, Nora. Such a lot of foolish pride you have. You aren't fighting for Tony anymore, don't you realize that? You're fighting to save your own pride. Pride is good to have, but not so much of it that it blinds you to everything around you and you refuse to see what is happening. When you find out that your pride is all you have left, you'll discover that it really isn't worth much. What good will it be to you when he isn't home and you are lonely, wanting someone to hold you close and chase away the shadows? Open up your eyes, Nora, now—while there still is time—while you still own Ravenwood. Don't lose Ravenwood trying to save Tony."

"Oh, get out, Sam!" I cried. "Why can't you leave me alone? I was enjoying myself out there in the garden. Why do you always upset me so? Make me feel things I don't want to feel?" There were tears in my eyes, threatening to spill over. "I want to hate you, Sam! Why can't I?"

"All right, honey—take it easy. I'm sorry." Suddenly Sam looked very tired. "I'm going to leave now. Go wash your face. The tears have streaked the dirt. But Nora, take time to think over what I've said to you and don't be too angry with me. We are probably going to be business partners very soon if you insist on thinking the way you do." Then he turned and started for the door.

"What do you mean, 'business partners'?" I asked cautiously.

Those damned hazel eyes mocked me slightly as he turned to look back over his shoulder. "That's why I asked you if Tony told you why he was going to Fairbanks. He has offered me half interest in Ravenwood. He needs money to finance a bar he wants to buy in Fairbanks. He heard it was for sale, and he went up there to look it over." With that, Sam disappeared through the door, leaving me staring after him with the wind gone from me as surely as though I had received a physical blow.

Tony returned from his trip to Fairbanks the next afternoon. I met him at the door and greeted him as though nothing had changed, but oh, I had done so much thinking since Sam's visit yesterday!

He was full of bravado, describing the country up there. It was the old Tony, full of enthusiasm, with eagerness glowing in his dark eyes as he talked of the town and the number of people living there now and the new families that were moving in. They had a schoolhouse, even a couple of churches and a fire station. "Just think, Nora! Stores to shop in. You don't have to depend on a freight wagon for supplies! And dress shops! Meat markets! Some of the restaurants are really modern. People up there have a lot of money, and they are spending it. If our bar and lodge were up there, instead of in this back country collection of bums, prospectors, and miners they call a town, we could get rich!"

I saw Abe and Maury exchange glances as they turned away but neither said anything.

Later that night, after the supper chores were done and we were in our bedroom, the conversation came up again. I sat on the side of the bed, absentmindedly watching Tony start to undress. "Come on, Nora," he joked. "You mustn't be so sentimental about this place. You worry so about money—you want to get rich. One place is as good as another. I promise you, we'll make it in Fairbanks. With the bar that I've got picked out up there, it will be a cinch. Won't be any time until we have all of the money we want! And it will be part yours, Nora. Don't forget that."

I didn't answer but began my preparations for bed, laying aside my hairbrush with a sigh and reaching for my nightdress.

Tony moved close to me. "It's about time we caught up on a few other important things," he murmured into my hair as he drew me near. "Lord, how I've missed you, Nora!" His hands began searching, slipping under my shift.

I held myself still, not responding, and I felt his muscles tighten as he kissed me roughly, pushing me back among the pillows. Tony had always been a patient lover, but in the midst of his growing passion, I felt his anger with me building. Try as I might, I could not bring myself to meet his kiss or match his embraces. I lay still and limp, unable to make any of the responses he expected of me. Tears welled up in my eyes and slid down my cheeks. Then, without warning, I turned my head on the pillow and began to sob with the abandonment of a hurt child.

"For God's sake, Nora! What the devil's the matter

with you now?" He drew back, his anger showing plainly in his eyes.

I could only shake my head and put my hand to my mouth to hide my cries.

"I thought you loved me. You've never acted like this before when I—"

I tried to control my sobs, hiccupping noisily, and wiped my face with the back of my hand. "I did, Tony. I still do—I think I do. I'm not sure anymore."

"It's Sam, interfering again, isn't it?" He got up from the bed and threw himself into the chair. "Bloody bastard! He hangs around here too much—always finding fault with something that I do. I should have stopped his interfering a long time ago."

"No, no, you're wrong, Tony. It's what you've been saying—about leaving Ravenwood, about selling the lodge. Don't you understand? I can't leave—I don't *want* to leave. I won't give up Ravenwood! I won't do it!"

He didn't answer but sat sullenly in the chair looking at me, his eyes like dark storm clouds, his mouth turned down at the corners in a bitter line.

"If this is what you think you want, Tony—really want—then I won't stop you."

He looked up, interest in his eyes, watching me, waiting for me to go on.

I wiped my eyes with the corner of the sheet and sat up. "You will be able to get a loan. I won't do anything to stop you. Half interest in Ravenwood should be enough to use as security for the amount you need. I won't sell it, but you can use the lodge as security for a loan. You can go up to Fairbanks and buy your tavern." I spoke low, in a monotone, as though I were reading the lines or they had been rehearsed. "But if you do, you will go by yourself, Tony. I won't go with you. I'm not leaving Ravenwood."

"You know about— Damn him!"

"Yes, Tony, I know. Sam told me part and I guessed the rest," I answered softly. "Did you really think you could sell a part interest in Ravenwood without my finding out?"

Tony got up swiftly and pulled on his clothes, not looking at me again. "Go ahead and get ready for bed," he said. "I'm not sleepy. I'm going down to Beth's for a while—where people are a little more cheerful to be around."

I turned toward the wall, a small bundle of misery curled under the quilts, and cried myself to sleep. I knew now that my life with Tony was beyond repair. If Tony left this time to go to Fairbanks or anywhere else, our life together was finished.

CHAPTER EIGHT

We saw a great many changes in the months after Tony left to buy his saloon in Fairbanks, changes I had not thought possible. Since that day the *Cordova Alaskan* carried the banner headlines, announcing to the world that the Copper River was conquered, the cry echoed up and down the canyons of our copper country, leaving a tumult of claim filing in its wake. A wild, unknown country was being invaded and brought to heel. I heard it rumored that more than four thousand gold and copper claims had been filed in the area. The ores being discovered were richer than any discovered elsewhere in Alaska, and few ores anywhere else in the world could surpass what was being mined here.

In October the railroad reached Chitina. Everyone turned out for the occasion. I went, along with Abe and Maury. Sam met us there, and we joined in the festivities. Almost overnight Chitina became a bustling transfer point for the freight and passengers moving from the railroad to the freight lines traveling into the interior. A modern hotel was built, along with several stores, and people moved in and built homes. The plans called for Chitina to become a junction point later, with the main railroad line going north to Fairbanks, while the copper spur turned eastward and ran along the north bank of the Chitina River. When this happened, who could possibly forecast what it could all lead to!

Maury and I started watching the newspapers as avidly as the men, eager for the latest word on the progress of the rails. It was the topic of every conversation, the subject of every argument. And late in March the railroad track was finally completed! It was an exciting time for our Copper River country.

Plans were made for a celebration, and everyone took part. It is traditional for the last spike driven in a railroad line to be a golden one that is later taken out and presented to a leading official after the ceremony, but up here, in copper country, the spike could be of nothing else but copper, and one was handmade for the occasion.

It was on a Monday—the last Monday in March— that the first train left Cordova to make a through trip all the way from the small seaport, past those fantastic glaciers, through the mountains, all the way to the Kennicott copper mines! Everyone turned out along the route, joining in, adding to the excitement. A private car was attached to the train for the officials, with a dining area for them and sleeping quarters. Aboard were a photographer to record the historic event and a newspaper editor, as well as reporters from our newspapers and from several "outside" publications. The train stopped in Chitina, the point where the rails would meet the freight lines for transferring passengers and freight going on into the interior. The manager of the freight lines was there to meet them, and he boarded the train to make the rest of the trip with them, up to the mines.

The train stopped at Kaskulana Camp overnight and then it started out on the last leg of the trip. It went to within a quarter mile of the end of the line. There the train stopped, and everyone gathered to watch while the last rails were laid into place. The sun was out with very few clouds in the sky. The temperature was in the high thirties, making the day seem even more like a holiday. The tension was building. All of us—the group on the train, the ones standing in the crowd—watched breathlessly as that last shiny copper spike was driven into place. Then the engines blew their whistles, the people cheered, bottles passed back and forth among the men, and the mountains echoed with the sounds of the victory.

The days, the weeks following the completion of the track up to the mines were even more hectic, more chaotic, than we had anticipated. They brought the bad as well as the good, new problems as well as the answers to old ones.

New people were appearing every day, some with a healthy stake, ready to work for more, others with an eye on someone else's cache. There were the prospectors, working alone with a gold pan and a sluice box, fiercely guarding the location of their diggings. There were the company people, brought in by the larger mines, the workers to burrow the tunnels back into the bowels of the mountains and bring out the rich ores. And there were the promoters, the laborers, the gamblers, the merchants wanting to set up stores, and the camp followers.

We had more women now in our Copper River country. Wives followed their husbands into the gold fields, carrying their share of the packs, doing their share of the work. They set up housekeeping in rough board-and-tent shelters, fighting the mosquitoes and the weather, and bore children. There was a schoolteacher or two, fighting to keep us civilized and educated.

There were several missionaries, anxious to protect our souls, and the women who wore a little too much makeup, cut their dresses a little too low at the neckline, who earned their own fortunes by singing and dancing their way across the country, traveling from bed to bed, collecting their pouches of dust, their nuggets of gold. Most of them preferred to move on, drawn by the dazzling lights and razzmatazz of the Klondike and Dawson, but some stayed and did their share in the settling of the country. They may have relieved the men of their cache on Saturday night, but on Monday morning a lot of it was lent back to men who found themselves broke, or hungry, or sick.

And with the people came the problems. There were the arguments over the ownership of claims, excessive drinking and brawling, thefts, and once in a while a shooting, with little law except what was delivered swiftly and defiantly by the people themselves.

But there were good things too. The people stood together, stronger than they ever had "outside," helping each other, forming a solid front against the elements, the hardships of the land. Cabins were always left unlocked when the owners were away. Firewood was left in the woodbins, kindling and paper already laid in the stove, and food was stocked on the shelves,

offering welcome to anyone traveling cross country
caught in an unexpected blizzard and in need of shelter. It was the unwritten law of the land that when he
left, after he had warmed himself and rested, the visitor
replaced what he had used from the woodbin and laid a
fire, for the next person who was in trouble and sought
the cabin for shelter.

People took time to know their neighbors and
weren't afraid to reach out a hand.

Of course, with more people there was a sudden demand for housing, food, lumber. . . . As a result, the
cost of supplies soared and lumber became scarce.

Ravenwood, too, felt the boom. Every room upstairs
was taken; sometimes the men doubled or tripled up
because of the shortage of lodging. Every evening the
main room filled, with men collecting around the bar,
smoking, drinking, telling stories, and doing a great
deal of speculation. For the most part it wasn't too
rowdy. Abe had a firm way of keeping everyone in line,
and the men respected him. It was only once or twice
that I saw him open the door and pitch a quarrelsome
customer out into the dark, to cool off.

Maury and I worked from early morning to late into
the evening, trying to keep ahead of the dinner orders
and to keep the rooms cleaned. It was an endless job,
and it seemed we were always tired, with work still
left undone. We had to have more help. The three of
us just weren't able to take care of it all by ourselves.

When a young man, somewhere in his late twenties,
who, disillusioned with prospecting, asked Abe for
work, he was put on as night-time bartender, to relieve
Abe. And we hired two Indian women from the village to help clean the rooms and work in the kitchen.

I ordered one of the new washing machines with

gasoline engines from the Sears, Roebuck catalog, and when it arrived we were ecstatic. We set it up in the backyard where the noise and the fumes wouldn't be a bother, and we filled the big, round tub with linens and hot soapy water. Abe started the engine, and we stood back watching the tub rock back and forth, belching sprays of hot water out at us sometimes, in time with the *ka-chug, ka-chug, ka-chug* of the small motor on the side. The work that machine saved was worth every penny it had cost to have it shipped up from Seattle. Maury and I were as happy as children at Christmastime. After Abe built a lean-to addition off from the kitchen as a wash room, we moved the washing machine inside, and we had a place to iron now too, close enough to the kitchen to carry the flat irons from the stove, but still far enough away so that we didn't have to stand near a hot stove to work.

One or two motor cars, dirty and noisy, had been driven along the Valdez Trail over ruts and through clouds of dust to reach the town, and they were the center of attention. I didn't care much for them, and I think I was a little frightened at the prospect of taking a long trip in one of them. There was too much open, wild country out here to be stranded in, if the car should break down. And I understood they did this quite regularly, with tires that blew out and parts that quit working. For the life of me I couldn't see how they were at all practical. Certainly not in the winter, when only dog-sled teams were able to travel the snowy trails.

At the lodge we had a flat-bed wagon for what hauling we needed done and a smart-looking buggy that I was very proud of. We had two horses to pull them. Rather tired old horses, but they filled our needs.

Another building was put up, out in back, to house
the horses and the buggy. We had a young Indian lad
working a few hours a day to keep it clean and care
for the horses and to do the other outside chores that
were too much for Abe.

All our freight came in by rail now, as far as Chitina,
where it was met by a freight line pulled by matching,
beautiful horses, to be transferred and moved on up
the Chitina–Tonsina road to the interior. We still saw
Logan Aldridge occasionally. He worked for the mining company now, hauling machinery from one mine
site to another with his freight wagon.

I spent my evenings alone, at the desk in my sitting
room, keeping the day's entries neatly recorded and
balanced, doing the ordering, paying the bills, planning ahead. Somehow there was never quite enough
time left over to do the reading I used to enjoy.

The stacks of money in the tin box grew, and each
week I visited Sam's office in the settlement with an
envelope containing a payment toward the loan he
had given Tony to buy the saloon in Fairbanks.

Finally, after a lot of hard work, the special day
finally arrived. I felt it, even before I opened my eyes
that morning, lying there in that sheltered place somewhere between sleep and wakefulness. A special day.
I slid from the bed and stretched luxuriously in the
patch of sun coming in through the window. The fire
in the sitting room was down to smoldering bits of
charcoal but the teakettle was still warm to the touch.
I splashed water into the basin and hurriedly washed
my face and hands. Letting my gown fall to the floor
around my feet, I scrubbed at my body with the rough
washcloth and took time to smooth oil across my skin,

along my arms, and down my legs, feeling the refresh-
ing tingle as I rubbed. A special day, and my body
felt it too.

By the time Maury came in the back door, I was
already in the kitchen. My hair was brushed and I
wore a clean apron over my blue gingham. I had the
fire already lit in the big wood cookstove and the
coffee water on.

Maury glanced up in surprise. "You're up and
around kind of early this morning, aren't you?"

"I've got a lot of things to do today" was my only
answer, but I hummed softly to myself as I worked.

I felt a touch of elation as I hurried through the
morning work, then went into my room to dress for
my trip to Sam's office with my regular weekly payment. I decided to dress up a little this particular day.
I chose a new dark-green skirt of a soft brushed wool,
copied from a San Francisco fashion magazine. My
blouse was crisp white, with a dark-green ribbon at
the neckline, holding the ruffles in place about my
throat. I took extra care with my hair, drawing it up
into a round roll on top, puffing out at the sides,
allowing a few soft curls to escape around my face.
An extravagant touch of perfume to match my mood
was added as an afterthought. Black kid gloves completed my outfit. The day was warm so I needed only
a light wool shawl about my shoulders.

Abe raised his eyebrows and whistled at me as I
came through the barroom. I looked over to where
he stood, polishing glasses, and I smiled, pleased with
his compliment.

"You want me to hook up the buggy for you?" he
asked.

"No, thanks, Abe. Not today. I feel like walking. It is such a nice day. I want to walk and enjoy it."

I felt that Sam had been expecting me, watching for me from the window. He met me at the door, greeting me with his warm, steady smile. When I opened my purse and took out the long white envelope and handed it to him, he tossed it casually in the top drawer of his desk.

"Not going to count it?" I asked.

"I don't see any reason to."

"There is today." I moved over to stand at the window and look down at the town. Lord, how it had grown in the three years since I had moved here. I heard people say that this was now one of the larger towns in this whole section of the country, but it was hard for me to believe. I could see horses moving along the road pulling wagons. There were women in yards hanging up the wash and children calling back and forth as they played. I used to know everyone in town, but now there were many faces I didn't recognize. Behind all of this show of domesticity, the mountains rose sharp and steep, forming a backdrop, ringing us in and holding us together. Aloof, rugged, beautiful, they dared us to push our boundaries out any farther. I loved those mountains and never tired looking at them, but I wondered if we were really successful in taming this wild, forbidding country—and if we were, what would be our penalty?

Sam's voice drew me back from my thoughts. "You really don't need to keep this up, you know, Nora."

I turned from the window. "Why? Have you heard from Tony? Don't tell me he has finally sent the money to pay off his debt?" Sarcasm was heavy in my reply.

"No. Not that," he answered. "I would have told you if he did. But this is his debt, not yours. You aren't obligated to me to pay it off. I don't like taking this from you and you know it."

"Yes. But I am obligated, Sam. You don't understand. It's very important to me that it gets paid. That's why I wanted you to count the envelope today. It's all there. The balance of the loan. Paid in full. It is a very special day for me. My Ravenwood is now free and clear! And . . . I owed it to Tony."

Sam was watching me, listening to me talk. I moved over and sat in a chair near his desk. "You know, Sam, Tony would never have come up here if it hadn't been for me. Oh, granted, he was anxious to leave San Francisco without his creditors being able to follow him, but I doubt that he would have chosen anyplace as demanding as Alaska. We were both so young—we thought we were in love. Tony proposed and my father refused to give his approval. I was a very willful person, accustomed to having my own way. My father is a very wealthy man, and I didn't know what it meant to not have everything that I wanted. When Father demanded that I stop seeing Tony, I slipped away and we met in strange little out-of-the way cafés, or in the park. I was caught up in the secrecy, intrigued by the bohemian, handsome artist, knowing I was envied by my sheltered friends.

"Then I discovered that my mother had not died when I was small. It was a shattering discovery for me—and I wanted to come up here to find her. Father tried to tell me that she was no longer living, but I refused to believe him. He had lied to me for so long about her."

Sam was watching me, listening closely to what I was saying. "Did you know Uncle Jim?" I asked him. "Did you live up here when he was still alive?" Sam nodded but didn't speak. "Then you must have known his wife, Amelia. She was my mother. She was married to my father—but she fell in love with his brother. She left with him, and I was told that she died. They came up here, found this spot to build Ravenwood, and here they found their happiness. That's why Ravenwood is so important to me. They wanted me to be able to come up here—to see it—and to live with them. When they died, it was left to me. That's why I can't sell it, as Garth Williams suggested. I can't lose it. I don't want indifferent strangers living there. Can you understand what I am trying to say?"

"Yes. I understand what you mean." He nodded. "I knew Jim and Amelia. Two fine people who were very much in love with each other. Knowing them and hearing them speak of you, I can understand what you are trying to say."

"I believe now that if Tony had known my father's lawyers intended to sell and I would have received the money, he would never have agreed to come up here. We would have married, I suppose, and settled right there in San Francisco—or traveled, until the money was gone." I gave a long sigh and shrugged my shoulders. "I wonder what my life would have been like if that had happened," I mused.

Sam was still listening intently, but he made no effort to answer, letting me ramble on with my story and my thoughts.

"Because I was strong-willed—and adventurous—and used to getting my own way—I was determined to come up here and find my mother. And Tony came with me, as my husband, to share whatever I found. And so I owed this to Tony—to pay off this loan—to give him a chance to do what he wants to do, now that he is up here. After today I can feel free. The debt is paid. Ravenwood is all mine now, just as Jim and Amelia intended. My obligations are over." I stood up, unable to sit still any longer. "Sam, I am free!"

Sam rose from his chair and walked over to me, putting his arm gently around my shoulders, drawing me to him. "I've hated to see you work like this," he said. "I never wanted to take the money."

I allowed myself the luxury of resting my cheek against the security of his shoulder for just a moment. The woolen shirt smelled faintly of tobacco and shaving lotion, and I closed my eyes, thinking how heavenly it would be to surrender myself without reserve to the broad shoulders and strong arms I had longed to have hold me.

"You know I want you, Nora," he said softly into my hair. "I've been in love with you for a long time now. I think from that first evening—"

"No, don't, Sam." I pulled away from his embrace. "Not yet."

"Why not, Nora? Tony is gone. You don't expect him back, do you?" He turned me around, to look directly into my eyes. "Or is that it? Look at me! After all that's happened, are you still willing to sit and wait for him to come back again?"

"No! No!" I cried out as I shook my head. "Anything that might have existed between us is dead now. I could never live with him again."

"Then what is it, Nora? I've waited for you for so long."

"The fact still remains that I am his legal wife." I

took several steps back, needing the distance to collect my thoughts. "I don't quite know what to do about it—or if I am ready to rush into doing anything right now. I feel a little frightened about the idea of a divorce, Sam. I'm not sure what I should do. I'm so confused. I think I'm going to take a trip down to see Garth Williams. I want to talk it over with him. As my attorney, he will know what I should do. As my friend, he can help me put my thoughts in order. I feel a little lost right now, Sam."

"Have you thought of joining Tony in Fairbanks?" he asked.

"No. Never!" I exclaimed. I turned toward the window with impatience. "Why all the questions today? Have you heard something of him? Tell me, do you know what he is doing? Have you heard anything at all, Sam?"

He shrugged. "Not very much. There were the rumors, of course. There always are. I think at first the saloon was successful, from all that I could gather. It was in a good location—was always crowded. He made a good buy on it. He might even have made the fortune he was talking about. But he is gambling again, and I hear that the stakes are running pretty high." His face was grim. "Oh, Nora, I might as well tell you. I heard just yesterday that he lost the place in a poker game. I don't know if it is true or not. It was just a rumor."

I felt the color leave my face. I knew Sam was thinking the same thing that I was. If the rumor was true— if Tony had lost the saloon and was out of money— perhaps he would be coming back to Ravenwood.

"How long ago was it that he is supposed to have lost the place?" I asked. "Do you know?"

Sam shrugged. "I don't have any idea. You know how rumors are. Hasn't he ever written to you? Sent a message of some sort?"

I shook my head. "Not a word. It's been over a year and a half—almost two years now. I can't believe where time has gone. At first I thought he would write and let me know if he had bought the saloon. I didn't believe he would just walk out of my life so easily, although we both knew there was little left of our marriage. Then my only thoughts were of paying off the debt—of clearing Ravenwood, because somehow I knew he had no intentions of sending any money. Now—" I turned and picked up my gloves from where I had dropped them. The special feeling for the day had gone. I stopped in the doorway and looked back. "Thank you, Sam."

"For what?"

"For just being you. For always being here when I need you." I wanted to say more, so many things. Instead I turned and fled, walking with short, quick steps back to Ravenwood.

I waited. One day melted into another. I dreaded each time the door opened, wondering if this time it might be he.

I knew for certain now that any love I might have had for Tony was dead. He had been a part of my life for a while, but the fires of passion burned low for lack of fuel and went out. Now there was nothing left but the ashes of memories to be shelved away in some dark place, along with other keepsakes of the past.

But Tony did not come back to Ravenwood.

I received another letter from my brother Tom.

Again, concern for me was his reason for writing. His letter told of receiving an invitation to an art exhibit in a new gallery. Because the showing featured landscapes of the Alaskan gold fields he went, hoping to see some representation of the country where I now lived. It was a shock for him to discover that Tony Lowery was the featured artist and that a large number of his paintings were displayed.

I placed the letter in my lap and stared out into the distance. So Tony had made it back to San Francisco and was painting again! I wonder what he must have thought, when he saw Tom at the showing. . . . I picked up the letter and began to read again.

"Either he didn't recognize me, or chose to pretend not to, because he looked right past me and made it impossible for me to reach his side to talk. There were a great number of people there, and any conversation would have been difficult—even if he were willing."

Tom went on to write that he had to find out if I was there with him, too proud to let them know and to come home. He hired an investigator, who reported back that Tony was living in the outskirts of San Francisco—with another woman. She was older, a widow, and reportedly very wealthy. She maintained a very large, fashionable mansion up in the hills overlooking the city. Tony was a guest, a "protégé" whom she sponsored in the art world.

I laid the letter aside thoughtfully and sat for a long time staring into the flames burning low in the fireplace. I knew the past was finished, and yet I had delayed going ahead with my plans for the future. Up until now I had found comfort in routine days, a sterile existence, keeping my mind so busy with the daily activities of Ravenwood that there was no room for anything else. I evaded any ties or commitments. The lodge was successful, the tin box filled, and regular deposits were dispatched to the bank in Valdez. My world was running smoothly, and I didn't want to face changes. The letter in my hand shook me into reality and gave me the incentive that I needed.

I had been thinking about making a trip to Valdez and meeting with Garth. The time seemed right and I prepared eagerly for the trip, choosing my clothing carefully. My outfit was warm but stylish; my hair dressed neatly in a fashion I had copied from a ladies' magazine. I stood back and critically inspected my image in the mirror.

I smiled my approval at the reflection. "You may not be a soft, green *cheechako* any longer, but you haven't become a backwoods bumpkin either." Satisfied with what I saw, I dabbed a bit of perfume from the tiny, cut-glass bottle to my throat and wrists, picked my valise up, and went out to find Abe waiting for me by the buggy.

This time I was to make most of the trip by railroad—a luxurious trip, compared to that first one on Logan's horse-drawn freight wagon. Abe took me south to Chitina in our new buggy, where I would meet the train. Other people were waiting in front of the hotel when we arrived. The big freight wagon from the interior was there, bringing passengers for the train and waiting to pick up others who would be traveling north. The horses were the pride of the freight company. Beautifully matched, they held their heads high and drew admiration from the crowd.

Chitina, the central distribution point for people and freight, had grown by leaps and bounds. I looked about in wonder at what had happened here in such a short time. Our town had grown rapidly, but this settlement had mushroomed beyond belief in the short time since I had first been here. A large, modern hotel had been built, and there were more stores and houses too. It was hard for me to imagine these things could happen in less than three years, and it all stemmed from man's greed for the brightly colored ores held within this country's hidden depths.

Abe helped me from the buggy and went onto the train with me, wanting to be assured that I would be comfortable and safe, before he left me. Taking a last look around, looking as though he regretted having to turn me over to this iron carriage, he promised again to be there, waiting for me, when I returned the day after tomorrow. I turned to the window to watch him leave and then settled down, determined to enjoy this unusual trip down through the mountains to the seaport.

The car filled rapidly with others making the same trip, although there was no one that I knew. Many were traveling just to see the mines and view the unbelievable scenery.

The seats were deep and comfortable—more like lounging chairs, with extra pillows available if you wanted. There were large windows, making it inviting to lean back and watch the panorama of mountains and glaciers that passed us by.

Maury had insisted on packing a lunch for me, worriedly wrapping several caribou sandwiches and a large piece of cake. It wasn't necessary because at noon the railroad served a delightful lunch. Indeed, every luxury was offered to us on this trip.

I never tired of looking at the ever-changing mountains that I had learned to love, so I settled back with my head against the plush cushion, looking out the window, drowsily half listening to the buzz of conversation going on around me as the tourists exclaimed over the glaciers.

The wheels clicked out a monotonous two-note tune over and over on the rails. The coach swayed back and forth in a deep rocking motion, and I swayed with the coach's gentle motion. We slowed for the curves, crawled across the bridges, and sped along at what seemed to me to be a breathtaking speed on the straight-of-ways, making our way down to the sea. I settled back, wiping all else from my mind, content merely to watch the beauty outside the window and to enjoy every minute of the trip.

The rails ended in Cordova. Valdez had lost the battle for a rail line when rich coal fields were discovered in Katalla, so along with all the others who wanted to ride the train instead of travel the Valdez Trail by stage, I traveled across from Cordova to Valdez by water.

This time I hired a carriage to take me from the wharf, up McKinley Street to the hotel. No one met me. I hadn't written to Garth to let him know I was coming. I wanted the time alone, to think out carefully what I was going to do.

A porter carried my valise upstairs. I asked to have supper brought to my room, and I spent a quiet evening by myself, reading some, standing at the window looking down on the streets at night, hearing their noises, remembering that first night here.

I did a great deal of thinking that evening, going over the past, remembering the good as well as the bad, until I finally drifted off into a restless sleep.

* * *

Garth greeted me as he always did, with warmth and enthusiasm. We visited casually. He showed no surprise at my unannounced appearance on his doorstep. He could sense, I think, that I had a great deal on my mind, and he waited patiently for me to begin whenever I was ready.

He brought out the coffeepot and we settled down in chairs. I told him about the trip to Cordova by train and how interesting it had been. I asked him if he had taken the excursion run up to mile forty-nine to see the Miles glacier. When he nodded, I told him how the engineer had slowed to a stop, letting us watch the huge chunks of ice fall into the water below, waiting while the tourists from the outside took their pictures with their new Brownie cameras.

Finally I brought out the letter from Tom and handed it to him wordlessly.

I waited restlessly while he read it over slowly, frowning at the words. When he finished, he laid his glasses aside and looked at me thoughtfully.

"That letter must have been very painful for you," he said.

"No. Not as much as I had thought it would be," I answered. "I knew he lost the bar in Fairbanks. I was afraid that he would be coming back to Ravenwood. He never wrote. I had no idea where he was until I received this letter from Tom. It's over, Garth. It's been over for a long time."

His voice was gentle. "What are you going to do now, Nora? How can I help you?"

"I want to get a divorce." I spoke with more determination than I had felt in a long time. "Will it be possible? Can you help me, Garth?"

"I see no reason for it not to be. You certainly have

had provocation. I have friends in San Francisco—a law firm I work with from time to time. There are sufficient grounds here in this letter. Yes. I can take care of it for you."

"Can it be done discreetly?" I asked, suddenly thinking of the hurt and shame I had already caused my father. "The word 'divorce' somehow carries a taint of scandal."

"Of course. Don't worry about anything."

I breathed a sigh of relief. "Good. Then take care of it for me, will you, Garth? I know now this is what I want to do."

"And then what next?" he asked. "Have you made any plans? Where will you go from here, after you receive your freedom?"

I shook my head. "I don't know. I suppose you are talking about Sam."

"He's a good man, Nora. And he's in love with you."

"I know. I've leaned on him so much already. But is it fair to him? I've got to take it just one step at a time. Right now it's hard for me to look beyond today and plan ahead." I sat quietly, my hands folded in my lap. "I need time. Too many things have happened."

Garth no longer spoke to me of selling Ravenwood and leaving Alaska. I knew this wasn't what he meant when he asked if I had any future plans.

My life became a studied routine, each day very much like the one before. Life for me could be described only as a comfortable existence, warm, friendly, casual, living entirely on the surface, with no emotional highs and no depressing lows. Sam came to eat supper frequently and often wound up staying through the evening. The four of us played cards, visited, or relaxed together in front of the fire.

I had the papers back from Garth on my divorce, and I filed them away carefully with other souvenirs of the past, not saying anything to the others about them. I wanted to keep my life just as it was, for the time being at least. I felt secure living in this vacuum, with no demands being made upon my emotions and asking none in return. I didn't want to do anything that might endanger this tiny fortress I had built so carefully around my little world.

Most of the time Sam seemed to understand. I knew he was trying to give me time to adjust. But there were times when his eyes met mine across the table, dark with the urgency he must have been feeling, and I felt my breath quicken. His hand would brush mine and I would draw back, frightened by the intensity of my passions begging to be released. At times I ached with wanting his arms to hold me against his hard body; nights I would wake up to the shrouds of darkness and lie there unable to go back to sleep, restless and hurting with loneliness. Nora—the girl who had spent a lifetime rushing into unexplored territories, caring little for the consequences—was suddenly frightened. I was afraid of passions so great that once I released them, there would be no turning back.

One evening, late in April, it all ended. I was shaken down out of that papier-mâché turret where I had hidden away. The walls came tumbling down around me, leaving me shaking. I stood among the ruins, no longer immune to the deeper feelings of pain or the stabbing jabs of jealousy, and I felt both in the agony of reality.

It was all caused by the door opening and Sam casually coming into the barroom with one of the prettiest, most sophisticated young ladies I had seen since leaving San Francisco. He helped her with her shawl and held a chair for her. I was in the kitchen with Maury, but we could both see them clearly through the passageway.

"Well, I'll be damned! Would you look at who Sam has with him tonight!" Maury clucked.

I was looking, my mouth open in surprise.

The firelight picked up the tiny bits of red gold in her lustrous, pale-blond hair. Soft blue eyes smiled up at Sam through heavy, dark lashes. Her skin was so soft and white that she resembled a piece of delicate Dresden china. She settled herself easily in the chair and looked about the room with interest. She made a lovely, fragile picture, in her silk gown, silhouetted by the soft light, and she was drawing a lot of attention, though she seemed unaware of it.

Not only had Abe noticed the newcomers, but the other men were watching too. In fact, some had turned in their chairs and were looking with open admiration. Sam didn't seem to notice the attention they were receiving as he bent his head forward, listening intently to what she was saying.

"You go take their order, Nora. Damned if I'd know how to talk to such a lady," Maury said.

"No! You go;" I answered. "I've got to check on the pies. They're ready to come out of the oven." I turned away quickly, not wanting Maury to see that I was shaken. I forgot to pick up a potholder before touching the oven door and burned the ends of two fingers. Snatching my hand back, I muttered one of Maury's choicer oaths.

Maury came back to the kitchen, swishing her skirts in exaggeration, her nose high in the air. "La-de-da but we have society favoring us with their presence tonight! Bet she pays more for that perfume than you or I do for our winter wardrobe."

"Wonder who she is?" I asked thoughtfully.

"Don't know. Sam didn't say when I was out there. But I'll bet you a pretty penny that she isn't from around this country anywhere," Maury answered as she busied herself preparing their plates. "Took her quite some time to select what she wanted to eat. Guess we didn't have nothing on our menu that she was accustomed to. She acted like she never ate macaroni and cheese or moose meat."

I noticed Maury took extra pains preparing the tray, making the dishes look attractive. One plate, obviously intended for Sam, had noticeably larger portions. As she worked, she fussed.

"Can you imagine? At first she told Sam that all she wanted was a large green salad. Now where do you suppose she thought I was going to get fresh lettuce up here? At this time of year?"

The girl was saying something, and she reached over and covered Sam's hand with her own as she talked. Even from this distance it looked pale and fragile against his tanned skin. Sam laughed at whatever she said, as though he greatly appreciated the remark. They seemed to be engrossed in each other's company. I turned quickly aside as Sam looked toward the kitchen, as though feeling my eyes watching them.

While Maury fixed the plates, she kept up her usual stream of chatter. For once it really annoyed me, but it was impossible not to listen. "Knew you shouldn't have held Sam off at arm's length the way you been

doing. Men being what they are, will only hang around
so long. With nothing there to hold them, they're
going to wander. No one can tell you anything though,
you're so stubborn!" She turned to look at me over
her shoulder. "Don't do you no good to look out and
speculate over who she is. The fact is, she is here. And
she wouldn't be here if you had the brains God gave
a goose to see what was right in front of your nose all
of the time. You've had him eating out of your hand
since you first got here—and him being worth two of
that good for nothing you had—but, oh no! You got
to moon around, trying to make up your mind what
you want to do. Well, you can see now where that got
you!"

"Stop it," I snapped. "Don't ramble on like such a
busybody! Sam is a bachelor—free to have dinner with
whomever he chooses." But inside I raged. It's true.
Sam is mine. No one else's. He has always been there
whenever I needed him. All I had to do was call.
Selfishly I had thought only of myself, thinking he
would always be there when I wanted him—and now
had I pushed him too far? Was he tired of waiting?
And this beautiful blond girl was standing by, just
waiting to step in when he grew impatient with me.

Maury paid no attention to my snapping at her.
"Here." She shoved the tray of dishes at me. "You
take them out. Go out there and defend yourself against
that claim jumper."

I glared at Maury but took the tray from her. Bright
spots of color burned on my cheeks as I left the
kitchen.

The girl was laughing as I approached the table—
the same light, delicate laughter that was so carefully

taught and practiced at Miss Robbins' Finishing School for Girls.

Sam stood, taking the tray from me and setting it on the table. "Evening, Nora." His eyes touched me with their special warmth, but I refused to notice. "I'd like you to meet a friend who has come to visit. Nora Lowery, Laura Williams."

Her "how-do-you-do, I am so glad to meet you. Sam has spoken of you so often" was very proper, but it was obvious that she was not all that interested in meeting another woman, even one who was as little competition as I.

"What a quaint place you have here. So very interesting . . ." Her voice had a lilt as she talked. For one horrifying moment I realized I had almost dipped my knees like a common servant at her compliment. I turned and fled to the kitchen.

Maury, of course, had been watching. "There's them that like the useless, ornamental type like that." She sniffed. "But not Sam—he's too smart for that!"

"Don't you ever mind your own business?" I snapped at her again, turning to attack viciously a stack of dirty dishes on the counter. For the first time I resented the lodge and the work it demanded, the country that had helped to harden me and make me independent.

Abe joined us in the kitchen to get a mug of coffee. "Boy, some looker Sam is having supper with—did you notice?" he said innocently.

I was rattling kettles and dropped a lid. He nodded his head in my direction.

"What's the matter with her?"

"Not a thing you stupid men would understand!"

Maury blazed at him, and Abe left quickly, shaking his head and wondering what he had done to bring Maury's anger down on him like that.

That night I slept fitfully, waking often and turning restlessly as the covers tangled and the pillow felt lumpy and uncomfortable.

They didn't come back to the lodge, but I saw her twice in town over the next few days. The first time I was quick enough to turn away to avoid a meeting. They were strolling along the boardwalk, her hand possessively on Sam's arm. She was smiling up at him and from time to time he bent his head as though listening closely to her talk.

The second time I was not quite so lucky. I was hurrying along the walk, already late with my errands, I rounded a corner and met them head on. Sam reached out to steady me.

"Hello, Nora." He turned to the girl beside him. "Laura, you remember Nora—"

"Oh, yes, of course." She smiled pleasantly. "It's the lady from the lodge, isn't it." I felt myself dismissed.

"Can you spare the time to join us in a cup of hot chocolate?" Sam asked. "I'd like for you to have a chance to visit with Laura."

"No. Really—thank you. I'm in a bit of a hurry today. Behind schedule as usual." I turned to the pretty blue eyes watching me in amusement. "I trust you are having a pleasant visit in our town."

"Oh, my goodness, yes, I am." She patted Sam's arm affectionately. "Sam, here, is such a darling. He's given me so much of his time, when I know he must be terribly busy. He has so much patience, explaining all of these things about the mines to me that I just don't understand at all," she simpered.

"Oh, yes, that's good old Sam." I tried to laugh. "Always there when a lady needs him!"

I saw Sam's eyebrows draw into a frown as I made my hasty good-byes and turned away to hurry home. Why did she make me feel like such a dowdy nincompoop each time I met her? I'll bet my family, my breeding, and my schooling were every bit as good as hers. She's just a—a—*cheechako*! Blast her! In fact, blast Sam too. "Sam is such a darling," I mimicked. That interfering, bull-headed egotistic—

It had been a long week for me and I was glad to see it come to an end. I welcomed the quiet evening. I had finished in the kitchen a little early and started for the fireplace, to relax and finish a cup of coffee, but when I saw Sam sitting alone at the end of the bar, I turned away and went into my sitting room, closing the door firmly behind me.

I had hardly seated myself at the desk and opened the ledger when Sam came in and pushed the door shut behind him.

"You've been a little hard to pin down in a conversation lately, Nora. You're always in a hurry to go somewhere."

"Oh, really? That's odd," I answered. "I thought you were unavailable yourself lately. You seemed quite wrapped up in your . . . new friends."

"Do I note a little tinge of jealousy?" Mirth lurked in his eyes.

"Jealousy?" I snapped. "Why should I be jealous? You're a free man. I have no strings on you."

"How well I know," he said softly. "You remind me

often enough." He crossed over to the stove and stood warming his hands, looking thoughtful.

"I tried to tell you the other night—when Laura and I had dinner here—but you left too quick to give me a chance—"

"Tried to tell me what?" I asked sharply. A dozen things he could have been trying to tell me raced through my mind, and I fought to remain calm.

"That Laura Williams is Garth Williams's sister," he said softly.

I raised my head with a jerk. "Garth's sister?" Oh, no, I thought. Garth and Sam are close friends. Garth's sister—and Sam—here it comes. I had a heavy, sinking feeling, and hoped my misery didn't show on my face.

"You really are a bit jealous, aren't you?" he asked. Somehow I felt that he was laughing at me, at a joke that only he knew, and it made me angry.

"Oh, now really, Sam. Why should I care if you enjoyed her company?"

"That's right. And I did enjoy being with her. But then why should you care?" He walked across the room to stand in front of me. "I thought you were happy with your life just as it was. When I reached out to you, you kept pushing me away."

"I was confused. I needed time to think. To adjust . . ."

"You wanted that divorce, didn't you?" Sam was very serious now.

"Yes. You know I did. It was a terrible mistake, right from the beginning. I was too blind—too proud—to see."

"Listen to me, Nora. Let me explain. Garth owns a huge number of shares in the copper mines. A large number of them are in Laura's name—"

"So," I flared. "In addition to her beauty and her fine clothes, she is also very wealthy. Well, good for you, Sam!" I spat. "Good for you." Tears filled my eyes and I turned away to hide them.

"Shut up and listen to me!" Sam's voice was harsh, demanding.

"Don't yell at me, Sam!" I spun around to face him.

"I wouldn't have to if you would keep still long enough to hear what I am saying."

I lifted my chin defiantly but kept still.

"Laura has been in Valdez visiting Garth for the past month. Since so much of her wealth is derived from the mines, Garth insisted that she visit them. He couldn't come up here himself so he asked me to do the honors—and look after her for the few days she was here."

I stared at him, my eyes wide, finally realizing what he was saying. His eyes were angry, his jaw firm, daring me not to believe.

"Then she's gone already?" I whispered.

He nodded. "She's gone. Back to her life in San Francisco."

His hands, which had rested on my shoulders, were moving around, encircling me, drawing me close.

Holding me against his hard, firm body, he murmured into my hair. "What are we going to do, Nora?"

"About us?" I rubbed my hands against his jacket, feeling the scratchiness of the rough wool, the taut muscles beneath the folds of the material, smelling the tobacco and the shaving lotion. "I don't know. I'm not the easiest person to get along with. I have a bad temper that is hard for me to control."

He was smiling down at me, laughter hiding in his eyes. "I know!"

"Well, you have faults too, you know! You are bossy, and bull-headed, and worst of all, you are usually always right!" Realizing what I had said, I added, "But not always." I sighed. "I guess sometimes I get moody and that doesn't make me very attractive company."

"And don't forget to add that you jump too quickly to conclusions," he said, laughter openly in his voice now.

We had done enough talking. I lifted my face, seeking his kisses. They were warm and tender, as I knew they would be. I took time to savor the swirling sensations as he led me unhurriedly to new passions.

"I need you, Sam," I whispered.

"Then why do you keep pushing me away?" he asked.

"I'm not pushing you away now—or haven't you noticed?" I breathed softly.

"You should be!" he threatened.

His fingers found the ties on my blouse, pulling it loose. I felt the roughness of his hands touch my bare skin, burning the flesh.

"Oh, Sam, damn you! Damn you!" Tears were flowing openly down my face. "Sam, will you marry me?"

He threw back his head and his warm laughter filled the room.

"Lady, I thought you were never going to ask!"

I was laughing or crying—I really don't know which, and it didn't much matter. He opened his arms to me and I closed my eyes in delicious surrender, to abandon myself at last without reserve to this man I knew I loved.

CHAPTER NINE

Abe and Maury took the news of our intent to marry in much the way I thought they might—as though they both had expected it to happen, just couldn't understand why it had taken so long.

Abe shook Sam's hand. "Don't know rightly if I should congratulate you or sympathize with you, Sam," he drawled, shaking his head seriously. "You're going to have your hands full, I guess you know. This little lady is headstrong, stubborn, and sometimes just plain aggravating! Tends to talk too much too. Sure going to take a firm hand to hold her in line. But you take good care of her and make her happy because if you don't, you'll have to answer to me."

Sam shook his hand solemnly in return, but I laughed out loud in my happiness and put my arms around Abe's neck and kissed him affectionately on the cheek. He pushed me away gruffly. "Just because you're going to get married, ain't no need to go getting so mushy." I could have sworn he blushed, but the lights were too low to be sure.

Maury took complete charge immediately, going off in a whirlwind of plans. The wedding would be held right here, she decided, in front of the big rock fireplace—where else could it possibly be but at Ravenwood? She started searching through her recipes for a wedding cake and checking the storeroom for supplies. She was in her element, glorying in the planning, the frustrations, the preparations for the wedding and the celebration that would follow.

Sam and I made our own plans, sitting together in front of the fire, with me curled deep in the shelter of his strong arms. I wondered how many evenings my mother had sat here in this same room and dreamed her dreams, feeling the arms of the man she loved around her, making her safe and secure, knowing that nothing else in the world mattered as much as the deep love she had found. I could finally understand how she must have been torn with the decision to leave me behind, but there was nothing else she could do. A love like this was so rare and so precious that she had to do all she could to hold on to it. It was not as though I had been abandoned. I had been left with a parent— my father—who gave me everything he possibly could, including his love, which I had not really understood until now. Her memory was very close to me at this moment, and I knew that somewhere she must be smiling, knowing that in Sam's arms I had found the legacy that she had tried to leave to me.

"Where would you like to go for our wedding trip?" Sam asked, interrupting my wanderings. "We can go down to Seattle and do some shopping, then we can go on down to San Francisco. I can get two months off from the mines without too much trouble. I haven't taken any time off for quite a long time. Would you like that, Nora?"

I turned in his arms, feeling the roughness of his shirt against my face as I rested my head on his shoulder, and I thought over what he said.

"Yes, it would be fun, wouldn't it. Just you and me. We could go to the theater—and there is a lot of shopping I could do. All of those big stores, seeing the new things. I wonder how much things have changed since I was there last." I twisted to look up into his face. "Sam, I would enjoy a trip like that, if that is what you want to do—but only because I would be with you. Don't plan it just to please me. I'm not homesick or anxious to return to San Francisco. My world is right here, at Ravenwood, with Maury and Abe, with you. You are my world, Sam."

He bent his head and kissed me tenderly. "I hope you will always feel that way," he murmured.

"I love you so very much, Sam. A kind of love I didn't know I was capable of feeling. I want you to be as happy as I am. I'll do everything in my power to be a good wife to you. I want us to live here at Ravenwood and always be together. I want to be with you forever and ever. I can't imagine life without you." I settled back down against his shoulder. "Sam? We can live here at Ravenwood, can't we? You wouldn't ask me to give up Ravenwood, would you?" Somehow this had never occurred to me before.

Sam didn't answer but a shadow crossed his face for a moment.

Sam is a proud man, and I knew he would have preferred to take me to a home that he had provided. However, since he was living in company housing,

owned by the mines—small houses without personality
—on this point he conceded to me, on the condition
that we redecorate our living quarters and that he
would buy the furniture.

I talked him into letting me keep most of my
mother's things that were in the sitting room, because
they were lovely pieces and I couldn't bear to part with
them. Seeing them there, knowing Uncle Jim and
Mother had selected them and loved them, helped keep
their memory alive for me. The bedroom, of course,
was a different matter. In that room no one mattered
but the two of us. I wanted nothing to be in it but the
things we picked together, and I wanted it to hold no
memories but the ones Sam and I shared.

The days before the wedding were hectic and seemed
endless, and yet there was hardly time to get everything
done. I ordered materials from Seattle and Maury and
I spent long hours designing, cutting, sewing our
dresses, wanting them to be perfect. We cleaned and
scrubbed the entire lodge and planned the cooking and
the baking. The sun was almost to the equinox and the
full days of sunshine lasted nearly twenty hours, with
only a few hours of gloom to call a night, giving us
that much more time to work. Bright sunshine
streamed in the window at three-thirty in the morning,
waking me. I found it hard to go back to sleep, so I
would lie in bed and think about the time when I
could turn and see Sam's head there on the pillow
beside me. Sam—who meant more than life to me. I
would usually get up and start my day early. In the
evening, even though I was sleepy and aching with
weariness, I found it difficult to prepare for bed with

the sun still streaming in. Hardest of all was to send
Sam home when the day was over. It was as though I
never really came alive until after the work at the
mines was done for the day and I heard his step
on the porch. I would stop whatever I was doing and
fly to the door, knowing his arms would be open to
me, oblivious to who else was there or watching. It is
hard to explain my feelings. Just the touch of his hand
—the sound of his voice—and I felt as high as though I
were sipping Maury's wild cranberry wine. When he
reached for me, the love in his eyes as he looked down
at me left me weak. I wanted to cry from the sheer
agony of knowing how much he wanted me—and I
wanted him.

"Sam," I whispered against his strong chest where
I was being held. "I love you so much!"

He would kiss me, and with his kiss I knew that the
day had been endless for him too, just going through
the motions of living until we were together again.

Finally the day arrived when we would exchange our
vows. The weather was mildly warm and the sky was
a clear, transparent blue. It seemed as though the
flowers and leaves were a little brighter and the birds
sang a little louder, reflecting our happiness.

All of our friends from miles around were there,
gathering together to share this special day with us. I
was as nervous as a schoolgirl, trying my best to stay
calm but not succeeding. Maury was even worse, trying
to be everywhere at once, finishing up the baking in
the kitchen and checking on all the last-minute preparations. Abe was trying to help and did his best to keep
Maury calm, gently kidding her, but it was hopeless.
She was thoroughly enjoying every frantic moment.

I was in my room when I heard Sam enter the lodge. Maury was fussing at him for the way he was dressed.

"For God's sake, Sam, what are you doing still in them clothes!" I heard her scold. "Here it is, almost time for this wedding to start and you're still dressed in your working clothes!"

"I figured Abe would need some help," he answered. "I got my suit over at your cabin. I'll go change in a few minutes. You don't want me packing wood in my wedding suit, do you?"

"Then just get out of here and go do it!" she ranted. "I don't want you hanging around here and seeing Nora before it's time. That's bad luck, don't you know?"

"You sure everything is all taken care of? Nothing you need me to do?" he asked.

"Everything is taken care of. Let me do the worrying, will you? Sam, you feel all right? You look a little shaky. You ain't feverish, are you?"

I heard Abe join the conversation. "Leave him alone, Maury. I'll fix him a drink and get him over to the cabin, out of your way."

I turned away, smiling to myself. So calm, cool Sam, always so sure of himself, was having his moments of nerves too, was he? I wanted to slip away without being seen and run to him, but I knew Maury would never stand for it.

The marriage ceremony took place in front of the big rock fireplace in the main room of the lodge, as Maury had insisted. The walls had been cleaned and polished until the dark woods glowed with a satin patina. The hardwood floors were waxed until they reflected the soft lights of the room. Abe had seen to it that the woodbin was filled, and the fire crackled and snapped, filling the room with the fresh smells of the forest.

Wooden benches had been built and now sat in rows for our guests. Dark-green evergreen boughs were twisted and twined into an altar and tall, white candles stood on the mantel, lending their soft light to the room. Everything looked warm, inviting, and beautiful.

The minister, an old friend of Sam's, had made the trip up from Cordova just for this occasion. His arrival had a steadying influence on Maury at last, and she began to turn her attention to our dressing.

From my place behind the door to the sittting room I could hear the people greeting old friends, children calling back and forth to each other, the scuffling sounds as the folks found a place to sit.

Garth and Sam had joined the others in the main room and Abe was with us, watching as Maury made the last-minute adjustments to my veil. I saw how his eyes were misty with pride as he looked at Maury in her new gown.

A hush fell over the group as Bill Howard began the notes of the wedding march on his accordion.

The door to our sitting room opened and Maury went out, dressed in the pale-green frock we had spent so many hours stitching for her. It was a lovely gown, with tucks and tiny embroidered roses on the yoke, falling to the floor in soft, shadowy folds. Her copper hair glowed in the candlelight. She looked radiant and her eyes were misty with happiness. Maury was beautiful.

We were next. Abe looked so stiff and uncomfortable in his high, starched collar and tie. Though he had chided the rest of us for being nervous, his hand shook when he took mine and placed it gently on his arm.

"Are you ready, Nora? They're waiting for us," he said softly, and I nodded back, hardly trusting myself to speak.

I was trembling as I walked slowly beside him toward our makeshift altar where Sam stood waiting for me with Garth Williams beside him as his best man. I heard small gasps from the benches and children's whispers as they first caught sight of me. Abe's arm tightened proudly.

My gown was of a deep, rich, ivory satin. The bodice fit snugly from a high neckline down to a tight-fitting waist. The skirt was of yards and yards of the same ivory satin, embroidered along the edge with tiny beige and pale-brown roses. It billowed out behind me, making a soft swishing sound when I moved. I had brushed my dark-brown hair until it shone, then coiled it back into a heavy chignon. My veil was of gauze of the same deep ivory color, fastened to my hair with a twist of pearls that I had found among my mother's things.

I raised my eyes and met Sam's warm, steady gaze, watching me, holding me with his eyes, enveloping me in love and tenderness. I moved slowly toward him, and Abe took my hand from his arm and placed it in Sam's.

The accordion music stopped. The minister cleared his throat loudly and began to read. The walls faded away, the room blurred, and I didn't hear the whispered hush among the group of our friends gathered there. Just Sam and I remained, each of us only aware of the other, as we exchanged our vows.

Sam slipped a thin gold band on my finger as a symbol of our love. I lifted the veil from my face and he bent to place a tender kiss on my lips.

"Hello, Mrs. Bennett," he whispered. "I've waited so long for you."

"I love you," I murmured, happiness swirling around me like a cloak.

We turned to face our friends as man and wife, and the magical spell that held us was broken as they rushed to our side, all talking, laughing, at the same time. Maury cried, as I knew she would, as she reached up to kiss Sam. Abe blew his nose and said he must be catching a cold as he bent to give me an emb̶a̶r̶r̶a̶s̶ kiss on the cheek. We were surro̶u̶n̶d̶e̶d̶ by our friends, all wanting to shake hands with Sam and kiss the bride. Garth finally man̶a̶g̶e̶d̶ to draw me to one side away from the others, where we could talk for a moment.

"Do I get to kiss the bride?" he asked.

I glowed happily as I turned my cheek up toward him. "Oh, Garth! I'm so glad that you were able to be here," I whispered. "It just wouldn't have been the same if you weren't here to share this day with us."

He put his arm about me and held me close to him. "You are lovely, Nora," he said. "Positively radiant. Jim and Amelia can rest easy now, and I guess I can quit worrying about my little *cheechako*, can't I."

I smiled up at him. "I tried to tell you to just have patience, that I would learn—grow up," I added softly. "But don't ever stop worrying about me. I still like knowing you are there."

He touched my cheek with his fingertips. "Be happy now, Nora. Sam is a good man and he loves you deeply."

"And I love him."

"Hey, you two! Why so serious?" Sam came up behind us and put his arm about my waist.

I turned to look up into his eyes. "My counselor was

just advising me that I am going to be very happy as your wife. He is a very wise man, isn't he."

Sam reached for Garth's hand. "You hand out sound advice, my friend. I'm going to do everything in my power to see that you are right."

While we were opening the gifts, Maury supervised the lining up of the tables. The other women all helped arrange the feast, adding specially prepared dishes of their own that they had brought with them.

...dding cake that Maury had spent so much time ...e wedd... ...passed around. The men pushed with was cut and ...rm a line around the room the benches back to fo... ...ning back and against the wall. Children were ru...ing back and forth, darting in and out among the grownups, shou... ing to each other as they played. Bill Howard started a lively tune on his accordion. A fiddle joined in. Soon everyone was laughing, dancing, eating, and drinking. I was passed from arm to arm, swung around the room with a great deal more zest than skill, to the rollicking, toe-tapping sounds of a polka.

I caught only glimpses of Sam, one time as he danced by with Maury, then with Mrs. Walker, and a fleeting glimpse of him talking with Garth and Abe.

He finally caught my arm between dances when I was standing near the tables, and placing his finger to his lips for silence, drew me away from the crowd, into the sitting room. He closed the door firmly behind us and leaned against it.

I gasped for breath. "What a madhouse it is out there!" I panted. "I don't believe I have any toes left, after that last dance!"

"I even saw Logan twirling you around out there." Sam chuckled.

"Oh, yes! I love him dearly, but it's actually dangerous dancing with him!" I slipped out of my shoes and stood in my stockinged feet.

Sam sobered. "Come here, Mrs. Bennett." He held his arms open to me and I melted into them. I felt the tall, rugged strength of this man as he held me so fiercely gentle, and my heart sang as I raised my face for his kiss.

Finally Sam held me out at arm's length, his voice husky with emotion. "Do you have your backpack ready? It's time for us to slip away."

I nodded. "Does seem a bit of a dirty trick, don't you think, to sneak out this way?" I murmured, wanting to move back into the fold of his arms.

"You wouldn't think so, if you knew what was going on out in the stable. I overheard them whispering. They think we're taking the buggy, and a couple of them are getting it 'ready' with old shoes and tin cans."

"All that work for nothing," I sympathized, with a conspiratorial smile.

"You're right. I have an idea," he answered. "But right now we have to change. I'll dress out here. You shut the door to the bedroom tight behind you. I don't trust myself too much, right now, and we've got to hurry if we are going to get away before they miss us." One last quick kiss, and then he pushed me away from him, toward the bedroom door.

In a few minutes we were in rough hiking clothes. Sam eased the window open and dropped our packs out onto the ground below. He went out next and then reached up to help me over the window ledge. As I dropped to the ground he kissed me quickly and handed my pack to me. "Here," he whispered. "You take this and go on up to the top of the ridge and wait for me. I'll be with you in just a few minutes."

"Where are you going?" I whispered back.

"Like you said, can't let all of that work go to waste. I'm going to sneak the horse and buggy out of the barn. I'll get one of the young boys to drive it on down the road and leave it in town. In the meantime, we'll be headed up the hill in the opposite direction."

I scurried away before some of the children that were playing outside saw me, up the trail to the rocky clearing, where I sat and waited. Very soon I heard Sam's quick steps coming up the trail toward me.

We reached a high hill, where we stopped to catch our breath and turn to look back down onto the lodge. Bits of music and sounds of voices floated up to us on the still air. We held hands and laughed mischievously as we thought how it must look—the buggy going down the road, almost covered with ribbons, papers, streamers, old shoes, tin cans, and a large "just married" sign tied on back—with a young Indian lad sitting alone on the seat, driving the team.

It took well over two hours, almost three, to hike back in on the trail to the lake where Sam had readied a cabin. We arrived there as the sun was getting low in the sky, bathing our world in a soft orange glow. It was a small cabin, just one room, built of logs. Sam had made a trip up here earlier in the week and it was swept clean, with fresh food supplies in the wooden crates nailed to the walls as shelves. There was a table with a kerosene lamp sitting on it, several chairs, and a barrel stove for heat and cooking. There was a bed, made up with fresh blankets.

I turned in the doorway and looked down at the lake as it lay like a mirror, reflecting the evening sky, the mountains, the setting sun. Except for the twilight sounds of birds, it was quiet, as though only the two of us existed in the whole world. I walked slowly down to stand at Sam's side, and together we watched the last bits of red disappear below the rim of the trees. The water turned from blue to almost black, with occasional white sparkling ripples made by jumping fish. Now everything was bathed in a silver light from the full moon. Even the birds were quiet.

Silently Sam turned, gathering me up in his arms and carrying me inside to the bed. Gently he laid me on the thick quilts and knelt beside me. His lips brushed my hair, my face, along my shoulder. Without speaking, I held my arms out to him.

There, in the mountain cabin, with the full moon streaming in through the open doorway, we repeated our vows in murmuring whispers and consummated our marriage.

The smell of coffee and the sounds of bacon sizzling woke me up. I opened my eyes slowly and saw Sam at the stove. He was already dressed, and his woolen shirtsleeves were rolled up to the elbows, as he stood turning the thick slices of bacon in the heavy cast-iron skillet.

"Come on, wake up, sleepyhead—out of the sack or I'll pour water on you."

"You wouldn't dare!" I stretched and yawned, feeling the luxury of lying in bed and watching someone else prepare breakfast. "I didn't know you could cook."

"Only when I go on honeymoons," he answered.

I pushed back the blankets and slid a bare foot out onto the cold floor, then shivered and drew it back quickly under the warm covers.

"It's cold out there!"

"Not over here by the stove, it isn't."

Sam tossed a heavy woolen shirt to me and I struggled into it. Then I leaned over the side of the bed and retrieved my stockings and pulled them on, still keeping the covers around me.

"I really don't want to leave this warm bed, you know," I told him reproachfully.

"If you don't, I'm coming over there, and then all this good bacon is going to burn," he threatened.

I pulled on the pair of men's pants I had cut down to fit me, and with the shirttail hanging out, my hair down loose around my shoulders, I slid out of the bed and ran across to the stove.

"I like burned bacon! Kiss me!" I demanded.

I spotted Maury's meddling hand when he set out the biscuits and jellies, but I pretended not to notice. We sat at the small table and ate our breakfast ravenously as we looked out through the open door toward the lake and watched a new day happen.

We spent two glorious days and three incredible nights there at the cabin, hidden away among the mountains. We took long walks, hand in hand, around the water's edge, and we talked.

"Not much like going to San Francisco, is it?" Sam said. "Are you sorry we put off the trip outside?"

"Never," I vowed. "Don't think that, ever, because truthfully I didn't want to go. I would have—for you—if I thought that was what you wanted to do, and I wouldn't have said anything, but I really didn't look forward to it. I don't think any woman ever had a lovelier wedding trip than we have had, coming up here to this cabin—just the two of us."

"We'll still make the trip—a little later," Sam answered. "I think it would be a good idea. The rift between you and your family has gone on long enough. It is time for it to be mended." He scratched a match on a rock and lit his pipe. I liked the smell of the tobacco he smoked and inhaled happily.

"How did you happen to choose this cabin for us to come to?" I asked.

"Jim first brought me up here, on a fishing trip. We packed in several times and stayed a few days. I used to come up here alone, after he was gone—just to get off by myself and sort out my thinking. It's the sort of place you only share with someone special."

Sometimes Sam fished for trout while I sat on the bank with a book open on my lap, idly watching him, dozing in the sun. We made love often, on the fresh green carpet of the forest and in the thick blanketed bed in the cabin, during the moon-bathed nights and in the warm, drowsy afternoon sun. I wished we could stay here forever—just Sam and I—but the time came when we had to close up the cabin and return to Ravenwood.

Abe and Maury had been busy while we were gone. The sitting room hadn't been touched, but the big brass bed that had been in the small bedroom since before I arrived was now stored in the shed. In its place was a carved rosewood bedstead that Sam had ordered. It and a matching dresser, with a large mirror, that almost filled one wall had arrived while we were gone. It was a beautiful set, polished and waxed until it glowed in the lamplight. The headboard was carved with scrolls of leaves and wild roses. Along the top of the mirror and across the front of the drawers a matching design was carved. Little half shelves, for holding candlesticks, were on each side of the glass, reflecting light to dress by.

The small tables, one at the bedside, the other beside

a rocking chair, held lovely lamps, their round glass shades hand painted with large pastel roses. On the bed was a new quilt, a gift from the Hills, sewn with loving care by Maury from scraps of materials she and I had used for dresses.

Sam brought his things down from the company housing where he had been staying, and I put his clothing in the closet, next to mine. Home at last. . . .

CHAPTER TEN

Though we still planned on it, and often talked of it, somehow our trip to San Francisco kept getting delayed, first by one thing and then another. Sam wanted to work on the lodge before the cold weather came. He was a master with machinery, and he and Abe built a generator for power. They ordered pumps and pipes, and before the fall was over we had running water right into the kitchen. Sam hired a man with plumbing experience to help with the work, and they installed an indoor bathroom upstairs for the lodgers.

Abe hauled lumber from the sawmill in the village, and he and Sam built an addition to our sitting room, adding a bathroom with a big white porcelain tub sitting on curling legs and another small bedroom.

The men ran pipes out to the Hills' cabin so they had running water out there too.

The first snowfall of the season came earlier than usual, bringing with it an urgency to finish the winter preparations. The mines took more and more of Sam's time. He left earlier than usual in the mornings and came home with tired lines around his eyes late in the evenings. I knew he was worried over the problems caused by the weather.

Everything—production, completion dates, transportation of the ores to the seaport, and schedules of the ships—was controlled by the weather, and the men fought hard to gain extra ground whenever they were able, to make up for the times their hands were tied by well below zero temperatures and wind-driven snow. Only one sawmill was in operation in the area, and the flashing blades worked long hours each day, trying to keep up with the demand for lumber. More was always needed.

Trams needed to be built to carry the ore down to the loading dock, and tram terminals, transfer bunkers, and snow sheds too. Bunkhouses were needed for the men who stayed at the mines all the time, and with the additional machinery being brought in, the need for a warehouse was becoming critical.

It was a race against time and the elements, and the men were giving it the best battle they could.

Maury and I were busy ourselves, picking wild berries, making jams and jellies for winter, canning meat, smoking fish, airing the bedding, and bringing out the winter clothes to check for repairs. All of Ravenwood was a beehive of activity; we all were taking advantage of the last of the summer hours to make ready for whatever kind of a winter lay ahead of us.

We delayed the trip to San Francisco once again, when we knew I was carrying Sam's child. He wouldn't allow me to undertake the ocean voyage until after the baby's safe arrival.

I wrote regularly to my family—telling them of my

marriage to Sam, the mines, the finishing of the railroad, the growing town, and, finally, I told them of the child that was on the way.

I received letters from Tom occasionally, and once or twice lately a note had been included from my aunt. I looked forward eagerly to those letters, watching for them anxiously, reading through them again and again. Each time I was a little disappointed that there was no small line added from my father. Though I pretended not to notice, the hurt still lay there, under the surface.

Even so, I didn't mind the constant delays in our taking the planned trip outside. My world was here at Ravenwood, with Sam, Maury and Abe, the friends we had made, the child that was on the way—and the tiny grave in the cemetery in the village.

Sam bought a new sewing machine for me—a lovely thing with a polished walnut top and a treadle that I pumped with my feet, making the stitches fly. What usually would have taken nearly a week to sew by hand I could put together in an afternoon. It was one of my fondest possessions.

After the first few snowfalls, when the temperature sank to below zero, the work slackened and Sam had more free time to relax. He and Abe went hunting together, bringing back a caribou. It was cold enough for the meat to keep outdoors in the meat cache, so they skinned it and stored the quarters for winter eating. Sam took the hide into the village to an Indian woman to have it tanned and made into gloves.

The men liked to go ice fishing on a cold, clear Sunday afternoon, when the work was all caught up. They would cut a round hole in the ice and drop their lines down to the murky water below. There were always other men out there, sitting by other holes in the ice, watching for nibbles. They would call back and forth and tell unbelievable stories, of nuggets they had found, bears they had seen, squaws they had enjoyed. Once in a while they would take a long swallow of whisky from a bottle being passed around by someone who had brought it to "keep the circulation going and prevent frostbite."

Many visitors came to the mines. Once in a while Sam would bring one of the men home with him to spend the night at the lodge—men who spent their lifetimes in the wildest parts of the world, building bridges, studying the composition of the earth and its secrets: geologists, scientists, engineers, and archaeologists. To them the home cooking and warm atmosphere of Ravenwood were a welcome treat.

After dinner they sat around the fire smoking, talking, having a drink together, as they unwound. Their talk intrigued me, and often I would take a bit of sewing and sit with them, quietly listening to the tales they spun.

A man by the name of Adolph Gunderson came home with Sam one night. They were sitting by the fireplace talking quietly as they enjoyed the warmth and relaxation after a long and strenuous day out in the cold. I had been reading, but when I heard them mention the Million Dollar Bridge, I laid aside my book and began listening to the conversation.

The Million Dollar Bridge across the glaciers was considered the number-one tourist attraction in the whole Alaskan territory at this time. It had been an almost impossible engineering feat, and though it had been named the Million Dollar Bridge its cost ran far beyond that figure. There were special tourist trains run out of Cordova, up to mile forty-nine, where they stopped for at least an hour and a half, sometimes longer, to let visitors see and photograph this amazing bridge and to view the spectacular performance of the glaciers calving.

I had seen the bridge when I took the train down to have Garth Williams apply for my divorce from Tony. As occupied with my problems as my mind had been at that time, I shall never forget the feeling I had inside when the train stopped. Miles glacier lay to one side of the bridge, Childs glacier to the other. We watched a wall of ice, three hundred feet high, vibrant in deep blues and greens, alive, working, moving. We could hear the rumble and cracking from the bowels of the glacier, and huge chunks of ice would break off. The thunder of them hitting the water, the giant-sized waves that were caused when they hit, had been overpowering and a little frightening to me.

"Is there something wrong with the bridge?" I asked.

"Nothing wrong with the bridge itself," Mr. Gunderson answered, turning toward me. "But the structure is in danger of being crushed by the glaciers."

"Mr. Gunderson is a scientist, Nora," Sam explained. "He has been brought up here by the railroad to study the forward movement of the glaciers and report on the danger to the bridge. He's spent most of his lifetime studying glaciers and their changes."

"I'm not the only one," Mr. Gunderson added. "There are some bridge engineers and a group of archaeologists, along with other scientists, who are up here taking measurements, making charts, trying to understand that monster of nature that seems intent on moving forward to crush that magnificent bridge."

I was listening intently to what they were telling me, because it affected the railroad, the mines, and could mean disaster to us too. The bridge was the only passage across that area. If the train could not cross the bridge, it could not continue up the route to the mines, and without the trains, the mines would close.

"Have you been watching the glaciers long?" I asked.

Mr. Gunderson nodded. "Several months. Without reason, the Miles glacier began to advance with the spring thaws. It usually rests some eighteen hundred feet from the railroad bed. By June of this year it had moved forward some twenty-five or thirty feet. By August our measurements showed it was only a little over sixteen hundred feet away and still creeping forward. It is a fearsome thing, Mrs. Bennett, to stand on a rock taking pictures and then to return the next day to find the rock gone, swallowed up by that living, moving field of ice. I have watched it push over trees, move boulders, crush rocks, destroy anything in its path as it moved forward inch by inch."

"How close is it to the bridge now?" My voice was low, filled with awe at the story he was telling.

"Less than one thousand five hundred and seventy-five feet right now."

"And still moving?" I whispered.

He shook his head. "No, it seems to be resting right now. The winter freezing has halted its forward motion. We aren't expecting any activity with it now until spring, so most of us are going home. I will be leaving as soon as I finish some notes I wanted to take up here at the mines, but I'll be back next March or April."

"But shouldn't the men be doing something now, while the glacier is immobile? Something to protect the bridge against danger in the spring if the glacier starts moving again?" I asked.

He spread his hands helplessly. "There is nothing we can do. That bridge is considered a masterpiece of engineering, but with all of our new technology, with all of our knowledge of building in this modern age, we are helpless. The Childs glacier is moving too, advancing from the other side, as though nature is intent on destroying man's iron trail into the forbidden regions of this land to remove the treasures that she does not want to give up."

"That's right, Nora," Sam explained. "If the glaciers reach the bridge, there is nothing that will save it. The Million Dollar Bridge will be destroyed."

To shake away the restless feeling I had from listening to the men talk, I put away my book and offered to bring coffee and fresh pie to them. They took me up on it with enthusiasm and the mood was broken, the talk changing to lighter subjects.

When the conversation turned toward politics, I excused myself and went into the bedroom to curl comfortably under the covers to read until Sam came to bed. I knew that once they started on politics, the talk would eventually get around to Gifford Pinchot, head of the Bureau of Forestry, in the Department of Agriculture, and the conversation could last quite a while. I was much too tired, and my back ached too much to sit out there and listen to it tonight. As far as I was concerned, after listening night after night to the discussions, it was not the creeping glaciers that were going to destroy us, it was the men in Washington like Mr. Pinchot. They were doing more damage to us than the glaciers, and they were doing it without ever leaving their comfortable, overstuffed chairs behind polished desks, in warm offices. Though Richard Ballinger, the Land Commissioner, was doing the best he could— raising objections, pointing out the rights of home- steaders and the urgent need for lumber now, not later, defending the miners who had claims all through that area—Washington still established the Chugach National Forest. The National Forest tied up all the lands from the Copper River to the borders of the Kenai Peninsula, following up the west and inland to the Chugach Mountains. Evenings in our bar- room were filled with angry protests and bitter dis- cussions after the forest's establishment.

I knew that tonight the conversation would turn to mining, the need for coal to run the smelters, the vast coal fields the government prevented them from using, the timber the government prevented them from cut- ting, the tax on railroads needed for transportation, and I was not ready to sit and listen to it.

I was dozing somewhere in that comfortable place of drowsiness, between wakefulness and sleep, when Sam came in.

"Still awake?" he asked in surprise.

"Ummh," I mumbled. "Did you get Mr. Gunderson settled in his room all right?"

"Yep. Everything's okay. The fire has a big log that should burn slow until morning. The lights are all turned down, and I checked the woodbin in the kitchen." He slid in under the warm covers. "Oh . . . I'm glad you were lying on my side of the bed. You got it all warm for me. Must be ten below outside to- night. Winter's moving in fast. Hope there's enough wood upstairs for the stoves. We're going to need it before morning or those guys will be climbing out of bed with icicles on their noses."

"I just hope someone wakes up to put the wood in the stove up there," I replied. "Our first year with indoor plumbing. I'd hate to see it all freeze up."

"One of them will. Someone always has to get up sometime during the night, and they're pretty good about stoking up the fire."

My head was resting on his shoulder and Sam was gently exploring my body as he talked. "You're getting a round tummy, Mrs. Bennett," he said smugly.

"I think I felt life today, Sam," I whispered. "I'm sure that's what it was. Your son is beginning to move around."

"My son? How do you know it will be a son? Maybe I'd like to have a daughter."

"I want a son," I answered. "I want to give you a son who will grow tall and handsome, a son who will be just like his father and make you proud. Then, later, if you like, we can have a daughter—maybe two or three. Who knows? Wouldn't it be nice to have a large family, Sam?"

Sam laughed softly in the darkness, reaching out to pull me close, holding me against him so that I could hear his heart beating and feel the hardness of his desire for me.

When I was with Sam, held closely in his arms in the big, ornate bed, surrounded by the warm, safe darkness of our room, there were no advancing glaciers, no railroad perils, no worry over coal or arguments with the government, no conservationists threatening to close up Alaska to its people. There were only Sam and I, our own protected world, and our love for each other that was too great for anything or anyone to touch. I turned to him, my need suddenly urgent, loving him, wanting him. And Sam slowly, skillfully, tenderly, led me to those dizzying heights of pleasure, until when I thought I could stand it no longer, together we found an explosive burst of ecstasy, leaving us weak and fulfilled, and ready for sleep.

CHAPTER ELEVEN

We were out in the side yard, Maury and I, tending to the plants and flowers in the little garden. Each year I had to try, and each year only a portion of the seeds grew. But I never gave up. By the middle of March all of the window ledges on the south side of the lodge had little trays of potting soil, sown with tomatoes, cabbages, and some petunias, along with different things I would try new each year. I had finally gotten some rhubarb to start, and now each year it came up, with thick, pink stems, so good cooked with wild strawberries in a pie. The cabbages usually did quite well, but the problem I had with them was the moose. It seems moose have a passion for cabbages.

The carrots, radishes, and beets we planted right in the ground, without starting the seeds indoors first. They usually did well for me, and the moose were not too fond of them. The last year or two we had been able to grow enough for the table, with some left over to have canned carrots and pickled beets through the winter.

The flowers were my real joy. The petunias adapted well to the climate, and I would start the seeds indoors and bring them outside late in May. Most of them would grow, and the flowers were larger than the ones I remembered from my father's garden. Logan said it was because of the long hours of sunlight—everything grew faster and larger. Things grew continuously with no evenings for rest periods. I had seen some fantastic gardens in Valdez and heard stories of what happened to gardens in the interior where the soil was better. Logan told me that in the interior valley cabbages would grow to weigh sixty pounds to a head, and only three strawberries could fill a fruit jar. Potatoes would grow, but they were a disappointment. Too much moisture, and too many hours of sunlight. The potatoes cooked too soft, making every panful good only for mashing. I was hungry for one of the large, firm potatoes my father's cook would bake, with crispy brown shells that I used to like to eat with butter and salt and pepper.

But though the end result was sometimes less than rewarding, I enjoyed the feel of the dirt, the warm sun. When some of the plants grew and produced fruit or the flowers blossomed, spreading their perfume out across the yard, I knew it was worth the effort.

I straightened up as a sharp pain ran across my back. Maury saw me wince, and she wiped her hands on her apron and came over to my side with a worried look on her face.

"Anything wrong, Nora?" she asked.

"Yes. No. I mean, no, nothing is wrong—but yes, I think the waiting is about over." I drew in my breath swiftly as I felt another sharp stab of pain. "We better pick up the garden tools. I think it's time to go in."

"I'll send Abe after Sam."

"No, wait awhile, Maury. Not yet. There's plenty of time yet. He worries so. Don't let's send for him quite yet."

"Sam ain't going to like that, Nora. You know he's going to expect us to send for him right away."

"I know. But men aren't much good at a time like this. Even strong men, like Sam. Let's wait just a little longer."

I bent to pick up my gloves where I had dropped them and felt a tightening through my middle. I looked over at Maury's worried face and laughed. "Maury, it's a birth we're expecting! Not a funeral. Now smile for me! And I think we better hurry. . . ." I had a feeling of urgency now. "Come on, let's go in, and you can help me get prepared to greet the arrival of this fantastic child of Sam's."

Once indoors Maury took command. She built up the fire in the wood stove, sent the young boy who worked around the stable after the doctor, and gave orders to the two Indian women who were doing the cleaning—getting her day organized so that she would be free to be with me.

I fixed a wash basin of hot water and washed away the dust from the garden. I brushed my hair, letting it hang down around my shoulders, free from its pins. I changed into a gown that I had ready and opened the chest to lay out my child's first outfit.

I checked the time between the sharp pains as I waited, pacing the room restlessly, doublechecking my preparations, trying to keep my mind busy. I was nervous but resolutely trying to shut away any fears.

When at last the sharp pains grew severe, taking away my breath, I pleaded to Abe, "Please, go get Sam. I need to know he is close by."

My time of labor was comparatively short, and the pain was no more than normal. Maury never left my side, and the doctor spoke softly to me, helping me, giving me instructions, as I struggled to give my baby life. Finally, tired and damp with perspiration, I heard a loud, protesting wail and knew my child was alive and healthy. Smiling to myself, I drifted off into a healing sleep.

Maury woke me by laying a tiny bundle, smelling sweetly of oils and wrapped in a downy blanket, in my arms.

My friend looked exhausted but radiant. "Wake up, Nora. Look at the most beautiful little lady ever delivered into this here country!"

I pulled the blanket down to see tiny hands, doubled into fists, flaying the air, a wrinkled red face, eyes squinted almost closed as she cried out in angry protest, a heavy thatch of dark-brown hair, and I knew Maury was right. She was beautiful!

"Where's Sam?" I whispered. "Is he here?"

"Here? Good Lord, yes. Pacing the floor and getting on everybody's nerves. Abe's been trying to keep him calm, and I think he's had his hands fuller than I have in here with you."

"Call him in, would you please, Maury? I want Sam."

He tiptoed into the room and over to the bed. He bent over and as he kissed me gently, I felt the tears on his face. Smiling up at him, I took my fingertips and wiped them away.

"My big, strong, brave Sam. Dry your eyes, my dearest husband, and meet your daughter," I whispered.

He turned and sat down on the side of the bed, his eyes filled with the wonder of the miracle lying in the crook of my arm making tiny mewling sounds as she nuzzled the side of the blanket. Sam reached out and touched the tiny fist, marveling at the perfection of her hands when she clasped her fingers around his one large one, and held on tight, binding Sam into slavery forever.

Samantha was a healthy, happy baby. She slept well at night right from the beginning, and everything seemed to agree with her. Her hair stayed a deep, rich mahogany and her eyes turned a bright, sparkling hazel color. She crowed in delight when she first discovered her hands and her toes. She struggled hard to learn to sit up, never content to lie still or stay in one spot for very long.

During the day Maury and I would take her into the kitchen with us, propping her in a wooden rocker, tying a dish towel around her middle to keep her from falling out as she watched us work. Abe found more and more excuses to come out there, releasing her ties and tossing her into the air with her squealing happily.

Though she slept well, she would wake early. She would pull herself up in her crib and sit with her face pressed to its bars, peering down with large, serious hazel eyes, studying her father. If he didn't rouse and smile at her, her tiny rosebud mouth would turn down at the corners in a pucker and her little chin would quiver. If this didn't work, tears would fill her eyes and she would send up such a plaintive wail that Sam would sit up sleepily and lift her down into bed between us. For a while she would be content to lie there, gurgling to herself as she watched her fat toes kick out from the blankets, blowing soft bubbles, experimenting with new sounds, and we would be able to get a little more sleep. But then she would tire of her games and turn over, reaching out to Sam, pulling on his ear, exploring the lines of his face with her chubby little fingers until he woke up and played with her.

Sleeping time was over. I would get up, change her diapers, and leave the two of them while I went out and started the water for the morning coffee.

Maury would usually meet me in the kitchen about the same time and have the fire going in the big wood cookstove. At this time all of our lodgers were working in the mines, so it was an early breakfast, and a hearty one, that we prepared every morning. And Mandy was in the center of everything, crowing happily as she ate her breakfast, holding court among the men in her life.

When she learned to crawl, Maury and I were nearly beside ourselves trying to keep track of her, keep her out of harm's way, because now she had a whole new freedom to explore. Pans tumbled from cabinets, and she would send up an alarmed cry for help when her explorations led her into corners that she couldn't find a way out of. She loved Abe, and more than once she found her way into the barroom, looking for him, following the sound of his voice.

Her first steps were taken from Abe's steadying knee, across to her father when he came in the door from work one evening. She learned early to work her wiles on Abe, and when it was necessary for Maury or me to reprimand her, she scurried to him for comfort, her face a picture of misery, hiccupping in her tears a little longer than necessary, just to be sure he noticed.

She took such a delight in every new thing she saw around her. Her first snowfall left her staring out the window in awe, watching the big flakes drifting down. Abe bundled her up and carried her outside, so she could hold out her hand and try to catch them, to feel their softness.

She had no fear of strangers. Soon the lodgers upstairs and some of the more regular customers who came in for their meals were among her court, bringing her small gifts, stopping a moment to play with her. Though I worried about it, the attentions she received didn't seem to spoil her. She never whined or fussed or pouted. She was a happy child, the whole world was her kingdom, and she eagerly tried to investigate every corner.

For a while things looked favorable in the battle being waged in the coal fields. The people who had staked the claims were fighting to meet deadlines that were unrealistic, but just when things were looking hopeless a circular was distributed saying that the time limit had been extended. They were being given until 1914 to apply for a patent. Hopes again were raised. With coal to run the smelters and the railroad, Copper River country could survive—not only survive but grow, with families coming in to settle. It would give the smaller mining operations that lacked the backing of big-money syndicates a chance to produce as well.

The setting aside of the area designated for the Chugach National Forest had caused a lot of bitter feelings, particularly among the miners and trappers. Some homesteaders were affected too. But it was the outcome of the battle over coal that would affect our lives at

Ravenwood the most. Our town had grown around the mines and the railroad. The mines needed the coal if they were going to be able to produce on any large scale, because it took coal to run the smelters.

When Sam came in one night I saw the tired sag to his shoulders, the faraway look in his eyes, as though he were with us but his mind was somewhere else. I knew something had gone wrong during the day to affect him so much, but I didn't ask until he was ready to talk about it. I wanted to give him a chance to relax first, to unwind and enjoy his dinner. Mandy demanded her share of his attention, squealing in delight when he tossed her in the air, happy at having her father home with her again.

It wasn't until later, after Mandy had been tucked in for the night and Maury and I were doing some hand sewing near the fire, that I heard about the new threat to our area. Several other men had come in and were sitting near the bar talking with Sam and Abe.

"Some of the coal claimants have received letters telling them they have one last chance to show 'just cause' as to why their claims shouldn't be canceled," Sam told the others.

"How can they do that?" one of the men asked. "They still got time left to meet the deadline, don't they?"

Sam shook his head. "The letters don't say anything about that circular that was supposed to have come out giving them an extension. Looks like they've missed the deadline for getting the patents."

"Well, looks as though they won another one, doesn't it?" another man said, slowly drawing on his pipe. "Those damned conservationists back in Washington are going to wind up locking up this whole territory

against us Alaskans who make our home here. How
much more of this red tape and harassment are we supposed to take?"

"I don't think it is Washington as a whole that is our
problem," a man visiting here from down near Cordova added. "It's that Gifford Pinchot and his band of
followers that are the leaders in this thing. I'm not
sure I know what they are trying to accomplish."

"It's just that they don't understand the waste," Sam
said. "They are just too far away from this territory to
understand the crime that is being committed against
us as well as against the land. If you don't harvest timber properly, it's just like any other crop. It rots where
it falls—and then it's no use to anyone except the bugs.
Those coal fields have enough coal to supply all the
power needed for the mines *and* for the railroads. It's
the twentieth century, for God's sake. None of us here
are asking for charity from the States. We aren't asking
for anything except to be allowed to develop our own
resources in a controlled and intelligent manner—to
supply jobs and provide a living for our own people
without raping the land while we do it."

Evidently a lot of people felt as Sam did, because
enough angry cables and letters were sent to Washington to finally draw attention. We heard that Gifford
Pinchot was going to make a trip to Alaska, to study
the problems firsthand. I listened to the men talk and
I read the newspapers, wondering if Mr. Pinchot must
not feel a little hesitant about venturing so far away
from the comfort of his office, particularly since most
of the reports carried back to him seemed to paint us
as savages or hostile, uncivilized outcasts and misfits
from the lower States, living in all sorts of makeshift
hovels under unsavory conditions. I suppose there

were some who still thought we lived in igloos and ate raw meat.

The newspapers kept us posted on the proposed trip. People read the stories and made guesses at what the visit would be able to accomplish. Everyone had hopes that a firsthand visit to our country would provide a better understanding of our needs and our demands.

Finally it was announced that the trip North would be made in September and that Mr. Pinchot would not be coming alone. A secretary and a senator would travel with him. We were told that they intended to visit the people and to listen to what they had to say. As of this date, temporary plans called for the trio to visit in Cordova, go by boat across to Valdez and on to Seward. From there they would travel inland to the Matanuska coal fields. On their return to the coastal regions, they would ride the Copper River and Northwestern Railroad up into Copper River country. We were going to be honored with a visit also. Katalla was not excluded, on the itinerary was a trip across to the coal fields in that region.

All the newspapers carried daily stories of the visit, adding their own wry editorials, not necessarily favorable to the travelers.

Secretary Fisher arrived first, as though to feel out the situation, before Mr. Pinchot followed a short time later. Though the Alaskans were bitter over the treatment they had received, disillusioned at being ruled by a government in which they had no vote, made wary by the diet of half truths they were fed, I was proud of my countrymen, for they conducted themselves with dignity, ready to listen and to discuss our problems, seeking a solution through understanding. The only outward show of their feelings was expressed with badges reading "Allow us to mine our own coal."

I'm afraid that Mr. Pinchot's trip to spread good-will did not have the effect on the people that he had hoped. The Alaskans were not impressed with him or his traveling companions, nor did they stand in awe of his slightly superior attitude. As could be expected in a situation like this, the jokes began to fly, with Mr. Pinchot the brunt of most of them. Even the news-papers took up the challenge, openly making sarcastic statements against the three. The *Valdez Miner* said, with tongue in cheek, "While it was probable that God made the U.S., Pinchot and his men would do a better job for Alaska."

Though I knew how Sam and the other men felt and I understood their reasons, as I listened to the conversa-tions and read the papers I began to feel sorry for Gifford Pinchot. The man just seemed to have a natu-ral knack for saying the wrong thing at the wrong time. It seemed to me that he kept stirring the people up every time ruffled feathers were beginning to be a little smoothed.

"Sorry for the man?" Sam had snorted, when I ex-pressed my feelings out loud. "Woman, what can you possibly be thinking of to make a statement like that?"

"Well, it's just the way things are going," I answered. "He's trying to impress everyone with what a power in the government he is, up here to straighten out all of the problems that are brewing, and each time he gives a speech he winds up causing more trouble, stirring up more hostilities among the people."

Sam laid aside his pipe, after knocking the ashes into the hearth, and looked at me in amusement.

"Never knew you to get interested in politics before, Nora. Thought the only periodicals you read were the women's magazines. What is it about Pinchot that has caught your attention?"

"Well, Sam, look at the paper here that I am reading. That man is really just beyond description. He and that senator—Senator Poindexter—were in Cordova yesterday. He just had to make a speech! Doesn't anyone tell him he would do better by listening than doing so much talking? Just listen to this. The newspaper says he told them: 'Contrary to general opinion, the conservation men are not responsible for tying up the reserves in Alaska. Since President Roosevelt sent his first message in 1906, we have been trying to get Alaska opened up under fair conditions—conditions that are fair to all of the people. We do not believe that development should necessarily mean monopoly.'"

Sam listened intently to me as I read, looking thoughtful. "People are so quick to shout 'monopoly' when they fear the power of big money, not knowing how to stop or to control them," he said. "And yet the little man, the small businesses, aren't able to build railroads, open up the bigger mines, develop the fishing industry—it is only the syndicates or the private corporations with unlimited financial backing that are able to afford to do the pioneering. The only other source with enough money to do it is the government, and it is obvious the government not only is not going to help the people to do it, it is blocking them at every turn. It will be the people who depend on jobs for wages who will be the losers." Sam reached for the paper. "What else does it say? How long is he going to be in Cordova?"

"I'm not sure," I answered. "I read it here somewhere but I can't find it now. I think they are leaving
today or tomorrow, headed for Valdez and Seward.
The paper said something about them going out to
visit the people, wanting to meet the pioneers of the
country, the businessman as well as the prospector and
the miner. Well, all I can say is that I hope we have an
early winter—a really rough one!"

Sam looked up in surprise at me. "What brought
that on?"

"Well, I do!" I declared. "I hope he finds out what
it is to ride on a dog sled in a blizzard, because that's
the only way to travel. If he hadn't set up such a fight,
he could be riding in a nice warm railroad coach all
the way, you know."

Sam smiled in amusement at me. "You're really getting serious about this whole thing, aren't you?"

"Don't laugh at me, Sam. Of course I am serious.
And I do hope he has a perfectly miserable trip."

We read the news items from time to time of Mr.
Pinchot and his small group of followers traveling
from Valdez to Seward, across to the Kenai Peninsula.
They brought no solutions to the problems the people
wanted to discuss with them and created new ones as
they went. The people were turning close-mouthed
and hostile, and I think Mr. Pinchot was beginning
to get a little nervous. The tension seemed to be worse
in the Kenai, and I wondered if he was beginning to
regret having that portion of the trip ahead of him.

It seemed as though Mr. Pinchot's visit was all that
the men could talk about when they collected in the
bar in the evenings. Though there was a deep worry
among them, on the surface they joked about the head

of the Bureau of Forestry and the problems that seemed to constantly plague this man who professed to be a seasoned outdoorsman.

One evening the door opened, bringing in a burst of cold wind and a new source of news. A parka-clad prospector stomped the light snow off his boots before he joined the other men.

Abe set a glass out on the bar. "Hey, Track, where you been? Haven't see you for a while."

The man dropped his parka across a chair and pulled off his heavy gloves. "Been down the line—in Katalla for a week or two."

"Katalla, huh?" Another man spoke up. "You must a been there when Pinchot was visiting that area. How'd it go?"

"You can sure as hell bet it wasn't what he expected." Track laughed as he reached for the glass. "They had quite a party waiting for him."

Sam frowned. "What do you mean? Things didn't get out of hand, did they?"

"Nah, nothing like that. You know the folks down there, Sam. Sure, they was all riled up, and they had a right to be, but they didn't want to hurt the guy. I mean, nothing serious like hanging him. Some of them got a little loud, but mostly they was reasonable. In fact, they went just the other way. They had a hell of a party waiting for him."

The men drew closer, listening, and Track took his time, enjoying being the center of attention, drawing the story out as he provided the details.

"You know how several of the businesses went belly up when they knew the railroad wasn't going to run out of there. Well, folks went around to all the empty storefronts and put up signs that said 'Out of Business—Closed Down by Conservationists.' Then the restaurant hung up a sign that said all their meals would be served cold 'cause they had no fuel for the stove. The newspaper took it up and printed an obituary. It said: 'DIED—ALASKA. CAUSE OF DEATH—TOO MUCH CONSERVATION. THE FUNERAL SPEECH TO BE GIVEN BY THE EXECUTIONER, GIFFORD PINCHOT.' The whole thing turned into a local holiday. Everyone had a lot of fun."

"Must have kind of confused the visitors, didn't it?" Abe asked.

"Well, don't rightly know what they expected, but it sure as hell wasn't what they met up with. I think they came over maybe expecting trouble, because Pinchot brought four men with him. Two of them he called guides, which was kind of confusing because he's supposed to be an ex-ranger, and you ain't going to get too far lost when the only route in there is on the boat. Don't know just what the other two men were there for. They just sort of stayed in the background like maybe they was ready to step in if anybody started anything. It was pretty easy to tell that Pinchot carried a gun too, even if it was hidden under his coat."

Sam frowned. "The thing didn't get out of hand, did it?"

"Hell, Sam, those men are smarter than that. They were havin' fun, not lookin' for a fight. You ought to see what the restaurant had on the menu that day. Porcupine soup, porcupine mulligan, and porcupine pie for dessert. Best they could do if there was no hunting in a national forest, they said."

"Must have been pretty confusing," Sam agreed.

Track laughed, remembering some new tidbit of news. "Oh, yeah. Right after he got there, Pinchot had the telegraph operator send a wire to his wife. He wanted to get word to her that he had arrived safe. Course telegrams are supposed to be confidential, but the wireless clerk got so tickled over it, he sort of repeated it to a couple of others and pretty soon the whole town knew and was laughing about it."

I followed Maury out into the kitchen where she was baking a new batch of doughnuts in case the men wanted something to snack on later.

"Wonder what all of this is going to come to." I sighed, rolling up my sleeves so I could start washing the mixing bowl.

"Probably nothing," she answered sarcastically. "The men know it too but they just keep hoping. Guess the only one not too upset about the whole thing is Abe. He don't say much but he hates to see so many people moving in. That's why he came here in the first place. To get away from people."

"But surely he's not in favor of such tight restrictions, is he?" I asked in surprise.

"No. Couldn't call Abe a conservationist like those other men. He believes in protecting the land, but like in most issues that are being fought, there's a happy medium somewhere in between the two. This is a hell of a big country up here. There ought to be room to hunt and do some trapping—even do what mining they want to do—without the government stepping in, acting like they're destroying everything in sight."

"Have you heard them talking anymore about the Miles glacier?" I asked her. "I haven't heard anything since Adolph Gunderson was up here last year."

Maury shook her head. "I heard them saying that

they been measuring it again this year but so far it isn't moving ahead. Think I heard them say it had even receded some. It's a crazy country we live in up here, Nora. Who knows what will happen next?"

It was about that time that I learned of other visitors that would be coming to Alaska. While they didn't attract the attention that Mr. Pinchot and his group received, to me it was an earth-shaking event.

Maury picked up the mail when she went into Walker's General Store for some supplies. The envelope was addressed to me, in my father's round, firm handwriting. Though I hadn't heard from him directly in years, I recognized his penmanship instantly. My fingers trembled as I tore open the side and slipped the folded letter out.

At last! He had written to me!

At the words on the paper, my knees weakened and I dropped into a chair. Maury looked at my white, shaken face and asked what was wrong, fearing the worst. I couldn't answer. I just handed her the page to read for herself.

September 10

My dear Nora,

It is time I saw my grandchild. Since you do not seem to be making any plans in the immediate future to bring her to me, I shall be leaving in three weeks to travel North.

I trust you will have accommodations for us at your lodge. Your Aunt Margaret and brother Tom will be accompanying me.

I have booked accommodations on the *Valiant* to Cordova. We shall take the train from there to Chitina.

Please have my son-in-law meet the train and convey us the rest of the way to the lodge.

> Regards,
> Your father
> Martin P. Crandall

I watched impatiently for Sam that evening, going often to the window to peer up the road. When I finally caught sight of him, I snatched my coat off the hook and flew out the door to meet him, waving my letter.

"Sam, you'll never guess who this letter is from! They're coming here—here to Ravenwood! Can you believe it!"

He caught me in his arms, stopping the flow of excited words by kissing me soundly on the mouth. I scrambled to get loose, my letter still foremost on my mind. "They'll be here in just a couple of weeks!"

"Slow down!" he insisted. "If you don't quit waving it about that way and talk so I can understand you, I'll never know who wrote the letter. And if I don't know who wrote it, how will I know who's coming to visit? Come on, girl, kiss your husband hello properly, and then let's go back inside out of the cold first, before we read it."

Once indoors, Mandy claimed his full attention. Jabbering in her own special language, complete with the blowing of bubbles, she demanded that he hold her and laughed in delight when he swooped her up into the air.

Impatient with my news, I took his coat from him and hung it on the rack. I felt a little as though he were putting me off deliberately, making me try to control my excitement. Then finally he put Mandy down on the blanket where her toys were spread and pulled me down beside him, as he reached for the letter I still held in my hand.

I waited while he read it, watching his face closely for signs of what he might be thinking.

"That's good," he said, putting the letter aside. "It's time you saw your father again. And I think he'll enjoy his trip up here."

"But Sam, what will I do?" I wailed. "How will I get ready in time?"

"Ready?" Sam laid his hands over mine. "What's to do to get ready?" He was so calm about the whole thing! "You're a good housekeeper. You always have things clean and polished. We have an abundant food supply laid by. What else do you need to do?"

I settled back, quiet for a moment, then I had another thought. "Where will I put them?" I asked, biting my lip.

Sam laughed at me then. "Now you're being foolish. With a whole lodge at your disposal, you're worrying about a silly thing like that?"

"But Sam, you don't understand. You've never seen their home. The big rooms . . . the splendid furnishings . . . the servants! They'll consider this as really 'roughing it'—like pioneers." I put my hand over my mouth. "What am I going to do?"

"If that is how they will see it, I can only say that it will be an interesting experience for them. It will be good for them."

"You are so practical. I love you, Sam." I settled

back again, my thoughts busy. Suddenly I began to giggle.

"What's so funny?" he asked.

"Oh, just thinking. I'm so glad you put in that generator and that we have an indoor bathroom, with running water! Somehow I just cannot stretch my imagination far enough to see my Aunt Margaret, in her silk dress with lace trim and her patent slippers, picking her way down the path to the outhouse. That is just too funny! Wait until you meet her and you'll see what I mean!" With that I went off into another burst of nervous giggles.

That night I couldn't go to sleep. I tossed and turned, my mind going from one thing to another. Finally Sam reached over and drew me into his arms.

"Please, Nora, neither of us is getting any rest this way. It's going to be another three weeks before they get here. By that time, at the rate you are going, you'll have both of us ready for a straitjacket."

"I'm sorry," I whispered. "It's just that I want them to like Ravenwood. . . . Oh, Sam, I want so much for them to like it here!"

His voice was so calm, so reassuring in the darkness. "They will. We'll bring Mandy's bed back into our room and set the brass bed up in hers. You can fix the room up for your aunt. She will be very comfortable in there. Save the two rooms at the quiet end of the hall upstairs for your father and brother. Now, see how easy it is? Go to sleep!"

I spent the next two weeks in a frenzy of activity. I sewed new curtains, new pinafores for Mandy, aprons for Maury and me. I cleaned, polished, and scrubbed until everything gleamed, and then I stood back and tried to see things through the eyes of a stranger. I wasn't eating right and lost weight. I drank too much coffee.

Finally Maury had enough.

"Are you that ashamed of all of us here, and of Ravenwood, that things aren't acceptable as they are? I feel like I have to straighten up and pass inspection every time you look at me. I had really looked forward to meeting them, because they're your folks. But if things here the way they are ain't good enough for them, I ain't so damned sure anymore that I want to meet them."

When Maury squared off, she knew how to direct her punches so that they landed where they hurt.

I put my arms around her, tears in my eyes. "I'm sorry. Honest I am. Ashamed? Never! Guess I really let my nerves get out of hand, didn't I. Forgive me, Maury?"

"Then just back off and simmer down, girl. Lord, it's a wonder that Sam has nerve to come home in the evening, the way things been around here lately."

Maury's lecture worked, where Sam's quiet reassurances had failed. We almost had a normal week before their arrival.

It seemed that winter was moving in much earlier than usual that year. Maybe it was because I wanted things to be so right when my family came to visit that I seemed to notice more the way the high winds whipped around the corner of the building, tearing at the shakes on the roof. The snow even seemed to be deeper, drifting across the roads and making travel difficult.

Sam laughed at my complaints against the weather. "Why, Nora! I thought you wanted it this way."

I turned to him in surprise. "What makes you say a thing like that?"

"Didn't you wish for Mr. Pinchot to have a miserable trip so he would appreciate our need for a railroad more?"

I *had* forgotten. "I've changed my mind," I answered. "I don't want my father's first visit up here to be plagued with bad weather the whole time. How long do you suppose this is going to last?"

Sam shrugged. "I imagine Pinchot and his group are wondering the same thing. He's already called off his trip up into the Matanuska coal fields. For an outdoorsman that he says he is, he's not too willing to venture up too far into the bush. The senator went on without him."

I reached across the table to hand a cup of hot coffee to Sam. I felt the oddest sensation for a moment, as though I were a little faint. Then I realized the coffee in the cup was moving around as though someone had jarred the table. I stared at Sam, not able to understand what was going on. "Sam, what is it?"

He grinned across at me. "You should have recognized that, Nora, after living in San Francisco. It's over now. The center must have been a ways from here, up in the mountains."

"You mean it was an *earthquake*?"

He stood up and reached for his coat. "I better get up to the mines. Something like that could raise havoc up there right now." He bent to kiss me. "Don't look so worried, honey. It wasn't hard enough to do any damage around here. I'll be back as soon as I can."

I waited anxiously for Sam to return that night to hear what he had learned about the earthquake.

"Not too much damage up around the mines," he

tried to reassure me. "Someone said that Mount Wrangell erupted. They saw clouds of black smoke coming out of the top of it. It's the railroad crews that have got the big worry. Evidently the quake broke loose a lake that had formed in one of the glaciers quite a ways down the line from here. It's spilled over and caused a lot of hell, taking out a railroad bridge and quite a stretch of track along with it."

I stood at the window looking out at the freezing rain beating against the glass, my face white with worry. "What about Father, Sam? What's going to happen?"

He came up behind me and put his hands on my shoulders. "He'll be all right, honey. He is still on the ocean, not even near here yet. If the track isn't repaired by the time he gets here, he will just take lodging in Cordova and wait." He turned me around so that I faced him. "They aren't going to start a train out from there unless they're sure it will get through, not when they are carrying passengers. Try not to worry so all of the time."

"But what a way to greet visitors!" I answered.

Sam grinned. "I imagine that's what Pinchot and his group are thinking. They're on their way up to the mines."

I turned back to look out of the window. The whole thing was a little terrifying, even to us who were used to the country and what it could do. I wondered what it must be like out on the ocean during this storm. This gave me a new worry. What if the seas were so high that my father's ship would be in danger? And, if he reached Cordova, what about the rest of the journey? The trestles washing away, the high winds? I heard a story about one canyon where the winds always were strong. They hung an iron chain on the last support of the bridge. If the chain stood out straight, the winds were too high for the train to venture out onto the bridge. Sam had laughed at my look of horror when I heard the story, and I have no idea if it is true or not.

From all reports Mr. Pinchot was still having a most unpleasant trip. We read where during one of the stronger gales his boat was weatherbound on a mud flat for several days. I'm sure he was eagerly awaiting the end of his trip, when he would be able to leave these people and this country with its miserable weather.

He was caught in several open debates. The people wanted answers and he attempted to define the reasoning behind what he and the government did. Everyone felt that when he debated the coal issue, he floundered badly, not sure of his facts. With Alaskans still bitter about the national forest boundaries, he insisted that they were established to protect us—to save the timber because it was going to be needed at some future date for local building.

And so the storms raged on, both on the debate stands and in the skies. One of the boats in the group being used to transfer the visitors from Cordova to Seward and back to Katalla was smashed to pieces in the angry waves. The boat that Mr. Pinchot was on wasn't damaged, but it was tossed about so roughly that I imagine he was badly frightened. The storm was severe enough that they beached the boat and continued the journey by mushing back overland. The newspapers had a field day with that one! Their headlines read: "PINCHOT CANNOT WALK ON ANGRY WATERS AFTER ALL."

Gradually the storm subsided, the waves losing force until they were docile. Though the temperatures remained cold, the sun came out, making our whole country look as though it were covered knee deep in sparkling white sugar. I stood at the window and watched the black-and-white magpies as they flashed through the trees and listened to the harsh call of the black raven. The only blemish on the fresh covering of snow was the single tracks of some wild animal where it had come up toward the back door, checking for scraps.

Sam had kept track of shipping arrivals and departures, so he knew approximately what day to expect our visitors. A message sent through the railroad dispatch office to Sam told us which train to meet.

The day had finally arrived.

Sam went alone to pick them up because there would not be enough room in the buggy for all of us on the return trip. Abe followed with the wagon to bring back their trunks. Despite the storms, the roads were passable and the temperature hovered just above zero, which wasn't too cold if you were dressed for it.

It seemed as though Sam was gone forever. I watched nervously from the window, unable to settle down to any one thing for very long. Maury didn't say anything, but she watched me with amusement and did what she could to keep Mandy entertained.

When I finally saw the buggy turn into the yard, I pulled on my parka and went out to meet them, walking a little slowly at first, not quite sure of how to greet them.

Father was the first one to step down from the buggy. We stood looking at each other for a long moment. I saw new lines in his face that I had not remembered, a touch more gray in his hair. His eyes were searching mine as we sought a bridge across the gulf between us.

"Hello, Father." I spoke at last, my voice soft with emotion. "Welcome to Ravenwood."

He held out his arms to me and I flew into them. He held me close, not saying anything as a tear slipped down his cheek and landed in my hair.

Sam jumped down lightly and came around to lift Aunt Margaret from the buggy, setting her dainty feet on the snowy path. Tom had been riding in the wagon with Abe, and they pulled into the yard behind the buggy. He jumped down, ran to me, and with a whoop lifted me clear off the ground, swinging me around and planting a kiss firmly on my cheek.

"Hello, little sister! So this is your Ravenwood that stole you away from us! I love it! Every bit of it! What a country!"

We started for the house, all trying to talk at once, when I looked back and saw poor Aunt Margaret holding her skirts up, helplessly floundering in the slippery snow. Sam noticed too, and he went back and scooped her up in his arms and carried her inside. He set her down on the floor in front of the fireplace, where she stood sputtering, her lacy hat tipped down over one eye, her hairdo askew, snow dripping from the edges of her skirts.

I ran to her, laughing at the spectacle she made. "Welcome to Ravenwood, dear aunt!" I hugged her warmly as I helped her with her wraps.

My father and brother were standing in front of the fireplace, drawing off their gloves and heavy coats. Tom was looking about the big room with lively interest. Father seemed unaware of us for a moment as he glanced around, almost as though he were seeking out reminders of an old memory, something to show that she had been here, had lived within these walls. I knew what he was thinking by the sadness in his eyes.

Aunt Margaret's eyes darted around like a tiny lost sparrow, taking in the tables set about, the bar built across one end of the room, tipping her head to peer down the passageway toward the kitchen.

"This is where you live, Nora? In a—a barroom?" she asked hesitantly.

"Yes," I answered without any apology. "Our living quarters—a sitting room and the bedrooms—are in the back, through that door behind the bar. This is the main room—or the barroom—yes, and it is the dining room too. The kitchen is off back through there. There are eight rooms upstairs, for the lodgers."

Abe and Sam had brought the trunks in, so I left the men together and took my aunt back to the bedroom where she would be staying. I knew she would be tired, that she would want to freshen up and maybe rest a bit before dinner. The long trip on the ocean must have been a devastating experience for her, without a chance to rest properly before making the journey inland to the lodge. After showing her around, I kissed her lightly on her soft, powdered cheek and left her, to go back out and join the men again.

Mandy had escaped from the kitchen and sat perched quite at ease on her grandfather's knee. She was looking up into his face, seriously watching him as the men talked together comfortably. I saw that Abe was with them so I went to get Maury, to introduce her.

Maury and I had planned that first evening meal with care. The long table in front of the fireplace had a freshly ironed white table cloth and was set for seven, plus a smaller plate for Mandy. I insisted that Abe and Maury join us, though Maury had protested that the first evening we should be alone.

My aunt drew me to one side and said quite discreetly, "Really, Nora! What has happened to your careful training? Do your servants always eat at the same table?"

"No, Aunt Margaret. Not servants. Very dear friends. Part of my family here," I answered.

The dinner was delicious: soup that had simmered on the back of the stove most of the day, until all of the flavors were blended together; a cabbage salad, made with a cabbage I had grown in the garden; thick, juicy caribou steaks that nearly filled each plate, still sizzling from the stove. There were mashed potatoes and fresh carrots, tall, fluffy biscuits, and wild currant jellies. Maury produced a deep, juicy blueberry pie for dessert.

Poor Aunt Margaret picked daintily at her food, as though completely overwhelmed at the heartiness of it all. My father and Tom ate with gusto.

"Must be the climate here," my father said. "Certainly does give a man an appetite!" Sam winked at me across the table and I smiled happily.

As we ate, we listened to our visitors describe their trip. Tom was jubilant in his description of coming into Prince William Sound and seeing the glaciers, the mountains, the waterfalls, for the first time. He told of the seals that basked on the rocks, the birds that followed the ship as it nosed its way into the harbor. I remembered when I had first come into this country, and I smiled to myself.

I asked about the weather during the sea voyage

and whether any of the storms that we had had so recently affected their trip.

"Absolutely perfect!" my father answered. "It was great sailing weather. Enjoyed every minute of it!"

"Really, Martin!" My aunt frowned at him. "How can you say such a thing? I could hardly leave my cabin the entire trip. I certainly was not able to eat." We all exchanged amused glances and hid our smiles.

Mandy refused to be left out of the conversation and chattered away happily, not caring in the least that she was not understood.

I saw my aunt glance nervously from time to time toward the bar at the end of the room, as it began filling with evening customers. Tom watched openly, straining to catch bits of the men's conversation.

Aunt Margaret retired early, understandably exhausted from her travels and all the new experiences. I washed a sleepy Mandy and tucked her into her bed, then went out to rejoin the others. The men were at the bar, talking with the group collected there as easily as though they had been there every evening. I went on by and joined Maury in the kitchen, where she was helping the two women in the final cleaning up.

"Whew!" I said, drawing on a clean apron. "The day's almost over! Well, Maury, that's my family. What do you think?"

"I like them," she answered with her usual directness. "Don't know why you worried so." She wiped her hands and poured us each a cup of coffee. "That Tom is going to fit right in. I overheard him and Abe already talking about doing some hunting and fishing. Your dad seems real interested in Sam and his work here. I don't think you have anything to worry about,

Nora. They are going to get along real good. But your aunt!" She chuckled. "I really love her. She's a game little lady. This whole trip and everything connected with it has got to be pretty confusing to her. You're going to have to have a little patience, but she is going to really enjoy herself."

During the day Father often went to the mines with Sam. He seemed vitally interested in everything that went on, wanting to know every detail, plying Sam with questions. Tom would go with them sometimes, but other times he went fishing or hunting with Abe. He was intrigued with the meat cache, looking like a miniature log cabin on its high stilts, out of reach of prowling animals. He listened to Abe carefully, following his instructions on how to dress the game, proud of any addition he made to the food supply.

There were other times when he just disappeared, finding amusement on his own. I fretted over the evenings he was away, wanting to know where he went.

Sam teased me about it. "You are his sister, not his chaperone. He's a grown man, he's a bachelor, and he's on a vacation. If he gambles some, drinks a little, and should happen to meet a girl or two and have some fun, it's his business, not yours." He turned serious. "Don't worry about Tom. He's a good man, Nora. He controls his life, it doesn't control him."

Tom spent a lot of time playing with Mandy. He would toss her into the air, and she squealed in delight when he settled her on his shoulders for a ride around the room. I watched them and remembered back to another time, another generation, when a little girl delighted in an uncle who played games with her. I smiled at the lovely memory. . . .

* * *

I knew it all must seem terribly strange to Aunt Margaret. I'm sure she felt quite daring to be spending a vacation in a "tavern" in the far North. The way we lived was so different from any life style she had ever been exposed to in the past. She would not bend her own rules, but she tried valiantly to expand them to include some of ours. Discretion and good breeding ruled over her critical tongue most of the time. Other times she looked bewildered and a little lost. She confessed confidentially to Maury that there were times when she felt she did not know her own niece in the slightest, I had changed that much.

She would always dress for dinner, as she firmly believed a lady should do, and then she would sit in the barroom with Maury and me as we listened to the men talk. Maury and I nearly suffocated with hidden laughter one evening when Logan came to call, wanting to meet my family, and stayed to spend the evening flirting outrageously with Aunt Margaret. She grew a little flustered with the attention, and when she finally excused herself to go to her room for the night she had soft pink roses in her cheeks and a twinkle in her eye that I could never remember seeing there before.

The men preferred to lounge in the barroom in the evening rather than do their visiting in our sitting room. Father liked to listen to the prospectors and the trappers talk. He plied Sam with questions, and not only did Sam not seem to mind answering them, he showed a certain pride as he explained our country. Father's main interest was shipping, of course, and they talked of the available shipping ports into Alaska. I listened to them with half an ear as I sat sewing.

"The scenery is beautiful—some of the finest you'll

find anywhere in the world," Sam was saying. "And
it is also the hardest to get to. The fishing is excellent.
Can't be beat anywhere. There are some pretty large
canneries going up, and they have a good chance of
succeeding. The fishing industry should boom as the
country grows. The real drawback up here is that only
a very few potentially good seaports exist. The rivers
run heavy with glacier silt, changing their beds, filling
in and narrowing channels. They're constantly shifting
and changing the shorelines. We have some of the
highest tides in the world, and there is a tremendous
force working when the tides change. It is hard to
imagine until you've seen it. When the ice goes out
during the spring breakup, it takes everything in its
path with it, bringing down more silt and debris—
including a few railroad trestles too," he added with
a smile. "There are not too many places a large ship
can get in close enough to unload right onto a dock.
Some say I'm wrong, but my guess is that Valdez will
eventually be the only real good remaining seaport
available where a ship can unload and have transportation for freight on into the interior."

Father sat drawing on his cigar thoughtfully, studying the flames in the fireplace, but I knew he was
absorbing every word Sam was saying.

Sam was in a reminiscent mood, encouraged by his
listeners. "When I came up here the first time, I was
about sixteen. Valdez was just a collection of rough
log cabins and tents overrun with every sort of half-
starved riff-raff you can imagine. That was the winter
just before the turn of the century. Boy, that was a
bad one! More snow than usual and the temperatures
below zero most of the time. Seems like the wind was
always blowing too, driving the cold right into the

heart of you. Think I remember the wind most of all.
All those poor devils up in the gold fields got snowed
out. They ran out of supplies, and it didn't matter if
they had found any gold—it didn't do them any good
up there—there was no place to buy supplies or warm
lodging. There were a lot of desperate men, and they
were all converging down through this country, trying
to get out. The only way down at that time was across
the Valdez glacier, and it was closed in with the blizzards. The snow was so deep they couldn't see the
crevasses and the temperatures were way below zero—
forty, fifty below, maybe worse. A few went ahead
and tried it anyway, at first. Then as the food ran out,
a panic just sort of took hold of the rest of them until
no one was thinking straight. I guess they all just
figured that if they were to stay where they were they
would either starve to death or freeze to death no
matter what they did, so they might as well go ahead
and take their chances. And they tried to make it down
across the glacier in the worst part of the winter."
Sam shook his head thoughtfully. "There weren't too
many of them that made it. The ones that did were a
sorry lot. I can still remember their faces—mental cases,
most of them. They had no money, no food, and their
eyes were haunted by the tales of the glacier demons
they said they had seen." Sam stared into the fire, as
though seeing it all again in the dancing flames.

I sat up and listened intently. I had never heard Sam
talk like this before.

"What happened then, Sam?" Father gently urged
him to continue. There was a hush in the room, for
others were listening too.

"There were several religious groups. They did what
they could, and between them and the Pacific Steam

Whaling Company, which furnished a whaler, they got
the ones that still lived passage outside. The ones that
would go, that is. There were still the diehards that
insisted on going back to their claims in the spring. A
lot of men died, even after they managed to reach
Valdez. The military was there trying to help too, and
they staked out a graveyard. It had almost as many
residents at the town did."

"What about you?" Father was studying Sam's face.
"You were pretty young. What were you doing up
there?"

"My folks were from the East. When Dad left to
come up here, Mother preferred to stay there with her
family. She just wasn't the pioneering sort. When I
came of age I received some money so I came looking
for Dad."

"Did you find him, Sam?" I asked. I had never heard
Sam mention his parents before.

"No. He was one of the poor devils who didn't
make it down the glacier."

No one in the room said anything; we were all waiting for him to continue.

"I went back East and finished my schooling. I
carried a picture of what I had seen, not able to forget
the stories I heard of the gold and the copper the
men had found, the persistent way the men told of
what lay beyond the glaciers. My mother died soon
afterward from an illness, and I was alone. I decided
to get a degree in mining. When I came back six years
later, Valdez had turned into just about the most important city in Alaska. I couldn't believe so many
changes—so much could happen in so few years! Houses
were going up everywhere—not just log cabins, but
nice homes, made out of sawed lumber. They had

electricity by now, and telephones, and a telegraph communication outside to Seattle. There were stores, a butcher shop, a couple of hotels, even a fire station with a fire wagon. A schoolhouse had been built. Men were bringing in their families or starting new ones. All this happened in three, four, five years."

Father was leaning forward, intent on the conversation. "Evidently there were others who were as interested as you. But something had to trigger growth like that. What was it?"

"Copper. Men came up here and went up into the interior looking for gold and they found some of the richest copper fields in the world. Those men who came back down that glacier that winter brought with them almost unbelievable stories of copper veins. A few of them had even lugged samples back with them. They were persistent, and they showed the samples and told their stories until finally they got someone to listen.

"The stories were pretty wild, hard to believe, but gradually they got what they wanted. Several groups of men got together and formed companies and backed the prospectors, sending engineers back with them. What followed next must have been a pretty wild time. Every man was trying to get there first. There were races out of town, claim jumping, stakes getting pulled up and moved in the dark, tents got burned. There were even a few shootings. Amazing what greed will do to an otherwise honest man."

Sam paused again. Then: "Copper country potential was big—bigger than anyone realized. As I said, different men formed groups—companies—and invested in the mining. Garth Williams, Jim Crandall's lawyer, was one of them. I wasn't wealthy, but I had a few dollars and bought in on some of the stock with Williams."

Father asked pointedly, "But copper or gold—either one for that matter—is no good in the ground. It has to be able to be transported out. Is that when the railroad was built?"

"Yes. But it wasn't that simple. There must have been forty or fifty railroad corporations that made some sort of attempt or at least showed some interest in building a line. The government blocked them by withdrawing subsidies or grants. When some still showed interest, the government set a time limit on completion, and imposed a tax: one hundred dollars for every operating mile, upon completion! That discouraged the most of them. It was unrealistic, no way it could be met.

"Out of all of those that displayed an interest, only five actually did start any building, but they couldn't handle the combination of the weather, the rugged terrain, and the battle the government gave them. Congress was dead set against a railroad being built in Alaska. You might say it forbade a railroad in Alaska."

"But one is here—we rode on it."

Sam nodded. "The CR and NR—the Copper River and Northwestern Railway. I had the good fortune once to meet Michael Heney. He was an engineer—really knew his business. He's built other lines up here—the one out of Skagway, I believe. He's a tough man, with the guts it took plus a lot of knowledge and commonsense to back it up. He got the job done when no one else could handle it. He died just before it was completed, but by then it was close enough that they could finish it without him."

"There must have been a lot of money behind him."

"Right. He was only the engineer. He had employers, and they had the money. The CR and NR is owned by the Guggenheim and Morgan Syndicate. They hold a lot of stock in fish canneries, as well as the gold and copper fields—yes, a lot of money—and they had a private ownership, which was to their advantage in a way. And yet it was almost their ruin."

"What do you mean?"

"Some folks thought they were out to control the whole territory of Alaska. Guess it did kind of look like it. Well, you know what a dirty word 'monopoly' is. And people started talking that way. With Congress up for an election before long, it kind of upset the boys in Washington, and the government gave them as hard a battle as did the glaciers, the blizzards, and the spring breakups that ripped out the work they had done." Sam shook off the mood. "But it got built. And what a mushroom followed behind it! Ask Nora. When she came up here, that town down the road was just a few cabins and a small store. Remember the day the railroad reached Chitina and then came up on the line to the mines?"

I took up the story. "Oh, yes, how could anyone forget! Uncle Jim had built this place as a hunting and fishing lodge. I'm not sure just what his idea was—to have guides, or what. When the railroad came, and the men came to work in the mines, Ravenwood felt it too. We filled the rooms upstairs, and Maury and I could not keep up with the work. That was when I hired the other help. The day the railroad came through there was some pretty wild celebrating! Along with the good, there was some bad too, of course. There always is. We got our share of the riff-raff. Some pretty unsavory characters hung around." I shuddered, remembering the two drifters I had met on the trail. I turned to Sam with a smile. "Even then Sam always seemed to be there when I needed him. That is, until one day I thought I had let him slip away. I thought someone else had stolen him right out from under my nose." I laughed merrily at the memory. "I solved it by asking him to marry me!"

Aunt Margaret gasped in disbelief, as Sam and I laughed together.

"Yep," Sam answered, his eyes twinkling. "Real fiery she was. I didn't stand a chance."

When Maury and Abe joined in our laughter, Aunt Margaret looked from one to the other of us with such disapproval that we laughed all the harder.

By this time Samantha had fallen asleep, and I started to pick her up to carry her to bed. Tom took her from my arms. "Here, let me," he said. "What an innocent she is when she's asleep." Mandy stirred only slightly, giving a little sigh and curling closer to Tom's chest. As I followed Tom across the room I heard my father ask Sam if he could somehow arrange a visit to the Kennicott copper mines, north of us.

Tom waited while I tucked her down under the covers, looking down at her with tenderness. "You are happy, aren't you, Nora?" he asked.

"Doesn't it show? Yes, I have a good life. I'm happy here at Ravenwood. Sam is a good husband. I love him, Tom. You and I haven't had any time alone since you have been here, have we?" I kept my voice low so I wouldn't wake Mandy. "I've missed you. We were always so close as children. But then it seemed we just grew away from each other as we got older."

"I know. I'm sorry I didn't write sooner. I wanted to."

"You haven't asked me anything about our mother. Can't we talk about it?"

"Is there anything to say, Nora? Isn't it better to just let the past alone and not bring up old hurts again?"

"No. I disagree with you. I think we should talk about it. Our mother found a very special love with Jim Crandall. Something so rare that few ever find it in a whole lifetime. To insist on bringing small children with her up into this country at that time would have been foolhardy. Tom, she loved Jim, but she respected our father. She only wanted her freedom; she didn't want to destroy him by taking away everything that was precious to him, and she would have, if she had taken us with her. She knew that if she left us behind, we would be well taken care of and loved. She wanted what was best for us and thought she was doing right by entrusting us to our father. It hurt her so to discover later that we thought she had died."

"You are able to justify growing up without her?" he asked. "You have found a way to forgive what happened?"

"Not only to forgive, but to understand," I answered. "I only hope that someday you will be able to understand too. She loved us very much. So did our father. We couldn't live with both of them, so she chose to leave us with Father. She didn't desert us, Tom, she left us where we would have the best advantages for a future. It was because she loved us and respected Father that she agreed to leave us behind."

I paused then. Tom was quiet, mulling over my words.

"Tell me, have you seen Tony lately?" I asked after a moment, trying to sound casual.

"How can you ask? Are you still thinking of him? After all you have here? I can't believe it."

"I only wanted to know if you had seen him, that's all. I wondered if he is doing all right now, if he is painting. There's nothing wrong in my asking. I hope he is happy—doing well. There are a lot of memories, Tom. Just because most of them are painful doesn't stop them from existing."

"No. I haven't heard anything beyond what I wrote to you in that one letter. I don't know where he is now." With that Tom turned and went back out to join the others, and I followed.

I felt sorry for my aunt, confined as she was to the lodge. I remembered my first winter here and knew only too well how the long periods of darkness could close in and smother a person. The few hours of daylight were just not enough, even when someone stayed busy. It must be very depressing for her. I promised myself to arrange my work better, so that I could spend more time with her, talking about things she would be interested in—listening to her tell of things she wanted to talk about.

I found her in our sitting room, listlessly thumbing through a magazine. I greeted her with a kiss and showed her my sewing machine.

"I am happy to see that you are sewing, my dear," she said. "I want to compliment you on the dress you are wearing." She reached out and lightly touched one of the ruffles I had added around the neckline. "It looks so nice on you. So feminine. You have no idea how distressed I was yesterday, when I happened to glance out of the window. I saw you out there, in the snow, in . . . men's trousers!" The last words were in a shocked whisper. I turned my head to hide a smile. I wonder what she would have said if I told her that those trousers had been a part of my wedding trousseau, what I wore when Sam and I made our escape to hike up to that wonderful cabin by the lake.

"Really!" she reprimanded. "If you must insist on living up here among savages, it does not give you the excuse to allow yourself to become coarse."

I disregarded the remark and went on to show her the dresses I had been making for Mandy. She asked if I minded if she worked some embroidery on the smocks, and I handed them to her gladly. I knew she would enjoy doing this for Mandy, and it would help to make the days go faster for her.

My father left with Sam on a two-day excursion to explore the larger mine sites. They were to stay overnight in company housing and return the next day, giving them more time for Father to see the operation. Tom and Abe were making ready for a hunting trip to restock the meat cache. Maury and I decided that with all of them gone, it would be a good time to take Aunt Margaret on a tour of the town. She had not been away from the lodge since her arrival.

The temperature was a little below zero, but the road had been cleared and the sun was out. It would be a good day for our trip. Abe hooked the sleigh up and harnessed the horse for us before he left. We laid out warm fur robes to put across our knees during the ride. Aunt Margaret allowed us to pull a pair of my fur-lined boots onto her dainty feet, but when it came to offering a pair of woolen underwear and a mackinaw, she would have none of it.

"Never! I shall never be reduced to wearing men's garments! I have my fur coat. It shall do nicely." Maury and I looked helplessly at each other as she pinned on a smart little bonnet that looked absolutely ridiculous for our trek to town. I laid out a woolen shawl, knowing all too well that before we went very far she would be only too willing to draw it up to protect her ears from the cold.

We left Samantha at home, in the care of one of the girls who worked for us. It was far too cold to take her out, no matter how she protested.

Our first stop was Walker's General Store and Hardware. I was certain Aunt Margaret had never been in a store quite like this, and I was right. She was fascinated with everything she saw. Things that were everyday to us, a necessary part of our existence, were curios to her. She went up and down the rows of leather, furs, Indian beadwork, stopping to examine the traps hanging on the wall, the scrubboards, the boots, the snowshoes, the heavy winter clothing, all mixed in with medicines and groceries.

She was a little nervous about the three Indians sitting around the pot-belly stove in the center of the room, and she walked wide circles around them, watching them out of the corner of her eye, taking in their strange dress, listening to their guttural, foreign-sounding conversation. I am sure they were just as curious about her—this strange little lady so obviously from a big city outside somewhere.

Mrs. Walker brought out some Indian art and jewelry, and Aunt Margaret was intrigued with the unusual designs. She purchased several pieces of the

delicate scrimshawed ivory and a carving small enough
to fit in her handbag. She drank coffee offered to her
by Mrs. Walker in a thick, heavy mug and chatted as
easily as if she were used to shopping there every week.

We walked a short distance along the board side-
walk, as we wanted her to see the bakery and the candy
store. Then we took her into the assay office so she
could see the samples of copper ore and the delicate
scales used to weigh the gold. Gordon Wright, the
assayer, was very obliging, explaining his work to her
and showing the precious ores. He let her hold several
gold nuggets in her hand and examine them closely.

We returned home while the sun was still out, careful
that we didn't keep Aunt Margaret out in the cold, dry
air too long. I had played with the idea of pointing out
the small church with the cemetery where my mother
and Uncle Jim were buried, along with the tiny grave
that held my first child, but I changed my mind. Aunt
Margaret still had not mentioned my mother's name,
and I felt she still would not be able to understand the
kind of love that had drawn my mother to follow a man
up into the wilds of an unsettled country. I suppose
in her own mind she blamed my mother for Jim
Crandall's break with the rest of the family.

I looked back to where she sat in the buggy with us.
Her cheeks were pink and her eyes danced with her
new adventures. I knew she had never spent such an
afternoon in her life, and I knew she was busy storing
away stories to tell later over tea to her friends in San
Francisco.

I decided that it was best that I leave things as they
were and just let her enjoy the afternoon. Aunt Margaret's knowledge and understanding of the outside

world was too limited for her to conceive of such strong emotions as my mother must have felt. As I thought about it, I felt a little sorry for her and how much she had missed from life.

CHAPTER TWELVE

It was late in the evening when Sam and my father returned from their trip to the Kennicott mines. They were both cold and tired, looking forward to a warm supper. Tom was, as usual, full of energy, waiting impatiently for them to get their coats off and give him an opening to tell of the moose he had shot, and how he and Abe had dressed it and hauled the enormous quarters back on a borrowed dog sled. He was proud of their day's work, and it was hard for him to keep from sounding boastful.

Father, who usually was quiet, preferring to listen to others talk, was irritable with Tom. Now he wanted the floor and wanted Tom to listen to what they had seen on their trip. It was obvious that he had been very much impressed, and he wanted to talk about it.

"Some of the most beautiful country I have ever seen! Spectacular!" he exclaimed as they sat down to eat. "The vein of copper they are mining is up at about five thousand feet—and those mountain walls rise straight up from the valley floor. There's a ledge up there, and they are hanging onto the side of that slope with their teeth. The buildings for the mines are all up there too. You would never believe how they built them if you couldn't see it yourself. The bunkhouses are on rollers, with cables anchoring them into the side of the mountain.

"They brought a sawmill in on a flatbed rail car and set it up, so they are able to saw their own lumber for the buildings right there at the building site.

"The one building that impressed me so is six stories high—and you know how they did it?" He demanded Tom's attention. "They cut benches out of the side of the mountain, like stair steps—one bench for each floor, and the building is built right into the side of the mountain. Amazing!"

"And you stayed up there, right at the mine, overnight?" Tom asked.

"Yes. Sam is acquainted with them and we stayed in the company housing. They have their own housing and offices, and they have just completed a large warehouse for the equipment."

Tom was openly impressed. "What do they use for power?"

"They dammed up the stream. Gave them all of the water they needed, and they built a power plant."

Sam winked at me. Both of us were amused to see Father so talkative, so insistent that everyone listen.

The men took their coffee cups with them to the more comfortable sofas near the fireplace. Sam lit his pipe. Father was still engrossed with his thoughts, his mind busily storing up data.

"Sam, how much ore did that fellow tell us they were hauling out of there?" he asked.

"I'm not sure," Sam answered. "I was looking at some machinery and didn't hear what he told you. But I understand they are capable of producing around seven hundred tons of ore a day right now. They expect to ship out better than sixty thousand tons before the year is out—depending on the weather, of course. Prices are going up all of the time, not holding stable at all right now, but at a rough guess I would say that should be worth somewhere in the neighborhood of thirty-two million."

Father was impressed with figures of that size. Tom took advantage of Father's thoughtful silence to tell of his moose hunt.

Even Aunt Margaret took a turn, wanting them to know they were not the only ones who had done something interesting. She described her shopping trip in detail and brought out the scrimshawed ivory to show.

I left Sam to lock up and check the fires for the night, and I was already in bed when he came in. He sank into the chair and tugged at his boots wearily. "Damn, I'm tired tonight!" He sighed. "My only consolation is knowing that Martin has got to be as worn out as I am. I thought I was in pretty good shape, but he managed to really wear me down. I noticed he went up to bed a little earlier than usual tonight."

"He does seem to be enjoying his visit, doesn't he?" I asked.

"Amazing man," Sam answered, hanging his shirt up on the hook. "He is interested in everything he sees. And, you know, he seems to understand most of it too, even though it has got to be all new to him. He has a remarkable mind for figures."

He groaned as he stretched his aching muscles. I pulled back the covers invitingly.

"Come here, Sam. Lie down and I'll rub your back for you."

Slowly I massaged his shoulders and down across the taut muscles of his back as we softly talked over the happenings of the past two days. I rubbed tiny circles across his temples and gently kissed him on the forehead.

"Feel better?" I whispered.

He sat up quickly and grabbed me in his arms. "Lady, if I felt any better, you wouldn't be able to stand it!"

Roughly he pulled me down beside him. I struggled and fought back, and we rolled and tussled among the bed covers, until I surrendered laughingly, melting into his arms, my responses matching his ardor.

Later, much later, I raised up on one elbow and looked down into his sleeping face. I bent and kissed him gently. "Stay by me always, my darling," I whispered in my mind. "Don't ever leave me. You are the only thing that is real. Without you I am nothing. You are my very life."

Father made several trips back to Valdez, sometimes alone and other times insisting Tom go with him. Among other things he wanted to send cable communications to Paul back in San Francisco, to keep in touch with the demands of the offices there. Each time he returned with his arms full of packages, which he stowed away mysteriously. Christmas was not far away and I guessed that most of the packages would turn up under the tree for Samantha. She had won him over completely.

Laughingly, I had tried to protest against the number of presents he was buying. "Father, you are going to spoil her shamelessly."

He turned my remark aside gruffly. "It is my right as a grandfather," he said. "Parents have to worry about whether a child is being brought up properly without being spoiled. Grandparents have license to do as they please. Besides, how do I know how long it will be before I see her again?"

"I hope that it won't be too many years." I sighed. "She is so fond of you, Father. Perhaps now, after making the trip once, you will come back again. Sam has talked about us coming down to San Francisco too. We meant to, since we first married, but somehow we just never managed to find the time when we could be away."

"You are happy, Nora?"

I nodded. "My only unhappiness was the rift between us my leaving caused when I left to come up here looking for Mother." I saw him turn away, his eyes distant, cutting me off from him, but I continued anyway. I felt it had to be said or it would always remain there as a barrier between us. "Mother didn't hate you, Father. She loved Uncle Jim but she never lost her respect for you. Otherwise she could never have left us behind. She didn't want to hurt you any more than she had to."

"It wasn't her respect that I wanted," he answered sadly. "But I knew I could never hold her when she wanted to leave. If she had taken you with her I don't think I would have wanted to go on living. I would have lost everything that meant anything to me."

I had never seen my father show his feelings so

openly, and I went across the room and put my arms around him. "Then let's bury the old hurts, can't we, Father?"

"It was in the same room that you stood, telling me that you were going. You looked so much like her. . . . It was as though it was all happening all over again. I wanted to talk to you—to tell you so many things—to beg you not to leave. Instead I shouted like a damned fool and drove you even farther away from me. Later anger and pride kept me from writing to you." He turned and looked around the room, his eyes lingering on the bookcases, the comfortable chairs, the needlework on the back of the sofa. "You have no idea what it took for me to come in here—into the home Amelia shared with another man . . . with my brother. To see her things around the room still here to remind me. To have you look so much as she did the last time I saw her."

There were tears in my eyes as I kissed him on the cheek. "But don't you see, Father? There is a difference between us. You haven't lost me. I haven't gone away from you. I am only living in a different place, a different home, but I am still your daughter. I still love you. And there is Sam. He is part of your family now too. And Samantha."

His voice was gruff, embarrassed by the open display of his feelings. "Then don't be scolding me for the gifts I am buying for her." He pushed me gently away from him. "Since I am the only grandparent still living, let me enjoy it. Let me spoil her for Amelia too."

He turned away and went out to look for Sam. I sighed with contentment. At last, in his own way, Father had managed to forgive and to understand, and the breach between us had ended.

* * *

This would be the first Christmas that Mandy would be old enough to understand and enjoy, and we made eager preparations. There was the tree and a large assortment of decorations I had collected over the past few years. Maury was in a flurry of baking. Aunt Margaret pinned on a white apron and joined in, making tiny cookies with dainty frosted designs. In his spare time Abe was busy making a sled for Mandy, and Sam had a small rocking chair, just her size, shipped in from Seattle. Beyond a doubt it was a Christmas we all would remember for many years, with all of us together, except for Paul. There was no doubt also that Mandy was the star. I dreaded to see it end because it also meant that before long our guests would be leaving. I truly hated to see them go.

Mandy was asleep. My aunt had retired for the night too, as tired as Mandy from the day's activities. My father, Tom, and Sam were sitting around the stove in our room, away from the others tonight, deep in conversation. My thoughts were on figures in the ledger as I sat at my desk going over the paperwork.

Sam called to me. "Leave what you are doing there, Nora, and come join us."

"I'm almost finished."

"Nora, please," my father said. "We are having a discussion that you should be a part of."

I looked at Sam. He nodded. I closed the ledger and went over to sit on the arm of his chair.

"My goodness, you all look very serious. What is it you are planning?"

Sam spoke first. "Your father wants to expand his

shipping and import business to include Alaska. He's planning a branch in Valdez."

"In Valdez?" I looked questioningly at father.

He nodded. "I can see a great future there. I like your husband, Nora. I have confidence in him. I have asked him to join the firm."

This was going a little too fast for me. I turned to Sam. "But what about your work at the mines?"

"I can cut my time back, turn it over to a junior engineer for now at least. To begin with I will only be needed in Valdez for a few days each month. Tom will be there all the time."

I looked over to Tom, who was smiling broadly. "Great, huh, Nora?" he said enthusiastically. "I'm going to live in Alaska too."

Muddled, I turned back to Sam. "Ravenwood?"

Sam took my hand. "I promised I would never ask you to give up Ravenwood. At first, while I'm only required to be there a few days at a time, I'll take some sort of temporary lodging. Later, if it develops as we expect it to do, we'll have a home down there. That won't mean giving up Ravenwood—it will just mean that you will have two homes. A home in Valdez for us to go to when I'm working there, but always Ravenwood to come back to."

"And you, Father?" I asked.

"I shall go back to San Francisco. Paul is nearly in complete charge there now. But I am growing older, and tired, and my home is there. I will always keep my hand in it, don't doubt that, but eventually I shall leave the active management to my sons and son-in-law."

"Well." I sighed. "It sounds as though a great deal

of thought has gone into this. Is this what you want, Sam? To gradually work your way out of mining?"

He nodded. "I've given it a lot of thought. I believe the shipping and import business has a sound future. Mines have a way of running dry. But only if you are with me in this, all of the way, Nora. It's your life too that we're talking about."

I looked at each of them slowly, these three most important men in my life, each confident, each strong in his own way. I looked back at Sam and suddenly realized how deeply I loved him. I knew I would follow him anywhere—even away from Ravenwood.

I stood up. "Then, gentlemen, it looks as though a toast is in order. Excuse me while I go and get a very special vintage—hidden away for very special occasions."

Later that night, as I lay in Sam's arms in the drowsy darkness of our bedroom, we talked again about his joining the firm with my father and brothers.

"Do you really feel sure about this, Sam? You aren't doing this for my sake? Thinking it is something I would want you to do?"

"My reasons are my own," he answered. "I admire Martin, and I respect him as a businessman. As we all know, mines are a guessing game. A vein like we're working on now can go on for ten years, or disappear tomorrow. Other times it will lead to a larger vein."

"It is pretty obvious, I think, that the railroad is going to end right where it is. I don't think there is any chance of it going on up to Fairbanks, as was originally planned. There are just too many obstacles in the way.

"I may be making a big mistake. I don't know. The mines may go on for years, the veins of copper rich enough to support continued digging. But I don't honestly see how it would matter. No matter how rich the veins of copper run, if they can't get coal, the mines can't survive."

I lay there, staring into the dark, trying to absorb all that Sam was telling me. It was very hard for me to try to look ahead into the future and see a picture as gloomy for the Copper River country as Sam did. Not for a country as rich as ours. . . . And yet Valdez, which had every qualification to be a major seaport, lost the chance to have the railroad to the interior begin at her docks because of the heavy coal deposits and oil discovered standing in puddles on the ground in Katalla. Katalla lost because of government regulations and opposition that made it impossible to extract the oil or mine the coal. Cordova was finally chosen as the starting place for the railroad—and it did have a good harbor, but without the railroad there was no route to the interior. And if the coal was not allowed to be mined, what would the railroad use for fuel?

Katalla already was showing the effects of the battle. People were moving away, businesses were closing. There was no reason to remain. Cordova was turning to other industry, and if the railroad should fail, the town could survive through its canneries. The salmon industry was just coming into its own and fish processing plants were springing up all through that area.

Not all of Congress was unsympathetic to our cause. One senator, Furnifold McL. Simmons, a Democrat from North Carolina, expressed his opinions in a speech given on the Senate floor. But what was one sympathetic voice among such a strong conservationist group? An annual tax of one hundred dollars a mile for every mile of railroad had been imposed, and this had a staggering effect.

The future development and growth of the Copper River country and its fantastic resources lay in the hands of the U.S. Government and the conservationists.

CHAPTER THIRTEEN

Our guests were gone now: Father and Aunt Margaret to San Francisco, Tom going only as far as Valdez. Once the decision had been made, they were all anxious to put the plans into motion. I was sorry to see them go, but I knew now that we would see each other periodically.

Tom found a building down on the waterfront that suited their purpose perfectly, and the remodeling began immediately. He cabled a list of materials needed and Paul saw that the carpeting, desks, light fixtures, and so on, were all on the next ship north.

Both Tom and Sam were enthusiastic over the progress being made. The new offices were modern, comfortable, and well lighted, designed with a careful thought toward the problems of heating in the winter.

Tom knew the fundamentals of the business very well, and Sam lent his knowledge of the country, the ways of the people in the North, and the problems caused by the weather.

At first Sam would be gone from me only two or three days a month. I stayed behind because I knew the men would be too busy to be any company to me, and it was for such a short time.

My brother had always lived in a large home, with servants taking care of all the details of meals and housekeeping. The small, impersonal hotel room and the eating daily in restaurants soon became an irritation to him. He disliked every part of it. He was unable to relax in the evenings with the sounds of other tenants walking up and down the halls, the scuffling sounds in the night, the lack of privacy.

Soon he found a small, lovely home with two bedrooms. When it was necessary for Sam to be in Valdez, he stayed with Tom. This made things a little easier for the men, especially after Tom hired a middle-aged widow to prepare the meals and tend to the housekeeping.

When they were finally set up and ready for full operation, it became necessary for Sam to spend one full week out of every month in Valdez. It was a very difficult time for me. I felt torn between Sam and Ravenwood. I didn't like being separated from Sam for that long a time, so I often arranged my shopping to match his schedule and would go with him. I felt useful, able to help Tom by redecorating and furnishing his home and overseeing the housekeeping. I fixed up the bedroom that had been set aside for us, adding a desk to give Sam a place to work, a rocker for me to sit and read. It was a comfortable bed-sitting room and became our temporary home away from home.

But while I was there I was always anxious to return to Mandy and Ravenwood. I was unhappy about leaving them behind and yet I missed Sam too much to let him leave without me.

At three years old Samantha was a caution, hard to keep track of, into everything. It took both Maury and me to keep her dresses clean and the tears in her petticoats mended.

One day, while following Abe around out of doors, she found a small baby fox, alone and frightened, near the edge of the woods. Its mother was gone, the victim of some unknown accident or hunter. Abe built a cage and showed Mandy how to feed and care for it. She named it "Saucy" because of its bright eyes, and spent hours in absorbed conversations with her new friend.

Saucy grew healthy and restless under the careful attention, and after a time was almost too large for the cage. Mandy was a little rebellious when Abe explained to her that it was time to turn Saucy loose— that wild things need to be free. Thoughtfully she watched her pet pace restlessly in its cage. We knew she understood when, sorrowfully, she opened the wire door and stood alone with tears in her eyes as she watched her little friend disappear into the woods.

Maury let her help make cookies, and she was always there to lick the frosting spoon. She helped Abe carry in the wood, one stick at a time held in her chubby arms, her short legs walking in Abe's tracks. She would dump her load in the woodbin behind the stove, then straighten up to dust the scratchy bark from her hands and tell Maury, "Okay, you can build up that fire now, me and Abe filled the woodbox for you!"

Evenings when he was home she sat curled in Sam's lap, her head resting on his shoulder, her fingers tracing the words on the pages as he read to her, until her eyes closed and he carried her into her bed. Mandy could not understand why there were nights when her father was away from us, and she would stand at the window, her nose pressed to the cold glass, watching down the road for him.

Occasionally Samantha went up to the mines with Sam, if he was on a routine inspection and only going to be gone a part of the day. It became a familiar sight around town to see Sam, his tall, muscular frame taking long, easy strides, and a pint-sized figure at his side in a gingham pinafore, shoulders back, ponytail bouncing, her small leather boots trying to match his stride.

I tried halfheartedly to intervene a time or two. "Sam, it just isn't . . . well . . . ladylike the way she follows you everywhere." He looked at me with surprise, so I tried to explain. "She is becoming such a tomboy. We—Maury and I—try to teach her manners." I was not doing a very good job of explaining because Sam just looked at me in confusion. Angrily I burst out, "Well, just look at her! She left this morning with her dress and her petticoats starched, her apron clean— and look at her!"

"It's nothing that won't wash off, is it?" he asked, looking a little hurt.

I glanced down at Mandy, who was watching us with interest. "Samantha, go to the kitchen and let Maury know you are back." As she left, I turned to Sam. "Some of it doesn't. You absolutely have no idea. You've got to be more careful when she is with you. Mandy is a very bright child. She picks up things quickly. It's her language, Sam! You wouldn't believe the words she has repeated!"

He tossed back his head and laughed, sounding relieved. "Is that what's bothering you, Nora? You worry too much about her, honey. She's full of life, and healthy, and interested in everything she sees. She may be picking up a few little bad habits here and there, but she'll forget or outgrow them."

Sam learned firsthand what I meant soon after that.

We were in the buggy, going into town. Samantha was on the seat between us, chattering away, neither of us paying too much attention to her. Suddenly she reached over and grabbed the buggy whip, switching it toward the slow-moving horse's backside.

"Ged up, ol' son-a-bitch!" she shouted in her shrill childish voice.

"Samantha!" I chastised in my most commanding tone.

"That's what Dad says, when he wants that pokey old horse to go faster," she answered calmly, her hazel eyes full of innocence.

I glared fiercely over the top of her head at Sam, and he turned away, but not before I saw his broad grin and his face turn a dull brick red.

Over the years Sam had staked a number of the prospectors who searched the hills for gold. Sometimes it was a total loss, and he never saw his money or the man again. A few came back, admitting defeat and acknowledging the debt they knew they were never going to be able to pay back. Then there were some who disappeared into the mountains with their gold pans, their picks and shovels, to return exuberantly months later to repay Sam with added interest. It was one such man who now had sent him an urgent message. At the time of the loan he had insisted that Sam hold shares in his claim. And now he had struck a

vein that promised to be greater than he had ever
dreamed. He sent Sam a message asking him to come
out to his claim site, and with the message was a pouch
filled with small gold nuggets.

In the years that I had lived there so close to the
mining country, I had never visited any of the digging
sites, either large operations or small, one-man camps.
I begged Sam to let me go with him this time. He was
reluctant at first. The travel would be on foot for long
distances where the terrain would be too rough to ride,
and there was always the possibility of being caught in
a storm. And, once there, it would still be awkward, as
he was sure there would only be a makeshift lean-to,
or a tent at best, for shelter. It was not a place to take
a woman. I pleaded, promising I could keep up with
him on the trail and not complain. I could see him
begin to weaken and went ahead enthusiastically planning for the trip. I was looking forward to the several
days out in the bush, just Sam and I. It seemed that we
had so little time to ourselves now. He was either gone
to Valdez or had so much to catch up on here that we
were never alone.

Mandy overheard us talking and automatically included herself in the trip. We stood in the kitchen,
Maury at the table mixing up a batch of dough and
Abe leaning against the doorway, both of them listening to us explain to Mandy that this time she could not
go. Her face was like a thundercloud, her tiny chin
jutted out stubbornly as she argued. Looking for re-
inforcements in her cause, she pushed a chair across
the floor to the table and climbed up on it, leaning
across to look at Maury. "You think I ought to go,
don't you?" she asked.

Maury never looked at the small, serious face waiting for her answer. "Here, flatten out this dough," she told the child. "Get it ready to cut out the cookies. I got too much to do. I guess it wouldn't matter too much if you went with them, but the cookies aren't going to have any of the frosting on them that Abe likes, 'cause I ain't got time to do it."

Thoughtfully Mandy patted the dough out smoothly on the table as she had been taught. Then, as though reaching a decision, she straightened up on the chair and turned toward us. "Damn!" She dusted the flour from her hands. "Sure would like to go with you." She brushed some flour from her apron with a long sigh. "But, you see, I got to stay here. Abe won't eat the cookies without the frosting, and that is my job. Guess they need me here."

Sam and I both solemnly agreed with her, forgetting to chastise her for her language.

We took the two horses, their side packs filled with the supplies we thought Vince Gentry might be needing, including some fresh vegetables. We were able to ride most of the way on the first day, but sometimes we had to dismount and lead the horses across loose rock, washouts caused by spring floods, or paths too narrow and dangerous to ride. I wore heavy boots, a pair of Sam's pants cut down to fit me, and a man's mackinaw. It was definitely not customary attire for a woman, but it helped me to move along easier behind Sam on this difficult trail. There was just enough of a breeze to keep the mosquitoes away, and the sky was blue and clear. The weather was perfect for taking this trek out into the bush.

We traveled at an easy pace, covering ground steadily but still slowly enough for us to enjoy the country we were passing through. Sometimes we stopped by a stream and drank deep of the clear, cold water. Once Sam stopped to point out a whole valley of fireweed, its color vivid against the dark green of the other underbrush.

We stopped for the night and made our camp high on a mountain ridge where the snow still lay in long gray patches up in the sheltered canyons. The trees were all leafed out, and underfoot was a carpet of spongy moss, freckled with tiny blue and red flowers. There were low-bush cranberry bushes everywhere, and the wild strawberries were just turning a blushing pink. Once in a while the silence was broken by the call of the magpie, upset with our intruding into their territory.

Sam built a makeshift firehole with rock, and while I cooked steak over the open fire, boiled coffee, and laid out thick slabs of bread, he unpacked our bedrolls and tended the horses.

We ate slowly, savoring the flavors of the outdoors, and afterward I sat curled in the shelter of Sam's arms, relaxed, content to watch the flames flicker and dance in the darkness, feeling their warmth on my face. Sam got up from time to time and threw more wood on the fire and kept going to check on the horses. I watched him curiously as he carried our foodstuffs a distance away from where we were to sleep. Then he brought back a dipper of water and warmed it by the fire before handing it to me.

"Here, Nora. I want you to wash your hands and face carefully. Get rid of any of the odors of the cooked food."

I looked at him, a question in my eyes.

"Bears," he answered. "That's why I carried our

supplies so far away. Always remember—wash off any smells of food from your body when camping out like this. Then you won't be so apt to have unwelcome visitors while you are asleep."

I shivered and looked out beyond our fire, into the darkness, but I didn't say anything.

Sam checked on the horses one more time, banked the fire for the night, and at last we crawled into our shelter of spruce boughs and fur robes. We kept most of our heavy clothing on, a necessity against the cold nights at this higher elevation, but it wasn't a hindrance. I turned to Sam, aggressive in my desire for his love.

"Eager, aren't you?" he teased.

I blushed in the darkness. "Must be the mountain air," I murmured against his shoulder.

"I must remember to bring you up here more often." He chuckled as he pulled me close to him.

Finally I slept—a restful, soft sleep, floating in and out of warm, pleasant dreams.

Sam must have gotten up several times during the night without my knowing it, because the fire still burned and the stack of wood beside it had gone down to almost nothing. I was alone when I woke, but I could hear the sounds of the horses being brought up closer to the fire and could smell the coffee. I slid out of the robes quickly and pulled on my boots.

"A bit stiff this morning? Ready to hit the trail again?" he asked, when he saw that I was awake.

"Sure! I'll be ready in a minute. Any kinks I have will work themselves out in a little while."

We ate cold biscuits and drank steaming hot coffee. The morning air was cold, and my teeth chattered against the cup, though I tried to keep Sam from noticing.

He kicked out the fire and threw dirt on it while I packed the utensils. We were on the trail again by the time the sun was fully visible over the mountain crest.

We followed the ridge for a long way, then gradually began making our way down a long slope toward a creek bed I could see far below on the valley floor. We were walking now, leading the horses. Loose rocks rolled beneath my feet, sending small avalanches over the edge of the trail. I could hear them, rolling, bumping, echoing, as they landed somewhere below. I hugged the rock wall, refusing to look over the side. I kept my eyes on the path at my feet, blindly following Sam, refusing to look or think any further than my next step, as the trail got steeper.

Grass replaced rock. Damp mud replaced dry dirt. We were down onto a level marshy meadow. My lungs ached and I realized I must have been holding my breath. I exhaled, breathed in again deeply, and smiled broadly at Sam.

"Nothing to it!" I boasted. Sam just grinned and shook his head.

The stream ran wide there, and shallow, with small eddies and quiet pools. Coarse marsh grass grew up through the water, and dead sticks protruded the surface here and there, a handy perch for birds waiting for mosquitoes.

Sam was closely scanning the canyon up ahead of us.

"Do you know where we're going?" I asked. "What is it you're watching for?"

He waited a moment before answering, then pointed off through the trees ahead. I strained my eyes but could not make out anything but the slight movement of the leaves in a gentle breeze.

Sam cupped his hands around his mouth and yelled. "Halloo! Gentry! It's Sam!"

An answering "halloo" drifted down to us. Five minutes later a man with a heavy beard and dried mud on his clothes broke out of the trees and walked toward us. "Figured that was you when I spotted you coming down that draw. Hadn't counted on you bringing anyone with you."

I took off my hat and my hair fell heavy down to my shoulders.

"And a woman, for Christ's sake! Beg pardon, ma'am. No offense meant."

Sam laughed. "My wife, Nora."

I held out my hand and smiled. "Hello, Vince Gentry."

He was obviously flustered and a little embarrassed at having a woman way out there, intruding into his territory.

We followed him back up the canyon for perhaps half a mile to his campsite, which was close to where he had been digging. The two men talked seriously now, Vince with a great enthusiasm, Sam listening intently. I was momentarily forgotten as I wandered around, looking at my first gold claim at close range. I could see where he had been digging away at the side of the mountain, dumping the dirt into a wooden sluice box that was about eight feet long, with ridges built into the bottom of it. A wooden trough, some five or six inches across, carried the water from a falls higher up, detouring it down and into the sluice box, where it washed around and through the dirt and rock inside and ran over to the creek bed just below.

Nearby was a fireplace built of rock, where he did his cooking. A crude structure of several long limbs covered with canvas on three sides, with the fourth side butted against the hill, appeared to be his only shelter. I went back and sat on a log, idly poking sticks into the low fire until the men finished their talking and remembered that I was there.

Vince cooked an excellent supper that evening—a stew of some sort, tasty with flavors I didn't recognize. He had a large pot of beans, savory with wood smoke. We added fresh-baked bread and potatoes, roasted in the hot coals, to the fare. We all ate heartily, Sam and I with appetites fed by the two days out in the open.

Though the men both tried to draw me into the conversation by talking of things I was familiar with, the talk kept drifting back to the gold dust and small nuggets Vince kept in little pouches buried behind the lean-to.

Vince noticed that I saw the rifle, primed and ready, never too far from his hand. "Bears been kind of grouchy this year," he explained. "I ain't been bothered none yet, but some of the fellows lower down on the creek are getting a little spooked."

Vince insisted that I take the small canvas shelter for the night, saying that he and Sam would bed down by the fire. Sam carried my fur robes in and dumped them on the rough bed of boughs. "Looks like you're going to have to harness those wild emotions this mountain air stirs up in you for tonight, lady," he whispered to me. He went back outside, chuckling, as I made a face at him. I fell asleep to the sound of their voices at the campfire and the noisy chattering of the stream. From time to time I awoke. I could hear the night noises—one of the men got up to feed the fire, a wolf called in the distance, another called in response. . . . I didn't like being alone and longed to get up and go out and join Sam, but after a while I drifted off back to sleep.

We left before noon the next day, after emptying most of the supplies from the packs to leave with Vince. The bags were reloaded with those precious pouches of dust and some ore samples and tied onto the horses.

"Travel easy, ma'am, them packs hold a fortune," Vince said to me by way of parting.

He went back down the canyon with us, to where we had first met him, and stood there shading his eyes, watching, as we started our slow, careful ascent to the top of the ridge. Once on higher ground we were able to ride for long distances, but slowly because of the rocky terrain.

That night we camped against the sheltered mountainside of large shale rock. After poking around, we found a natural cave running back about ten feet deep and six or seven feet wide, high enough for us to stand. Sam unloaded the saddlepacks, carried them inside, and settled the horses for the night. We fixed our fur robes into a bed on the sandy floor and built up a fire at the entrance.

Sam gathered more wood while I boiled the water for the coffee and set out thick slices of cold meat and fresh bread. The moon was almost full, drifting in and out from behind clouds, so that it cast changing shadows against the rock. Nervous, Sam made several trips outside, checking the horses and glancing around before finally banking the fire and moving toward the bed we had made.

"What is it, Sam?" I asked, a little edgy by his caution. I saw that he had moved the rifle, putting it beside the robes where he could reach out and touch it easily.

"Nothing. Sitting by the fire last night listening to Vince spin those bear stories kind of spooked me too, I guess. Bad as when we were kids and would sit around a fire outdoors and tell ghost stories. We'd scare each other until we all had nightmares."

He pulled off his boots and slid in under the fur robes beside me. As he turned and twisted a little, matching the lines of his body to the sandy floor beneath us, I felt his hard, lean muscles, the solidness of his chest, the warmth of him beside me. We lay side by side in the dark, watching the moon half hidden by smoky swirls of thin clouds, seeing a star here and there, listening to the sounds of the fire burning low near the entrance to our shelter. I rested my head on his shoulder. His hand strayed across my breast, paused as it explored the fastening on my shirt, then touched my flesh. I turned to him as his hand moved slowly, idly lower, touching, tracing patterns, bringing my emotions alive. My body quivered in anticipation.

From Tony I may have first learned the ways of a man and a woman, but from Sam I learned what it is to *be* loved, to know that his arms were always there, waiting for me, and that I was the only one who could fill them. Sam gave me warmth, security, a knowing that I was wanted and that he needed me. In return I gave myself completely to him, with no reservations, no hidden private corners kept secret, no fears that I might turn to reach for him and he wouldn't be there.

And there, on the sandy floor of the cave, beneath our pile of fur robes, Sam gathered me in his arms and made love to me, making me feel like such a wanton woman because he was such a seductive man.

* * *

When finally we slept, neither of us noticed that the fire had burned down to a few sputtering coals and warm ashes.

I sat bolt upright to a piercingly terrified scream. I had never heard a horse scream before, but I knew instinctively what it was. Sam was on his feet instantly, the rifle in his hands.

"What is it?" I whispered, my voice shaking, the words sticking in my throat.

"Be quiet," he snapped. "Don't move. Maybe he won't realize we are in here," he whispered.

"Who won't?" I clenched my teeth to stop their chattering.

"I think it is a bear. Stay where you are." He went to a crouch and moved toward the entrance to the cave. Carefully he reached over and threw a piece of wood, heavy with pitch, onto the fire. It sputtered hesitantly for a moment, caught, and burst into flame. He added several more pieces of wood. They caught and started to burn. I looked beyond Sam, past the fire, out into the dark, and I saw the bear on its hind feet, moving toward the cave.

At first glance I swore it was twenty feet tall; then as reason took over I cut that figure in half. Twelve feet, maybe fourteen, of menacing fur, walking upright toward us. I tried to scream but the sound froze in my throat. Sam took careful aim and fired. The impact of the bullet only caused it to pause a moment, then that huge mountain of angry bear kept moving closer. I heard Sam shove another shell into the barrel but not quite fast enough. A long arm, ugly with sharp claws, a vicious swipe, and Sam was knocked off balance, his shirt sleeve shredded and stained as blood flowed in red spurts. The sight of Sam in trouble shook me loose from my frozen panic. I seized one of the flaming chunks of pithy wood and hurled it dead center into those black, gleaming eyes. The bear grunted in pain and moved a few steps backward. I was reaching for another torch but Sam already had the edge he needed. He fired again, and this time the bear dropped in a heap, not six feet in front of us. I stared at it, disbelieving, and started to tremble. I turned to run to Sam. His arm was badly damaged, and at the sight of it I began to cry.

Sam tried to laugh, but his voice was weak and shaky. "What a woman I have! One minute she is a fierce tigress, hurling flaming torches to protect her mate, and the next a weeping female."

"Don't tease." I sobbed. "Not now. Let me build up the fire so I can see your arm. You're hurt."

I tore my spare shirt into strips, and working with that and the water we had brought in the night before for morning coffee, I managed to stop the flow of blood and bandage the wound securely. I was afraid of infection from those dirty claws, and I knew we had to get back into town to a doctor. I kept the fire built up. Sam will never know how frightened I was as I stole a few yards away from the mouth of the cave, jumping at every sound, until I found the spring flowing out of the rocks, refilled the coffeepot, and fled back inside. We sat up the rest of the night drinking hot coffee and waiting for the sunrise.

My panic left with the arrival of daylight, and I began to plan ahead.

Sam asked, "Should we skin it and take home the hide? Make a nice rug."

"Not on your life!" I exclaimed. "I never want to
see that fellow again, dead or alive!"

One of the horses was lying mangled and dead not
far from the cave's entrance. The other horse had
broken loose and was nowhere in sight. Each time Sam
moved around, fresh blotches of red appeared on the
bandage. Finally I persuaded him to sit quietly on a
log while I searched for the horse, promising to call
out so he would know where I was all the time. I found
it, grazing on fresh green grass near the creek, not too
far from where we camped, and I led it back to the
cave. I hid part of the ore samples to be picked up
later and packed the pouches of gold dust and the most
important supplies, leaving the rest behind to lighten
our one remaining saddlebag. I left behind our extra
change of clothing, but brought the coffeepot and
enough food for the day ahead of us.

I insisted that Sam ride. We argued, but I won by
telling him that if he started bleeding again and lost
consciousness I wouldn't be able to find the way home.
He realized that I was right. I knew he was trying to
keep me from knowing the pain he was feeling, but his
face was pale and his hands were shaking. I helped him
up into the saddle, watching him anxiously as he
swayed uncertainly.

I carried the rifle firmly in my hand, mentally re-
hearsing the lessons Abe had given me long ago. I kept
going, leading the horse, pacing myself to last out the
long distance. I watched Sam carefully, moving along
swiftly when he dozed, stopping to let him rest from
the jolting when he roused from time to time.

My legs ached, my head throbbed, but I kept going,
one foot ahead of the other, knowing I couldn't stop.

I sought familiar landmarks, hoping I was following the right trail. Again and again I wished I had paid more attention on our way out.

Midday, while the sun was still high in the sky, I stopped beside a stream. I helped Sam off the horse, worriedly noticing how he clenched his teeth and shook with a chill. I let him lie flat on the ground, using my coat for a pillow, and covered him with a robe, hoping the rest would help.

I built a small fire and boiled some water. Carefully I cleaned the wounds again, better this time now that the was light enough to see, and readjusted the bandages. I bathed his face with the cool water from the stream, trying to make him comfortable so he could sleep as long as possible.

Slowly I drank a cup of hot, strong coffee and studied the terrain ahead of me.

Finally I had to rouse him. "Sam, darling, wake up. We have to be moving. I'm sorry—I can't lift you by myself. You've got to help. It can't be much farther, but we've got to get started. I don't dare risk letting us get caught out here by dark."

He gave me a crooked, one-sided grin, trying to reassure me. Together we got him back up onto the horse and I put out the fire.

"How about a drink of that cold water before we start out?" he asked, and I hurried to fill a coffee cup for him. I refilled the canteen from the icy stream and hooked it onto the saddle. I was anxious now to be on the trail, fear creeping over me like a cloak.

We reached the lodge just before nightfall.

Maury had been watching, and she and Abe ran out to meet us, sensing something was wrong. I saw Abe reach up for Sam and help him off the horse. I knew he was safe now, and I fainted dead away, into a heap on the ground.

The next morning Abe, Maury, and I sat in the kitchen and I recounted the story to them. The doctor had sewed up Sam's arm the evening before and had instructed him to stay in bed for several days. After a good night's rest I was fine, other than a few scratches and blisters.

Maury and Abe teased me goodnaturedly about our appearance the evening before. "What a scare you gave us! We could see plainly enough that Sam was hurt, even from a distance. But you—you were walking right along, brisk as anything, leading that horse and carrying the rifle. You didn't have a scratch on you, leastways none that we could see. You just looked up at Abe helping Sam and down you went in a heap!"

I had to laugh along with them. "Guess I just never had the time before that to give in to how frightened I was."

I carried the breakfast tray into the bedroom to Sam. Mandy was up on the bed, patting his cheek and cooing to him. Pronouncing herself his nurse, she wanted to read to him from her picture books.

Sam was strong and healthy, and he mended fast, but even so it was almost a week before he was able to be up and around, back to work again. Even then his arm stayed stiff for a long time, the muscles tiring easily. He was left with several long white scars as a memento of my first visit to a gold claim.

The pouches of dust were sent to the bank in Valdez for safekeeping until Gentry could come to town to claim them. The ore samples were taken to the assay

office. The report back matched Vince's enthusiasm.
Sam sent word out to him by a trusted friend who also
found our cave shelter and brought back the supplies
we had left there.

CHAPTER FOURTEEN

The next year seemed to fly by so quickly that I could not catch up and hold on to the moments that were so precious. I was left feeling frustrated and dissatisfied. I wanted to stop time for just a little while, to be able to savor slowly the things that meant so much. Mandy was growing so fast, changing every day, and these were things that Sam and I should be sharing together. I resented Sam missing so much of her childhood. It didn't seem fair! He should be there, ready to reach out when I was lonely or to laugh with me over the happenings of the day when I needed someone to share them with.

Mandy was sprouting longer legs and starting to lose her chubby baby fat. Every event in her day carried an intense importance to her that somehow the rest of us had forgotten. She found such delight in the smallest things, sometimes nothing more than watching a ray of sunlight dancing through a bit of colored glass. Other times she had her moments of despair, her tragedies. She was a small bundle of misery, running to Abe for consolation, when she lost two of her front teeth. He took her up on his lap and told her a delightful story about a tooth fairy who would come in the night and replace the missing teeth under her pillow with a bright copper penny. Mandy was enchanted with the story, and she carefully stowed the two baby teeth away before going to bed that night. On his return from Valdez she proudly met her father at the door with a wide jack-o-lantern smile and two copper pennies clutched in her small hand.

My resentment over Sam's being gone so much of the time grew worse as the firm of Crandall and Bennett Exporting, not only did well but grew in size, demanding more and more of both Sam's and Tom's time and energy. Sam seemed always either to be going to or coming from Valdez, and was never home long enough to suit Mandy and me. We missed him terribly when he was gone, and in the short periods he was home he had to try to catch up with all the problems that had accumulated at the mines while he was gone, so he couldn't give us the time we wanted. My tongue grew sharp, and precious moments that should have been spent in love and understanding were wasted in petty quarrels that I was sorry for immediately afterward. The last time Sam was home I had noticed little tired lines around his eyes, and for the first time I saw a few scattered gray hairs beginning to show at his temples. What was happening to us?

Maury and I were in the kitchen doing the last cleaning up and putting away for the day shortly after Sam had left on another of his trips to Valdez. I stood at the window looking out, far beyond the mountains of our Copper River country. My thoughts were in Valdez with Sam, my heart empty with loneliness. I was wondering just what he was doing this evening, if he missed me as much as I longed for him, when Maury's voice interrupted my thoughts.

"I swear, Nora, sometimes I don't know where your thinking is. I'm getting pretty darned tired of your long face moping around my kitchen every time that man leaves to go to Valdez."

I turned to look at her and saw that she had poured two cups of coffee and set them on the table. I went over and sat down wearily across from her.

"I get so lonesome for him, Maury," I said softly. "It just seems that he has to be gone so much of the time now. And it's getting worse, not better. I want us to have a normal life—I want more children. We were going to have three, maybe four. We had such a full life planned. Nothing is working out like I thought it would."

"Well, what about him?" she snapped back at me, no sympathy in her voice. "Why don't you give him a thought, instead of feeling so sorry for yourself all the time? Do you suppose he likes trying to keep up two jobs at once? Do you think he likes staying down there, with only that sour-faced old housekeeper to take care of him? Does she know what he likes to eat or give a damn if he is eating what he ought to? Have you ever thought that maybe he gets lonely down there, wanting a little companionship too?"

I sat looking down at the bubbles floating around the rim of the coffee cup, listening to her, realizing that what she said made sense but not knowing how to answer.

"Humph!" she snorted. "You can be so smart about some things and so damn dumb about others! I ain't

much for bookwork, but I sure do know that it isn't
smart for a woman to send a good man like Sam off on
his own like that all the time. He may love you, and
he idolizes Mandy, but he is still a man. And men need
their women nearby. And if she ain't willing to be
around—if she's too wrapped up in her own life to see
his needs—there are always them others who are, just
waiting to catch him when he is feeling lonely and
weakening a little."

I looked up, startled, to stare at her. Whatever was
she talking about? Not Sam. Not my Sam!

"Fat chance Abe ever going off like that," she continued. "Where Abe goes, I go. There wouldn't ever be
anything in the world important enough that I should
stay behind and not be with Abe if he should need me.
There's no other woman, no matter how old or ugly
she is, ever going to cook and clean for my Abe. That's
what lovin's all about, Nora."

Maury was right. Sam was trying to work two jobs—
the mines and the new company—to insure our years
ahead. Then he spent days traveling back and forth to
be with us as much as he could. Life wasn't easy for
him, that was certain. Yet never once did I consider
how lonely *he* might be. My thoughts had been fo-
cused entirely on my own needs and desires. I knew it
was time to make a decision. Mandy would be starting
school next fall. I wanted her to be where there would
be good schools and her studies would not be interrupted by the weather. And I wanted Sam. Not part of
the time. Not wedged in somewhere between Valdez
and the mines. I wanted him all of the time!

"What am I to do about Ravenwood?" I asked her.

"The obvious thing. Leave Abe and me here. We
managed before you moved here. We can do it again.

Between the two of us we know almost as much about running it as you do. We can send the receipts and paperwork down to you once a month. We can get along. The trains run regular. It will give you a place to come back to, when you and Sam want to get away. Real often, if you want to. Ravenwood will always be here, waiting for you, honey." For a moment a shadow of sadness crossed her eyes. "Hate to think about Mandy not being underfoot all the time. I imagine it will kind of hurt Abe too to have her gone. She's been kind of like our own kid, you know." She gave a sigh and then the old smile returned. "What the heck. She can come up here in the summer and stay with us. We'd take good care of her—you know that—and it would be a real vacation for her. Abe and me would like that, having her spend her summers with us."

I was thoughtful, carefully thinking over all that we had said. "Of course, Maury, if I am living down there, I will still be alone when Sam comes up to the mines."

"Maybe," she answered. "But after listening to him and Abe talk, I'm betting that if Sam has his family down in Valdez with him, so he can work full time at the company office with Tom, he won't be wanting to keep traveling up to the mines. He's about ready to wind up his career as an engineer and go to exporting. He's pretty proud of the way the business down there is going. Can't you tell?"

How could I answer her? I had given so little time to wondering about Sam's feelings lately and I had scarcely listened to him talk about the firm of Crandall and Bennett.

I reached over and hugged her, my eyes a little misty. "Thank you, Maury. Whatever would I have done all these years without you, dear friend? You've always been there, ready to lend a hand to me when I needed it or didn't know what to do. It just seems like whenever I get my thinking all tangled up and I can't seem to straighten out the threads by myself, you and your earthy logic served over a cup of coffee seem to make it all sort itself out and look so simple."

My mind was busy the rest of the evening—not with trying to cross the miles to be with Sam in my thoughts, but plotting and planning on how to be with him in body too. When Sam returned two days later, I had my arguments all rehearsed, my speech prepared. I was impatient. I hurried through dinner and was eager for Mandy to be put to bed and the work around the lodge finished. As soon as we retired to our sitting room I would tell him of my plans.

I watched Sam pull off his boots and slip his feet into slippers and light up his evening pipe. I had taken the pins out of my hair and stood brushing out the tangles, wondering how to begin. Sam was the one that broke the quiet first, however.

"I was watching Mandy tonight doing the chores you had assigned to her," he mused. "I can't believe how she's growing. It seems like only last week when she was still just learning to walk."

"She'll be starting first grade next fall," I answered.

"Isn't that a little soon?" he asked. "She's still pretty young. There's no reason to push her."

"She's old enough. There is no reason to hold her back either."

"I suppose you're right, Nora, but it worries me. Do you think about it sometimes? I wonder if we have done right by Samantha, letting her grow up in a country that holds so few advantages for her. Aren't we being pretty selfish?"

"What on earth are you talking about?" I asked in surprise.

"I'm just wondering if we should have gone back outside because of Mandy. You and I are happy here, doing our bit to help push back the wilderness. We're creating our own little place in things, trying to find our own answers to our reasons for being. We both seem to have found all that we need right here, but are we being fair to her? Now that she's starting to grow up, doesn't she deserve to have friends her own age, to know something of a world outside of the Copper River country? She's entitled to proper schooling—to be able to take advantage of a city and all that it offers."

"She will have friends when she starts school. The one in Valdez is very adequate for the lower grades. When she is ready to go on after that, she can always go to San Francisco and stay with my family while she finishes high school. They would love to have her, and they would see that she is finished properly—and she'd only be gone from us during the winter months."

"What about her religious education?" he asked. "We haven't done too much for her on that score."

"Oh, Sam, how can you say that?" I replied, shaking my head. "If we had gone back outside and were living in a city as you say, she would have gone to church on Sundays—probably to the large cathedral where Aunt Margaret took me as a child. And as she grew up she would be spending more time wondering what to wear because of the people she would be seeing there than in thinking of her prayers. Here she has met

God in the greatest cathedral of all. He has been here for her in the mountains, in the lakes, in the sunrise. No, Sam, I don't think we've held her back at all. I think, in her own way, she knows more about God, understands Him, than most of us. She learned when she first reached out her hand to catch a snowflake and wondered where it came from. Remember how she would bend over and study a new flower poking its first spear of green up through the dirt? It broke her heart to turn her pet fox loose that day, but she understood how wild things were meant to be free and she opened the cage herself and let it go. Samantha is learning values. She knows what it means to love, to care about other people's feelings, to hold life in her fingertips and to know its meaning. No, I don't think we have failed her, Sam. She has so much. . . ."

I sat on the arm of his chair, resting my cheek against his hair, my fingers tracing patterns on the back of his neck. "But speaking of her education . . . Sam, I really think it is time we decided to take a home of our own in Valdez. I'm sick of being away from you so much of the time. I don't want to live like this. I feel as though I'm being torn apart, trying to decide whether to go with you each time you leave or to stay here with Mandy and Ravenwood. You are spending too much time traveling back and forth, when you could be doing other things, and it's wearing all of us down. We have to think of Mandy too, as you said. She will be starting school next fall and I want her to be able to go for a full term without interruptions. She needs a full-time father too. And . . . I need you, Sam. I insist that you let us move to Valdez and be with you!"

Sam reached up and drew me down onto his lap. "Since you feel so strongly about it, I have something to show to you." He reached over the side of the chair and drew a roll of paper out of his satchel. I watched as he spread it out in front of us, across our laps. It was a drawing of a house showing a front view and a floor plan with the rooms all marked out, with little notations for measurements, the way an architect does. I stared at it in surprise, slowly realizing what he was showing to me.

"Sam!" I sputtered. "You've been planning on this already? This is to be our home? Oh, Sam, I've been so blind!"

He drew me close to him, holding me so that I could feel the gentle strength of him. "I haven't much enjoyed the time I've had to spend away from you either. I kept waiting, hoping you would find it in your heart to leave Ravenwood without me asking you to. I don't like the way we've been living, but I knew how much this place means to you. My work at the mines is finished now—I can leave it at any time. I could stay in Valdez permanently if you were there." He had a worried expression on his face. "You won't be really giving up Ravenwood, you know. You can come back here any time that you want to—to visit, to rest, to vacation. It will still be yours—waiting here for you."

"Nothing is as important as being with you, Sam. I love you more than anything in the world. And by loving you I have learned the true secret of Ravenwood. It is not by living in any certain place, but it is knowing the love, the trust, and the happiness that my mother found by living here with Uncle Jim. For me it would be living *anyplace* where you are. You have helped me understand why she left."

"I'll do my best never to make you sorry for this decision, Nora," he whispered.

I placed my fingers across his lips. "I know," I whispered. "How can you forgive me? I am so addled sometimes. Why didn't Maury pour that cup of coffee sooner?"

He looked puzzled. "What do you mean by that?"

"Nothing." I smiled and nestled closer down into the crook of his arm. Tomorrow we would spread out the blueprints again and go over them. It would be exciting and I looked forward to it, but not tonight. Tonight I had other plans for us. I ran my fingers inside his shirt, tracing lines across his chest. I saw his eyes twinkle and felt his muscles tighten as he responded to my suggestion. He picked me up in his arms and carried me through the doorway into our bedroom. Tonight belonged to just the two of us.

Just before drifting off to sleep, as we lay in the big carved bed with my head resting on his shoulder, I thought again of the house plans Sam had taken from his briefcase. "Sam? You still awake? Can I talk to you?"

"What about?" he mumbled sleepily.

"About the house."

"I thought we were going to wait until the morning," he grumbled.

"I was just lying here thinking about it. It looked pretty large. Can we afford to build a house like that? Do we have enough money?"

"We can afford it." He turned over, wanting to go to sleep.

"But Sam," I persisted, "it isn't just the cost of the house. There will have to be things like curtains, and dishes and pans—and what about furniture? It will take all new things because we haven't anything suitable to

move out of here. Otherwise it would leave Ravenwood bare. Have you thought about all of that?"

He was awake now. "You are a natural-born wor-
rier, woman. I wish you would wait until morning to
start going over the finances. But I guess you have
reason to wonder. As much as we have talked, I don't
think we ever sat down and discussed money, did we?
I always tried to see that you had whatever you needed,
and you never asked if there was more. But put your
mind at ease. We can well afford this home that we will
plan and build together." His voice was gentle in the
darkness. "I imagine there will be enough left over so
that when it's finished, we can finally take that trip
together outside, to Seattle, and you can pick out all
your furniture right there on the showroom floor without trying to choose from pictures in a catalog. Would
you like that? We can take Mandy with us. She's old
enough to travel. We'll make it into a real vacation.
What do you think?"

I put my arms around him, curling closer to his side,
happier than I had been in some weeks. "Start the
workers building on it right away, Sam. I don't want
to wait any longer. We've been apart long enough."

The home that Sam was building for me in Valdez
took almost a year to complete. A great deal of thought
went into it, with Sam constantly checking and recheck-
ing the construction. The spongy soil needed extra
fill dirt for the foundation because the country is subject to shifting lands and recurrent earthquakes. Sam
worried about the drainage, not wanting to finish the
building and discover that we were settling slowly
down into the tundra. He chose the location carefully,

wanting a spot sheltered from the high winds in the winter and yet where we would have easy access to the town when the snows drifted ten to fifteen feet deep, blocking the roads. Not being as practical as Sam, I wanted the house built where I could stand at a window and see the mountains, the waterfalls, and where the ships came into the dock from Prince William Sound. I wanted to be able to see the glacier.

The spot he finally chose was toward the edge of town, within easy walking distance of his office and shopping areas. I could stand at the kitchen window and see across to where the sunlight played along the high peaks and was caught in the waterfalls.

Compared to my father's home in San Francisco, it was not a grand house, but it suited the Alaskan countryside and climate. It was large for this town. There were three bedrooms, a separate dining room, a sewing room for me, and a study for Sam. The kitchen was roomy, with many windows and plenty of room for a small breakfast table where we ate most of our meals.

Sam planned on a large fireplace in the living room, built entirely from the native rock found on the cliffs at the edge of town. Bookcases, of course, would be built right in, large enough to hold all the books we had collected over the years and cherished.

The yard around the house was a comfortable size—large enough for us to enjoy, small enough for us to care for easily in the short Alaskan summers. We had it planted with shubbery native to the area, with a spot left for me to garden. As a special surprise, Sam added a small greenhouse where I could start the little seedlings to set out in the spring after the last freeze, giving them a headstart against the race to produce before the first snowfall.

I spent many happy hours poring over books, studying pictures, picking wall coverings and paint colors.
The lumber for the framing of the house was cut at
the sawmill at the other side of the town, but all of the
finishing materials—the glass for the windows, the
curved wood moldings, the lighting fixtures, the plumbing—had to be shipped in from outside. It seemed that
our most urgent requirements for the next step in the
building were always "on the next boat from Seattle."
I came to dread that phrase.

But even with the frustrations it was a happy time
for us. We worked together, planning and building
the home we would share. Often I went to Valdez with
Sam. We stayed at Tom's home while we were there,
and many times Samantha accompanied us.

Mandy, of course, loved these trips. To her each one
was an exciting adventure, full of surprises. To the
adults in the group it was often full of unexpected
surprises too, though to us not nearly as exciting as
Mandy thought them to be. We used the Valdez Trail
most of the time because the train went to Cordova. If
we took it, we would have to travel across to Valdez
by boat. And the trip across the water could be frightening when the weather was bad and the wind whipped
the waves into swells. The Valdez Trail had been taken
over as a military route to carry supplies to Fort
Egbert, at Eagle, far in the interior, so it was being
maintained year round. A stage traveled the road and
a number of supply stations and roadhouses had
sprung up, offering shelter and meals to the traveler.
They were positioned from ten to twelve miles apart,
sometimes farther, so we always planned the trips from
one roadhouse to another, stopping at the most convenient one before night. Often this meant we had to

come to a halt earlier in the day than necessary, because there weren't enough daylight hours to reach the next stop. Camp Comfort Roadhouse was probably one of the most popular and the most crowded because it was only twelve miles from Valdez. Tourists would make the trip out that far to have dinner, get a closer look at the glacier, and still be able to return to Valdez in the same day.

No matter how many times I traveled that route with Sam, I never ever tired of the scenery or ceased to wonder at the Keystone Canyon and its beauty. The canyon walls rise as sharp and high as a giant corridor, and any number of waterfalls tumble down into the waiting stream below. In the winter, when the cascades of water are frozen, they resemble something from a fairy castle, full of spirals and unexpected caverns, catching the light, reflecting back hidden rainbows.

Since the first motor car made the trip in 1907, others accepted the challenge. Brave souls forded streams that crossed the trail and got out to push when the cars bogged down, axle deep in the mud. Crews of men worked year round to keep the road open, fighting the mosquitoes in the summer, the winds and drifting snow in the winter. Yet it was still the sleds, pulled by dogs, that got through the easiest when the snow drifted and the temperature dropped below zero.

Mandy adjusted easily to her new life in the town and was looking forward to being able to start school with the other children. She was ecstatic that now not only did she have her father close by to follow around and talk to, but her uncle also, and she adored him.

Mandy had never been a spoiled or a selfish child, but she showed her first signs of jealousy when Tom began spending more of his free time with a certain young lady who lived there in Valdez. The first night Tom brought Sarah Huntington to his home for dinner while we were staying there, it became necessary for me to reprimand Mandy very sternly, reminding her sharply of how a guest was always treated in our home.

As Tom's courtship became serious, it was obvious to all of us that Mandy was going to have to learn to share her uncle's affections. We put new energies into finishing our new home, knowing that Tom would be wanting his own house for his bride.

I liked Sarah, and when Tom brought her over one evening so she could shyly show us the diamond glistening on her finger, I welcomed her with open arms, knowing she would be a good wife for Tom. I would love having her for a sister. With tears in my eyes, I hugged Tom, so glad that he had found a happiness of his own and would be settling down close to us.

The wedding date was set to be a week after Sam and I returned from our furniture-buying trip to Seattle. As soon as we moved into our own home, Tom and Sarah would be married and would leave immediately by steamer for San Francisco, for about two months.

All of us would be married now—first me, then Paul, and now Tom. Paul didn't have any children yet so Mandy was the only grandchild, but I still hoped the situation would change. I wanted a boy so much, a son for Sam. But so far I had been disappointed each time I had let my hopes rise, thinking this time, maybe. . . .

Our home was nearly completed. It was time for Sam to secure our reservations, and we made our plans excitedly. The furniture would, we hoped, return on the same ship that we did, and so as soon as we arrived we could begin unpacking and settling into our new home.

I insisted on bringing many personal treasures from Ravenwood, wanting to keep them near to me, so this necessitated one last trip back up into the Copper River country before I turned the responsibility of running the lodge over to Abe and Maury. I felt a bit sad, knowing that this was the last time I would be returning to Ravenwood as my home. It would not be the same anymore, and I wanted to make my own private farewells to the lodge I had learned to love so dearly.

While the others were visiting, I slipped away quietly, wanting to be alone for a while. I walked through the late-afternoon sunshine down to the cemetery in the village for a few quiet moments with the tiny grave in the corner, near the fence. My small son, who had not lived long enough for me to hold in my arms, rested there. Because of him a part of me would always remain at Ravenwood, no matter how far away the life ahead of me would lead. I saw that the grass had been cut recently and I knew that either Maury or Abe had done it.

I strolled back through the village, glancing at the shops but not going into any of them. So many memories were rushing around inside of me. I didn't want to talk to anyone right now; I just wanted to be alone to say my farewells in my own way.

I remembered the first time I saw Ravenwood, an isolated lodge in the bush. A place where my mother had lived and found a happiness and complete love, so deep that she had wanted me to be there to share it with her. But that was never to be. I thought of how I had come up there, green and inexperienced, seeking a mother I had grown up without knowing, and had arrived too late. She had left Ravenwood to me, hoping that somehow I would know security and happiness and find a love to match her own. And it was there that I had made a home, found friends like Abe and Maury, tried to discover what I wanted out of life. I thought of the celebrating when the train came through up to the mines, of the way the village had grown, of the way the people had moved in, pushing back the wilderness with their homes, their families, their children. Of the heartbreak I had known and learned to control, the lessons I had learned. And of Sam—that wonderful, strong, quiet man who had come into my life and changed everything for me.

I raised my eyes and looked off toward the ridge of mountains. Somewhere up there was the lake with the small log cabin where Sam and I had spent the few days after our wedding.

Yes, my mother had left me a heritage beyond price, because it was there at Ravenwood that I had lived and learned, and it was there that I had found a love such as most women never know.

When I reached the yard of the lodge, I sat on a log, not quite ready to go inside and join the others. The sun was warm on my shoulders and I could hear the birds in the wood, calling back and forth.

I thought of Tony, a handsome, laughing man who did not belong in the harsh, demanding, sometimes serene beauty of Ravenwood any more than I would have belonged in his bohemian world. The hurt was healed now and almost forgotten, and I felt no bitterness when I thought of him.

I remembered, with a faint smile, the aching muscles,

the broken fingernails, the tears, as I learned to pick berries, to make jams and jellies, and I recalled the wonderful feeling of accomplishment when I succeeded in holding my own here in the bush country.

"I'm not leaving you, Ravenwood," I promised. "I'm only going to Valdez to be with Sam. I will live there and make a home there. I will be happy because I'll be with Sam. But I'll be back from time to time. Sam will too. We'll both be back whenever we can. Sam is building a lovely home for me. I know I am going to love it too, and we will be happy there. But nothing will ever replace the very special place in my heart that belongs only to Ravenwood."

I went inside then. I had said my farewells, and now I wanted to be with the others, a part of their laughter and their talk, to start packing.

I shook away the memories of the past and began preparing for the future. We were to leave for Seattle on Monday and there were so many things that needed my attention before I could leave.

The steamer we took to Seattle was luxurious compared to the one I had traveled on on my way to Alaska. I drew back in surprise when Sam led us to the cabin where our trunks were already waiting for us. It was large, soft lighted, and draped in warm, rich colors. There were two comfortable chairs and a small carved writing table. The bed seemed huge, with fresh, clean-smelling bedding and large, fluffy pillows. There was a small dressing room, and there was a bed for Samantha against one wall. I spun around the room, crying out in delight. Suddenly the trip became more exciting, more interesting, and I was eager to begin unpacking and get us settled in our quarters.

Samantha was unusually quiet, staying close to either Sam or me, watchfully taking in all of this new world. When we dressed and went to dinner in the large dining room, she still hung back a little, suddenly shy. Sam winked at me in amusement over the top of her head as she sat at the table, eating with exaggerated good manners and solemnly studying everything around her, not missing a thing.

The weather was in our favor, holding calm for the whole trip. Deck chairs were placed around so we could sit out in the sunshine and watch the rolling seas or read lazily and nap. Mandy's curiosity finally took over and she could hold back no longer. We had to keep a close eye on her, because her adventurous nature led her to want to explore parts of the ship where she knew she was not allowed. She made friends easily and soon had won over even the deckhands, who spun yarns of their travels at sea while she listened, wide-eyed, believing every word.

A number of other passengers were making the trip with us, but the group was different from the ones I had seen on the journey north. Then it had been men anxious to reach their destination, filled with stories of the discovery of gold, discouraged by the lack of work at home, ready to take on a new, dangerous adventure and fill their pockets with their dreams of easily gained wealth.

On this trip there were schoolteachers going back outside for a vacation. There were businessmen, like Sam, returning to their home offices with briefcases filled with handwritten reports on what they had found. There were other women with small children in tow going out to visit their families, showing the stress of the hardships they had endured in the tired

lines of their faces but knowing they would return because their men were in Alaska. There were a few men
in uniform, a priest, and tourists, their Brownie cameras still conspicuous in their hands. Enthralled by
their adventures, they were ready to take pictures of
everything that met their eyes, and they exchanged
stories of what they had seen and where they had been
as they sat in the lounge in the evening.

There were several prospectors who, boisterous in
their tales of the color they had found, were anxious to
reach a city and start spending. Others had not fared
so well and had little to say. There was a red-headed
newspaper reporter, returning to her desk in Seattle,
who spent her hours writing notes as she sat out on
one of the deck chairs, paying little attention to what
went on around her.

Most of all I enjoyed having Sam beside me, sharing
with me. We talked and laughed together or just sat
quietly without saying anything, just knowing each
other was there. When the big ship nosed its way into
Puget Sound and the port of Seattle, I almost hated to
see the voyage end.

We were greeted by throngs of people on the docks.
Some were there to greet the passengers, others just out
of curiosity. Everything seemed so vital: Stevedores
waited to unload the freight, while the pushing, shov-
ing, irritable noise of cabs waiting to pick up fares
filled the air. Streetcars wanted the tracks cleared so
they could get through, and horns were blowing. The
sights, sounds, and smells of industry were inescapable,
and everywhere one turned there were people!

Sam took my arm and led me through the mass,
heading toward a waiting taxi. Samantha clung to his
other hand, not taking any chance on being separated

from us. Here on these wharfs were more people at
one time than she had ever dreamed existed.

The skyline was rimmed with tall buildings, and
smoke rose in tall, winding spirals from factories. Our
driver pointed out where the large shipyards were,
building ships for the war the United States was involved in but that had not quite touched our northland. Here in Seattle the war was very real, changing
people's lives. The city was in a period of transition,
with various political parties and organizations struggling to gain power. I learned of all the different ones
—the Industrial Workers of the World, nicknamed the
Wobblies, a group that made speeches in the streets
and dared to fly a red flag next to the Stars and Stripes;
Radicals; Conservatives; Socialists; Democrats; Labor
Party; Republicans. So many groups, with so many
beliefs . . . I was a little frightened when our cab
took us near speakers on soap boxes shouting out their
angry speeches to crowds of people passing by. Groups
of men in navy uniforms from nearby Whidbey Island
mingled with the listeners and were openly hostile to
the lectures they considered slanderous against their
flag and their country.

For the most part, the various groups did their cam-
paigning in the poorer sections of town, along skid row,
but once in a while they went into the business dis-
trict, where they were accused of inciting riots among
the sailors by deliberately hurling insults at them and
their country. Military men, urged on by citizens,
whether for patriotic reasons or for their own amusement, traveled in groups, seeking Wobblies out, smash-
ing Socialist meeting places and headquarters. . . .
Sometimes an innocent group such as a waterfront
gospel mission was damaged by mistake.

I worried about Sam when he left Mandy and me to
go on some business dealings that took him near the
shipyard. I felt threatened by this noisy city more than
I ever did by the wilderness.

Sidewalks were filled with people; streetcars clanged
along their noisy tracks, ringing bells for attention; fire
engines raced through the streets during the night,
waking me with their sirens.

I was not the only one finding things new and
strange. Mandy turned away in distaste from the fresh
fruits on display on a vegetable stand. The famous
Washington apples had natural blemishes, caused by
the rains or the sun, but she didn't like the looks of
them. All that we were sent up in the Copper River
country were free of these marks because only the best,
most perfect fruits were sent on the long journey, in
order to prevent spoilage en route.

On one of our walks through the park she stopped
and bent over in sudden alarm, her attention riveted
on a small, green garter snake wriggling away to safety
under the leaves. She had never seen a snake before—
we had none in Alaska.

The rows of fine department stores in the downtown
area held a fascination no woman could resist, particularly one who had been away from them for as long
as I. I came back from each expedition with my arms
full of packages, with more to be delivered to our
hotel later. I bought gifts for our friends and new
clothing for myself, Sam, and Mandy, as well as the
basics for our new home—curtains, cooking utensils,
dishes, and new electrical appliances just on the market
that intrigued me and I thought I couldn't do without.
Finally I grew ashamed of the way I was spending, and

a little worried of what Sam might say when he saw the bills. But he only humored me with a smile, encouraging me to enjoy myself.

Sam took me to restaurants, a different one each evening, and we dined in a luxury I hadn't enjoyed since leaving San Francisco. We had salads with lettuce so crisp it snapped, and asparagus spears tender and green. Mandy drank ice-cold milk and was introduced to her first dish of ice cream with thick chocolate syrup, topped with whipped cream. There was no end to the fun things I discovered again through the delighted eyes of my daughter, such as hot buttered popcorn in the park, bought from a vendor pushing a two-wheeled cart, and motor cars. Oh, yes, Sam insisted on renting one of those smelly vehicles and taking us for a ride at a breathtaking speed through the countryside, racing up and down the back roads, a little too recklessly, I thought, showing Mandy her first cow, large farms growing lush and lazy, without the threat of an early snow. We went to the beach and picnicked on the warm sand, then strolled along the shoreline looking for shells.

Sam went with me to shop for furniture. Beautiful things were displayed for us, and I drew back a little hesitantly, staggered by the price tags. But Sam insisted that I pick what I wanted—not for its price tag but because it was something I felt would fit into our home, something we would be comfortable living with.

There were days when we did no more than roam without plan through the city, visiting libraries, museums, and art galleries or visiting the parks. It was on one of these trips, while going through a large gallery, that I saw a roomful of oil paintings that attracted me like a wave of homesickness. The mountains, the rugged coastlines, the gulls watching small fishing boats, all looked familiar and I drew Sam toward it.

"Look, Sam! It looks like home, doesn't it!" I exclaimed. "Let's go in and take a closer look."

As we went through the large arch leading into the display room, I saw an easel in the doorway. On it was a large placard reading "Featured Artist—Anthony Lowery." *Tony.* He was here. It was his paintings that were on display.

I raised my eyes and on the wall directly ahead was a large, beautifully framed painting of Mount Wrangell, a lovely piece of work catching the deep beauty and silence of the country. Lounging beside it was a figure all too familiar to me, even after all this time. I felt the color tinge my cheeks, and for an instant I wanted to turn and walk away. Then I felt Sam's steadying hand on my arm.

Tony was watching us approach, an amused smile on his face.

"Hello, Tony." Sam spoke first, his voice as calm and steady as always.

Tony held out his hand. "Well, what a surprise. Hello, Sam. Nora—"

"Tony," I answered softly. "How are you?"

"Doing well enough. And you?"

I felt Sam moving away from my side and I heard my daughter's voice asking, "Daddy, who's that man Mom's talking to?"

"Someone she knew once, a long time ago."

"Do you know him too?" she quizzed.

"Yes. I know him. He used to live up in the Copper River country for a while."

"Then why don't we stay and talk too?" she persisted.

"Because I saw a case of dolls on display over there that I thought you would really want to see. Come along, baby. Mother will be with us in just a moment or two."

I stood looking at Tony. "Your paintings are beautiful. That's what drew us in here. I didn't know that you were here. I'm glad you're working with your oils again," I said softly, not sure just what else to say without sounding awkward.

He grinned—the old, familiar smile: a little sarcastic, a little reckless. "Yes, I have been painting for several years now. Can't get away from the turpentine and oil, I guess. Keep going back to it."

"I am glad. That's what you always really wanted to do."

"I suppose so. When you were looking at them, did you notice the price tags? A little staggering, isn't it? And, believe it or not, they are selling for those figures."

"Do you live up here—in Seattle?"

"No. I only came up here for the showing. I spend most of my time outside of San Francisco—a little town right on the coast."

He hadn't changed too much, really. And yet he was different, not the same Tony I had known. The dark hair still curled boyishly but there were a few—only a few—gray hairs showing at the temples. His dark eyes still laughed even when he wasn't smiling, but his face was fuller. There was a coarseness to his features that hadn't been there before, as though he had seen a little too much of the world and it had left its mark among the lines. I wondered if he still drank as much, still

liked to gamble. His taut boy's body had grown heavier. There was even a paunch, ever so slight, but notice-
able. Lord, how he must hate that.

"How have you been, Nora?" he asked again. "You
look well. You've changed though. You are still lovely
but in a different way. You look happy."

"You have changed too. But then we were so
young. . . ."

The grin came back. "Young—and foolish—thinking
we knew all of the answers. Are you married?"

"Yes. To Sam."

"I expected that."

"Did you? Why?"

"Because he loved you long before I left. It was something he couldn't hide. That was one of the reasons it
was so easy for me to walk away and leave you. I resented it—hated him for it. . . . Are you happy with
him?"

"Yes." I paused. "We have a daughter. She's five and
a half now. Sam isn't with the mines anymore, Tony.
He has joined my father's company and we live in
Valdez. And you? Have you married again?"

"Yes. But I'm not right now. It didn't last too long
either." There was another long pause as he studied
me. "What are you doing in Seattle? Do you still own
Ravenwood?"

My eyes glowed at the thought of Ravenwood. "Yes.
Abe and Maury are there, taking care of it. You
wouldn't recognize it though." I went on to tell him of
the changes Sam had made—the indoor bathroom, the
other remodeling—and we talked about the railroad
finally reaching the mines and the carloads of ore that
were being brought out.

Tony nodded. "I know. It's been in the newspapers.

The railroad didn't go on any farther though, did it? Have they scrapped the idea of going on to Fairbanks?"

"I don't know. I think so. It isn't mentioned anymore. They didn't win the battle to mine the coal, you know. I think that had a lot to do with it. A lot of people feel pretty strong about it—that it will stop the development of the Copper River country. I don't know what will happen now. They aren't even going to go ahead with building a connecting line over to Valdez. You have to go by boat from Cordova still." My eyes strayed across the room to where my daughter stood, fascinated by the dolls. "Do you remember the old Valdez Trail we took, riding in Logan's freight wagon, to get to Ravenwood? It's a regular road now. A stage makes the run between Valdez and Fairbanks. And there have even been some motor cars traveling on it. They keep it open the year round. . . ." I broke off, then asked quietly, "So you are doing all right, Tony?"

"Sure, couldn't be better." His eyes were following Mandy as she walked beside Sam, tugging at his arm as she chattered away to him. "She's a cute kid. She looks a lot like Sam, doesn't she? He's a lucky guy." And I knew that he was thinking of another time, another infant, another dream built on sand.

I looked across at Sam: tall, lean, firm muscles under a smooth, well-tailored jacket. He was strong and rugged, yet full of gentle patience as he listened to his daughter talk. His back was to me, bending slightly to point out something to Mandy. I took a deep breath and smiled. "Yes. That is my family." How much they both meant to me and how much I loved them! Suddenly I turned away, impatient to be back with them. "Good-bye, Tony. Take care. . . ."

I walked slowly over to Sam. When I reached his side I slipped my hand onto his arm, brushing my cheek against his shoulder.

He looked down at me, his eyes warm, tender, loving me. "Everything all right, Nora?" he asked softly.

"Everything is fine, Sam," I answered huskily. "Do you realize just how much I love you?"

His only reply was a tightening of his hand over mine where it rested on his arm. Together we moved on through the gallery, out into the sunlight, laughing at the impatience of our daughter.

Two days later we left for the return trip to Alaska. Though it had been a fantastic vacation and I had loved being there with Sam—shopping, seeing a large city again, picking out our furniture and the things for our home—I was impatient to be back. I had had enough of the crowds and the rushing about, the noise. I felt an urgent need to walk along a wooded trail, stop to pick a few berries, hear Maury laugh. I wanted to go home.

Sam was anxious to return also; he didn't want to be away from his office any longer. He was thinking of the work that needed to be done, the things awaiting his attention.

Tom would be waiting for us too, because he wouldn't be able to go ahead with his plans for his future until we returned.

CHAPTER FIFTEEN

Tom and Sarah were married in the new church that had just been completed at the edge of town. Sarah's family had lived in Valdez for a number of years. Her father had come up here before the turn of the century and had seen Valdez grow from a tent town to the busy little seaport that it is now. She and her mother came up here several years later, after he had established the hotel and made a home for them. They had many friends and Sarah was an only child, so the wedding was large and well attended.

The church smelled of new lumber and fresh paint, mixed with the perfumes of flowers that somehow had been coaxed into bloom in time for the late June wedding. I sat on the bench next to Garth Williams, with Mandy beside me. Abe and Maury were there, having made the trip into town especially for the affair. They were staying with us, in our new home, which had finally been completed and furnished. Mandy sat on the edge of her seat, for once silent and wide-eyed, as she stared in wonder at the beautiful church, the rows of flowers, the candles. Sam, the best man, was standing up front near the altar beside Tom. He looked so handsome in his formal suit. My Sam. My heart swelled with pride. Tom was obviously nervous, and he attempted to hide it by smiling too broadly, too often.

The music started and we stood. Sarah drifted up the aisle holding on to her father's arm to meet Tom. She was a vision all in white satin and netting, like a fairy princess from one of Mandy's storybooks. I looked down at my daughter as she watched the bride, completely entranced by what she saw. My heart went out to Tom, my dear Tom, who had come to Alaska to find me and stayed on himself. His love for Sarah showed openly on his face as he stood watching his bride move toward him.

Tears came to my eyes as I remembered my own wedding to Sam, before the homemade evergreen altar at Ravenwood, and the happiness it had brought to me. My thoughts wandered back, and as Tom made his vows to Sarah, I could hear Sam's voice softly promising to love and cherish me. His eyes met mine across the rows of people and I knew he was remembering too.

I was brought back to the present abruptly as Tom kissed his bride and the group of people came alive, laughing, shouting, talking, pushing out from their seats to watch Tom and Sarah run down the aisle. Everyone was trying to catch a glimpse of him lifting his bride into the waiting motor car. We threw rice, and everyone shouted wishes for happiness as the car pulled away from the curb.

A reception was to follow at the home of Sarah's parents. Garth and I waited for Sam to join us. Then,

with Abe and Maury, who now had Mandy with them,
we got into our automobile to travel across town to
take part in the festivities. Yes, in our automobile. Ever
since Sam had driven that one in Seattle he had been
determined to own one himself.

Many people were there when we arrived, making it
difficult to work our way into the main parlor where
the newly married couple waited. Blinding flashes of
light filled the air as a photographer took pictures of
Sarah cutting the cake with its tiny bride and groom
standing on top. The cake was served on delicate china
plates, and champagne flowed like water.

A long table, covered with a cloth heavy with embroidery and lace edging, was heaped with presents. I
could hardly believe the assortment of lovely things
they received, ranging from fragile china and crystal to
gifts of handiwork—crocheted tablecloths and hand-
sewn quilts.

The bride threw her bouquet, and finally Tom and
Sarah made their escape to begin their trip to San
Francisco on a ship sailing that very evening.

Our own group returned to our house, tired, eager
to kick off our shoes and sit in front of the fireplace
and visit. Garth came with us for the evening because
he had not had a chance to visit with Abe since we
moved to Valdez. The men wanted to talk politics and
copper mines, railroads and lost coal leases.

It seemed as if it had been such a long time since
Maury and I had talked together, and I looked forward
to the evening. Mandy fought to stay awake but finally
her eyes closed, and with a sigh she nestled her head
on Abe's shoulder and went to sleep.

"Can't believe how this young one has grown!" he

said as he stood to carry her to her room. Maury and
I followed, then slipped out to the kitchen to have our
own visit over a cup of coffee, away from the men.

While the men discussed the way folks were moving
out of Katalla even though the coal deposits still were
unmined and oil lay in puddles on the ground, Maury
and I talked about the trip Sam and I had taken to
Seattle. She was full of curiosity about the streetcars,
the large buildings, the theater we had attended. I told
her about the department stores where I had gone
shopping and how shockingly short women's skirts
were. And I told her about seeing Tony.

"How was he?" she asked.

"Says he is doing fine. His paintings were beautiful—
so real that you could almost feel the cold of the snow
or hear the seagulls. They were drawing a lot of attention."

"How did he look?" she wanted to know.

"The same. A little heavier, a little older. He's still
good-looking but the boyish charm is gone. He looks
very—what word do I want? Worldly? There was a
hardness there that I don't remember."

"You think he is doing all right?"

"I think so. He's doing what he wants to do now.
And his paintings were selling at quite a price."

The talk drifted to gossip from the village, and
Maury talked about Ravenwood. It was good to have
my friend near, and I hated to see the evening end.

Mandy began her schooling in Valdez. Each morning
I sat at the breakfast table with a cup of coffee and
watched her and Sam as they walked down McKinley
Street together. The school was on the way to the docks,
and they always walked that far together. Even though

we had a car, Sam insisted on walking because it was about the only real exercise he was able to get, now that the office was keeping him so confined. In the summer when the weather was nice, Mandy would walk down to the docks in the evening and meet him, so they could walk home together. In the winter when the temperatures ranged well below zero for days at a time, she waited at school for Sam to stop by for her. We had deep snows here in the wintertime. Sometimes it was necessary to walk down the sidewalks in front of the stores, after the streets had been cleared, and not be able to see the traffic at all. You could hear the sounds—the horses, the dog sleds, a few automobiles, so you knew they were there—but the high banks of snow were like walking in a tunnel. Sam felt better about it if Mandy didn't walk the bitter-cold route alone. They were very close, those two. Samantha adored her father, and I don't think Sam missed not having a son. If he did, he kept it from me.

Though I missed Ravenwood, I was content in the home Sam built for me. I could stand at the kitchen window, near the sink, and see out across the water to the beautiful mountains with their cascading waterfalls. I could watch the large boats moving slowly into the docks, bringing supplies from the outside or leaving again, heavy with Alaskan fish from the canneries. Gradually I became involved in town activities. Because of my love for books, I was one of the volunteers who helped create a library. It started out quite casually; a number of us traded books from our own bookshelves. From there the idea grew until more people became interested, people without home libraries of their own but who wanted to read. We formed a group, adopted a set of rules to govern our lending library, and moved our new venture into an unused room in the Alaska Road Commission building. Between twenty-five or thirty of us were willing to volunteer our services, and I found myself working at the lending desk or sorting books and putting them on the shelves several afternoons a week. We kept up with the work indoors quite easily, but we were constantly looking for volunteers to help us keep the walkways shoveled during the winter months. Sam came over several times and helped, and other young men lent a hand, but it was during the week when most of the men were working that we had our worst problems. The snow just kept filling in every path cleared.

I made new friends among my neighbors and somehow always seemed to be working on some project or other, active with this group or that. So much needed to be done, and though I kept busy and content, nothing ever quite replaced Maury and the summers of berry picking, the preparing of jams, the canning—all the things involved with living and surviving in the bush.

I enjoyed taking care of my warm and loving home filled with mementoes of our life together. We each had a favorite chair—mine was a rocker, Sam's was a large, overstuffed chair with an ottoman for him to rest his feet as he read. The living room was never as orderly as it should have been. There was always a half-read book lying on the table, waiting to be picked up again. Or at times the pillows on the sofa were disarranged, easier to rest against that way.

We had indoor plumbing in the whole house! What a convenience! Water faucets ran hot and cold water, not just in the kitchen but in the bathroom too. In the bathroom we had a large white enamel tub sitting on curling ornamental legs that was deep enough to sink in water clear to your shoulders. And a toilet that flushed when you pulled the chain. City living did have definite advantages. I made a braided rug for the floor to take away the chill when you stepped from a hot bath out onto a cold linoleum-covered floor. And we had hot water in such good supply that we never ran out unless I washed clothes when the others were home, but this seldom happened.

We had electricity wired into every room, but I still kept my good old dependable lanterns handy for the times when the wind came down the canyons in a gale force, knocking over the poles and blowing trees into the power lines. I cooked on a wood stove, preferring it to the new, more modern electric ones, so even though the winter weather would turn for the worse, we did quite well, using my kitchen stove and the fireplace for heat.

My favorite room was my sewing room, where I spent many happy hours during the day making dresses for Mandy and myself or sewing things for the house. It was a light and airy room, with a small, enameled stove to keep it warm in the winter when extra heat was needed.

It is a little hard to go back through time and sort out the years that followed in an organized manner, because they were such busy ones and there were so many changes in our lives.

The offices down near the docks took more and more of Sam's hours as the business grew—particularly in the summertime. He stayed tall and straight, his muscles lean and hard, but I watched as more gray hair gradually appeared at his temples and tiny lines appeared in his face.

I saw less and less of my beloved Ravenwood. Sam and I tried to go there at least two or three times during the summer, but we never made the trip during the winter anymore. After school let out for vacation, Mandy would go up with us and stay with Abe and Maury, returning with us on our next trip. She loved the summers spent at Ravenwood, and I know Abe and Maury hated to see her leave. Tom and Sarah loved to escape there whenever it was possible, but their trips too grew farther and farther apart as they had their children, first a boy named Martin after our father and then a girl named Elizabeth.

The work at Ravenwood tapered off. Most visitors were tourists traveling through to the interior, covering longer distances now that the road was better, so they would stop for a hot meal and leave again, eager to cover as many miles as possible in the long daylight hours of summer. Only a few were venturesome enough to travel the road in the winter.

Road maintenance crews stopped in when they were working in the area, and for a few days it would be hectic, with Maury working almost around the clock trying to keep up, but then they would move on to another stretch of the road and it would quiet down again.

The two Indian women weren't working there anymore. Each had families of their own now, and the work was light enough that Maury chose to take care of it alone, with only some part-time help on laundry days.

The one year that I shall remember as being a very

difficult time for all of us was 1929. It was the year that
Samantha left us to go to San Francisco to finish her
schooling. It was something that Sam and I both
wanted for her, and yet it was so hard to give her up.
A bit of sunshine went out of our lives when she left
us, and the house seemed to suddenly become too big,
too empty, too quiet.

That was also the year that we lost Maury. She had
caught a cold during the preceding winter, and no
matter what she tried, it just seemed to hang on and
on into the spring, with a racking cough that left her
tired and pale. Then when she thought she was feeling
better and finally getting over the lingering illness,
it suddenly turned into pneumonia. Within a few days
she had slipped away.

We left for Ravenwood as soon as we received Abe's
message. Mandy was there with him, as it was still a
month before her school term would start. Tom and
Sarah left their children with her parents and made the
trip with us. We took our car, the two men changing
off with the driving so we were able to travel straight
on through, making the trip all in one day. We covered the 186 miles in only a little over nine hours,
which included our stops to have lunch and to stretch
our legs, while the men tinkered with the car.

I thought back to the first trip up Richardson Highway, then called the Valdez Trail. The freight wagon
had taken three days, and we had spent two nights in
rough, makeshift roadhouses along the route.

Along the way I tried to keep the tears from my eyes,
but it was so hard to do. Everyone was quiet, deep in
thoughts and memories, and the monotonous turn of
the wheels lulled me into remembering my first days
at Ravenwood and how Maury had taken me under

her wing and taught me so much about life, love, and survival in the bush. Without her how different my life might have been. With misted eyes, I silently grieved the loss of a dear friend.

The loss was not mine alone. I knew that Sam felt deeply about her too. He was very quiet on this trip, his eyes shadowed, his face cold and withdrawn.

And Samantha had lost a second mother. From the day she was born, it was Maury, as well as I, who was there to kiss her hurts, tie on a freshly ironed pinafore, scold if it were needed, and mend cuts and bruises with cookies warm from the oven.

The funeral services were plain but attended by more people than I realized lived in this bush settlement. Maury's final resting place was in the small cemetery behind the town's church.

Abe, his eyes dry, stood silently at the gravesite. His face was unreadable, his thoughts withdrawn into a place where we could not reach him. There was nothing any of us could do to ease his pain. I saw Samantha move over to stand at his side and slip her hand into his, but no words passed between them.

We did what we could for him, staying on at the lodge for several days so he wouldn't be alone. Samantha and I carefully packed Maury's clothing away in a trunk, but Abe refused to let us take it from the cabin.

It was then that we decided it was time to close Ravenwood. With Maury gone and without us there, it seemed the only thing to do. We put dust covers on the furniture and did a final cleaning. Once again Ravenwood would be used as it was originally intended —a retreat, a hunting and fishing lodge, a place for us to escape.

We begged Abe to come back to town with us. We

had a large house, and he was a part of our family. We wanted him close to us. But Abe remained firm. He hadn't liked cities before and he didn't like them now. He preferred to go on living in the cabin he and Maury had shared for so many years, fishing and hunting when he felt like it, close to the country that he loved. He would take care of Ravenwood, keeping up the repairs, and would be there waiting when we came to visit.

When we returned to Valdez, Mandy began her plans to make the journey to San Francisco where she would finish her schooling. She was going to make the trip alone. Even though she would be on one of the ships working for the Crandall-Bennett firm, and Sam was reassured over and over that the captain himself would watch over her, he nearly backed out of letting her travel by herself. It was very hard for Sam to give up his daughter and realize that she was growing up.

Finally Mandy left us, an excited, chattering girl-child of fifteen. She returned to us two years later, a tall, slender, extremely attractive young woman with hazel eyes, rich brown hair cut short and marcelled, her skirts far too short for me to approve of, a hat pulled down over one eye. She carried a sophistication of the city about her, a poise that was foreign to the bubbling tomboy we had sent away to school.

The day of her homecoming was a red-letter day for Sam and me. I had been up early that morning, giving her room a final airing, tending to the preparations for the dinner I wanted to have ready when we returned from the wharfs. My work was interrupted by my frequent stops at the window to see if I could catch sight of the ship coming into the narrows.

Sam was up early too and dressed to go down to meet the ship hours before it was time to leave.

Even the house itself seemed to echo "today Mandy is coming home" from room to room.

The ship was not expected to dock until sometime around noon, but Sam was pacing the floor and checking his watch by nine o'clock. I teased him a little about it, but I was just as nervous.

The arrival of a ship from outside was always awaited with interest, and there were already people standing around on the docks when we arrived. But instead of prospectors carrying packs, anxious to get ashore so they could start the trek to the gold fields, our ship was filled with tourists, carrying their cameras, brochures in their hands, pushing their way ashore, looking for transportation up to view Valdez glacier and Keystone Canyon, before they returned to the ship to continue their trip on north to the new town of Anchorage that was springing up on Cook Inlet, or even farther on, to Nome and the Bering Sea.

Sam found a place to park the car, and we made our way down to the ramp the passengers would use. The large ship was settling into its berth now, and the stevedores moved in to begin unloading the freight. Cartage wagons stood by, the horses pulling them nervous from the noise and confusion. People were shouting back and forth to each other. Children, excited by the arrival of a new ship in the harbor, were dodging about, chasing each other, playing their games.

I spotted Samantha first, standing by the rail waiting to be allowed to come ashore. She looked so lovely standing there in the sunlight, the wind ruffling her hair, her eyes eagerly scanning the crowd as she looked for us. I pointed her out to Sam but it took a moment for him to find her, and then he let out a long, low whistle of disbelief.

"Are you sure, Nora?" he exclaimed. "What has happened to her? She looks so different! My God—her hair! What happened to her long hair?"

I reached out and touched his arm. I felt sorry for Sam in a way. "She has grown up, dear. That's what has happened to our Samantha," I answered softly. There was something else I had seen that Sam was still too stunned to notice. I had watched the young man who had been standing beside Samantha on the deck, and I noted that he was following at her side, down the gangplank, but I decided against commenting on it. One blow at a time, I thought to myself. There was time enough for Sam to realize that growing up meant that there would be other men in her life now, men who found her an attractive woman. Poor Sam. This wasn't going too easy for him.

She walked toward us, slender and graceful, holding her head proudly, every inch a proper lady. However, in the last five steps she became our own Mandy again, flying into her father's outstretched arms, laughing, crying a little, reaching her face up to be kissed.

"Oh, it's so good to be home," she bubbled happily. "To see you again—I've missed you so much! Oh, Daddy, you have no idea the things I have stored up to tell you!" She wriggled loose from his arms and turned to hug me around the waist and kiss me on the cheek. "Mom, you look positively radiant! Grandfather sends his love—I'll tell you all about them when we get home. I am so glad to be back!"

Suddenly, as though remembering, she turned then to the young man who had followed her from the ship and who was standing back, looking a little unnecessary and very uncomfortable. She reached out a hand and drew him into our circle, bringing him to Sam's attention for the first time.

"See, Edward," she cried. "Aren't they just beautiful, just like I told you they were!"

I looked at my daughter's glowing face and I knew she had grown up indeed, and I knew that my poor darling Sam was in for another upset that he must somehow learn to accept.

She stood with her hand resting casually on the young man's arm, making him a part of our group. "Mom, Dad, I want you to meet Edward. Edward Mott." Edward looked stiff and ill at ease as he reached out to shake hands with Sam. When I looked at Sam's face, now it was Edward whom I felt sorry for. What an intimidating experience this must be for him, to arrive in such a strange new land and be met by such an imposing figure as Sam was right now. I smiled and held out my hand to him, hoping some show of friendliness might help the poor young man.

"Edward and I were in the same business classes at college," Mandy explained. "After we graduated, he received a position as an accountant for one of the canneries right here in Valdez so we traveled north on the same ship. Wasn't it nice that I had someone on the same ship whom I knew?"

Under the circumstances, Sam had no choice but to nod in agreement without seeming rude. There seemed nothing else to do but to ask if we could drop Edward off somewhere. Samantha readily accepted for him because he seemed to be having some difficulty in speaking up.

"I told him that Huntington's Hotel was the best place for him to stay if he was going to take perma-

nent lodging. The others are all right if you are staying
overnight or just for a few days." Mandy chattered
on, oblivious to her father's dark face. "They are more
for tourists—and after all, Huntington's is almost family. Sarah's father owns it, and she is married to Uncle
Tom. We can drop him off there, can't we? It's right
on our way home anyway."

When the men left to collect the trunks, Mandy
turned to me with her eyes soft and glowing. "What
do you think, Mom? Tell me, quick, before they come
back. Isn't he absolutely dashing? Isn't he handsome?"

"Mandy, just how well do you know him?" I asked,
wondering how much she hadn't told us. "I don't
remember you mentioning him in your letters."

She shrugged, twisting the long rope of beads around
her fingers, her face serious. "We had classes together,
as I said. He likes all the same things that I do. We
exchanged books . . . we've gone to several parties
together, and we went to the theater. Aunt Margaret
invited him to dinner and Grandfather likes him, but
I think that is because he listens instead of talking all
of the time. It isn't anything serious yet. Mom, I think
he picked this job up here because of me. He had
several offers to choose from. He was the top of his
class, so he could have gone to work almost anywhere
that he wanted. He is positively brilliant!" And then
she giggled, reaching out to hug my arm, her face alive
with mischief. "Edward doesn't know it yet, but I am
going to let him chase me until I catch him. I am
going to marry Edward Mott!"

"Mandy!" I reprimanded sharply. "Don't be so forward! That is not the way for a young woman to talk."

"Oh, come now, Mother, don't give me that severe
look of yours. The women in our family know what

we want, and we are determined. I know the story
about Grandmother and how she came to Alaska, and
I've heard all about Daddy chasing you until you
proposed to him!"

My cheeks turned a bright pink and I turned away,
glad to see Sam coming toward us. The trunks were
loaded in the back of the car and he was ready to take
us home.

The first week that Mandy was home was an absolute
delight for Sam and me. Our home had grown too
quiet, too neat, too routine. Our telephone rang a lot
more now and we became used to young people coming and going, filling the rooms with their sophisticated
chatter. We didn't see as much of our daughter as we
would have liked—she seemed always to be so busy,
wanting to see her friends again, to visit around the
town, to see the changes. But once in a while we would
catch glimpses of the old Mandy, when she would drop
the brittle covering young people seemed to find
necessary. Then she would pick up an old sweater and
go for long walks alone as though her eyes were
thirsty, to drink in the sight of the high mountains,
the waterfalls. Wandering along the shore to watch
the fishing boats and listen to the seagulls—all of the
things she had missed while she had been away—this
was our beloved Samantha.

These walks usually ended near the docks and her
father's office, about the time he was ready to leave for
the day, so they came home together—just like when
she had been in school in town. I knew how much
this meant to Sam and how he looked forward to those
few moments they spent alone, strolling back up the

street toward the house, talking about small, unimportant things that had happened during the day.

She was eager to see Abe, and one of the first things she did was to sit down and write a long letter to him, telling him about her trip home, asking pages of questions about Ravenwood, telling him about Edward Mott. I was certain that this last part of her letter would cause Abe to visit—perhaps he'd show up casually in town to stay at our house for several days—and I was right. Abe could not imagine that Mandy was old enough to show such an interest in a young man, and he intended to judge for himself if Edward was worthy of her.

I gained a new respect for Edward the evening Mandy invited him to our home for supper. He was such a quiet, almost shy, fellow, but I knew what staunch courage it must have taken for him to face both Sam and Abe at the dinner table.

I heard the respect in his voice when he spoke to either of them, and I saw the way his eyes softened when he looked at Mandy. I was beginning to like this young man and to understand what attracted Samantha. I hoped that Sam and Abe would not be too severe with him.

Samantha was seeing Edward nearly every day, I knew, and several evenings during the week he called to take her out. But no matter how busy she was, Mandy always found the time to appear at Sam's office about the time he would be ready to start his walk home. I would stand at the kitchen window and look up McKinley Street and watch them approach, talking quietly together. I would smile to myself in contentment at how I had been so deeply blessed.

If Mandy was eager to be home and renew old friendships, I was just as interested in hearing her tell of my family still living in San Francisco. Her grandfather, such a proud man, still went to the office every day although he was past seventy years old now. He walked straight and brisk without the aid of a cane, was alert, and still controlled the company with an iron hand. Though he was a very stern man, Mandy was very fond of him and spoke of him with a deep affection. How she must have brightened that big, empty home and how much he must miss her now that she had left!

Aunt Margaret still took care of the household, and Samantha said she reminded her of a delicate piece of old lace—fragile looking but made of strong threads.

Paul evidently had attained what he wanted from life—a senior position in the firm, marriage to a prominent socialite with an excellent family background and an independent wealth of her own. They lived in a lovely old mansion that had its own distinguished history to add to Paul's status in society. They had no children. Mandy wrinkled up her nose and said Paul's wife was much too busy with her benefits and her clubs to have any time left over to give a thought to children. If Paul was a success in the world of finance, at home he was but a corporal with his wife the commanding general.

After Mandy had been home for two weeks, I could sense her growing restless and I wondered what she was planning. I knew something was on her mind but she hadn't taken me into her confidence. Abe was still in town, supposedly waiting for some supplies. One morning he and I were sitting at the breakfast table having a first cup of coffee, waiting for Sam to finish dressing and join us. The bacon was already fried and a pan of hot biscuits was just about ready to come out of the oven when Mandy came out of her room, earlier than usual.

She was neatly dressed in a suit of dark wool with a crisp white blouse. It was a new outfit, one that I hadn't seen her wear before. Her hair was in careful waves, and she wore silk stockings and a pair of high-heeled shoes. She carried her hat and gloves.

Her father came into the kitchen about the same time and raised his eyebrows slightly at the sight of her. "Up and off so early, baby?" he asked. "Must be something special. You look extra pretty this morning."

"Yes. I'm going with you," she answered as she laid her hat and gloves on the counter and picked up a glass of orange juice. She talked with a studied calmness that caused me to look up, alert, wondering. "I am all settled in now, and I am ready to start my new job."

I was watching closely now, sensing something was about to happen but not sure what.

Sam's eyes flew open in surprise. "Job? What job? What are you talking about?"

"Why, Daddy," she answered sweetly, as though he should have known all along what she was talking about. "My job as your secretary. Goodness, you spent all of that money on my education. Now it is your turn to benefit from your investment. Just look at what a beautiful and well-trained secretary you are about to have, groomed to your specifications."

So this is what she had been planning! Leave it to Mandy to come up with something like this. No wonder she had been so preoccupied these last few days, wondering how best to approach him. I watched Sam's face over the rim of my coffee cup. How would he handle it?

He did just what I might have expected—he yelled a lot.

"Never!" he roared. "Absolutely not! Whatever gave you an idea like that? You are not going to go to work! Don't you have everything that you want? Don't I provide for my family? Work? I won't hear of it!"

Samantha answered him quietly and with a great deal of dignity. "If I had been a son, I would have returned from my schooling and joined the firm. There would have been a place for me. I would have been welcome."

I caught Abe's eye. He winked at me and we both turned away, studying something out the window. They didn't need us to enter into their argument, offer opinions, or take sides. I already knew the outcome, even if Sam didn't. This was my daughter talking.

Samantha learned her new job in the shipping office quickly. She took charge of the paperwork and the bills of lading that seemed always to be stacking up, needing attention. She took a delighted interest in everything that went on around her and though Sam fought a hard battle, I knew he was proud of the way she understood the work and fit so easily into the routine.

CHAPTER SIXTEEN

Sam and Mandy walked to the offices together every morning, taking advantage of the late-summer weather, but there were times when he came home alone with a frown on his face. These were the days when Edward had called at the offices at closing time, and he and Mandy had gone off together to have dinner at one of the restaurants in town. After a quiet supper Sam would spend a restless evening, glancing up at the clock often, until he heard Mandy's light step on the porch. Those were difficult days for Sam. It was hard for him to recognize that our Samantha was a woman now, and one of these days another man would come into her life and he would have to share.

At the close of summer the weather had stayed warm, as though reluctant to withdraw and let winter have its turn. Everyone was enjoying the nice weather, staying outdoors as much as possible, knowing that all too soon we would be buried in snow and unable to stay outside any more than was necessary.

One Saturday Samantha was in the kitchen, humming happily to herself, packing a giant picnic basket. Pouring himself a cup of coffee as he waited for a sample, Sam watched her put the finishing touches to the frosting on a cake she had baked earlier.

"Something special today?" he asked. "Looks like you got a good idea. The three of us can go on a picnic. Where do you want to go?"

"I'm sorry, Daddy. I was packing this for Eddie and me. I can't go with you—not today. Maybe we can later." She tried not to see the disappointed look on his face as she handed him a slice of the cake, hoping it might help a little. "Eddie and I are going to hike up toward Mineral Creek. He has been working so hard, trying to get caught up on the new work at the cannery. He hasn't had a chance to get out like that very much. We thought we would take a picnic basket with us and maybe even pick some berries. The currants are gone by now, I suppose, but there might still be some blueberries. Maybe we will be lucky and find enough for some pies. Would you like that? Do you remember how we used to always pick berries at Ravenwood—and Maury would let me help make the jellies? Do you remember how good they tasted?"

After they left Sam was restless, wanting something to do. He suggested that we go for a drive, and I asked if he wouldn't like to go up toward Keystone Canyon. I loved to drive up there, past the glacier, up toward the waterfalls, away from the town and other people, just Sam and me. This time of year it would be particularly beautiful, with the leaves turning color, the hillsides alive with the bright reds and golds of autumn.

We drove away from the streets of the town and

followed the bay around to the wide, shallow stream
where hundreds and hundreds of salmon came each
year to spawn. After he stopped the car, we got out
and walked to the edge of the bank to watch the
churning, boiling water as the fishes' bodies wriggled
and dug at the gravel bottom of the streambed in a
last frantic turmoil of reproduction. The water was
milky white with their efforts. Once the eggs were
deposited in the rocks and had been fertilized, the fish
died, their scarred and lifeless bodies to be fought over
and picked at by the hundreds of seagulls who collected
there and ate until they had to waddle away from the
feast, too heavy to fly.

We returned to the car and drove on up the winding
road, away from the small fishing boats, the buildings,
the people, the noise. The Valdez glacier lay off to our
left, looking deceitfully calm and at rest, defying man's
urge for progress to touch or to change it.

From there we entered the narrow canyon where the
road followed the stream. The air smelled fresh and
clean, and though the leaves had started to turn the
foliage was still thick with patches of dark green. Sam
found a turnout and pulled the car over and shut off
the engine.

"Want to get out and walk for a bit?" he asked.

"Oh, yes, let's," I answered. I was basking in the
warmth of the sun and hoping that Sam was as relaxed
and enjoying the day as much as I was.

There was a flat area here, following a gully that led
back out of sight of the roadway, and we started walking toward it. Ahead of us I could hear noisy water
tumbling on the rocks, hidden from view by the lush
dark-green overgrowth. I knew there had to be a small
falls back there somewhere.

Sam had walked on ahead of me and he turned now, watching me try to untangle my skirt from a berry vine. He was laughing at me.

"I guess this outfit was not intended for tramping about in the woods, was it?" I called to him. "Wait for me."

When I got free and reached his side, he took my hand. "No, I was just thinking back. You looked so young there in the sunlight, it brought back a lot of memories. Do you remember that first hike we took together? On our wedding day. We sneaked out of the back window and hiked up to the cabin? You were wearing those ridiculous men's pants and that heavy shirt that was two sizes too big for you."

I made a face at him. "You didn't think I looked silly then!" I turned and sat down on the soft grass. "Let's rest for a while, Sam. I'm out of breath after that climb."

He sank down onto the grass beside me. "What's the matter, Nora? Not able to keep up like you used to?" he teased.

"Don't be funny," I answered tartly. "I notice you were getting a little winded too." I reached out and patted his midsection affectionately. "It seems to me that I can feel a little weight there that wasn't there on that first hike either."

"Well now, if you want to be that way and talk about a few added inches, Nora . . ." He tipped me playfully back onto the soft grass and I frowned at him, trying to look stern.

Sam was laughing, teasing me goodnaturedly, but as he looked down at me his face grew serious and his eyes went tender with emotion. Slowly he bent down until his lips found mine. I put my arms around his neck, drawing him closer to me, my pulse suddenly pounding in my throat. I felt his fingers fumbling with the buttons on my blouse as his lips traced a pattern against my breast. After all these years, Sam's touch could still set my blood on fire, filling me with desire.

"Nora?" he whispered huskily.

"Yes," I murmured, moving closer into his arms.

We lay side by side on the hillside in the warm sunshine, looking up at the fluffy bits of clouds that were drifting lazily overhead. I could hear the sounds of the stream through the trees and once in a while an impatient bird calling to its mate. Sam was idly chewing on a blade of grass, lost in his thoughts.

"I suppose we should be getting home," he said at last. "We didn't leave a note and Mandy will be wondering what happened to us."

"I doubt that she will be home this early," I answered. "It's been such a lovely day. I hate to see it end so soon. It has been a while since we just took off, the two of us, without any plan. You work too hard, Sam. You need to get away more."

He chuckled. "Yes, and look at how we spent it. Look at us, rolling and tumbling around in the weeds like two kids—and at our age!"

"What about our age!" I exclaimed with a great show of indignation, as I sat up and glared at him.

"Well, look at us. You have got to admit we're a little old for this sort of thing. Have you noticed that I'm getting a few gray hairs around the temples? I didn't pay much attention to it myself until Mandy came home. It's hard to believe that she is almost grown up. Where has time gone, Nora?"

I bent over and put my fingers to his lips. "Hush.

Don't talk like that. When you hold me in your arms and make love to me, I feel as though I shall never grow old. We may both mellow a little and change with the years—we may even slow down and reach the peaks a little less often—but our love will never let us grow old, Sam. It just gets richer and more meaningful with the years."

We kissed then—not a kiss of urgent passion, but a kiss of satisfaction, satisfaction with our lives, with our love for each other.

Sam glanced at his watch and rose, brushing the clinging grasses from his pant legs.

"My God, do you realize what time it is? Come on, Nora, we've got to head back home. What's Samantha going to think if we come in with grass stains on our clothing and you with briars caught in your hair?"

I laughed at his concern. "I doubt that she will even notice. She is busy with her own thoughts nowadays. But if she asks, I will tell her that I have been on a secret tryst with a handsome man—that I have a lover."

"I wonder how her day went?" he said as he helped me pick up the remains of the lunch I had brought with us.

"Whatever she did, I doubt very much that she spent much time wondering about us, so quit your worrying, Sam."

"She spends too much time with that Edward fellow. She should be seeing some of the other boys in the town once in a while. Don't you talk to her about it?"

"Samantha is a grown woman now and she knows her own mind. There isn't much either of us could say that would influence her one way or the other about Edward. Besides, he's a nice boy, Sam. Give him a chance."

His answer to me was a scowl. Together we started back down the hillside toward where we had left the car and the moment passed. Soon he was smiling again, helping me over the fallen logs, holding back the branches until I had passed.

He checked the oil and the water in the car, took a last look at the tires, then we were ready to leave.

Sam was eager to get home now. We drove along the dusty road in contented silence, and I knew his thoughts were on Samantha. I rested my head on his shoulder, and once in a while he would look down and smile lazily at me. It had been such a lovely day for us.

Samantha was already home when we returned, her face closed and dark as a thundercloud. I pretended not to notice, waiting to see if she wanted to talk about it. I put our coats away, unpacked the remains of our lunch, picked up papers and pillows on the sofa before I went into the kitchen to join her.

"It was a beautiful day for as late in the year as it is, don't you think?" I asked lightly. "Your dad and I went for a long drive. Something we haven't done in a long time—just go off like that by ourselves."

Her only answer was a nod and a careless shrug as she went ahead with setting the table for supper. She had a Swiss steak cooking in the Dutch oven and the potatoes were almost done, ready for mashing, so I knew she had been home for a while. Mandy liked to cook, and though I prepared most of the meals, she often helped or once in a while took over completely, preparing some dish she liked to make. Tonight, however, she had little to say, and our evening meal was a little awkward, with Sam and me doing most of the talking. His eyes went often to her gloomy face and he looked puzzled, but at least he didn't mention it or ask questions.

After the dishes were cleared and the kitchen cleaned up, Mandy headed toward her room.

"Going to bed so early, baby?" Sam called after her.

"Yes, Dad. I guess all of the fresh air tired me more than I thought. We hiked quite a ways and I have been sitting in the office too much—out of shape, I guess. I have a book I want to finish reading so I thought I'd just curl up in bed and read for a while."

I watched her go into her room and close the door behind her. Thoughtfully I wondered what was troubling her. Well, she would work it out somehow. She wanted to be alone right now, but she knew that if she needed us, we both would be there for her to talk to.

Sam was restless. I put my arm around his shoulder as I bent over the back of the chair where he was sitting. "Please, Sam, let her alone. She'll tell us what's wrong when she is ready. Mandy is all grown up now. Her hurts can't always be something that she can bring to us, to be cured with a hug and a cookie. Don't meddle."

"It's that young fool Mott," he growled. "He takes up too much of her time. Can't you talk to her about it? He shouldn't be around so much—he should give her a chance to see her other friends. My God, he's even there when we lock up at night down at the offices." His thoughts went to the hike they had taken this afternoon. "If he has done anything to hurt her—"

"Please dear, relax," I begged "She is a young woman in love. Love isn't always moonbeams and laughter. Even the deep, lasting love can mean a lot of tears and hurts. For the young, love can be a very painful experience—or can't you remember back that far?"

"It is because I remember too well that I don't like it," he answered. "That Edward had better keep in line." He glowered.

That night, with the lights out and the house so very quiet that even a creaking board caused by the house settling sounded loud, we heard soft, hidden sobs coming from Mandy's room.

Sam sat up in bed and turned on the light. "For God's sake, do something, Nora! Go in and talk to her. You can find out what's wrong. If that Edward has—"

"Hush!" I tugged at his arm. "Don't imagine things, Sam. Turn the light out, dear. I'll talk with her in the morning, if she wants me to. But tonight leave her alone. She will not want either of us to interfere." As much as I wanted to put on my slippers, go into her room, and sit down on the side of the bed, to try to take the hurt away from her and mend it, I knew that I had to wait until she wanted me to intervene, until she wanted to confide and was ready to talk about it.

The next morning was Sunday and we had a lazy, late breakfast. Mandy had dark smudges around her eyes and I knew she had not slept well. Sam went into the living room to read the Sunday paper in front of the fireplace. I waited until we had the dishes washed and put back in the cupboard before I poured two cups of coffee and set them on the table, one in front of Mandy. She looked up at me with a question in her eyes.

"What's that for? I've already had two cups, and you know I don't drink that much coffee."

"Sit down, Samantha, and listen to me," I answered, my voice a little stern. "One time, a long while ago when I wasn't too much older than you are now, when I thought I had come to a complete impasse with my problems, Maury would pour two cups of coffee, set them on the table, and order me to sit down and talk with her. Then with that earthy wisdom of hers, we talked over what was bothering me. Somehow, after a session with Maury's coffee, my problem seemed not so large after all, and the answers would be there, just as plain as could be. I don't have Maury's wisdom but maybe it will work for us anyway. So sit down," I said firmly. "I'm not going to spend a whole Sunday looking at your gloomy face—and I won't have your father upset this way."

"Oh, Mom," she said reluctantly, but she sat back down, absently studying the small bubbles that formed at the side of the cup.

"It must be very serious. You don't usually allow things to upset you so deeply. Or, if they do, at least you have always been able to talk to one of us about it before. What is it, Mandy?"

"That's just it, Mom. It's so stupid! It was just a silly argument over something that wasn't that important— that shouldn't have happened at all! But neither of us would back down. Somehow from there it just sort of ballooned into an angry fight with both of us saying things we didn't really mean. Oh, Mom, I said some awful things. Hurting things—and Eddie did too."

"Then maybe he was thinking about it during the night too, and if he feels as bad as you do, he'll come over today and it can be patched up."

"No. It won't turn out that way. I said terrible things to him." Tears filled her eyes. "He didn't even walk me to the gate." Her face was filled with misery. "Well, to be honest, I guess he couldn't because I turned and ran away from him and didn't wait."

"Why don't you call him up and apologize?" I suggested. "Just say that you are sorry for losing your temper?"

"I couldn't do that! Never! Besides, I can't be the first one to say it. It's this pride of mine. It wouldn't work, anyway. If I did, he probably wouldn't even talk to me."

"Does it matter?" I asked. "Perhaps it is for the best. You've been with him so much lately. There are other young men around the town eager to know you better. Why not date others for a while? Maybe that might be a good idea."

Her face looked stricken at the very thought. "Oh, no, Mom! I couldn't do that. There will never be anyone for me but Edward!"

"Do you really love him that much, Mandy?" I asked gently.

She nodded. Tears were in her eyes again, threatening to spill over. "I'm afraid so. As much as you love Dad, I think. When I am with him, I have that same warm, loved feeling that I've always seen you and Dad show for each other. When I am away from him, I feel . . . empty." Her eyes were pleading. "What am I going to do?"

I studied my coffee cup, thinking seriously before I answered. "Hmmm. Well then, if that is the way it is, you had better learn to swallow just a little bit of that pride. A little bit won't hurt you at all. I know. A truly deep love is something most women go through life without ever experiencing. If you think that you have found it, then it is certainly worth fighting for. The women in our family are like that—we love deeply. My mother left her husband and children to follow the one man that could bring her such a love and happiness. I almost lost Sam once because of my pride. Don't let your pride stand in the way of your reason, Mandy. Don't give up that easily—if you are certain Edward is the one. Go to the phone and call him."

"Do you really think I should?"

I nodded.

"What if he doesn't want to talk to me?"

"You'll never know, will you, if you don't try."

She hesitated for a moment, indecision on her face, and then she got up and walked slowly down the hallway. The telephone rang just before she reached it.

"I'll get it, Dad. I'm right here anyway," she called out.

I heard just enough of the conversation to know that everything was going to be all right. At least for now. With a sigh, I went into the living room and settled down in my favorite chair to read the paper.

Mandy came flying into the room, her coat over her arm, her face wreathed in smiles. "That was Edward on the phone! He wants me to meet him down at the coffee shop." She reached over the back of the chair and kissed my cheek. "Thanks, Mom—for serving a cup of Maury's coffee." Then she turned and ran out of the door.

Sam looked up, startled. "What did all of that mean? 'Maury's coffee'?"

I smiled across at him. "Nothing you men would understand, dear. It's women talk. A very special brew."

"Hmmmph," he mumbled as he returned to his paper. "Well, whatever it is, it must be potent. It's good to see her happy again."

CHAPTER SEVENTEEN

Samantha's marriage to Edward Mott gave us the son
we had never had. Edward was a fine young man and
we were proud of him. He had no close family of his
own and he accepted us as his, with an eagerness that
was touching. Edward left his position with the fish
canneries and joined the firm of Crandall and Bennett.
He lacked the knowledge of the country and knew almost nothing of the export trade, but his thorough
training in accounting was a great help to Sam and my
brother Tom.

Samantha didn't work after her marriage. At first
she was deeply involved in redecorating the small home
she and Edward rented on the other side of town.
Then they had two sons, scarcely a year and a half
apart, and three years later a tiny daughter named
Maury.

Things were not going very well back up in the
Copper River country. The veins of copper still lay
heavy in the high ridges of the mountains, but the men

grew restless and dissatisfied with the working conditions and the pay. This grew into open tension, and the tension burst into angry arguments between management and employees.

The price of copper began to drop, yet operating costs stayed high, with transportation fees even higher. In the late thirties the economic disaster that swept across the lower United States reached our coastal regions, and the mines were closed. Almost everyone thought that it was a temporary thing, with the mines closed just until an agreement could be reached, until financial problems could be solved. They believed it was so temporary, in fact, that when they left the copper country many of them didn't take all of their belongings. Dishes were left in cupboards; some were even left on the table, as though waiting for the occupants to return at mealtime. But the problems were never solved. The mines never reopened.

With the mine closures, the railroad made its last run. Without the railroad or the mines, towns died. Almost overnight it happened. The little villages that had taken root in the bush and blossomed so quickly into thriving towns died an even quicker death. A few people remained, scattered here and there, but they say it is only the winds that cause the doors to open now, and it is only the ghosts who walk the boardwalks and whisper in the deserted buildings. The copper and the gold is still there, rich veins lying undisturbed, but the diggings are gradually being covered with the young birch trees.

The railroad tracks have mostly disappeared, partly carried away by the ice and the mud of spring breakups —nature reclaiming her own. The roads back into the villages have not been well tended. Now they are only deep rutted dirt trails, almost impassable except in summer. However, the old Valdez Trail remains the well-traveled Richardson Highway, a concrete ribbon flowing right on by with barely a pause at the turnouts we used to take back into the villages and the mines.

The Million Dollar Bridge still stands at mile forty-nine out of Cordova, still touted as one of man's greatest engineering feats of the time. Though it is ineffectual without a serviceable connecting route on either side of it, it stands in good repair, without even the paint peeling, like the last word in a lost argument.

There were other changes too. We saw the young, unmarried men in our town wearing uniforms and leaving to join the war. There were military installa-tions here in Alaska—not army camps, sprawling out in the open, but hidden in the Chugach Mountains, ready for defense if the war should move up in this direction. There were rumors, of course, and many of them no more than that. But we heard whispers of undercover groups using the mine tunnels as hiding places and storage shelters.

It was during this period of tension and change that we lost my father. He was followed closely by Aunt Margaret. Her charges all raised, her duties done, she slipped away quietly in her sleep.

There were the good things, though, to offset the un-rest. Samantha's children were a joy to us, and we found many excuses to have them around the house. I would watch from the kitchen window for Sam to come home in the evening, walking a little slower now, but with two young boys beside him, stopping while they tossed rocks into the water or bent to inspect some newfound treasure, tipping his head slightly as he listened to them talk.

Abe finally resigned himself to buying a car—a Model T—for the long trips into Valdez. He still used a horse around the lodge to haul the firewood on the sled or to get through the drifts when the roads weren't cleared enough for the cars. When the weather was permissible, he would drive into Valdez and stay with us for a week or two at a time. He grumbled about having to come in for supplies so often but we smiled to ourselves. We knew that it was the tiny Maury, with her hazel eyes and thick mass of auburn curls, that drew him into town.

Ravenwood belonged to Samantha now. She loved to go up there with Edward whenever they could get away. Sometimes we kept the children so they could have some time alone, but most of the time they all went together. Abe looked forward to the visits, patiently teaching the boys how to fish, telling them stories of earlier days in the Copper River country. Baby Maury saw through his gruffness and held his heart in her tiny hands.

When we got together for a holiday now, we made a good-sized family group: Mandy and Edward with their three children, Tom and Sarah, accompanied by young Martin home from college in San Francisco, and their daughter, Elizabeth, with her brand-new husband.

Thanksgiving this year was at Tom and Sarah's, and their home was filled with running children, young people talking and laughing, older men arguing politics and discussing the war that threatened to reach our shores. The women collected in the kitchen, creating the good smells that drifted throughout the whole house as we gossiped about babies and recipes.

We were all there, plus several others who were such close friends that they were almost family.

It had been a good day, full of warmth and fun and love, but it had also been long. I noticed Sam was growing very quiet, as though he were tired. I knew I was. We had been up since early morning, so that I could bake pies at home before we left. I think we were both ready to settle down in our own deep, comfortable chairs, by our own fireplace, for a restful and quiet evening—just the two of us.

It had snowed off and on throughout the day. Edward put on his fur parka and walked with us out to the car to be sure that it started and that no shoveling of the driveway was needed. There were lots of hugs and good-byes said, kisses blown by the children, and then we were on our way to our own home across town.

Sam built up the fire and picked up his glasses to settle down to read while I went into the kitchen to fix us hot tea. He looked so tired this evening, and I thought perhaps the hot tea would help him to relax. I hated to admit it, but Sam and I were beginning to show our years. As much as we loved our grandchildren and wanted them around us, after a long day with them we both looked forward to the quiet of our own living room, our chairs placed by the fire, our books nearby, pictures of the children scattered about—the mementoes of our life together all around us.

I called to Sam when the water was ready for the tea. Part of our nightly routine was that he would carry the filled tray into the living room. He didn't answer. Thinking he didn't hear me, I put the teapot and cups on the tray and added a few of Sam's favorite cookies before going to the archway leading into the living room to call again.

"Sam?" A sense of foreboding washed across me when he still didn't answer.

His book had slipped to the floor unnoticed. His head was tipped forward and his face had an unnatural flush, as though the room were too warm. Spellbound, I watched him struggle to undo his shirt collar and listened to his breath coming in short, difficult gasps.

"Sam? What is it?" Suddenly terrified, I rushed to his side and dropped to my knees beside his chair. "Sam, are you ill? What's wrong?" I felt my breath caught in my throat as panic took over. My eyes searched his face, begging him to laugh at me and tell me he was all right.

He groped for my hand. It was cold to my touch, even though the fire was crackling and the room was warm. He was trying to talk, trying to tell me something, but the words were coming in short, painful sounds and I had to bend closer, trying to understand.

"Call . . . Dr. Fletcher. Quickly now, girl. I think . . . it is . . . my heart."

"Oh, my God!" I sobbed, and flew to the telephone, not wanting to leave his side even for a moment but knowing I had to get help. All the while I dialed, I prayed that the doctor would not be away for the holiday.

Dr. Fletcher was there, thank goodness, and answered the telephone himself. I begged him to hurry, having to repeat myself when he told me to slow down so that he could understand what I was saying. He promised that he would be there in just a few minutes. He would leave immediately, and he lived only a few blocks away. I ran back to Sam's side.

Tears blinded me and I was filled with such a helpless panic. Sam was in terrible pain and there was nothing I could do to make it easier for him.

I didn't know if I should move him or not, but he looked so uncomfortable in the chair and there wasn't room for him to lean back far enough. Somehow, with a strength I didn't know I possessed, I was able to get him from the chair onto the sofa. I unbuttoned his shirt, removed his shoes, and tried to make him as comfortable as possible by stacking pillows around him as he struggled to breathe.

"It will be all right, Sam," I pleaded as I knelt beside him and cradled him in my arms. "It will be all right. Dr. Fletcher is on his way. Just a little bit longer, dear, just a little bit longer and we will have some help." Beads of perspiration were on his forehead, and I wiped them away as I brushed his hair back from his face and crooned to him. "Rest easy, my dearest. Just try to rest. The doctor will be here soon and he will know what to do."

His breathing seemed to become a little easier. He turned his head toward me and smiled weakly as he reached for my hand. "I love you," he whispered. "You have . . . given me so much." His voice was low and the words came with an effort. "We have had . . . a good life, you and I."

"No!" I cried out. "No! Don't talk like that—I won't listen to you!" I cradled his head to my breast, rocking gently back and forth in my grief. "You're just tired. There was too much excitement today—too many people. And you ate too much. The food was too rich, too heavy." I was crying now, my tears falling on his face. "Dr. Fletcher will be here soon. You mustn't leave me, Sam. You can't go away and leave me here alone.

I need you too much. I don't want to go on living without you. I don't want to be left alone."

His voice was very low now, barely a whisper. "Don't, Nora. I don't want to see you cry."

"I'm not." I tried to wipe my eyes with the back of my hand, but each time more tears replaced the ones I scrubbed away.

"Always remember," he murmured, "how much I love you. How much we shared, and don't grieve—don't be sad. My love will . . . stay on with you . . . even when I am gone."

He became very still then, as I held him close to me and rested my cheek against his face. We were there, in that very position, when the doctor gently put his arms around me, lifted me to my feet, and led me from the room.

CHAPTER EIGHTEEN

And now I am sitting here in this comfortable old rocker, the treasures of our life together all around me, my memories spread out for you to see, telling this story of a green *cheechako* who dared to come to the great northland in search of a dream and who became a part of the country's growth and found a greater wealth than was ever uncovered in the fabulous mines of Alaska.

Someday Ravenwood will go to little Maury. I hope that she will be able to find a love that will fill her life and know the peace and contentment that goes with it, as I did, and my mother before me.

I keep hearing Sam's last words—that I was always to remember the way he loved me and the life we shared—and I am not sad or lonely. I live each day to the fullest, enjoying the days that I am given until it is my turn to leave, knowing that Sam will be there, waiting for me.

VOLUME I
IN THE EPIC
NEW SERIES

The Morland Dynasty

The FOUNDING

by Cynthia Harrod-Eagles

THE FOUNDING, a panoramic saga rich with passion and excitement, launches Dell's most ambitious series to date—THE MORLAND DYNASTY.

From the Wars of the Roses and Tudor England to World War II, THE MORLAND DYNASTY traces the lives, loves and fortunes of a great English family.

A DELL BOOK $3.50   #12677-0

Breathtaking sagas of adventure and romance

VALERIE VAYLE